Nightriders
by
Ashley Blake

Writer's note:

Welcome back friends! Thank you for your continued support.

I'd like to offer some insight into my latest venture, *Nightriders*, a tale that is parts truth and fiction, set entirely in 19th Century Louisiana.

Nightriders is a story based on events that happened shortly after the Civil War, when a group of ex-Confederate soldiers created a home guard. Their sole purpose was to protect their communities from criminals set upon disrupting their way of life, in a predominantly lawless territory.

Proper credit must be given to Mr. Richard Briley III, who detailed the rise and fall of these outlaws in his book, *Nightriders: Inside Story of the West and Kimbrell Clan.* Professor Jack Peebles deserves credit due to his research on the bare-bones history of the clan, which provided grist for his subsequent book, *The Legend of The Nightriders.*

I utilized both books to conduct my research for this novel, as well as collecting information from elderly folks whose relatives were alive during that time. My grandparents John M. Blake, Sr. and Ezona Gibbs were raised in Goldonna, Louisiana, located in the central part of the state, where a fair share of the clan's activities took place. I visited the sight of a clan member's grave. I even spoke with a grandchild of one of the accused riders. This happened sixteen years ago, in 2000, when the grandchild was 87 years old. I asked him about Abram (Ab) Martin, a reputed nightrider. The man looked up from his wheelchair, gave a wrinkled smile, and said, "Son, he'd kill you dead."

So this was my introduction to the story of the West Clan, or West-Kimbrell Clan, as they were initially called. Over the course of time in this piney woods area, the group became informally known as the nightriders.

Quite intrigued to learn more, I further researched the West Clan. I mean, I grew up two hours from this area and was perplexed as to why I had never before learned of this gang. Maybe my parents were trying to protect my fragile mind from the horrors of this world, past and present. I can't blame them for that. But I like horror stories, so I set out to learn more.

When I first read Mr. Briley's book, I was altogether curious, in awe, and downright disgusted that the riders had robbed and killed more people than any other villainous outfit operating during that time, including Frank and Jesse James—the famed outlaws of the Wild West. Cited in these books, the reason why law-abiding citizens outside Louisiana had never heard of these men is detailed in their methods of execution. By robbing and killing at night, once someone saw their faces, the gang followed the pirate's creed of "dead men tell no tales".

Consequently, their names were not known to the public in sensationalized newsprint, as were the hijinks of other outlaws during that time.

I'll admit I added a fair amount of fiction to this 143 year old tale. Because of the retelling of these stories, imagination had to be applied in order to create a sequential storyline. What I found unbelievable, and disheartening, is that most of the stories told down through the generations were *true*.

I have strived with attentive care to recreate believable dialogue between real characters responsible for some of the goriest murders in Louisiana history. If it entertains, offends, yet makes you feel empathy towards their victims, then I've accomplished what I set out to do—show these outlaws' perpetual greed and willingness to commit unimaginable violence gained at the sacrifices of innocent people.

So interested in the rise of these outlaws, and their ultimate downfall, I felt compelled to create my own version of this local legend. My goal was to produce an entertaining story that showcased these villains at the height of their power, with my friends witnessing such chaos from the safety of the page.

Here's hoping you'll enjoy reading it as much as I enjoyed writing it.

This story is dedicated to the innocent men, women, and children who perished at the hands of the West-Kimbrell Clan. May your souls rest in peace.

Tales of John West and his nightriders, and the crimes committed by this gang, were constantly whispered about the countryside. In the "No-Man's Land" between Winnfield, Louisiana and the Arroyo-Hondo, just then a man had to be careful.

—excerpt from *Nightriders: Inside Story of the West and Kimbrell Clan* by Richard Briley III. c. 1963.

"Most of the robbers were Masons and Deputy Sheriffs."

—excerpt from *The Legend of The Nightriders* by Jack Peebles. c. 2005.

"With the nightriders around, the devil's out of work." –Copeland Yates, 1871.

And for your lifeblood I will require a reckoning: from every beast I will require it and from man. From his fellow man I will require a reckoning for the life of man. "Whoever sheds the blood of man, by man shall his blood be shed, for God made man in his own image."

Genesis 9: 5-6

Prologue

Atlanta, Louisiana - April 1872
Will Drake's General Store

Laws Kimbrell stood at the counter nursing a glass of whiskey, looking through the window at the townspeople slowly gathering in the middle of the muddy street.

The folks talked among themselves, then began focusing their attention in unison on the second floor of the store. It seemed they were waiting for something to happen, something exciting, and somewhere in his suspicious mind Laws figured that maybe they were directing their gaze up at him.

This can't be, Laws thought.

When it came to the clan, folks around here minded their business.

Why, on *this* of all days, were men walking the town carrying rifles? Others freely gripping pistols as though threatened? Why were they congregating in the streets . . . moving closer to the store?

In a short time the crowd below had grown larger. He saw the faces of local citizens, several strangers, even clan members wandering about, some looking up at the second-story room of Will Drake's General Store.

Currently swapping nods and stories with Lec Ingram, a fellow member of the notorious West Clan, Laws turned to the door leading downstairs. For some reason, one he could not directly get a handle on, he waited for it to open, but nothing happened. The door remained shut.

Lec Ingram wondered aloud why all the commotion.

Laws finished his whiskey. Demanded another.

The room was hot, the only ventilation pulsating from three opened windows filling the saloon with crisscrossing breezes. He was dressed in a dark vest, a beige long-sleeved shirt and gray trousers over cleaned boots—save red dirt riding the soles' edges. His long black hair drew down in a wave at his collar, covering the nape of his neck. Clipped to the sides of his waist rested twin Army issue Colt .44 cannons. If a foolish man tried his hand at a duel with Laws Kimbrell, Laws would kill him quickly in the exchange, for he was known in this area as a professional gun-thrower. This happened to be the case even before he joined the Confederacy and fought for the South in the 12th Regiment Louisiana Infantry.

The door flew open, and in walked a boy no older than twelve years old. The boy leveled a rifle at Lec Ingram and Kimbrell.

Others in the room sat still nursing their drinks and playing cards, wondering, of course, what this kid had in mind.

"Nobody move!" the boy yelled. "You there, Mr. Laws Kimbrell! Put yer pistols on the table." He aimed the gun barrel at Lec Ingram. "Both of ya!"

Laws swallowed his whiskey and slammed the empty glass on the counter. *Bam!*

"What's the meaning of this, boy? Put that gun down or I'll do it for ya!"

"You men are under arrest by the good citizens of Winnfield and Atlanta Louisiana! Y'all set yer guns on the table nice and slow, now . . . I mean it!" he warned. "Or I'll shoot."

Laws saw the fear in the boy's eyes and relished in it. He laughed out loud, as he was not to be taunted by a mere child.

Reaching slowly for his sidearm he knew what he had to do.

And the outlaw had no problem in this world with his decision.

Chapter 1

Atlanta, Louisiana
July 1913

There it is. Shiny as ever.
Sun-bleached bone staring out at the world through empty sockets over a devil's grin.

I look at it often, that skull on the fencepost. Makes my stomach turn to look at it, but knowing how it got there gives me a measure of satisfaction that some form of justice was done.

The things I've seen some folks will find hard to believe, and that's okay. But these eyes don't lie, and the wicked tale I have for you won't sit right with the non-believers. And that's okay, too.

My name is Caleb "CS" Cole. When I became a carpenter by trade in my younger years I settled my family in the Saline Bayou region of central Louisiana between the towns of Natchitoches and Winnfield. Days here are slow and easy, much like they were at times back then. It's just that back then you often heard the thunder of hooves denting the earth on any given evening and sounds of heavy metal thumb-busters blasting the life out of some poor soul who happened by the wrong group of men.

This gang I speak of was part of an intelligent network of thieves called the West-Kimbrell Clan. For years they worked this area over good. This clan included some of the most notorious psychopathic killers to ever walk the state. Masters of disguise, this breed of monster dispatched many, many people. And for every victim, they granted no quarter.

There's no doubt they were a formidable outfit. They hated their fellow stranger with a purity that rivaled most men's love for a beautiful woman. Their collective goal was to go about their days as upstanding citizens of the territory, while secretly progressing as thieves after sundown.

I suspect they truly loved no one—not even, perhaps, themselves. They hid behind the night's shadows to kill for profit, and in the process left no witnesses.

Folks around here called them the nightriders.

Chapter 2

Jackson Lawson (Laws) Kimbrell learned from an early age how to rob folks, leave no witnesses, and evade justice.

I believe a certain evil flowed through this family's bloodline that allowed him to show no respect for another's very life or even feel remorse for his wrongdoings. Whatever the reason, he was taught well.

You see, Laws came from a family who had performed their share of atrocities upon unsuspecting travelers well before the nightriders rose to prominence as a full-fledged gang.

Lawson's father, Dan S. Kimbrell, and mother, Mrs. Mary Kimbrell, once ran a boarding house just off the Natchez Trace, and it was here they rented any of their four extra rooms to wayfaring strangers at a reasonable overnight fee. Of these temporary lodgers, a few lucky ones came and went without incident. The unlucky among them (those whom the Kimbrells suspected had possessions worth stealing—an abundance of gold coins or material wealth) were murdered and buried in the back field or shifted downstream in the Bayou Rouge.

Aunt Polly, as Mrs. Kimbrell was known among family and friends, had three sons who did her bidding—and they followed orders without question. These cutthroat gunslingers were named William, Shep (named after his Uncle Shep), and Lawson Kimbrell.

Just to bring you up to speed, allow me to show you a glimpse into these young men's psychotic mentality:

At the insistence of his sister, Uncle Shep Williams moved from Arkansas to the Wheeling Settlement outside Montgomery. Aunt Polly claimed he'd be closer to family as he grew in age, and also convinced him of the fertile land of central Louisiana, which would easily accommodate another farming business. So, Shep Williams finally made the decision to relocate. He bought a spread of farming property and began where he'd left off—filling the area with heads of cattle to raise for the meat hook.

An Irish farmhand named Kenneth worked for Uncle Shep and usually accompanied Shep to the Kimbrell homestead on monthly visits. While living comfortably working the farm, burdened by little extra expense, the Irishman saved his money like a miser.

Word got around that wherever he roamed, the Irishman weighed down his saddle bags with an abundance of gold coins. When the Kimbrell brothers caught wind of this rumor, they invited their Uncle Shep and his farmhand out for an afternoon of deer hunting.

Never having had much interest in hunting anything beyond a hot meal and a soft bed, Uncle Shep always declined the invitations.

But one fall day while visiting the Kimbrells, the Irishman accepted the brothers' invitation to go hunting Virginia Whitetail.

Next morning, Kenneth polished and primed his rifle and joined Uncle Shep Williams' nephews at Will Drake's Store. They found a secluded area of woodlands known to be well-stocked because of lack of human traffic, and set out to bag a deer.

At the end of the day, the Irishman did not return to Uncle Shep's farm. Two days passed with no sight of the farmhand, and Williams grew exceedingly concerned for the welfare of his old friend.

Shep Williams visited his sister's home again, fearing the worst, and searched for Lawson Kimbrell, the eldest brother—and the one who had incessantly offered up the hunting invite.

When his uncle rode up, Laws was sitting in a rocking chair sipping tea from a tin cup.

"Lawson? What happened to my farmhand? He ain't been to work in two days! Ain't like him to miss work and he was last seen with you! Where the hell is he?"

Laws set his cup on the planked porch and stood. "He's where you'd be now if you'd gone huntin' with us."

Dread came over Shep Williams. He realized now that the Irishman had been murdered by his nephews for his money purse. Wasting no further time discussing the matter with his reckless kinfolk, Shep returned home and ordered his wife to pack their essentials. They were moving.

"Why Shep? Why the rush?" his wife asked. "What's happened?"

"Those mad dog sons of my sister are dangerous. Nobody's safe around them. They'll kill anyone for a nickel and a chuckle. Now get going!"

By the end of the week, Uncle Shep Williams had moved his family and cattle south of Lafayette, severing all ties to Aunt Polly and her brood of bloodthirsty highwaymen for the remainder of his life.

Chapter 3

Along with the assistance of their three sons and daughter, Uncle Dan Kimbrell and Aunt Polly enlisted brutal ways of dispatching their victims.

Usually said victim was caught off guard while in deep slumber by an axe to the head. Uncle Dan was in charge of dealing with the men, and he used a variety of tricks to put a man's back to his blade before striking. His one failsafe routine was to offer them a drink of whiskey and then show them a healthy horse he proposed to sell. He would then lure them into the barn near the main house, remove his axe from the wall, and embed the blade in his victim's skull.

If an entire family stayed overnight, it was Aunt Polly's responsibility to dispose of the women and children. She kept a sharpened butcher's knife nearby to silence the women.

Aunt Polly would tie a woman's hands behind her back and force her to kneel on the kitchen floor, head hung over a metal milk pail, and then slice the meat of her throat crossways so swiftly that the pail filled within seconds. Her young daughter, Mattie, caught most of the mess.

"Hold her steady, Mattie," her mother would say. "I don't want blood on my floor, girl. Not one drop!"

But regardless of Mattie's stronghold on their traumatized female victim, there was always a mess to clean, and the kitchen's floors served as a darkened, fluid-stained reminder of past slaughters.

Aside from the inevitable cleanup, the one thing Aunt Polly disliked most of all was the screaming. "These womenfolk scream so loud they sound like a stuck pig. Can't *wait* to shut 'em up!" she'd say, then stab them in the heart.

Aunt Polly murdered children in their sleep by holding a pillow over their face until they perished from suffocation. She always managed to put children in separate rooms, and there they would spend the night on lone cots. This way there stood less risk another child might wake to noises beyond the walls.

Infants were poisoned intravenously with a healing remedy concocted from a huge amount of alcohol, herbs, and crushed coca leaves called Dr. Tolli's Miracle Healing Elixir. When the little ones perished they were unceremoniously stuffed into a burlap sack and chucked in the bayou.

Uncle Dan went to great lengths clearing the property of evidence of a dead body. He buried his victims in shallow graves by the bayou, knowing from past experience that in time, the animals of the forest would feast on the remains, leaving only offcuts of a skeleton. He'd then place the bones in a potato sack, use rocks to weigh it down, and throw the sack into the slow-moving stream of water.

Why they did this to their fellow man, I can't tell you. Surely greed provided intense motivation, but to maim and kill in cold blood? . . . that's another level of evil entirely.

How these two pulled off some of the goriest murders in regional history and were never caught for their deeds is beyond my grasp of comprehension. I believe in God, but these folks probably never heard of Him, never believed in Him, or figured they'd ask His forgiveness for their sins at the Mt. Zion Baptist Church every Sunday morning.

And the strangest thing was that they were perceived as respected citizens of the community. Yes sir, nothing more than God-fearing folks struggling in the farming market; so kindhearted, this generous couple sometimes showed goodwill by opening their home to wayfaring travelers.

Will Drake's General Store and upstairs saloon near Two Sweet Gums Road both served as a stopping place for weary travelers seeking goods and services on their Westward way over the Old Indian Trail. Those who needed a comfortable night's rest were politely directed to the Kimbrell home.

During the early stages of the West Clan's misdeeds and adventures, my father was told a story about an elderly couple who passed through on their way to the Promised Land of Texas.

One day Ira and Jean Mabelvey arrived at the Kimbrell home in their clean, sturdy buggy and nice threads. Welcomed like lost relatives, the Mabelveys were invited in to wash up and partake in that evening's supper of cornbread and beans, squash and fried squirrel.

The Kimbrells, always exceptional hosts, asked of their travels from Georgia.

Excited in the prospect of settling in Texas, the Mabelveys described their travels with poetic grace, confirming that they'd seen unknown areas of the southern territory in vivid detail. They had also met several kind hosts along the way, enjoying themselves throughout it all.

After the meal and fellowship, the couple was shown to an upstairs room that exuded the warm comforts of home and bid goodnight.

By all accounts, their hosts appeared natural in their hospitality and forthcoming in their eagerness to please travelers searching for shelter. Unaware that they were in the company of ice cold killers, Ira and Jean Mabelvey did not feel they were in any danger.

Ira informed his wife that Mr. Dan Kimbrell was in the market to sell his fine mare. Ira agreed come morning that he'd purchase the beast to help the old man financially in these hard times.

At daybreak, the couple woke from a peaceful night's sleep, ready to continue on their merry way. Aunt Polly whipped up some homemade biscuits and squirrel gravy that her guests ate to contentment.

The couple thanked the Kimbrells and were about to settle up for their night's stay when Uncle Dan invited Ira out to the corral.

"We'll settle up later. Let's take a look at that horse."

"Oh yes, of course," said Ira. "If it's as fine a breed as you say, I'd be glad to take it off your hands."

Uncle Dan smiled at the man's enthusiasm. "Won't take but a moment to size her up."

While the men retired to the back field, Aunt Polly asked Mrs. Jean Mabelvey if she'd like to see her garden. Mrs. Mabelvey followed her host to the side garden where Aunt Polly showed her row after row of ripe tomato plants, squash, bell peppers, and turnip greens.

"If you're so inclined, you're welcome to take a basket of food on your trip," Aunt Polly offered.

"Why, that's very kind of you, Mrs. Kimbrell. It'd be a joy," she said.

A plump red tomato caught Mrs. Mabelvey's eye. She knelt in the soft dirt to pluck it from its root, when Aunt Polly sidestepped her crouching body and slid the blade of her butcher's knife across the woman's throat, cutting cartilage with one sharp cut. Aunt Polly shuffled back as blood splattered the tilled dirt in a gush of bright red.

At the corral, Mr. Ira Mabelvey studied the black and white horse that looked well-fed and strong but aged in ways that might hinder future usefulness on the trails. He frowned. "I'm unsure, Mr. Kimbrell. Looks like crow bait in six months or so, but I appreciate the offer."

"I have another steed in the barn if you'd like to see. Selling that animal for much less anyhow."

Ira followed Uncle Dan through the large opened doors of the spacious barn. Stacks of hay filled the loft. Farming tools hanged from the walls.

As Ira searched the area for another pony, Uncle Dan removed his pole axe from its hook and stepped away.

"Where's this horse? In the field?" the perplexed man asked.

Uncle Dan swung the axe's blade into the back of Ira's head, splitting his skull clean open. He left his guest lying on the straw to bleed out. Later, he and one of his sons would strip their victim naked of clothes and personal affects (watches, rings, folding money), then drag the body to the bayou. The man's buggy would be hidden in the barn until it was either sold out of state, or burned to ashes.

Cleanup of this kind was meticulous and carried out in such a fashion that after a few hours no one might suspect a dual murder had occurred on the property. Uncle Dan and Aunt Polly found pride in their ability to silence their victims quickly, and in very little time remove any and all evidence of these horrific acts.

The Kimbrells had many neighbors and friends within earshot, so they had to be cautious in their delivery, never shooting their victims, as a series of echoing gun-blasts might summon unwanted attention. Careful in their execution, Aunt Polly's tainted butcher's knife ensured death at the throat, while Uncle Dan utilized the lightning force of a steel blade.

But sometimes familiar faces stopped by unannounced.

Shy of an hour after the Kimbrells disposed of the Mableveys, Pastor James Weeks of Mt. Zion Baptist Church arrived for an afternoon visit.

Blood in the garden had barely soaked into the earth when Aunt Polly met the preacher and his wife at the front gate, welcoming them enthusiastically. Uncle Dan shook hands and ushered them inside for coffee and slices of pound cake.

While their guests enjoyed the snacks, Aunt Polly picked up a beige overcoat that had been thrown over a chair.

The pastor's wife touched the soft fabric. "My, what a handsome coat, Polly. Dan has impeccable taste!"

Their visitors had never seen any of the Kimbrells in such attire, and Aunt Polly was concerned the preacher's wife would grow suspicious.

"Oh, Dan couldn't afford a coat this nice," Aunt Polly said.

"She's right about that," Uncle Dan affirmed.

"You see, just yesterday an older gentleman and his wife boarded the night. He bought a newer coat in Ruston because he said he'd outgrown this one," Aunt Polly explained. "So, he left it with us. I figured one of the boys would wear it, but they're sworn to their ugly dusters, like boys tend to be. Perhaps Pastor Weeks might enjoy it."

"It is a nice piece of fabric," the pastor said.

"It's yours if you'd like it, pastor," Uncle Dan offered.

Pastor Weeks politely waved off the offer, instead directing his host's attention to the tanned mare in their corral. He claimed he did not notice the horse there a couple of days ago when he passed through on his way to Sunday services and was curious where they found such a beautiful animal.

"That's a fine horse you've got out there. Where'd y'all purchase it?" he asked.

In a community where everyone had a good idea of what everyone else owned, it was necessary that Aunt Polly explained in false detail how she acquired the horse and that soft coat, to hide the reality behind their actions.

She recalled how their visitor, the old man, traded his horse for a more mature mare they owned. "Ol' girl we traded for that beauty has a kinder nature . . . to endure long trips."

The pastor and his wife stayed nearly an hour, thanked the Kimbrells for their hospitality, and then continued their trip into Natchitoches.

*****

Later on, when the town folk discovered the truth of how the Kimbrells murdered the Mableveys and stole their buggy, horse, and suitcase full of clothes, the pastor claimed that something was definitely amiss in the Kimbrells' attitudes that day.

"They were cordial, accepting of our company as always. But we believed the Kimbrells were hiding something they wouldn't entrust to another soul," the pastor claimed. When he found out the ulterior motives behind their gift-giving and those passing explanations for newer things, he declared he wasn't absolutely convinced at the time but took Uncle Dan and Aunt Polly's word as truth.

"My wife and I could have easily become victims in that family's boarding house of horrors," Pastor Weeks told a farmer named Wallace Cole. "They created a carnival of bloodshed that I heard spanned the length of ten years."

Chapter 4

The gang was not created overnight.

Around 1835, an American outpost was established in the Sabine territory of Louisiana, during which time social conditions improved for quite awhile. But as the war with Mexico erupted, this affair brought with it men of all types and all temperaments into the Southeast, making gradual, civilized progress a sudden playground for the cruel-minded.

Army engineers for General Zachary Taylor created a highway of the Natchez Trace. The name Natchez was derived from the Natchez Indians, who originally settled the area. Trails they blazed were marked by directions "notched" in the bark of trees, which provided successive guided pathways, or "notched trails", to assist tribe members in accurate travel.

When both the Alamo massacre and the final annexation of the Great State of Texas had become one for the history books, a lawyer and Methodist minister named John A. Murrell from Franklin, Tennessee (who preached the Good Word for well over twenty years), suddenly turned to banditry and enjoyed the pleasures it employed.

Murrell arrived on the strip and joined up with the Copeland gang. The Copeland brothers, Frank and Jim, were a pair of narrow-minded fools who displayed average talents for robbing wayfaring strangers. Slaves to the drink, they were never very reliable and prone to failure. Messy and unorganized in their methods to lead a bunch of cutthroats, John Murrell knew, if given the chance, he could outperform as the gang's leader.

Fortunately for Murrell, the brothers were caught for their misdeeds and hanged by lawmen in Coushatta, Louisiana. To escape justice, their members dispersed into different territories of the state.

At this point, in the year 1842, John Murrell ushered in his own gang (which included some of the older Kimbrells), and took over activities on the strip. His robbing and murderous adventures eventually won him the title of "Reverend Devil". For more than twelve years, Murrell's Mystic Clan—as it was known—robbed anyone worth a nickel.

One young man who joined this clan was none other than John Robert West, a rebellious thirteen-year-old ready to take on the world. Through Murrell, West learned the basics of thievery, poised as a prodigy to someday take over Murrell's Mystic Clan.

But when John Murrell died of tuberculosis in Pikesville, Tennessee in 1854, the Mystic Clan dissolved. John West worked his father's farm awhile and then enlisted in the Louisiana Infantry. He went on to fight his fellow brethren in the Civil War, earning lifelong skills of military tactic and survival, which he later put to use.

John West grew into a heavy-set man with thick shoulders, a round face and fire-stricken red hair that bled a light touch of blond. Underneath a field hat—some called it a cowboy hat—the man's sharp green eyes looked upon the world in constant wonderment. He possessed a disarming gentleman's charm that misled folks into a false sense of trust. Like the "Reverend Devil", West was adept at gaining people's confidence while simultaneously hiding the evil that controlled his desires.

And West would ultimately outdo the corrupt minister in acting out a believable religious, God-fearing lifestyle, all while mastering the art of highway robbery—not to mention killing more than the Murrell gang ever thought possible.

The clan leader owned a farmhouse overlooking Little Hill Bayou, complete with numerous chickens, horses, and roaming cattle under the watchful eye of a healthy bull. He also tended a bountiful garden and ran a cotton gin that generated a satisfying monthly income from sales in Monroe and Shreveport.

His wife, Sara West, was a sweet woman. She cooked and cleaned and kept house, but her main duty was raising their three daughters, known at school as the West girls—Elly, Ginger, and Faye. Sara West loved and respected her husband. She did not know of his Dr. Jekyll and Mr. Hyde personality as a respectable man of the community by day and a trained thief by night.

In the beginning, at least, that was the rumor.

When the story of the nightriders bloomed into full-fledged legend, it's funny how folks in later years could not believe that the wife of one of the most proficient killers in southern history had no knowledge of her husband's late-night business. The fact of the matter was that John West guarded his home life from his darker side. Unlike some men of the era, he did not feel the need, nor have the urge, to inform his wife of his affairs.

She did not nag him when he arrived home late. Sara took his word that he'd been at the General Store visiting friends or playing cards at the Kimbrell's ranch down the road. She played the part of silent housewife and questioned nothing.

Early on, West became a member of the Mount Zion Baptist Church of Atlanta, and would one day serve as its Sunday School teacher. It was while sitting in those hard-backed wooden pews, singing the praises of Jesus Christ, that he met Uncle Dan Kimbrell.

West and Kimbrell had similar interests in hunting, and in a short time became acquainted.

West looked up to the old man, who was very knowledgeable about the area and the sport of tracking deer and leading ducks. The elder Kimbrell had also taken a liking to the young man, and welcomed him into the community as one of his own.

Before long a level of trust had been gained between the two men. West regaled Kimbrell with tales of his time running with John Murrell's bandits, and later at war with the Yankees.

Kimbrell admired West for his aggressive nature and winning charm. The older man saw John West as a mirror image of his younger self—hungry to make a fast dollar by any means necessary. Stories of hijinks in the Mystic Clan and fighting a bloody war were impressive, yes, but Uncle Dan Kimbrell wanted to witness firsthand this boy's true grit.

"There's only two ways in which to kill a man," Uncle Dan said. "Take him by surprise, or get to know him."

Kimbrell introduced West to the art of murder-for-wealth one rainy night when a lone stranger on horseback traveled down the Trace.

As a way to ensure they were bonded by unwavering trust, Kimbrell supervised from the forest, while West was expected to kill, then dispose of the body himself.

West trotted up alongside the stranger. Surveyed his satchel bag and horse. Old and tired, the animal was nothing to brag about. The man was clean-shaven and healthy in appearance, and by all accounts looked as if he had coins on his person.

As planned, West struck up a conversation with the man. His name was Louis Wright, an out-of-work barber hoping to secure employment in Baton Rouge.

John West did not rob Louis Wright that night. He did not harm the man. He listened and rode along, then bid the traveler farewell.

When West returned to the prearranged spot to meet Kimbrell, the old man was not there. He waited for a spell in the darkness, then heard a gunshot ring out.

A rider approached from the direction in which West wandered just minutes before.

Rain-soaked and angry, Uncle Dan Kimbrell pulled the reins to his horse. "Why on earth did you let him go free? I told you what to do!"

"That man had nothin' worth takin'. He's out of work. Ridin' a old nag, to boot." West shook his head. "Didn't seem like we'd get much out of the deal, 'specially if I went off and killed him. Sore back s'all after diggin' the grave."

Kimbrell sat quiet atop his horse. He removed a black saddle bag off the horse's rump and opened the long flap, revealing a flask of whiskey in the rain, surrounded by gold coins. "Out of work or not, men on the road got to have a way to get by. Look here at what you almost missed."

"*Shit!* What about the rider? Mr. Wright?"

"You know his name?"

"Yes sir. Louis Wright. That's what he told me."

"Louis Wright fell off his horse, son." Dan Kimbrell sealed the bag and threw it to West. "But he left enough coins in that satchel to allow you a comfortable season, if you know how to spend it. There's more where that came from . . . and it all comes down this road."

West nodded, feeling disappointed for letting the old man down.

"Let me tell ya, West. When you get in deep, don't ever let them go. If you're going to rob a man, you might as well do him a favor and dispatch him in a quick fashion . . . because believe me, if they live, they'll talk. If they talk, they'll find you. If they don't find you, the authorities they talk to *will*. Clean up your mess. Enjoy your find. Don't complicate these endeavors with bothersome feelings or muddled thinkin'."

Chapter 5

Later in their criminal career, Uncle Dan Kimbrell and Aunt Polly (efficient and vicious killers to be sure) slacked off bringing human prey into their home. Negative rumors had begun to spread about the couple, most notably that they may have robbed a few guests in their farmhouse. "Few" was an understatement indeed. Uncle Dan and Aunt Polly and their sons disposed of several more folks in their time.

How this rumor started was unimportant to Dan Kimbrell. Harsh consequences of being hanged got the elder Kimbrell's attention, and so he demanded the butchery cease immediately—before his family was caught. If authorities suspected these allegations to be true, they'd sniff out the farm and look over the grounds. They'd stumble across a femur, or jawbone stuck up out of the earth from the rains, find assorted clothing in the house that did not fit the Kimbrell's taste of style.

During this time, instead of luring folks back to the safety of a warm house with the promise of lodging and an evening's supper, Uncle Dan's son, Lawson Kimbrell, managed to step the organization up a notch with the help of John West, creating a gang that rode at night and robbed folks on the roads. In contrast to how Uncle Dan and Aunt Polly operated in processing mass murder, Lawson's gang cut out unnecessary greetings, initiated more clever tricks to blindside, and put on airs to gain people's trust. Thanks to her oldest son's clever designs, Aunt Polly's stained floor remained free of blood years after the West-Kimbrell gang was formed.

Uncle Dan did not regularly ride with the West Clan, but on occasion he had the impulse to once again take advantage of his fellow man. So one evening he decided to go tracking on the Old Sparta Road alongside Ab Martin, a fellow clan member.

A few miles east of this road was a well-known camping area called Clear Spring, created for the benefit of weary travelers moving through Winn Parish. This location also served as a hotbed in finding targets for West and his clansmen.

The two riders slowed as they passed, their interest peaked by the sight of a fine horse and buggy.

It was in a lone clearing on Clear Spring that Dan Kimbrell and Ab Martin held up a roving horse trader and his fifteen-year-old son.

Uncle Dan killed the man using his old ball and cap pistol.

Waited for Ab Martin to shoot the son.

But Ab Martin's gun misfired.

Seizing his chance to escape, the boy hopped on the saddle and kicked his horse in high gear. He rushed through the woods and out on Sparta Road, where other travelers created a crowd of security, then hightailed it like lightning.

A month later, Uncle Dan and another clansman, Wendell Riley, returned home from Winnfield on business and crossed Clear Spring. They noticed two campers resting near the water. Tents had been set up, and an iron pot of beans hung over a fire.

Uncle Dan felt the urge to indulge himself. Maybe they had some gold. "Wait here," Dan told his partner, and turned his horse in the direction of the campers.

The crusty old outlaw's intent was clear, his partner decided. The old man would rob the campers and most likely shoot them before they enjoyed their supper.

A few minutes later, as the clansman waited for Uncle Dan's return, a single shot thundered over the pines.

Uncle Dan rushed out of the forest, leaning far over the saddle, and rode hard past his partner.

"Come on! Get outta here!" Dan yelled.

Dan Kimbrell gave no explanation why the rush. The confused rider caught up to Dan down the road, looking suspiciously beyond the dust for other men on horses. But they were alone in the fading light as they rounded the Old Sparta Road and cut through a wooded path that bled onto the Natchez Trace.

Arriving at the Kimbrell farmhouse long before his partner, Uncle Dan stumbled up the stairs and through the front door. He said nothing to Aunt Polly, who was currently braiding Mattie's hair in the kitchen by lamplight. His two sons, Shep and William, relaxed in the front room.

They later admitted to Laws that they had never seen the old man move so fast.

Uncle Dan found the nearest bedroom and shut the door, unwilling to answer his family's concerned inquiries.

"Dan? What's wrong?" Aunt Polly asked. "Supper's gettin' cold, so you best come on outta there quick-like or these boys'll empty the pot of stew I been bawlin' all evenin'. You hear me Dan Shaw? Dan!"

"Pa? Is there somethin' amiss? Open the door, Pa," Shep Kimbrell pleaded.

"You all right in there, old man?" William asked, trying the door for the third time.

"Leave me be!" yelled Uncle Dan. "Cain't you vultures allow a man rest?"

Aunt Polly finally noticed the other rider standing at the door, hat in his hands. She recognized the rider but couldn't recall his name.

"Well? Come out with it. What'd that fool husband of mine get himself into?"

Wendell Riley shrugged. "We were comin' back from Winnfield, ma'am, just runnin' errands s'all. Halfway up the Sparta Road, Mr. Kimbrell saw some campers out on Clear Spring and turnt his horse t'wards the woods in a flash. I heard a shot. Just one. Not rightly sure who got the wrong end of the gun."

"So that's it, huh? He went and got himself shot?" Aunt Polly asked.

Wendell Riley looked at the hateful expressions on Shep and William Kimbrell, knowing that he had to choose his words carefully, or this just may be his last conversation. "I don't know exactly, Mrs. Kimbrell. It all happened so fast. Mr. Kimbrell came flying out on the road like a banshee. He told me to get on outta there. That's all I know, ma'am. God's honest truth."

Aunt Polly looked at her two sons and their gun belts hanging on the coat rack high above their heads, as if to give an unspoken order. Mattie was curling her fingers through the half-braided knots in her hair, curious eyes on her big brothers. Shep and William relaxed in their chairs (which was a good thing for Wendell Riley), William running the edge of his thumb over the blade of a sharpened hunting knife, Shep pulling on a high-riding leather boot (which was a bad thing for Wendell Riley).

"Well, fine. Let us alone, will ya?" Aunt Polly asked. "This is a family affair and we don't need the likes of another rider here right now. Unnerstand?"

"Yes ma'am." The rider propped his field hat on his sweaty hair and turned the horse toward the gates.

Because Uncle Dan refused to discuss the matter, his family left the patriarch alone for the better part of the evening.

When Laws arrived home, Aunt Polly told him what transpired.

Then they all watched with apprehension as Laws beat on the door, demanding his father open up.

Chapter 6

Around midnight, Dr. Tom Harrison, the best surgeon and medic in Winn Parish, was awakened by hard knocks at the front door of a bricked colonial home he shared with his wife and daughter.

Dr. Harrison was a thin, balding man who wore home-sewn shirts that his wife created on her step-pedal Singer sewing machine. He enjoyed the sturdy feel of cleaned black trousers cuffed neatly at the ankles, the assurance every step provided while walking about town in his classy dress shoes, and how those precious, hand-crafted spectacles he had shipped in from Rhode Island made him appear much smarter than he actually was. Quiet and studious, he ran a prosperous business in Natchitoches. Like scores of other healers over the years, he hadn't allowed the temptation of mind-altering stimulants and rambling women destroy his livelihood—instead focusing on the health of his fellow man (in return for fair payment) to see that his family survived these weathered times.

He blinked sleep out of his eyes, found his eyeglasses, and walked the long hallway in long-johns and leather boots stained by a history of animal shit, gray hair frizzed out in all directions. He hoped this wasn't an emergency. Oh sure, he'd figure out a way to help someone after office hours, even when they're banging on his front door, as he possessed an almost maddening empathy for his fellow, ailing man. Always wanted to help.

But Dr. Harrison had already worked a full day at the office, and when he got home his wife asked him to clip the front bushes, so by the time he ate supper and slipped under the covers, he was just plain tired. At this hour he wasn't feeling very sympathetic to smile it all away and even begin to care.

He opened the front door and was met by three men in boot-dragging duster coats that wrapped around their bodies like drapes, their faces covered by potato sacks. Slits had been cut out of the tough, scratchy fabric, and Dr. Harrison immediately honed in on the evil in the men's eyes.

One of them pulled a pistol. "Dr. Harrison? You're comin' with us. *Now*."

Fear taking his heart, the doctor said, "Gentlemen, please, there's no need for drastic measures. Tell me the reason for your visit, and I'll try to help."

"Get in the wagon."

"If you seek medical attention, I'm glad to assist you where we stand, but I will not leave my home at this hour. My wife's asleep."

The man put the gun barrel to the doctor's forehead. "Get in the wagon. Or the next time your wife *and* your daughter sees you, you'll be under a stone." He cocked the hammer. "Got it, Doc?"

Dr. Harrison's eyes lit up in understanding. "Why of course. Anything you say, yes . . . just let me get the um, I'll get my tools. They're ah, right here, right behind me."

Using the barrel of his pistol, Laws Kimbrell pushed the door wide, kept watch as Dr. Harrison retreated into the foyer and retrieved his medical bag.

The doctor was then blindfolded and ushered onto a waiting coach and instructed to remain silent. A half-hour later, the carriage came to an abrupt stop. He was pushed at gunpoint up the steps of a house, the smell of spicy black-eyed peas roiling on the stovetop suddenly making him feel queasy.

Someone removed the blindfold.

Dr. Harrison found himself in a bedroom lit by candles and lamplight, looking at a man lying on his back on a large mattress. Like his captors, this man wore a mask, the middle of his shirt covered in crude, blood-stained bandaging.

"Well? What're ya waitin' for?" asked the gunman. "Look him over and give us the news. Can you fix him?"

The wounded man kept both hands flat over his stomach, wheezing as he breathed, his large brown eyes below the cutout holes in the mask tired and old and fading fast.

Dr. Harrison placed his medical bag at the foot of the bed. Carefully lifted the bandages. He studied the explosive wound across the stomach, then slowly shook his head, knowing that the man lying before him was not long for this world.

"Do something!" demanded the agitated gunman.

His captors did not want to hear the truth, but damn the consequences, he was prepared to give it to them. Dr. Tom Harrison was a caregiver, not Jesus Christ.

"Sir, at this point, there is little I can do. This man has suffered a fatal gunshot wound to the abdomen, the area where blood concentrates to digest food and dispose of bodily waste. Most of his stomach has been punched out. He's lost several pints of blood. Best I can do is assure he's as comfortable as possible." Dr. Harrison reached for his bag, and felt the silence in the room weigh down on him.

None of the men seemed choked up about the news. No one cried out or shed a tear, and (thankfully) no one asked the good doctor further questions. He unfastened the flap of his bag and rummaged through for a needle and a vial of clear liquid that had MPHN stamped on the side.

"What'll that medicine do?"

Dr. Harrison turned to the masked psycho. "If you'll allow . . . this injection will make him *comfortable*. He'll feel no more pain from his wound. He'll pass."

"You can't save him then?" another psycho asked.

"The only man who can save him now is the man upstairs," replied Dr. Harrison. "Do I have your permission to administer morphine? Or would you rather this man remain in excruciating pain?"

"Make it quick," Uncle Dan whispered hoarsely.

Dr. Harrison rolled up the man's shirt's sleeve on his left arm and found a blue vein in the crook of his elbow. He stuck the tip of the needle into the vial, sucked up liquid. Quick, escalating comfort, the medicine would send the wounded man into a fog of numbness and blissful pleasure. The doctor squirted drops out of the needle to clear it of air bubbles, and aimed for a vein.

Before the tip of the needle pricked skin, the man before them coughed violently and hacked a line of black blood into the threads of his cloth mask. Choking, his body writhing terribly, Uncle Dan's eyes (alive with shock) pleaded for mercy.

Jolted by the outburst, Dr. Harrison pulled back, holding the tip of the needle inches from the man's skin.

"Pa!"

But Pa didn't answer.

Pa died.

And he died in all the torturous pain his victims may have wished upon that sorry son of a bitch.

*****

The next day his sons lay to rest "Uncle" Dan Shaw Kimbrell, an event that lacked the usual fanfare of sympathizers. No one read scripture from the Holy Bible. No one shared their thoughts in a Eulogy. Not one member of this scarred family dedicated any meaning to Dan Shaw Kimbrell's life.

I'm guessing that's how it should have been. I stood there at the edge of the woods holding a stringer of fish while Uncle Dan Kimbrell burned like seasoned wood in the depths of Satan's Hell.

They wondered about it, but Shep and William and Lawson Kimbrell would never discover who actually shot their father that fateful day.

I sure wasn't going to tell them that the gunman was Jacob Bayless, the fifteen-year-old son of the horse trader Uncle Dan killed on Clear Spring only a month before. I find it fascinating the boy had the gumption to return to the scene of the crime and that he had such respect for his father to wait patiently for the scoundrel who committed his murder, and then avenge his father's death.

Angered to a point of no return that Uncle Dan was gone from this earth, Laws saw red. He grew meaner, more irritable, unsatisfied with his meandering life. Without the direction of Uncle Dan Kimbrell, and seeing as how Aunt Polly totally lost her will to live after her husband's death, Laws Kimbrell was well on his way to becoming the area's most notorious killer.

Chapter 7

This would not be a poetic (nor accurate) story, if I did not reveal the presence of one Daniel Arron Dean, an ex-Confederate soldier who made the trek as a Prisoner of War with Lawson Kimbrell from the foothills of Georgia to the swamps of Louisiana.

Dan Dean was of medium height and handsome, with dark, closely cropped hair, calm blue eyes, and an easy smile. After the war, he worked the family farm, raising cattle and chickens. Dan and Laws were friends, but when they returned to their homeland in Louisiana, the two men took very different life paths.

While Dan made an honest living, attended barn dances, and occasionally indulged in the company of ladies, Laws Kimbrell was fast becoming a powerful member of the West Clan, spending most nights planning robberies, his days drinking whiskey and looking over the account books at Will Drake's General Store.

Now, to be clear, Dan Dean had once been a member of the nightriders, but his actions were not of the greedy or sadistic nature. Dan truly believed he was serving his community as a nightrider by watching for carpetbaggers and thieves and ex-Yankee soldiers who might arrive to disrupt his fellow neighbor's way of life. The Reconstruction Era was in full swing, and the country was overrun with wicked minds who willingly took advantage of God-fearing, hardworking folks. Protection from these twisted souls was of utmost importance.

Dan Dean and Laws Kimbrell were not as close as they had been once upon a time, but they kept in touch. Dan saw him at Will Drake's Store from time to time, or walked in on Laws at the barber's shop, then struck up a brief conversation of no matter. Even though Dan knew of his old friend's involvement within the West Clan, one thing was certain: so adept in his talents, from an outsider's perspective, Laws appeared as just another good ol' boy trying to ease back into an honest, work-a-day civilian life. Nothing more.

Another thing Dean and Kimbrell had in common was how well they handled a pistol. Both were skilled gun-throwers, and some believed Dan Dean quicker on the draw than his friend.

But I'm getting ahead of myself.

Yes sir, Dan Dean was a sure gentleman. An honest man. He could be a mean gun-thrower, too, let me tell you. When he got wind of the robberies on the main road from Natchitoches through Winnfield and Atlanta, he did not saddle up and ride out to play the hero.

He minded his business. Even though he heard that John West and his nightriders might be responsible for these events, Dan Dean kept his mouth shut. Even if he suspected John West of running an inner circle of killers within a supposed group of honest men, Dean knew that by voicing his opinions about the subject to the wrong person may lead to a fight he couldn't win.

Word of the roadway robberies finally reached the ears of Parish authorities, who would not stand for this type of shit to continue anywhere near their town. The search to apprehend these ruthless cutthroats kept officers occupied for quite some time, but sadly, no one in connection to the nightriders was apprehended.

Winnfield's sheriff, however, spent hardly any time investigating the matter. Sounds cowardly, yes, but Sheriff Hayden Rose was smarter than most people will have you believe.

Sheriff Rose knew about the clan's "inner circle". The men in that group wouldn't think twice about ending his career in law.

It was common sense, really. If Sheriff Rose arrested John West, Laws Kimbrell, Lec Ingram, and Abram "Ab" Martin, among others without substantial proof, the courts would throw out the case because of insufficient evidence. Then it'd be too late for Sheriff Rose. By the time he left the Natchitoches courthouse, his family would be dead, and he'd be lucky to make the trail back to safe haven in Winnfield before the gang rushed out of the shadows.

And if he tracked these types of men in vigilante fashion, he'd certainly lose the battle.

So it stands to reason and served his best interest why Sheriff Rose decided to hang back and let it ride. He neither saw nor heard evil. In his mind, he ran a smooth operation. He kept the town safe from outsiders. By not tracking down every last member of the nightriders, some may have called him a coward behind his back, but

Sheriff Rose felt he was doing the right thing—protecting his family from those who might destroy them, should he dig too deep.

The longer Dan Dean stayed in Winnfield, the more he understood why Sheriff Rose played it safe. Whoever ran this outfit, whether it be John West or a complete stranger, the fact of the matter shown clear: they'd kill you after dark, for even a few gold coins, or a fine horse.

Friend or foe.

Chapter 8

Unlike hundreds of other soldiers, Laws Kimbrell survived the bloody Battle of Shiloh in Tennessee. He went on to fight the Union until he was captured and held as a Prisoner of War in Georgia.

After the Civil War, Laws returned to Winnfield and the Atlanta and Montgomery areas to begin again. Lawson's father, Dan Shaw Kimbrell, introduced him to John West, and together the men created the clan with the assistance of a few notable cutthroats in the area. This gang was initially created to ward off criminals of all types, especially thieves interested in moving in on their territory.

Soon, adjoining towns found a decent level of peace.

For a while.

Laws Kimbrell and John West agreed to keep the gang together—not by utilizing a home guard. They were more interested in robbing wayfaring travelers on the main thoroughfare.

The El Camino Real, or original Natchez Trace as it would be formally known, swept up from eastern Mexico through Central Louisiana, and then cut through Mississippi into Tennessee.

In a span of six years, some of the most brutal murders in Louisiana's history were committed on this road—as one after another, countless people lost their lives to these outlaws.

The West-Kimbrell Clan killed so many innocent people that the gang did not have the time (nor resources) to bury every last body. They created a better method for disposing warm corpses in the form of several strategically placed round, bricked wells that had been dug ten feet into the earth.

Here they would deposit their victims in the wells, then go about the business of removing any trace of their handiwork. They repainted wagons and sold them to naïve Texas buyers; emptied their stables of stolen horses to connections in Arkansas and Mississippi. They gained monetary value at all costs and in any form, from expensive jewelry and gold coins, to clothing and living accessories.

The nightriders either hid or used goods accordingly. The clan ran a modern day racket of stolen goods, gaining huge profit margins. At the time no one knew who was behind these awful dealings. No one in central Louisiana suspected their neighbor or a passing stranger. The nightriders, local folks said, was made up of ghosts.

The truth was far more disturbing than your average citizen might think. Culprits behind these horrific crimes were the same folks you'd see on any given day in any neighboring town: having lunch inside a hotel lobby, buying goods, paying two bits of silver for a shave and a cut, or at church serving the same God you believe in.

In a short amount of time the nightriders accomplished scores of dirty deeds. If the West Clan believed you had something worth their time, they'd waylay you. They accumulated so much wealth that they needed an accountant to keep the books.

Laws Kimbrell was not only a leader of this gang, he was part of the group of men who executed the murders. This "inner circle" was made up of sixteen trusted men. The rest of the hundred or so members were mostly lookouts, including couriers and others who believed they were still providing a home guard, as Mr. Dan Dean once had. Other members obeyed orders by dealing out whatever goods the clan made away with, in exchange for a slice of the pie.

Turning profits through the redistribution of horses and wagons and valuables served the gang well. Blacksmith shops dotted along the Trace were important to the gang's industrious progress. Here, wagons were modified and repainted for selling. The vast majority of the West Clan members did not know the names of those in the inner circle, and members of that group did not advertise such incriminating information.

In effect, they were ghosts, invisible to the curious eye.

Because there were so many of them, when meeting another rider on a beaten path, a secret password was used to identify the rider as a fellow clan member. If a nightrider said: "The clover is blooming," the other man would reply: "Spring is here."

A different response may result in the wayfaring stranger's immediate death. Then the nightrider would steal all his valuables, take this horse and clothing, and leave him in the bayou. Or find a nearby well to rid evidence of a crime. Travelers did not have to appear as though they had money. As long as they had a healthy horse, they'd likely be killed for it.

As a way to communicate with other members, different signs were notched into trees—some that designated meeting areas, others that directed a nightrider down secret trails toward hideouts, or to even mark places where a body lay. Before a robbery, they even mimicked the sounds of owls and fleeting birds to communicate their locations.

John West's most prized possession was a bullhorn inlaid with jewels and carved with the initials J. R.W.

Whenever West came across a potential victim, he blew this horn to summon riders. West's ability to organize the clan was evident in his use of signals cut in the bark of trees and identifying passwords such as "Spring is here". This ancient way of communicating served him well in expanding the gang and knowing exactly who was a member (and who was not) simply by their knowledge of such implementations. If he needed his men to gather at an unscheduled meeting, he'd puff out specified signals the gang understood by sound. Six blasts from the horn meant a meeting at his home above Little Hill Bayou. Other predetermined blasts meant either he needed men at his Prescott Gin or at Will Drake's General Store, or over at the Kimbrell Farmhouse.

Each sound had its meaning, and at the sound of that horn every rider of the circle was expected to put on hold their daily affairs and join the group—lest they face an angry John West, who showcased no patience for excuses and expressed little emotion in understanding tardiness.

Chapter 9

July 8, 1866

"Got one comin' up the road and he's lone." John West looked back at Laws and spat a wad of chew on the forest floor. "Let's make time and see where the young man's headed."

The two clansmen ventured out on the main road, their horses kicking up red dust in the summer air, and met up alongside a uniformed man. He looked to be in his late twenties, maybe early thirties. They weren't sure, but didn't really care about his age. He wore a Union soldier's uniform, and that alone made him an enemy of the South, especially considering the war had ended.

"Good evening sir!" John West said, touching the brim of his field hat in greeting. "How are you getting along this fine day?"

"Well enough to ride, I'd say."

"Ain't seen a fine filly around this road have ya? We lost her 'bout a mile or so back. Got through that old fence I been meanin' to fix."

"Can't say I have, mister," the man replied. His uniform was free of wrinkles, the Union cap slanted just over his brow so that Laws and West were unable to see his eyes. "You say you're from around these parts?"

"Yes sir. Why, I've got a homestead here full of cattle. Got me a cotton gin. Nice area for cotton," West said. "Are ya just passin' through our small territory of Louisiana?"

"Yes. On official business," the man said.

"My name is John West. This is my business partner, Mr. Lawson Kimbrell."

"Lieutenant Simeon Butts. Good to meet you gentlemen."

"Likewise, Lieutenant Butts," West said. He could not help but notice the heavy saddle bags hanging on either side of the horse's rump, and wondered what they held. There was only a practical reason why a military man on the El Camino Real was traveling south through this land of pine trees and swamps: he was destined for the City of New Orleans. "Coming from out of state, are ya Lieutenant?"

The Yankee soldier did not have any reason to believe these men were anything but good-natured. They were just curious to see a man in uniform, spend some time talking as they searched for their missing horse. The Lieutenant had experienced war firsthand and felt that he knew when evil was near. And so he thought his new company posed little threat.

"Down from Pennsylvania, to be direct. There's a post in New Orleans where I'm expected in two days' time. Forgive me should I sound rude, gentlemen, but I am conducting military business, and not at liberty to discuss the matter any further."

West raised his hand. "Forgive me for prying. We just don't get many soldiers down this way, what with the war over and all."

"I completely understand, Mr. West."

As the three men traveled down the wide dirt road, the heat wrapped around their skin like a wool blanket. West opened a canteen of water and passed it along to Laws, who took a big gulp. West reached into his own saddlebag and produced a flask. He took a nip. Passed that to Laws.

When Laws offered the flask to Lieutenant Butts, the man smiled and shook his head.

"Thank you, but I do not partake in spirits on duty. What will make my day is water for my friend here," he said, patting the horse's black mane. "Do you happen to know of a watering hole nearby so I can replenish my steed? He's awful weary."

"You are in luck, sir. There happens to be a spring about a quarter mile over yonder. We're set right for it. You and your fine animal can rest there awhile before y'all continue your journey."

"Thank you kindly, Mr. West. That'd be of great assistance."

Sometime later the men came across a clear running spring through the pines, just off the main road near a cemetery that held exactly ten tombstones, most of which were occupied by Confederate soldiers who perished in battle.

John West got down from his trusty horse and knelt at the spring. West put his lips to the stream and drank, then smiled up at Lieutenant Butts, water falling in rivulets over his bearded chin. "Right clean water here, Lieutenant. Help yourself."

Lieutenant Butts watched his horse drink to contentment. He then replenished his canteen. He bent over toward the water's surface and splashed his sweaty face. Sipped eagerly out of his cupped palm.

Then, in the reflection of the clear stream he saw the lengthened shadow of a man approach at his back, and fear gripped his heart.

Kimbrell fired a bullet through the back of the Lieutenant's head, the gun blast resounding across the land.

The Lieutenant fell into the spring, limp and gone. The man's horse jumped back, then returned to lapping up a colorful mixture of dirt, water, and blood.

West and Kimbrell made quick work of getting rid of the body. They undressed the soldier. West opened the Lieutenant's heavy bags, and his evil grin stretched wide into his cheeks at the find.

That evening, West and Kimbrell burned the Lieutenant's uniform and identification in a bonfire behind West's farmhouse on Iatt Creek. Next, they hid the man's horse for safety overnight in West's stable, intending to profit from the sale of the animal next day or so.

Taking stock in the back room of the house, they found several gold bullion in the soldier's bags along with two hundred coins he'd been carrying on his person. They delighted in their take. The bullion alone netted them over twelve thousand dollars.

But this was no ordinary robbery. The riders were well aware they had killed an active military man. When he did not show up as expected at the post in New Orleans, the Army would send out soldiers to investigate the whereabouts of the missing Lieutenant.

West and Laws Kimbrell had to lay low for a spell, let the storm pass. They did not want to be tracked by Army officials. If that level of authority caught them, forget seeking trial—the state militia would hang these riders from the nearest Oak.

*****

A month passed and any investigation into the Lieutenant's disappearance that may have commenced, never led back to the clan leaders.

While hunting squirrel for dinner an elderly gentleman discovered the body of Lieutenant Butts lying beside the flowing spring. By now the body had been consumed by the animals of the forest, leaving a skeleton of the man, the only apparel left to see a copper button ripped from his uniform and the tattered remains of stained underwear.

This murder marked the definitive beginning of John West and Lawson Kimbrell's bloody, six-year crusade throughout central Louisiana. Their dealings would strike fear in those who heard of the gang, and leave travelers dreaming of a better life beyond the Texas line dead and bloated at the bottom of a deep, dry well.

Chapter 10

1870

One afternoon when Laws heard the call from the hunting horn, he strapped on his gun belt and saddled his horse, ready for hell. He met John West and the notorious Frame brothers, James and Dave, at a designated location in the woods, where the jungle-like thicket provided ample cover from wandering eyes during daylight hours.

They watched the wagon come down the road. Instead of surprising the man on this well-traveled thoroughfare, the four nightriders befriended him and struck up polite conversation, explaining that they were searching these parts for missing cattle.

"Haven't seen any cattle," the man said.

"I assume you're just passin' through our little town?" West asked.

"Yes. I've a cousin over in Alabama interested in buying my land for two thousand dollars. I'm making this trek from my wife's family home in Texas to finalize the deal. Then I shall return to Texas and build a new cabin for us."

"Fine plan indeed!" West said. "Why, my name's John West. I have a settlement just down this road a couple miles, on Iatt Creek. We have a stove, food and water for your horse, plenty of extra room. Take my offer and stay the evening. I have not been out of this country in a witch's spell. For room and board, you may enlighten me on the things you've seen among your travels."

"Thank you, Mr. West. I'd like to take you up on your kind offer, but I must make time. The sun is still high and I have camping gear for the evening. It only makes sense that I keep moving along."

"I understand. Say, what do you go by?"

"Oh, I'm Ward Lecht. Pleasure to meet you."

"Likewise, Mr. Lecht," West said. "When you come back through the area, you should stop in and have dinner with us. My Sara is a heckuva cook, bless her heart. There's excellent deer hunting in this part of Louisiana, too, lemme tell ya! You should partake in a hunt before going on to Texas. It is quite delicious eating."

"I'd like that, Mr. West," said Ward Lecht. "When I return in October, I think I'll take you up on that offer."

"As Mayor of The Wheeling Settlement and a well-read teacher of the Christian faith, I believe it is only right to be hospitable to passersby through our area. Mr. Lecht, just look for the big cotton gin up this road here a bit. My settlement is gated and has J.R.W. aligned on the posts. You are welcome through those gates any time."

The nightriders bid Mr. Ward Lecht farewell and rode on past him at a faster pace.

Then the riders switched back on winding trails.

As they watched what could have been a profitable robbery of a strong horse ride out of sight, a disappointed Laws asked why West did not press the issue.

"Jesus Christ, West, why didn't you persuade the stranger to stay the night? Late night girl incentive or something . . . . "

"Way I see it, if we'd've waylaid him here and now, we might have gotten some coins he's using to get along the trails. His horse, sure, but not much more. I'm betting when he comes back through he'll stay at our settlement and join me on a deer hunt. Come that time I'm willing to bet he'll have a couple thousand dollars for us, too. Maybe more." John West hocked and spit. "That's what I'm betting on, anyways. If he don't come back this way, he's a lucky dog."

*****

Mr. Lecht turned out to be a savvy business man. He traded real estate for a living, and from what I heard later on, the man made good on his transactions.

After that meeting with West and his men, I'll admit I wished Mr. Ward Lecht would have avoided the Natchez Trace altogether, and taken another route. But Mr. Lecht not only returned in late October across this path to Texas, he remembered the promise of a home-cooked meal and an early dawn hunting trip, and so rode right up to John West's sprawling homestead.

Just thinking back on this story makes me shudder.

It was as if John West had been waiting that entire month for the businessman to arrive.

West greeted his visitor with a strong handshake and that wide, crooked smile of his.

"Welcome back Mr. Lecht," West exclaimed. He was dressed down in an un-tucked flannel shirt and navy blue trousers, his red hair hidden under a wide-brimmed hat that shaded wild green eyes. "I presume you've had a good trip so far?"

"Why yes, Mr. West. It's been exceptionally productive. Thank you again for the invite. I brought some homemade fig jellies for your missus. So, tell me, what time should we get to trackin' them deer?"

"Ha! Good show of character! I favor a man with spirit. We'll get us a fast start on the beasts. Say, right before dawn?" West suggested. "Come now, Mr. Lecht, secure your horse and let me carry your bags. You're my guest, you're probably tired as all get out, so you'll be happy to know Ms. Sara has supper on. Afterwards, we'll uncork a bottle of brandy and chew on whatever comes to mind."

"Thank you Mr. West. After all that, I will need my rest."

"Oh, don't be concerned. We've got plenty of bedding." West tied Mr. Lecht's horse to the porch railing.

That evening, Mr. Lecht dined with John West and his wife and daughters.

Once the family retired for the night, West and Ward Lecht spent time by the wood-burning stove, sipping brandy out of small round glasses. They discussed various topics ranging from the final days of the war and those damned Yankees, to the virtues of women and raising children. West explained how he'd found this piece of fertile land while still a soldier in the infantry and had continuously profited from his twin cotton gins.

In turn, Mr. Lecht offered information that he should have kept to himself.

"Speaking of land, Mr. West, I just happened to sell my homestead in Alabama a few weeks ago."

"Congratulations, Mr. Lecht. That's grand. Sure is."

They relaxed awhile longer, then turned in for the evening.

Sara prepared breakfast the next morning—piping hot biscuits 'n gravy, crispy bacon, skillet grits, sliced apples and pears, along with a pot of hot coffee. The jars of jelly offered up by their guest was also a welcomed addition.

After satisfying their hunger, West and Mr. Lecht collected their rifles and left at the break of dawn.

West showed Mr. Lecht a trail that wound through the forests of his back field, where he claimed he'd killed many big bucks in years past, right there beyond the property line.

Shadows grew with the bleeding sun, and deep inside the woodlands they secured their horses to pine trees that had been tagged by red ribbons flapping in the chilly wind.

"We'll progress a stretch then hike down to a marsh up yonder," West whispered. "You go off that way, see that trail? Leads you right to the water. Them blessed deer love that marsh, lemme tell ya."

Without hesitation, Mr. Lecht rested his rifle on his shoulder.

It wasn't long before he lost sight of John West in the thick wilderness, and continued walking the narrow, beaten path alone. Autumn's blanket of leaves sank underfoot and twigs cracked as he searched for the marsh.

He was having a good time, sure, but his rambling thoughts once again focused on his wife, Elaine, back in Texas. Oh, how wonderful it'd be when he felt the warmth of her loving arms after so long. It had been a demanding round trip staying with strangers and relatives and suffering loneliness along the way. He'd grown tired and restless (often disillusioned at times) until he finalized the sale of his Alabama home.

A little further down the path Mr. Lecht found the bayou, just as his host directed.

Currents rippled lightly across muddy water, and he noticed dried hoof prints marking the dirt.

Mr. Lecht found camouflage behind a mighty cypress tree. Waited patiently for the first sight of deer.

He decided should he kill one he'd give the meat to his gracious host, so that Mr. West could provide for his wife and little girls . . . and why not be so kind? He was on a trip. He couldn't very well carry the dead creature to Texas and expect a proper meal. The meat would go bad. His time hunting was sporting fun, nothing else.

Mr. Lecht flicked opened his pocket watch.

Nearly an hour had elapsed since he last saw Mr. West. He'd heard no shot ring out, so apparently they were having the same luck.

This was better than riding the trails, though. He listened to critters scuttle throughout the forest, felt wind at his cheeks . . . heard the click of a pistol's hammer lock into place.

Mr. Lecht stepped around the tree, his hand gripping the rifle tightly, and walked into the long barrel of a gun.

"Mr. West! What are you—?"

"You sold your land over there in Alabama," West said.

"That's correct, I—last night, I told you I did, yes I did."

"How much didja get?"

"For my land? Quite a bit. Little over three thousand. Why? Why are you doing this?"

"Where's the gold?"

"Gold? I don't have any gold."

"Look here Mr. Lecht, this back and forth'll go smoother if you tell me what you got for your business deal over in Alabama."

"Federal reserve notes. They're easier to carry. . . please, Mr. West, if your aim is to rob a man trying to make his way back to his wife, then go ahead and take my money. They're in my saddlebags. I'll hand over every bit, just let me leave this place. I will not speak a word of this incident. That's a promise."

"Well! Aren't we generous today? And I have a promise for you as well," West said. "I promise that you won't speak of this to anybody . . . because you're the big buck I've been huntin'."

West shot him in the forehead.

*****

Ward Lecht's attractive wife, Mrs. Elaine Lecht, a preacher's daughter in her forties, with curly black hair and dark eyebrows that accentuated her blue eyes, waited patiently for her husband to arrive in Texas . . . but having no way to contact him to hear of his progress home, days turned into weeks, weeks into months—and during this time of rebirth for America (what with all the chaos and hardship hurdling forth from the aftermath of the Civil War) she accepted the possibility that he'd been selfishly waylaid for his fortune.

And so, Mrs. Elaine never saw her husband again.

Chapter 11

Lawson Kimbrell had never been married, but during his time leading the nightriders he became smitten as any man might be with Miss Annabelle Frost, a local butcher's daughter.

Annabelle was a fiery red-haired beauty bearing sharp green eyes, a curvy body, small nose, and a clean smile. A girl of only seventeen, she lived with her parents and sometimes worked by her father's side at the butcher's shop he owned in Winnfield.

Occasionally she and Laws attended local barn dances, perused retail shops in Winnfield's square, or picnicked on the riverfront of Cane River. She loved taking relaxing carriage rides with him through the bricked streets of Natchitoches. Always the quintessential gentlemen in her company, always willing to please, Laws spent seemingly endless amounts of money on dinners, fine clothing, and Shakespearian plays held at the Historic District Stage. Anything to make her happy.

Laws liked her. Annabelle, he believed, enjoyed his company, too. For quite some time they were as steady as summer doves.

Before gearing up for another night of destruction in mind, Laws often stopped in Frost's Butcher Shop to buy meat for his family's supper. Brothers Shep and William always requested strip steak. Laws favored thick-cut sirloin steaks, seasoned with salt and ground pepper.

Garrett Frost, the owner, threw in a few beef tenderloins on the house because, well, Mr. Frost thought a lot of Laws Kimbrell. He even told his wife, Mrs. Shannon Lee Frost, that if God allowed, he could definitely see this Kimbrell gent as his son-in-law. "Fine young man, fine young man," he'd say. "Dresses sharp. Handles business. Good thinkin' head on his shoulders. Money and a fine horse to boot? Ha! Our Annabelle could meet a suitor worse than the likes of Mr. Kimbrell, that's fair to say."

And if she were working at the shop when Laws showed up, Annabelle was permitted to leave early.

Depending on his mood (and whatever nightly activities he'd planned with the clan), Laws spent time with his girl until he either tired of the affair, or had to split and see to business. Eating raw oysters and crackers on the riverfront lawn, watching the day pass, would come to an abrupt end if Laws heard the call of West's hunting horn blast over the countryside.

Not nearly as apologetic as Annabelle thought he should be, Laws Kimbrell would cut short their visit and be on his way, promising to rekindle courtship at a later date.

The man she was beginning to fall for had a lot on his plate. She was too youthful, too trusting, to debate his sudden disappearances during their get-togethers. She never questioned his actions, for fear he'd lose interest in their romantic relationship.

Another problem is that Annabelle and her parents had no clue she was being courted by a calculating, merciless killer.

As part of his demeanor to receive acceptance in the pleasing eyes of Annabelle, Kimbrell behaved the gentleman, which served only as personal camouflage meant to disguise his true self—the heartless, gun-slinging leader of the West Clan Outlaws.

I remember one particular Saturday evening when Annabelle accompanied Laws on horseback to the Kimbrell farm. They visited on the front porch (him drinking corn whiskey, she sipping sugarcane tea) as the sun sent bruised pink rays over the bordering pine trees.

This episode happened several times in their courtship. On these evenings, Annabelle may stay the night, or she'd bid the Kimbrell family farewell, then follow Laws to the main road. From there she'd make the two mile journey back to Winnfield.

To assure she made a safe trip wherever she roamed on the Natchez Trace, Laws equipped Annabelle's saddle with a bright red sash that hung down the horse's side. This sash served as a signal to other gang members that the lady riding that particular horse was to be left *alone*. During a nightriders meeting Laws explained that if someone attempted to rob Annabelle Frost, at any time of day, he'd find the scoundrel, lodge the barrel of his gun down their throat and send them away.

This statement was more fact than a mere threat. Laws Kimbrell's name and reputation was known far and wide as a man who took no spit in the eye, and he'd kill anyone for a nickel and a chuckle should the psychotic reasoning overcome him.

Like other members of the inner circle, Clyde Judkins had a healthy fear of Laws Kimbrell. Clyde was a fat wild cat with freckles across his face, and long, scraggly hair that fell over his shoulders. He had an itchy trigger-finger, and like others living in one of the worst regions to gain prosperity in the nation, Clyde was on the hunt for men with gold.

I saw Annabelle leave the Kimbrell home that spring evening, breezes parting her red hair as she made her way down that dirt road.

Clyde Judkins and Darren Forte were out looking for trouble—any target, any gain—when Annabelle Frost crossed their paths.

"We got us a peach," Darren said. "You come up behind her."

Clyde nodded.

Darren Forte rushed out on the road, his hand held high. "You there! Stop your steed!"

"What's the meaning of this?" Annabelle asked. She turned and saw another man approach from her left. "Move out of my way!"

"Fine horse," Clyde Judkins declared. "Not sure which one I should take, ma'am. The pretty filly or your horse. "

Annabelle sucked in a breath.

The two men came closer, inspecting her horse and saddlebag.

"If you got money on ya, we'll take it and let you be on your way," Clyde said.

"I have no money!" Annabelle said.

"No gold?" Clyde asked. "But you've seen our faces. We've got to take *something* . . . so how about that something be you?"

Annabelle trembled.

The men stood inches from her horse. If she tried to ride away, they'd surely take shots at her. She thought better of that. Calmed her voice in an attempt to dissuade their plans.

"Please, gentlemen, this isn't right! You shouldn't do this!"

"Get her!" Clyde said, grabbing her ankle and yanking her off the saddle.

Annabelle fell into the fat man's arms, hitting her toes on the hard ground.

She tried screaming out. Clyde clamped his big hand over her soft mouth to muffle the cries, dragged her into the woods.

"Don't just stand there, you fool!" Clyde beckoned.

Darren did not move. He froze in place, looked at the girl's horse. His vision finally caught the moon rays shining across the horse's back, at its tanned saddle, at the red sash hanging down its leathery side.

"Oh my Dear God," Darren whispered. "Clyde, get back here. Leave that girl be!"

But Darren's words fell on deaf ears, as Clyde was well into the woods by now, tearing the clothes off of Annabelle Frost's slender body.

Clyde pulled her to the ground.

"No!"

"Shut your mouth, gal!" Clyde slipped his hand down her stomach and forced a knotted finger inside her vagina.

Lying helpless, crying under the stars, Annabelle prayed for mercy. The man squeezed her plump breasts and planted firm, sloppy kisses over her neck and lips. She'd rather the men kill her and get it over with than have to endure the indignity and pain of a disgusting intimate encounter.

The stranger unbuckled his belt and shucked his trousers, laughing all the while at Annabelle's attempts to fight him off.

Tears rolled out the corners of her eyes. She understood that no matter what she did, how tough she fought, however loud she screamed, no one was coming to her rescue. She'd been physically challenged miles away from the nearest ear, forced to deal with a fat, hair-bellied, half-naked man lingering above her, ready to penetrate her body.

Annabelle closed her eyes. Prayed she'd live through this.

Clyde laughed, spittle flying out of his mouth and across her face, when he was suddenly pushed off of the girl.

Clamoring about, Clyde yanked up his trousers. "Dang it, Darren! Wait your turn!"

Darren pushed him against a tree. "Leave her alone, Clyde!"

"What're you gettin' at? You gone soft? Is that it, ya crazy fool? Are you a pigtail now? Look at this treasure of flesh we got here. Get you a taste when I finish! Now go hide her horse."

"I ain't touchin' that horse," Darren said. "And I sure as rain ain't touchin' that girl."

"Why the hell not?"

"Because of this," Darren said, holding up the red sash. "Found it on the horse's saddle. Laws Kimbrell put it there. That there's Kimbrell's girl you're wrestling with."

I wish you could have seen the look in Clyde Judkins' eyes when he heard those words.

Clyde quickly stepped away, stumbled onto the main road, apologizing under his breath: "Jeez, ma'am, forgive me. I didn't mean no disrespect. Please, here . . . here's your horse, safe and sound. Go on home and have a peaceful evening. I—I'm so . . . ." Clyde's words trailed off. He untied his horse and turned the animal toward the darkness of a westbound path.

Darren watched him go, then turned his back to Annabelle. "You can get dressed now, ma'am. I sincerely apologize for my friend's actions. He didn't know. He uh, didn't see the sash."

Annabelle walked out of the woods, shaken but alive, listening to the stranger's adamant apologies. Climbed on her horse.

"You should be ashamed of yourself, the both of you!" she said, wiping tears from her cheek. "How could anyone be so cruel? What kind of animals are you to take on a defenseless woman in the dark? You! . . . You goddamn *cowards!*"

Feeling the need to explain himself, but knowing damn well more talk might lead to his demise as a member of the nightriders, Darren mounted his brown horse and tipped his hat in a kind gesture.

Darren Forte understood that he and Clyde had really messed up, and the longer he lingered in the girl's sight, the better she'd remember the details of his face in the stark moonlight. He had to get a move on, and quick.

With a swift kick to his horse's side, Darren disappeared into the woods, leaving Annabelle Frost alone on the Natchez Trace.

Chapter 12

Early on a February morning in 1872, Dan Dean fried eggs and country ham and drank two cups of black coffee. Dressed in black trousers and a gray shirt, he sat on the edge of a flowery-patterned loveseat and polished his boots to a glowing shine, staring off in deep thought.

For the better part of three months he had gone through a difficult time rediscovering the bachelor lifestyle. His steady lady friend, Ezona, had decided to move back home to Kentucky and care for her ailing mother. Since the war ended, Dan had settled back in the Winnfield area. By nature, he was not a man who made hasty decisions—including packing up and moving away. He liked living in central Louisiana. He knew the people here. He had family here. He was a popular man about town, with powerful political connections, a nice home, and a good life. Dragging up stakes and starting over was simply not an option.

So, Ezona Veltrea journeyed east without the man she loved. Her departure left the usually composed, industrious Dan Dean in a state of immediate shock and undeserved sadness. Unless he went into town for supplies or attended services at Mount Zion Baptist Church, Dan spent days speaking to absolutely no one.

Fortunately, Dan was growing accustomed to his single status and was even finding his way out of the house more often. He wasn't one to waste much time sulking around and living in the past. What's done is done, he thought, and it was time to move on.

Dan finished up some farm work, fitted on his leather riding gloves, then rode into Atlanta.

At Will Drake's General Store he bought a bag of beans, some feed, cornmeal, matches, lantern oil, dried meats, salt and pepper, and sugar cubes for his horse, Quaid.

Dan was putting the items in his saddlebag when Laws Kimbrell approached.

"Mighty fine day for a drink, don't ya agree?" Laws asked, giving Dan a hard clap on the shoulder.

"Lawson. How're ya doin'?"

"Ever go up to Saline Bayou and try for them fat bream?"

Dan smiled knowingly. As kids, he and Laws used to camp out on Saline Bayou and catch large-mouth bluegill and bullfrogs. It was a gentle reminder of how things once were, before they grew into teenagers and then soldiers going to battle in what would be remembered as the bloodiest war in America's history.

"Haven't got up there in quite awhile," Dan said. "Fishin' sure beats workin', though."

Laws thumbed at the back entrance of the store, which led to the upstairs saloon. "Feel like takin' a break?"

Within a few minutes they were sitting at the bar looking at reflections of themselves in the clear glass mirror. Without asking their preferred poison, the bartender, Milt, poured two finger shots of Old Crow Whiskey and set them on the counter.

Laws raised his glass in a toasting manner and wet his lips. "Here's to old friends, Dan."

"And fishin' on Saline," Dan added. He clinked his glass against Lawson's drink. "Good to see ya, Laws."

"Same here."

"Any news of late?"

"Aww, well, you know my story."

Dan lowered his voice. "Shouldn't be doin' those things, Laws. It ain't right, you know that."

"Say whatcha want. Gets me to the next day. Or month. Depends." Laws took the bottle of whiskey and poured himself another haymaker. "Settlin' in this town after the meat grinder we went through, ain't like folks are givin' me much of a chance to go straight-laced and all. Opportunity knocks, I open the door."

Dan Dean did not agree with Laws Kimbrell's business of robbing, but he understood his friend's willingness to do so. During tough times, any opportunity to appropriate wealth was an opportunity worth seeking.

But to murder some poor sap after stealing his gold—that was just pure evil.

"I can't imagine," Dan said.

"It don't get to me if that's what you're getting at. I'll shoot a deer. I'll pop squirrels out of trees. A man? A man ain't nothin' I can't handle. Just a bag of water and workin' muscle."

"I thought you left that kinda thinkin' back in the war."

Laws looked down at the empty glass in his hand, slowly ran his finger around the clear rim. "I left a lot of things back in war, Dan, but knowin' how to put a man down for the count wasn't one of 'em."

Dan noticed that the bartender was wiping down a large beer mug with a white cloth, seemingly minding his duties. "Maybe we should change the subject. For prying ears."

"Anybody who comes in earshot of whatever I say will not talk out of place, else they're a fool . . . a goddamn *dead* fool."

"I can understand defending yourself, Laws, that's what we do. Even goin' after a scoundrel drawin' a gun on you in the name of winning a doggone war, I get it, but . . . stoppin' folks on their travels? Takin' their valuables and then . . . you send them to the Promised Land because you think they might identify you? It's insanity."

Laws gave that curt smile again. "They'd get all mouthy. If they see this face, they'll talk. Why take chances? That's my reasoning."

"You know I don't agree with you or what you're doing . . . but at least admit that what you're doing is wrong."

Through the opened windows, Laws heard familiar blasts yell out from John West's hunting horn—two long ones, followed by a short *hermmph!*

"Somebody must've bagged a big buck," Laws said. This time he did not smile. This time he reached into his shirt pocket and pulled out a rolled cigarette. Milt the bartender immediately found a match and struck a flame at the tip of it. The rider breathed in, shot a V of smoke out of his nostrils. "Free for the next hour or so, Dan? I want to show you something."

"Where're you plannin' on us goin'?" Dan asked.

"There's a friend of mine went huntin' deer this mornin', said he'd let me know when he got one. Whaddayasay we ride out to see that animal?"

The deer or your friend? Dan thought, reaching for the bottle. He poured another full shot of whiskey, and drank it down like a man being led to the gallows.

Chapter 13

A sense of foreboding came over Dan as he followed Laws by
horseback down the Old Indian Trail, towards Goldonna.

He wasn't quite sure why his old friend wanted him to tag along.
Dan Dean had seen many a deer in his life, several he'd killed, so
this journey did not constitute an experience of epic proportion. The
hunter who killed the big buck needed a wooden sled roped to the
back of a horse, some assistance getting the deer secured, and that
was that. Then he could go home.

Of course, there lingered the feeling something wasn't entirely
positive about this jaunt. Somehow, someway, if things went afoul
(and he had a feeling they would) he'd have to eradicate his presence
from a quandary using skilled force.

"Bit further yet," Laws announced, removing a flask of whiskey
from his vest pocket. He uncorked the top and knocked back a shot.
"*Ahhhh*. Want a swig?"

Feeling increasingly sloshed, Dan wiped his shirt's sleeve across
his forehead, soaking up sweat. Although he gave in to drinking
from time to time and was used to its fantasy-like influences, those
three glasses he emptied at the General Store proved enough
wavering stimulation to put him down for a long nap.

Still . . . that feeling kept him alert . . . the feeling of knowing
that he may not return from this trip made him suspect. Surely it was
the alcohol making him think such absurd things. Laws Kimbrell
was an outlaw, and Dan Dean knew of his cold heart . . . .

But Laws Kimbrell wouldn't place him in danger.

Would he?

Christ, what if he—?

*Stop it, ol' boy. You're thinking nonsense. You're just going to
help someone remove a deer from the woods so they'll have meat for*

the season. You've done it before. Quit turning this trip into a personal nightmare.

The long-distance horn sounded again, this time with more urgency. Laws turned back. "Almost there!"

Dan followed him off the main road and through a stretch in the forest, where a wooden fence had been cut away to allow entry. The sun glinted off the steel frame of a cotton gin set far off in a field. Dan looked away, blinking the glare out of his sight.

At the far left corner of the vast property, Dan saw three people . . . and not one deer in sight. As they moved closer to the cotton gin, Dan made out John West and Dave Frame leaning against a water well.

A man and woman, their mouths gagged with rope, had been forced to their knees.

"What the hell is this?"

"West wants to see ya, Dan. Hear him out, will ya? It's just business."

John West slapped a mosquito on the back of his hand and wiped the tiny blood streak on the side of his gray pants. He stepped around the dried up water well, hand extended. "Dan Dean! Glad you could join us today. How've you been, Dan? Good, I reckon?"

Dan didn't respond with a friendly handshake but instead looked beyond the gang leader at the frightened couple. In their eyes he believed he saw hope . . . hope that he'd save them . . . hope that they'd walk away from this affair alive.

"Answer me, Laws," Dan said, ignoring John West. "Why're those folks tied up and gagged? What'd they do to y'all?"

"Oh nothing, nothing. Believe me, they've done nothing Dan," West interjected. "It appears Mr. and Mrs. Menifee here, *hahaha!* They found themselves in the wrong place at the right time."

The poor man at their feet struggled against restraints and bit into the rope in anger. His wife, a lovely blonde, appeared to have given up and accepted their current predicament.

Dan saw in her eyes whatever fight once glowed there had burned to ash. She'd been crying and tracks of salty tears had cut through the face powder patted on her cheeks like twin razors.

Feeling deeply sorry for them, he wanted to tell them that no, he wasn't their hero. He couldn't change these men's decision to carry out the terror they had in mind. But he was willing to give it a try.

"Look here, West. I know about you and your riders. Laws knows I'd never speak a word of your late-night activities. So I refuse to bear witness to this deliberate show of unforgiving ruthlessness. Goddamn it, these folks are innocent of any wrongdoing! Let them go."

"You're correct, Dan. These folks *are* innocent. And I know you've never talked about our special group of men, that's a given. I see no need to explain my actions on the matter before us," West said. "But to satisfy your curiosity, Mr. and Mrs. Menifee here came along in a real nice buggy led by a fine horse, so I thought to myself, because I'm a thinking man, '*what else might these good folks have in their possession?*' Well, my thinking was not in vain. I landed a good lot. Pearls and a diamond ring. Folding money. Trinkets I'll sell sometime. Found some splendid clothes, too, and a pocket-watch inlaid with—hey, let's not get into specifics. I'm just tickled as all get out that you've joined us today. I've wanted to meet with you in private for some time now. How about we talk business?"

"What business?" Dan asked, turning to Laws.

"Looks like you came to town at the perfect time, old friend," Laws said. "Now you've seen what we do. By happenstance, you're witness to this kidnappin', whether you like it or not."

West stepped forward. "Become one of us, Dan. A member of the inner circle. As you've heard, there're great benefits to being in that elite group of men. There's money to be had in this gang. Gold and all kinds of fancy jewelry. Silver and bronze and copper. Yes sir, you never know what you might come across when a traveler trots down the Trace. You take what you want, and you destroy the rest. Like this."

John West pointed his pistol at the face of the kneeling man.

The gun blast exploded over the land. The man slumped over, landing hard on the ground, his left eye turned to a red/blackened mush of busted muscle and bone, the back of his opened skull spilling forth a mixture of brain matter, ferociously pumping out a geyser of blood.

Jolted from the gunshot, Dan stepped back in disbelief.

The woman screamed behind her gag, a high-pitched sound that pierced Dan's ears.

She swayed just enough to fall beside her husband, landing on his stomach; tried with all her strength to look at his face. She shut her eyes tight and cried, her lips curling back over her teeth in anguish.

"Awful as it sounds, you get used to it," John West said, stepping around the squirming woman. "The Lord calls home all his sheep someday. Just so happens today is their day."

"How can you even speak of the Lord our God in this manner? Those words shouldn't even come out of your filthy mouth! How in this world can you go to church and teach bible class and have folks believin' you're filled with goodness? With righteousness! When you go on the sly and do things like this? You're the devil reincarnate!"

"Ha! Not hardly."

"I don't want nothin' to do with the likes of you, West. To hell with your clan, and to hell with you!" Dan turned to get on his horse. Heard the familiar click of a hammer being set on a gun.

"Don't rush off."

"Are you gonna fire down on me?"

"I'm not as fast as you," West replied.

"You've already got your weapon in hand. No man I know of can beat that draw."

"It's only a precaution. Laws? Tell your friend here what's next."

"This is your show, West. You tell him."

"Fine then. Dan, since you've witnessed the death of this poor sap, you now have a choice. Kill the lady here and become one of us . . . ." West grinned. "Or we kill you."

"John West, you can burn in hell for all I give a damn. I ain't gonna hurt that lady. I'll be glad to hurt *you*, though."

West hurried toward Dan, gun extended. "You will follow my orders, or I'll—"

Click!

Laws put the barrel of his Colt .44 an inch from John West's ear. "Ease up, West."

In that second the gang leader realized he'd gone too far in the presence of Lawson Kimbrell.

A bead of sweat dropped from his temple. He sucked in a deep breath, eyes wandering to the black hole of the barrel, gently turning so as not to startle his fellow clan leader with a sudden move. "Lawson, if you'll listen . . . I'm trying to—"

"Dan Dean's an old friend, West. I won't allow him to be harmed by you or anybody else. Asking him if he wants to be part of the circle is one thing—we discussed that. Having him hurt this lady to be a member was not part of the deal."

West nodded. "I see, Laws. But you do agree that your friend has witnessed a murder?"

"He doesn't have to perform one. Not like the other members. Put the pistol down and leave Dan out of this, or I'll put you beside Mr. Menifee."

Thinking now of self-preservation amid the sobs of the lady lying across her dead husband, knowing full well Laws Kimbrell would send him away, (not to mention that Dan Dean could draw on him any second), West came to his senses and lowered his pistol.

"All right, Laws," West said.

Laws holstered his gun. "Dan? Get gone."

Dan looked at the helpless woman. He wanted to take her with him. "Let her go first."

West grinned again. "Dave? Let her go."

Dave Frame turned his gun on the woman and shot her twice in the heart.

West looked at Dan Dean. "There. She's gone."

Dan held his hand close to his guns as he led Quaid away, never losing sight of John West, Dave Frame, nor his childhood friend Lawson Kimbrell.

Farther down the center of the field, he saddled his horse. By the time he got home Dan was breathless, a bit more sober, and filled with regret that he did not kill John West when he had the chance.

Chapter 14

Following the murders of Mr. and Mrs. Menifee, Laws, West, and Dave Frame dragged their bodies to the well and dumped each of them in, head first.

They heard the bodies hit other skeletons, making cracking noises rise up through the tunnel of stone.

Laws took charge of hiding the buggy at a livery to be repainted.

West rode off with the Menifees' black mare, hid the animal in his barn. In the morning he'd arrange to transport the horse up the Red River, where it would be sold in Shreveport for profit.

Although he could have lost his life, West did not comment on Lawson's willingness to protect Dan Dean.

The leaders were mean, selfish men responsible for the nightriders' successes and failures . . . and that kind of power and pressure came with its share of intimate disagreements.

At the barn beside his house, West removed his blood-stained shirt and hid it in the loft. He'd burn the article later to erase evidence that he'd committed murder. Adept at covering his tracks, West took keen measures to keep his activities secret from his wife. As far as his family was concerned, he could do no wrong.

West entered the back door of the big house. He put on a fresh shirt in his bedroom and walked into the front room.

Sara sat on a yellow velvet couch, knitting a sweater for their daughter, Faye. She barely glanced in his direction. "Supper'll be ready shortly. Roastin' a couple of tenderloins Laws dropped off this mornin'. You want yours cooked through?"

"Yeah. No blood," West said. "Where's the girls?"

"Elly and Ginger went over to play with the Blanton kids. They'll be back before sundown."

"Is Faye here?"

"Faye!" Sara yelled.

Faye stuck her head around the door of her bedroom. "Yes, momma?"

"Come see your father."

Faye walked down the hallway, her wide brown eyes catching the falling rays of the sun, her red hair curled tightly into pigtails that bobbed across her shoulders at each step.

"Hi daddy," Faye said.

"There's my sweetheart." West lifted her up easily and held her close to his chest. "How'd you like school today?"

Faye rubbed her eye. "Ms. Vernor talks a awful lot about things that happened a long time ago."

"That's called history lessons, Faye. History tells the stories of things that happened long before you were born."

"History makes me sleepy," she said. "I got good marks on my arithmetic today. What's five plus eight, daddy?"

West feigned a studious look. "Uh . . . hmm. Thirty?"

"Ha! It's not *thirty!*"

"Then you tell me just how much is five plus eight, smarty-pants."

"Thirteen!" Faye exclaimed in a high-pitched voice.

West laughed along with his daughter, then put her on the floor. "Well, seeing as how you get such good marks in school, I got you a surprise."

"A surprise?"

Sara looked up from her knitting, suddenly interested.

"Hold out your hands and close your eyes."

Faye did so, smiling.

West reached into his pocket, brought out a piece of jewelry and set it in her cupped palms.

Faye opened her eyes. "Wow! A bracelet!" The beaded turquoise bracelet was inlaid with silver that reflected the sun along the walls in long, sharp lines. "Oh my! Thank you daddy! Thank you!" She reached up for a hug.

He bent down to receive a soft kiss on his cheek.

"Come here, child." Sara took the bracelet and strung it around Faye's wrist, clasped the ends together. The bracelet was a bit too large for the child's wrist, but not so large that it might slip off her hand.

"I love it!" Faye exclaimed, admiring the bracelet. "I love you, daddy!"

"You keep up the good schoolwork, darlin'," West said.

Faye skipped away down the hall. "I will!"

"So, where'd you get that lovely piece of jewelry?" Sara asked.

"Over in Natchitoches," West lied.

"How much didja spend?"

"That's my business, woman. I wanted to get the child a gift, so I did. Why the questions all of a sudden?"

"You came in here asking for the girls. What if all three of them had been home? Do you have surprise gifts for your other daughters?"

"Perhaps I have a gift for you."

Sara raised her eyebrows. "Oh?"

West slipped his hand into his pocket and brought up a pearl necklace. He handed it over. "I hope you like it."

Sara beamed. "I do like it, John. I really do. But I don't go to school. I didn't make good marks today. Why do I get a gift?"

West t hought a moment. "You deserve something like that every so often for being a good mother and a darling wife."

Beaming at the compliment, Sara got to her feet. "Come here, you silly man." She kissed him full on the lips, the necklace hanging over her hand. "You're so good to us. I don't know what I'd ever do without you."

"Don't worry yourself, Sara. I ain't plannin' on goin' nowhere. Didja cut up any potatoes and onions to go with that meat?"

Chapter 15

Still shaken by the disturbing scene he'd witnessed at the Prescott Gin, Dan didn't put it past John West to send his nightriders after him on the road, or even later this evening.

At home, Dan unloaded his store purchases and filled a trough with feed for Quaid. The horse, indifferent to the ordeal in which his owner had been spared, started munching down.

Dan fixed himself a cup of coffee and sat back in a rocking chair on his front porch, looking out at the expanse of his front yard leaning against the curve of the Old Sparta Road.

Without anyone to bounce his opinions off of, he got lost in his own thoughts about what he'd witnessed—the senseless murders of two people at the hands of those ruthless cowards, John West and Dave Frame.

It was useless to seek out the authorities for justice. West and his men would no doubt hear about it, and no doubt they'd come for him. Dan Dean was a crack shot, but no man alive could fend off an entire posse, and he wasn't fool enough to try it.

Laws Kimbrell had saved his life. Dan not only felt grateful, but knew he was indebted to the man.

No matter what he's done, no matter how much I deplore his outlaw ties, someday, somehow, Laws will ask me to pay back the favor.

Dan watched the road and listened closely to the surrounding woods another hour. When he believed it was safe to return inside, he got up from the rocking chair and bolted himself in the house.

He roasted two ears of corn and made a bowl of bean soup for the night, but did not eat right away. He looked around the place, at the fireplace in the front sitting room, the cooking area, the bedroom and up at the opened loft area, which served as an extra bedroom.

The house was lonely.

He was lonely.

Both needed a woman's touch.

Dan had attended barn dances in Olla and Clear Creek, and although he'd found girls to spend time with, they never panned out into a live-in partner. And that's what he wanted. Someone he looked forward to spending time with. Someone to hold dear, day in and day out.

Ezona had been such a nice girl; funny, pretty, a talented cook. At one time Dan thought she was the one for all time, but homesickness got the best of their relationship. There were no hard feelings. Ezona felt she had to go see to her mother, and so Dan did not hold her back.

After months of life without the company of a woman, though, Dan was getting restless. He needed to feel the soft firmness of a woman's kiss, the reassurance in her voice that he'd never be alone. Sure, there were loose women about wanting nothing more than an evening foray into carnal knowledge, and Dan knew where to meet them.

But Dan respected women. He was in search of a lady friend, one with whom he might create a lasting relationship, not various ladies of the night.

Ezona may not have been the one, but their relationship had been partly successful. He'd learned the ways of a woman like never before. In a closet near his bedroom Ezona had left a dress, a powder makeup kit, a near-empty bottle of perfume, a pair of high-heeled boots, and a long tanned cloak she hardly ever wore.

Every time he walked by he could still smell her scent confined to the closet.

Sometimes he fooled himself into thinking that maybe she'd returned, ready to give their relationship another go.

He stood in the front room holding his cup of now cold coffee and looked out the side window as bluish dusk fell in a brisk wave, throwing shade along the yard.

Wished for pleasant company.

Chapter 16

Laws woke before dawn, drank his coffee and rode into town to go over the books with Will Drake, the clan's bookkeeper. That's right. The clan made so much money in their illegal operations that they kept an account of all revenue, guarding the allocation of every stolen coin.

I actually liked Will Drake. He dated my cousin, Emily, back in '52. She said he was a righteous fellow, had a sharp mind for money. Maybe that's why he broke off their engagement. Because Will loved money more than anything—even my cousin, a beauty from the cotton fields of North Louisiana.

Will became a successful businessman in the area. At one time he owned the nearby livery, a bed and breakfast in Winnfield, and four cotton gins in Atlanta. He sold all that stress and responsibility to purchase the General Store.

The man just knew how to run a business, which impressed John West enough to bring Will onboard early on in the clan's ventures.

Will Drake was not a member of the nightriders. Nevertheless, his connection to the clan was blood-bound, and remained as secretive as the identity of the members themselves. He knew exactly how John West and Lawson Kimbrell made their money, but Will did not ask questions, nor pass judgment on their activities. For his part he was paid handsomely under the table to keep the books private and his mouth shut.

Gathered in the back office of the store, Laws and Will reviewed the past month's recent entries inside a leather-bound ledger:

3 gold bullion: $1,642.00
248 gold coins: $717.00
11 diamond necklaces: $2,840.00
6 pearl necklaces: $600.00
8 painted wagons: $5,875.00
14 horses: $7,400.00
2 gold pocket watches: $365.00

Misc. items (clothes, trinkets, trunks, weapons): $1,776.00

Laws left ten gold coins on the desk. "All right, Will. Where'd you put the most recent take?"

"Over at Horsehead Rock," Will replied, gathering the coins in greedy hands. "John's orders."

"I'll be back for a drink."

Laws stepped into the sunshine, feeling the warmth on his face. He got on his horse and rode toward Natchitoches. On the way he ate three boiled eggs and a few pieces of dried beef he'd brought along for lunch. He turned eastward onto the Harrisburg Road and miles later rounded the Goldonna Road, finally coming to a location deep in the forest where most of the clan's treasure was buried. Central Louisiana, like the rest of the state, was scarcely populated with earthen rocks unlike territories of Arkansas and Tennessee, but there was one location, an oddity in the area's geology, that stuck up ten feet out of the earth like a giant, misplaced thumb.

Horsehead Rock was aptly named because the long, smooth formation resembled a horse's head in a windblown sprint. Behind this rock, hidden in wooden lockboxes, lay treasures of all kinds: gold coins, gold bullion, and silver. Necklaces, bracelets, rings, pendants, watches and brooches created from expensive stones; diamonds, pearls, rubies, and emeralds stood out especially. These treasure chests held more than seventy-five percent of the clan's stolen goods from those poor folks unfortunate enough to cross their path.

Miscellaneous items that Will Drake recorded in the clan's ledger did not find a home in the lockboxes, as they were either sold on the cheap or somehow employed among the gang.

Laws kicked away a scattering sweep of pine straw and dug two fingers deep into the earth until he touched the surface of solid wood. He pulled up the case by a rope handle that had been strung around the body of the lockbox—just enough to be free of its clay-encased shell.

He unlocked the box and looked intently, in awe, at the colors and shimmering vibrations of its contents. He removed a diamond necklace that sparkled brightly in the sunlight. Helped himself to fifty gold coins—ten to pay himself back for giving Will Drake his share, forty for when he needed to use them—and secured the box.

Laws pushed the treasure back into its resting place, covered it with clumps of dirt and camouflaged the surface with pine straw, until the ground was somewhat level and non-distinct to the passing eye.

He listened to the wind for any sounds on the trail, for men on horses. Always careful to keep watch on the road when he dipped into this collective bank, Laws was deservedly paranoid for many reasons—as anyone might follow him through the woods, wait him out, then get their greedy hands on the prize.

Or, like his unlucky cohorts at the Bingham farmhouse, get shot down in a gunfight. When he heard of the recent murders of Jake Dodson, Mickey Fontaine, and Irvin Broussard, the only question he asked was *who killed them?*

The thought that no one (not even John West) had the answer did not surprise Laws—it only left him disappointed. Someone knew the location of their horse-thieving operation and now the gang would need to adjust logistics accordingly; stay far from the farmhouse a long while, speak nothing of the dead riders, and endure the inconvenience of moving the hushed operation to another location in the coming weeks, when time and opportunity availed.

One undeniable fact that disturbed Laws more than any detail concerning the whole bloody issue was that whoever killed those nightriders had not presented a badge. A man with a badge would have announced his authority. Men wearing badges swelled with pride and hungered for ink and recognition. Whoever did away with Lawson Kimbrell's partners did not crave notoriety. Only blood.

He lit a rolled cigarette and watched smoke drift before his eyes in a thin, lazy cloud. The humidity made him sweat, so he removed his coat jacket down to his white shirt and suspenders, got a canteen of water from his bag and drank deeply.

It was agreed between himself and John West that when either of them had the need to seek out the treasure at Horsehead Rock, they were permitted to go about their business discreetly but with respect to the other's share of supply. There were more gold coins available than that of other valuable items—currency they could easily replace by plying their trade as highwaymen.

When Laws finished his smoke, he stamped it out under the heel of his boot, digging the paper and burnt tobacco into the dirt so as not to start a fire that would surely bring unwanted attention to

Horsehead Rock. Feeling it was safe to leave, he led his horse back through the wooded path.

On the return trip to Atlanta, passing the Old Sparta Road near Dan Dean's house, Laws turned his horse toward Winnfield.

He had a hankering for steak and onions tonight.

Chapter 17

Bells chimed against the door of Frost's Butcher Shop as Laws walked in and crossed a hardwood floor topped with sprinklings of sawdust. Cattle and pig carcasses hanged around the room like pink-and-white meat decorations. Links of sausages, bundled and tied tightly for transport, dangled freely above the entrance to the back room. Packaged dried meats were stacked near the long counter, where Garrett Frost's meat cleaver, freshly wiped down to show a clean shine, lay beside separated turkey legs.

Mr. Frost strolled out of the back door, his white apron stretched all the way to the tips of his boots. He was a nice man, always welcoming, with graying hair that swept back on his head in wisps to make room for the balding intrusion of age. He had manicured a long mustache that curled around the corners of his mouth into two sharp points, and had the muscular shoulders and arms of a man who accepted physical labor as a necessary part of life.

"Ah, Lawson. How are you today, son? How's that sweet mother of yours?" Mr. Frost shook Lawson's hand.

"Since you asked, sir, Aunt Polly's fell quite ill. She ain't been the same since my father passed."

Mr. Frost gave an expression of sympathy and shook his head slowly. "My, my, I am sorry to hear that, Laws. You fairin' okay?"

"It's tough." A pause. "We'll pray."

"I'm sure you will, I'm sure you will. Here to see Annabelle?"

"Thought I might."

"She's in back cleaning. Go on, son. She'll be happy to see you."

Laws stopped short of the door and turned to the old man. "Do ya think you can cut me up a few sirloins, Mr. Frost?"

"Sirloin! Of course, of course. Thick as you'd like."

"How's this?" Laws said, making the depth of an inch with his thumb and forefinger. He placed two gold coins at the end of the bloodied counter.

Annabelle was sweeping an area in the corner, her apron colored with red specks and stringy entrails from carving up freshly slaughtered animal parts. She did not put too much energy into the motions of her task. She was distracted by her thoughts, the busy end of the broom barely collecting dirt and sawdust.

"Laws?"

"There's my girl." He cupped her face in his hands, kissed her lips. "I got something for you, Annabelle."

She put on a kind smile. "What is it?" she asked, her voice a hoarse whisper, as though she'd spent the afternoon screaming.

"Close your eyes." He produced a silver necklace from his coat pocket and clasped the ends around her neck. "There."

She looked down at the sparkling jewelry, her face lit up in amazement. "Oh my. Laws!" She stood on the tips of her toes and kissed his cheek. "But why? . . . What's this for?"

"Cain't a man get his lady-friend something nice every now and then?"

"You bet he can, silly! And it's so nice. I'm grateful you thought of me." She smiled with true happiness then, her fingers touching the diamond pendent at the center of the chain. As quickly as it appeared, the smile morphed into a trembling frown and Annabelle could no longer contain herself from her overly sensitive emotions.

Her hand weakening, the broom fell, smacked the floor. "Laws, I'm—" She tried hugging him.

Laws put his hands on her shoulders and held her at bay. "Annabelle, what's wrong? Why are you crying? I hand you a gift, and you *cry*? What kind of behavior is that to showcase?"

Shaking her head, she untied the apron and threw it on a four-legged chopping block. She hooked her arms around Lawson's waist, face pressed sideways against his chest. "It's not the gift. No, not at all. That night," she said, "the night I left your house. There were two men on the road. They stopped me . . . dragged me off my horse. The one with that awful breath, oh God Laws, I can still smell his stinking breath! The bastard, he—"

Laws gently pushed her away. He tilted her chin up, met her eyes. "Annabelle. Who were these men? Did you see their faces?"

She looked at the door to make sure she and Laws were alone. If her father heard this story he'd go after the bandits with his old Greener shotgun. Annabelle couldn't bear the thought of him going up against evil souls who wouldn't think twice about killing a protective father.

"Annabelle! There was a full moon that night. Did you see their faces?"

"Well, it all happened so fast I can't remember exact details! They had hats on. Looked like, they looked like highwaymen out for trouble, and they found *me*."

"Where's your horse?"

She pointed at the window.

Laws went outside. Her horse was tied to a Sweetgum tree by a water trough, the red sash hanging from the saddle and getting batted by a stiff breeze.

"They stopped me out of the blue . . . demanded gold," Annabelle said, now standing wearily behind him. "The one who took me in the woods, he hitched up my dress."

"What did you do, Annabelle? When that happened, what did you do?"

"I—I screamed. He put his hand over my mouth and I . . . all I could do was pray God would save me, that it wouldn't hurt. Kept wishing you were there, Laws. That bastard put his fingers in my— he put them . . . *inside me!*"

Alarmed at the release of this detail, nothing else mattered. Laws didn't know who maliciously attacked his girl, or would have deliberately disobeyed his orders, but during the last meeting he made his point clear: ". . . and that's that. Any one of you boys stop a girl on a horse that has this here sash tied to it will be dealt with on a personal level."

He now realized that the two men who heard his orders weren't concerned about dire consequences. They disregarded his warning like a fart in the wind, and in turn disrespected his lady friend.

I figure out who it is, their lives won't be worth a Confederate dollar.

Recalling the incident aloud made Annabelle burst into tears again.

He hugged her. He did not whisper that it'd be okay, or tell her to hush, or make-believe it was something they should forget. He'd fallen silent at the thought of any man touching his beloved Annabelle. Warm tears wet his skin. Thought long and hard about how he could relieve her pain and thus regain respect among his men.

Laws decided then and there it was high time he held another meeting of the West-Kimbrell Clan's inner circle.

Chapter 18

Sunday morning spread golden light over Mount Zion Baptist Church and clear skies promised a beautiful day for fellowship. The red-bricked structure was nestled at the northeast corner of St. Maurice crossroads, where townspeople traveled by buggy and horse (or simply strolled) to serve their God.

Dan Dean exchanged pleasantries with charming womenfolk who prepared the day's luncheon (which would take place immediately following the closing prayer) and politely answered old timers' questions regarding the war—jumbled memories of ripped-out guts stuck to the soles of his field boots flashing alive in his mind, images he couldn't forget, experiences he'd never bring up in conversation. He sat in the middle pew, his hat and Holy Bible at his side, waiting for the service to begin.

Dressed in their Sunday best, folks talked among themselves about the gorgeous weather and the tasty food waiting in covered picnic baskets on the back pews. From behind the small wooden podium that had the Cross carved elegantly into the grain and read: 'This Do in Remembrance of Me,' a choir of six ladies and six men began singing the hymn "I Love To Tell The Story" to an accompanying piano, played by Mrs. Jude Eggerson.

Dan stood with the congregation of forty or so, singing along by memory. He recognized men whom he considered respectable; men who worked hard to provide for their family, who protected their homes from heartless scoundrels. These men believed in the fruits of farming, the love of family, and the blessings of God. They also believed in the power of guns, using their weapons for hunting game or to ward off personal threats. They were not in the business of robbing people on the trails, nor dispatching married couples in a field by a well—as some men whom Dan knew of.

Jim Maybin was one of those family men Dan respected. Maybin was an old friend of the Dean family. Dan's father, Abel Dean, helped Maybin start a successful blacksmith business. Jim Maybin,

Jess Cady, Fred Boss and Antone Luke were among the citizens in the Atlanta and Winnfield area who minded their business.

Yes, much like Dan, these were humble, good-natured men. They had been part of the nightriders in the beginning of the home guard initiative; protecting their territory, fending off unsavory characters. Unlike Dan, though, these men strayed clear of the clan's affairs as the nightriders' name gradually became synonymous with evil works.

Dan thought it an absolute disgrace that John West moved freely among the innocent and easily deceived—going around pumping hands, presenting fake smiles, putting on a show as the respected Constable of the Wheeling Settlement, and even a spiritual leader to several in this congregation . . . when in truth John West was a snake in the grass, capable of far more terror than any parishioner could have imagined.

When the singing ended, Pastor James Weeks walked up to the podium and asked that everyone remain standing for the opening prayer. He bowed his head. "Oh Gracious Heavenly Father, we come to you on this day, Your day, with open hearts to gain your message of love and grace. Be with our community in these difficult times, oh Lord. Be with our families. Protect our farms. Keep us safe from the forces of Evil so that we may sow only that which is righteous and good. Allow each new day to bring happiness and grace only You can provide in our meek lives. We ask this in Jesus' Holy name, Ah-men." He asked the congregation to be seated. "Folks, this morning we're going to start services a bit different than most glorious Sundays, with a testimony of Faith from one of our esteemed members." Pastor Weeks looked at the crowded front pew, which was mostly occupied by West, his wife, and daughters. "Brother West?"

West got up from the pew and approached the pastor, smiling proudly. He laid his beefy hands on the sides of the podium, looked out at the congregation.

"Good morning Brothers and Sisters! I hope everyone is in good spirits today. Why, you should be, for two reasons as far as I can think of: we are here to praise the Lord . . . and take part in after-service fellowship to eat some of the finest food this side of Texas!" He smiled again, that big alligator grin showing a mix of straight and crooked teeth, his cheeks flush red from excitement. "I don't know about you, but I can't wait for some of Mrs. Hathaway's cinnamon apple pie. Don't worry, I'll try to leave some for the rest of y'all." A few chuckles erupted throughout the crowd. "As most of you know, God has blessed me with a beautiful family, a wonderful home, and the joy of having friends like you. Over time I have seen my share of nightmares, that's for sure. Through it all God stood as the one true light who never forsake me. As most of you know, I am a friend to my community. I try, with the Lord's strength, to help my fellow neighbor any way I can through their trials and tribulations. I believe." He pounded his fist on the wood, saying: "I *believe* because I know the Lord with my heart! My very *soul.*"

"Amen!"

"Tell it Brother!" someone yelled in back.

West leaned away from the podium and moved his hands as he spoke. "Jesus Christ is my savior."

"Amen!"

"A savior helps people. A savior protects." West touched his thumb to his beard, appearing to concentrate in deep, deceptive thought. "And so I realized, as a sworn peace officer, that I have much of the same duties to help protect my community. You see, a lot of concerned folks have visited me regarding a group of rebel no-gooders called the nightriders. I do not speak of the riders who helped clean this town of Northern scum and the carpetbaggers after the war. That gang was honorable, out there doing an honest job to safeguard our local towns.

"But that gang is no more, and this fairly new adaptation of the nightriders appears to be a close-knit match of cutthroats. You've surely heard stories of this gang's stranglehold on the Natchez Trace . . . robbing folks in the middle of night?"

Many nodded.

"This gang is rotten and what they're doing is unforgivable. I declare that whoever's out there carrying the guilt of these sins will definitely burn right side up in Hades!"

"Yes!"

"Amen."

"As a servant of the people, I promise that you're safe from these rogues. I promise you I will put forth every effort within my political power to rid our towns of these devils. God will make them pay for their earthly wickedness. As God as my witness, I will see to it that they perish by the rope."

"Amen!"

"Those cowardly fools out there making a mockery of the law and harming folks after dark had better prepare for the Lord's vengeance. Because when God hands down the orders, the grim reaper comes out of the shadows!"

"Preach on John!"

"Friends, feel free to visit me with any concerns you have about these savages. I will protect you. That is my pledge. May God bless us all."

Dan watched John West shake the pastor's hand, that smile of his nothing more than a perfect disguise. He returned to his seat beside his wife, who looked so proud of her husband, patting his arm and telling him he did such a fantastic job.

*****

After closing prayers the churchgoers gathered in the side yard of the church, where blankets, picnic baskets, and pots of food were set out on the grass. The air smelled of cold fried chicken and turnip greens, sweet perfume and lit pipe tobacco.

There were pots of squirrel mulligan, sausage gumbo, chicken n' dumplings and raccoon stew; pans of meatloaf and mashed potatoes, butter beans, roasted corn, and skillet-fried green beans. Someone brought an entire turkey, the skin browned by bourbon brine and spices. A few baskets contained only cornbread and biscuits. Bottles of root beer, jugs of sweet tea, and lemonade in pitchers were lined up on the wooden tables. And for those taking in a light lunch had their pick of fruit baskets full of apples, pears, muscadines, plums, pecans and dry-roasted peanuts. For dessert the ladies of the church had baked a variety of apple, cherry, and chess pies—the whole buffet a feast for fifty, ready to consume.

Dan sat under the shade of a loblolly pine tree, looking out at the cemetery, his eyes automatically focused on the tombstones of his parents, Abel and Ettie Dean.

The flowers he set out a few weeks ago had wilted and gone brittle, most of the petals picked apart by weak breezes. He made a mental note to bring out more flowers sometime soon, and sit and visit them. The couple died within a month of each other while he was away at war, his father succumbing to pneumonia, and his mother, he believed, of a broken heart. The family physician, Dr. Thomas Harrison, found no other natural cause for his mother's demise beyond depression during those icy winter months of 1863.

He still kept the letter his mother had written him that February folded neatly in an empty cigar box. Composed in her slow, fragile handwriting, the half page detailed how terribly sick his father had become . . . suffered high fever, coughing fits, went through blackouts and memory loss. Shit himself.

"When he's awake he hacks blood. I have a premonition he won't make it to spring," she wrote.

Dan received the letter in time to return for Abel Mason Dean's funeral. He stayed at his mother's side for a couple of days afterwards, then reported to his regiment in Georgia.

That April, his friend Jim Maybin sent another letter notifying Dan that his mother had recently joined his father in the afterlife. Struggling to mentally and physically survive the chaos of war, Dan received the letter too late and was unable to travel the hundreds of miles to attend Ettie Althea Dean's funeral.

For years after, the devastation of losing his parents weighed heavily on Dan's mind. Having no siblings to turn to, the only family left for him was his mother's sister and a handful of cousins over in Sterlington and East Texas.

Dan dipped a biscuit in a bowl of gumbo.

John West walked up. "Well, Dan Dean. It's sure good to see you here on the Lord's Day. How are things?" West asked, his eyes barely hiding pointed animosity.

Dan looked around at the women in their lively dresses and the men in their jackets, happily enjoying themselves. He wondered if any of them knew of the soulless John West. Dan believed he was the only person in this crowd who knew the many faces of Deacon West . . . from the self-styled, righteous Sunday School teacher and family man he appeared to be in front of the masses—to the wretched, calculated killer he became at sundown.

"You've got some nerve coming over here," Dan said in a hushed tone. "Folks here have been deceived. They see something about you that ain't really there. Can't blame 'em, really. How would they know different? But you ain't nothin' but a put-on, and they'll know soon enough. Right now, it'd be to your advantage to walk away and leave me be."

West held his smile in place, his eyes as cool as river water, and knelt on the blanket by a picnic basket. As he spoke he remained cheerful, his tone calm, direct, making sure Dan heard the ferocity in his words.

"Just to let you know, Dan, if you speak of anything you've seen in recent past, I will cut you down. And if I fail to do it, my men will succeed. Make no mistake, the only reason you're alive today is because I told them to stand down. Listen, I know you won't talk. You're smarter than to go off and talk." He plucked a pear out of a basket and left a huge bite-mark in the skin, spoke as he chewed. "You want me to walk away, fine. But here's my counteroffer: it'd be to *your* advantage to join us. You'll be flush beyond belief, that's a certainty.

"If you don't join us, well, you never know what kinda fight might knock on your door."

"Tell ya what, West, if any of your men try to bulldoze me, they'll leave in a pine box. There's your certainty."

John West laughed. "Oh, you are a stubborn man, Dan Dean. Fool-hearted pride to the gills." He waved at Permilia Bordeaux, who claimed in passing that she enjoyed his testimony during the service. "Why, thank you, Miss Bordeaux. It's always a pleasure to speak of the blessings God has bestowed upon us."

She smiled knowingly. "It is, Brother West, thank you. Enjoy your day."

"Miss Bordeaux, my day will only get better once I get me a slice of your homemade cherry pie." West watched her move on to speak with other folks, her hands clasped over her Bible, hair done up in a tight blonde bun. He turned back to Dan. "Worst pie I ever put in my belly. My eight-year-old daughter can bake better mud pies." He sniffed, took another bite of the pear. "Concerning this issue between us, Dan, let me put it another way. Laws might've saved your hide that day in the field, but don't kid yourself. Laws ain't always gonna be there to protect you, a friend as he says. I respect Laws, so me and my men won't come after you.

"But now . . . since you've witnessed firsthand what we're capable of, if you ever stand in the way of my operations, Laws Kimbrell or whoever else won't be able to save your skin in time."

In response to West's threats, Dan Dean looked up from his bowl of gumbo, the light in his eyes a hard blue under his hat.

"Pine. Box."

Chapter 19

Over the course of three days rain danced down in pellets, flooding his property. By the end of the week, after the sun had dried the land, Dan planned to complete a project that had been on his mind ever since he and some friends built his new barn—tear down the *old* one.

It had been a fixture in his family since years before the war, a structure his father and uncle braced together on the east side of the field using cheap wood and sheets of corrugated tin. The small, rickety barn slanted to one side like a sick puppy. When he moved back to the homestead, he'd been lucky to shelter his horse, all his tools, and twenty bales of hay in the blasted thing.

Now that he had the opportunity and resources, it was time to clear the land.

He was not in a rush, as his days were filled with steady work on the farm to make an honest living, but he disliked the building—for no other reason than that it made his property appear shoddy and ill-kept. With hammer and crowbar in hand and a canteen of water looped by a leather strap around his shoulder, he rode Quaid out to the eyesore of a building, ready to destroy.

One of the twin doors leaned open drunkenly on large rusted hinges and the heat of the day amplified the stuffy scent of hay dust riding the air. Ancient tools hanged on the wall: a sling blade, a hatchet, two pole axes, and a variety of metalsmith devices. A wooden ladder resting against the far wall led to the loft. Dan figured he'd begin with the roof and work his way down. Knock out the support beams and shed the tin, create a hollow top.

He ascended the ladder and stepped on scattered hay straw on the loft floor. Through the bare square window he saw Quaid slowly roaming, snout to the earth, nibbling whatever tempted his appetite.

Then something strange caught Dan's attention.

He looked closely at a loose bundle of hay across the room. He blinked, disbelieving his vision. The hay seemed to be moving—no, it *was* moving . . . up and down, in sure repetition, gracefully. He waited for the movement to cease but the steady repetition mocked his wishes, kept on. It was as though the hay was breathing, in and out, up and down . . . then reality set in and Dan shook off the notion that this was happening without assistance.

Naked flesh flashed at him.

Dan squinted in the dimness, trying to make out the small shapes. When he realized the shapes were dirty toes, a scowl broke over his face. He walked over, grabbed an ankle, pulled.

"Oh!"

He let go.

A young girl scooted out on her rear, backed into the bundle of hay. The fear in her big brown eyes was evident. She was shaking.

"Ma'am?" Dan stepped forward, palms out in a non-threatening gesture. "Don't fear, I'm not gonna . . . I just want to talk to you."

The girl started kicking, giving off defensive grunts, landed a foot hard against Dan's crotch.

"Oh! *Jesus*," Dan whispered, covering his privates. He banged the wall headfirst, nearly knocked himself out cold.

The girl scrambled to the ladder. Down she went.

"Wait!" Dan yelled. "C'mere!"

Feeling the raw pain of the hit rush into his intestines and lay there like a lead weight, Dan did his best to give chase. Barely regaining his balance he missed a few rungs on the way and landed violently on the naked ground.

His visitor ran like a lightning bolt towards Quaid. She grabbed the saddle horn and pulled herself onto the smooth, blanketed seat, took the leather reins and slapped the back of the horse's mane. "Hiyah! Hiyah! Run, you damn beast!"

Quaid sashayed a bit to the right and decided against the screeching order.

Dan limped toward the girl. "Who are you! What're you doin' in my barn?"

Instead of responding vocally, the girl kicked her bare feet back out of the stirrups and dropped to the ground on the other side of Quaid. Took off.

Within seconds Dan was on his horse.

He watched the girl run as fast as those skinny legs could carry her across the field. He patted Quaid's mane. "C'mon ol' boy, let's get after her." A gentle kick to the side, and Quaid was off like a shot.

Dan rode up beside her, slowed his horse, looked down at the girl's dress, which was now colored in scattered buds of wildflower. "Hey! Stop!"

She kept running, her dress impeding her stride.

Dan kept at a steady trot. "You can run 'til you give out. Can't reach the road and not ease up for a breath. I ain't gonna hurt ya, now . . . slow down! Let's discuss the matter."

Tiring out, she slowed to a jog then fell to her knees.

Maybe she's coming to her senses and will act reasonably, Dan thought.

"I can't—can't go on," she said, sucking in a deep breath of country air.

Dan heard her crying.

He dismounted and knelt at her side, moved a curtain of brown hair from her face. She was attractive despite the tough hair and specks of grit on otherwise clear skin. She'd had it rough, he could tell, and did not recognize her from around town. He felt sorry for her. The nurturing part of him wanted to provide her with food and warmth and hospitality, especially a long, soapy bath.

"What's your name, Miss?"

She looked up at his eyes. "What does that matter, mister? You got what you want. Get it over and done with! I've nothing to live for anyways!"

"Why would you say such a thing?" he asked, surprised at her outburst.

"Go right ahead and shoot me! That's what you're gonna do, ain't it?"

"No ma'am, not at all." Dan reached out and gently touched away hair that had stuck to her tear-soaked cheeks. Studying her up close, the girl was pale and thin, skin flushed, her face drawn out in exhaustion. She was around sixteen or seventeen (he couldn't tell) but she was surely old enough to explain herself. "Answer my question. What were you doin' in my barn?"

"Hiding!"

"From who?"

"I don't know. Not exactly. Not their names, anyhow. I saw their faces and I know they're out to kill me. Not just hurt me. *Kill* me.

The big one, he even said he'd put me in that well, too, when he finished me off. But I didn't give him the chance. Daddy told me to run, so I ran. I ran forever through those woods. Ran 'til I came to that creek back yonder.

"That's when I saw the barn. Figured it was just a good a place as anywhere to hide from those savages. I didn't have the energy to go on, and my feet were blistered something awful from those hard boots. I been," she wiped her eyes, "I've been in your barn for many nights, waiting for them to forget about me. Figuring on my next move . . . so I could leave this awful place."

Dan scoped out the great field to assure they weren't being watched. "I'm sorry you went through such an ordeal. Listen, come on up to the house and I'll see if I can find you some fresh clothes. I've got a tub you're welcome to use. Matter of fact, I was about to make some lunch. Do you like souse meat?"

"Wild berries and pecans is all I've had for days. That, and creek water. Souse meat sounds delicious."

Dan took her by the hand and helped her to her feet. "Then souse meat it is." He escorted her to the house. Quaid followed behind, stopping here and there for a nibble. "I imagine you're not from around here. What's your name, Miss? Where's home?"

"I'm Contessa Menifee. From the Carolinas."

He felt a chill lay into his shoulders.

"Who are you?"

"Dan Dean."

Chapter 20

Upon entering the front room of Dan's farmhouse, Contessa held the handsome stranger's arm as if she were chilled, a look of awe in her weary eyes. The high-ceilinged arch and expansive, opened living space was a far cry from her own living quarters back home, and much larger than the barn loft where she'd spent days hiding from her parents' murderers.

She stood there dazed, looking around the front room; the seating area, the mirrors hanging at opposite walls, at unlit lanterns perched on wooden-carved shelves in the corner.

Poor girl must be thirsty after that full sprint across the field, Dan thought.

He removed a carafe of purified spring water among bottles of root beer, bourbon, and apple cider arranged on a shelf. He could not help but look her over. The afternoon sun lit her shapely body, pronouncing the curves of her slender hips and thrust of erect breasts through the fragile threads of a frayed dress.

Familiar desire stirred in his body, a strong yearning he hadn't felt for quite some time. Something primitive and animalistic begged him to satisfy the sudden, raw urge creeping up inside . . . to *feel* her.

He handed her the glass. "Drink this. You need it."

The girl drank so fast that water dripped in steady lines from the corners of her mouth, dampening her blouse. "*Ahhhh.* Thank you, Mr. Dean. You're a kind man. May I sit?"

"Make yourself comfortable."

She sat in a wicker rocker in the middle of the room. "You have a real nice house."

He sat across from her in a straight-backed burgundy chair. "It's suitable for me."

She glanced at his left hand, noticed he wasn't wearing a wedding band. "A whole family could live here."

"That was the plan, for a time. As it stands, though, my lady friend's mother fell ill and so she moved back home to see after her." He took a breath. "Kentucky." He couldn't believe that within the expanse of a few sentences he had explained away his prior relationship to a complete stranger.

He collected his thoughts, stood.

He did not know Contessa Menifee from Adam, and in the space of a brief conversation had already released more personal information than he'd offered freely to some folks he'd known many years.

"I'm sorry to hear that," she said, turning away. "I hope her mother feels better." She stared out the opened window at the bright sunshine, a breeze lifting her hair across her eyes. "You know, my mother was healthy as ever less than a week ago . . . then those savages killed her *and* my father for no good reason." The edges of her eyes crinkled at the horrific memory.

Dan expected her to cry but she produced no tears—only expressions of sadness he knew all too well in the faces of those suffering unbearable pain. He considered her statement.

Just how did she know her parents were deceased? If she ran like the wind, as her father instructed when the family encountered John West and his nightriders, how could she have known for certain that her parents were murdered?

Unless . . . Contessa *witnessed* the massacre. And if that was the case, then she had seen him among the other riders.

It's no wonder she was scared beyond control. She thought I was aiming to kill her because the poor girl believed I was part of the gang!

"I tell ya what, let me fix us those sandwiches," he offered, changing the subject. "Then I'll boil water and draw you a bath." Dan returned to the kitchen area and got a loaf of bread from another shelf. Opened a can of souse meat. "So . . . where were you and your parents traveling to?"

"Texas. My father worked at a lumber mill back home. He got work with the U.S. Postal Service in a town called Fort Worth. I remember he gathered us at the supper table and told of his plans to move us out of Charlotte. I didn't want to leave. I have lots of friends there. My grandparents, girlfriends, a boy I fancied. I did not put up much of a fight because I thought if I was ever gonna see any place besides my home town, then setting up roots in Texas would be that chance to experience something different.

"But I had a bad feeling . . . the morning we left home, my momma passed out ham biscuits to get us through 'til we made camp that evening, and there was something I felt just wasn't right. Fear of the unknown, fear of what lay on the other side of the hill . . . what kind of folks we'd meet along the way, things like that. Other than people we'd known for so long, who could we trust? We set out to see. Our trip was going well. I really enjoyed spending time with my mother and father, right up 'til we got to Louisiana."

Dan spread mayonnaise over two thick slices of French bread, covered it with tomato and a peppered layer of souse meat. "Do you remember how many men stopped your carriage?"

"There were three."

"Do you remember seeing their faces?"

"One fella was big and fat and had red hair. His beard was red, too. The other one, he was short and ugly and had scars on his face like he fell into a bucket of straight razors. The third one was tall on the saddle, black hair, had a trimmed mustache. Man with the red beard walked out on the road holding the bridle to his horse as though he was lost. So my father stopped to see if he might help. The man gave us some story about losing a calf and asked if we've seen it. My father said he hadn't seen any animals on the loose, and just when the man let us by, those other two came across with their pistols, shouted out orders they'd do away with us if we didn't obey."

Yeah, that's how the riders in the circle operate. More than likely Lec Ingram or Dave Frame assisted in the robbery. It's possible even Laws had a hand in it. Laws would have had enough time to assist in the hold up, then go to town for a drink. Just so happens we met up because I had trading to do that day. When he heard that bullhorn sound off, Laws created a convincing lie—all because John West had been waiting for the perfect opportunity to ask if I'd join his gang.

He brought her the sandwich on a plate.

She took it eagerly. Instead of eating, she set the sandwich aside and continued her story: "Those men had us at gunpoint and forced us back to that field. They stole my father's rifle so he couldn't protect us. They were so fast we couldn't outrun them if we tried. When we turned off the main road, the riders were talking among themselves, paying no direct attention to us. My father turned to me and whispered, '*We love you, Tess. We'll meet again in Heaven. Now you've got to run.*'

"I couldn't move at first but I did not disobey. I got up the courage, crawled in back of the carriage, and jumped through the split in the canvas. Ran through the high grass and next thing I knew I was in the forest, layin' on dry leaves—bugs crawlin' on my skin, ants stingin' me, but I stayed quiet. I was so scared they'd shoot at me, I just put my head down and stayed quiet.

"It wasn't 'til they got to that well and led my parents down off the carriage that they realized I was gone. I heard Red Beard say, 'Find her! Find that gal and bring her back here!' His men spread out through the woods and it was only by God's grace they never caught sight of me. I hid in some thick bushes. Waited them out.

"That's when the riders forced my parents down on their knees, bounded their hands and gagged their mouth with rope. I wanted to stop the madness, but what in the world could I have done? I was completely helpless."

"I am sorry for your loss, Contessa. I don't know what else to say."

"When Red Beard tied up my parents, all three men disturbed our luggage. They found my mother's jewelry box and my father's life savings—twenty-six hundred in gold coins and folding money stashed away in a leather satchel he'd hidden in a bedroll. Red Beard told the others to go on, that he'd 'take care of our visitors' and 'split the take later'. I was sick to my stomach. I just knew he was gonna kill them then and there.

"He sat on a tree stump and swigged on a canteen full of fresh water that we fetched from a place called Clear Spring. I saw my father lean over to kiss my mother. They did the best they could with that rope tied around their heads, snagged between their teeth. They loved each other *so* much." Contessa picked up the cold sandwich and took a small bite, chewing slowly, her eyes taking on that far-away look again. "That's when Red Beard blew on a sparkly-looking bullhorn. An hour or so later I ran through the woods towards the sun and found your old barn."

"Ms. Contessa, I'm proud you made it there safe. Eat up, now, you need your strength. There's plenty."

She bit into the soft bread and cold, salty meat.

Dan went out the back door. He returned a few minutes later carrying a steel pot of water. He set it on top of the wood burning stove and lit a match, waving the flame across pine needles bunched up underneath a stack of dried hickory limbs.

"I'll bet you could use a hot bath. I've got bars of lye soap, wash rags, and a clean robe for you to wear."

"Mr. Dean?"

He turned to her. "Call me Dan."

"Why were you there, Dan?"

"Why was I where?"

"In that field with those men. After a while, I saw you ride up with the one who sat tall in the saddle, the man that had a smart mustache. Red Beard even called out your name. I saw him slap his arm and say, 'Dan Dean! Glad you made it out today.'"

Dan's fear proved correct. Before she ran away and found refuge in his barn, Contessa Menifee *had* seen him among West and Kimbrell.

"Contessa, I am not a part of that gang."

"Then why were you there?"

"The man with the mustache? That's Laws Kimbrell. The big fat one you call Red Beard? John West. They're the leaders of a gang of robbers called the West-Kimbrell Clan. They robbed your parents because y'all came down the Natchez Trace like any other family, and figured y'all had somethin' worth takin'. From what you told me, they were right." Dan stoked the fire. "Laws Kimbrell's an old friend of mine. We were in the war together. I didn't plan on being in that field that day. I was lied to. Met up with Laws in town by chance. Said his friend needed help moving a deer out of the forest. I figured I'd help, so I followed him out. That's when I saw your parents tied up by the well and knew something was wrong.

"This'll sound strange to you, Contessa, but John West wanted to see me that day. He wants me to become part of his gang. What I mean is, he wants me to become a cold-blooded killer . . . like him."

"But why?"

"They think I'm something special behind a pistol."

"Are you?" she asked cautiously.

He thought of the several men in blue he'd killed in the rolling hills of Shiloh, Tennessee, and on the riverbanks of Vicksburg, Mississippi, then said, quite convincingly: "I'm accurate enough." He raised his hand. "Don't panic, now. I am not one of them. I wouldn't hurt you for all the gold in America."

Contessa put her barely-eaten sandwich on the plate. "Dan, I believe if you intended to do me harm you wouldn't've wasted all this time asking how I got here."

Dan filled a long steel tub with heated water and left Contessa to bathe.

He relaxed on the porch and kept a steady eye on the Old Sparta Road, a Liege brand long-range rifle resting across his lap, expecting the nightriders to show any minute.

Chapter 21

Supper at the Kimbrell home was light. For the past week Aunt Polly had fallen ill to debilitating fever and a severe cough she believed the result of "bronkey-itus", instructing her sons to avoid her bedroom—unless, of course, she rang the bell. The bell had a handle on it, like those the schoolmarms up the road used at Goldonna Elementary School.

The bell meant bring me water. The bell meant bring me food. The bell meant bring me medicine (Dr. Tolli's Miracle Healing Elixir will do just fine, thank you). That damned ring-a-*ding! ding! ding! ding!* meant more blankets; damp cloths for my forehead; come in here and open that winder; come in here and close that winder; bring me my knittin' basket; and Laws' favorite: where's my hug?

The young men had been cooking for themselves the past week. This evening William was busy skinning four fresh squirrels he'd blown out of tree boughs in the backyard. He seasoned the pink meat with salt and pepper, then softened it in a large bowl of cow's milk. Shep sliced and heated potatoes for a greasy skillet of home fries. Laws tried frying homemade biscuits but messed that up gloriously. He cut up a loaf of bread instead and wiped the slices through butter, browned them on a heated iron skillet. Then he put chunks of mush melon in a bowl.

The brothers did not know exactly what was wrong with their mother, but the consensus held that she was depressed from being alone after their father's death. To have a deep bond with another loved one for so long—only to have that person snatched away in a flash, could very well dampen the spirit and cause the warmth of the heart to melt cold in their absence.

Aunt Polly hadn't left the comforts of her bedroom since she caught sick.

The brothers took turns changing her bedpans. They assisted in bathing her in the steel tub off the bedroom. They were worried about her health, obviously, but despite their efforts Aunt Polly showed no signs of improvement.

Dr. Tom Harrison was called on to examine and evaluate her wellness. The good doctor explained that not only was Aunt Polly suffering from bronchitis and painful migraines brought on by an unhealthy diet (she wasn't eating when she was supposed to eat, and when she did eat she picked at her food), the woman had also slipped into a dire state of depression. When asked why she felt depressed the brothers shrugged ignorance, neglecting to speak of Uncle Dan Kimbrell's death. Explaining how their father passed on would give them away as the culprits who kidnapped the doctor that night not too long ago. They decided to let him live.

"Not sure why she's feelin' sad," Laws said. "It's a shame."

"Well, she needs to get up and around, fellas. If only for a walk around the yard, to get the blood flowing," Dr. Harrison suggested. "If she doesn't try, her bones will grow too weak to hold her weight, light as she is. If and when she does rise, she might fall and break a hip."

"We'll see what we can do, doc," Shep said. "Mother can be stubborn as all get out, ya know."

Laws paid the doctor ten gold coins for his services.

"I hope your mother gets to feeling better," the doctor said. "Call on me if her condition doesn't improve."

The problem lay in the fact that Aunt Polly wasn't getting any better. She had recessed to nothing more than a warm body on a bed, sleeping off and on all day and night, and continuing to cough up blood during her waking hours.

The sound of the ringing bell (at first a gentle nuisance that increasingly bothered the brothers), had now become a signal that their mother was still alive.

They sat down at the long wooden table and began eating fried squirrel over bread, topped with skillet gravy. The brothers did not talk much while having supper. They ate in silence, each son wondering what might become of their caring mother . . . how long she'd be around . . . .

"Damn these 'taters are tough!" William griped, chewing on the fried skin. "How hot didja fire up that grease, Shep?"

"Hot enough. You try makin' 'em."

"I've cooked 'em up better than this, for sure. This's like chompin' on tree bark."

"Say whatcha want about my cookin', it don't matter. If I went out huntin' some squirrel I'd've dropped at least a dozen of them bastards. Not a prissy little four count to satisfy three grown men, ya dang idjit."

"You sorry shitbird!" William snapped. "I would've had more time to hunt 'fore dark if I hadn't worked the fields all day . . . while you sat up here drinkin' hooch on your *dead ass.*"

Shep scooted out of his chair quickly, making the legs scratch marks on the planked floor. Unsheathed a knife. "Better shut that mouth, brother, or I'll split you from neck to craw!"

Laws reached across the plate of fried squirrel legs and grabbed Shep's wrist, twisted the blade away from William's jaw. "You fools simmer down or I'll gut the both of ya." He nodded toward the back bedroom. "Mother's sleepin'."

Shep pulled away from Laws, anger burning in his eyes. He slid the blade in the leather sheath strapped to his belt.

William ate, staring at Shep with contempt.

"William's right," Laws said. "Them tater's are tough as rawhide, but that don't make a difference in the rest of the meal. The meat's got pellets in it, bread's burnt, and the gravy's too salty. Only thing here worth goin' down is the melon, and we didn't even make that." Laws sipped his sweet tea, set the glass on the table. "Aunt Polly can't cook for us now, boys, so if we've gotta make way and do for ourselves there's no need being negative about the process. Now *eat.*"

They did.

There was something to be said for being the older brother. The older brother was routinely respected in a bloodline hierarchy of male bonding. And because of this genetically-blessed clout within such a rowdy bunch, neither Shep nor William believed Laws was lying when he threatened he'd lay into them.

Brother or no brother, Lawson Jackson Kimbrell would erase what he perceived as the problem, and then hide their bodies in the nearest well.

When they finished supper, Shep lost the coin toss and had to clean dishes. William cleared and wiped down the table, because that's what he usually did to assist his mother. Laws went outside, took a seat in the rocker, and lit up an after-dinner cigarette.

That's when the bell rang.

William looked at Shep, who in turn looked at the smoke drifting through the open door, thinking Laws might step through. Laws sat still.

That high-noted annoyance invaded their ears again.

"I went last time," William whispered. "Momma don't favor me no how."

Shep didn't make a big deal of it. He threw a brown rag over the back of a chair and walked the hallway toward the dimly lit bedroom.

Candlelight danced in orange flames around the corners of the room, outlining his mother's covered body in trembling shadows.

His stomach fluttered. Not from the squirrel meat and salty gravy—it's just that he hated seeing his mother in such frail health. She'd lost a lot of weight and seemed closer to death than she did even yesterday. Her face was a prune of wrinkles, eyes blinded by cataracts, absent and far away. Shep couldn't believe she'd had the strength to reach over, find the bell, pick it up and shake it.

"Mother? What is it you need?"

"Laws?" she asked.

"It's Shep."

"Shep, my dear Shep," she said. "Come here, darlin'."

He stepped closer to the bed, still steaming over William's wiseass remarks. His mother had refused baths for three days now, and her skin put off a musty odor of uncleanliness that made Shep nearly upchuck the contents in his stomach.

"I'm here, mother."

She pointed at an empty jar. "Fetch me some water, darlin'."

Waiting to see if she'd say anything else, Shep swiped the jar off the fragile nightstand and left.

"Shep?" she called.

"Yes, mother?"

"Tell your brother to come in here. I wanna see Lawson."

He left the room angry. Laws was still outside relaxing, puffs from the cigarette creating plumes of smoke that hung heavy in the blue moonlight.

"Laws, she wants to see you," Shep said.

"I'll be there in a bit."

When she was awake and half-alert Aunt Polly always wanted to see him. It was no secret among the brothers that their mother favored Lawson.

He finished his cigarette and flicked it in the yard, watching the fiery embers fade to black in the grass.

Laws entered the room and approached the bed. "How're you feelin' mother?"

"Laws?"

"I'm here."

She reached up and felt for his hand. When she found it, she pulled him closer with all her strength. "Don't let them take me, Laws. I beg of you, son . . . kill them so they don't take me off."

"Who are you talking about? Mother, you're home. You're safe here with us. No one is going to harm you."

"You don't unnerstand, son. They're aimin' to get me . . . for the things I've done. They're here, in this room. They're watchin' . . . waitin' for the time when they can—oh, they'll snatch me away! For the folks I hurt, they want their due. They're after my soul!"

As tiny and frail as she appeared, Aunt Polly gripped his trigger hand with such strength that Laws gently pulled back from the pain.

"Who is it says they're coming to take you? Did somebody threaten you? Was it one of the riders? Tell me, mother, I'll take care of it. What's got you spooked?"

Aunt Polly pointed at the floor. "Down there Laws. Do you see them? They're swirling around, just a waitin'. It's the devil! I shut my eyes and see fire. Flames and flames and flames of fire! When I open them, I see demons holdin' the keys to Hell's gates. Them spirits swirl around my bed like rattlers. They're ready for my soul, Laws, and there ain't nothin' I can do to turn it right.

"God won't forgive me for the things I done. Already had many a long talk with Him and He don't believe I deserve the Kingdom of Heaven. He told me so, told me I will *burn*. He left me to Lucifer, and Lucifer sent his spirits to get me. On my death day they'll drag me down there, and the good Lord has no reason to stop 'em."

"Mother! Stop talkin' this way. There's nobody in this room besides me and you. No demons are coming to get you. This nonsense, it's all in your head."

"I've confessed my sins to God. I've repented. I've asked for forgiveness. Not a damn thing's come of it, either, because I still see those spirits . . . they're waitin', son . . . waitin' for me to die so they can take me off!"

Laws sighed heavily. "What is it you want me to do, mother? I can't get rid of something I can't *see*."

The Kimbrell's were not religious like a majority of their community neighbors, but they did believe there was a God. The thing is, they had chosen the path of evil for so long even Laws realized that a righteous God could never forgive their deceitful, horrendous actions toward their fellow man. Aunt Polly had just as much blood (if not more) on her hands as any one of her sons. If she recalled her deeds to a minister in the name of Jesus Christ, she'd give herself away as a murderess. Deepening depression and seeing wild phantasms was between her and God, and it looked like God had made His decision.

Her fate was now in the hands of Heaven's fallen angel, Lucifer.

"You can't see them now . . . those spirits . . . but you will, son. I'm sorry, but one sad day you will see them."

Shep walked into the room carrying her refill of fresh water. He set the jar on the nightstand and stood there looking at Aunt Polly reaching for Lawson's hand.

"Here's your water, mother," he said, and leaned over and kissed her dampened forehead.

"You're a good boy, William."

"It's Shep. William's in yonder washin' dishes."

"He's a good son, too. Laws?"

"Yes, mother?"

"Pray for my soul."

"I—"

"Pray for me, son. I've done all I can since Dan died. I'll tell you right now, the only way out of this world is going up, or going down . . . and I'm—I am so sorry I filled your life with tragedy."

"Shhh, mother, drink your water and get some rest. I'll pray for you."

"I will, too, mom," said Shep.

"Thank you, William," she said.

Shep shook his head and walked out.

"Laws? Where's my hug?"

He reached down and held her frail bones in his arms, kissed her cheek.

"Good night, boys. If you can help it, try not to do the things I've done. Ain't worth it in the end." Aunt Polly let go of Lawson's hand, closed her eyes, and fell into another deep sleep.

Before Laws blew out candles he searched along the floor for swirling images of evil spirits that his mother claimed she'd witnessed, but found nothing more than trembling shadows fanning out from the light of wax candles.

"G'night, mother."

Laws leaned over the nearest candle and blew out the flame.

Chapter 22

Aunt Polly died the next morning.

The brothers buried her beside Uncle Dan Kimbrell's grave underneath a great Oak in the back field, just a few feet from the tombstone of their older brother, Guy Kimbrell, who died at three days old in 1842. This little one survived Christmas eve, all of Christmas Day, and a hint of the morning sun the day after before he suffocated in his sleep.

Aunt Polly's funeral was a somber event, gaining the sympathy of fifteen people, including neighbors and old acquaintances of Mary Kimbrell. Pastor James Weeks officiated, ending the ceremony by reading a passage from Romans 14:7-9—"For none of us lives to himself, and none of us dies to himself. For if we live, we live to the Lord, and if we die, we die to the Lord. So then, whether we live or whether we die, we are the Lord's. For to this end Christ died and lived again, that he might be Lord both of the dead and of the living."

Flowers were set upon the grave and when the sky opened its flood, Laws stood alone in the field, head down, silent. If you were to look at the man's face you'd wonder if the streaks of water falling from his cheeks were rain, or long overdue tears.

If I had to bet, I'd say tears. There just had to be some good in Lawson Kimbrell's rocky heart. At the very least I wanted to believe this. He did not shed a single tear for his father, Uncle Dan, but I wanted to believe he greatly missed his mother. I hoped he understood what his mother had said on her deathbed, that one day he too might see those evil spirits swirling around him . . . that if he was in any pain now, it was because his mother had been escorted to Hell during those early hours.

It has to be said (at least from my perspective) that when Laws Kimbrell lost his mother, something snapped inside him. Oh, he was a clever, thrill-seeking madman even before then, and Laws would continue as the co-leader of the West Clan . . . but if there had been a soft spot for anyone in his heart, namely Aunt Polly, that spot was now drenched in blackness forevermore.

Laws walked away from the gravesite on that rain-drenched afternoon knowing whatever may come, he had nothing to lose.

Chapter 23

Later that evening Laws held a meeting of the inner circle at his home.

Eighteen men sat around in the front room and spread out along the front porch, some smoking imported cigars, most drinking whiskey or tea out of glass jars. Present were Lec Ingram, Ab Martin, the Frame brothers (James and Dave), Hank Wright, Gus Rivers, Clyde Judkins, Zeek Crutchfield, Arthur Collins, Darren Forte, Jurd Vines, Maurice Washbow, Copeland Yates, along with West and Kimbrell and a handful of others.

Several members asked John West why the reason for the meeting. But this was a rare occasion where even the co-leader was in the dark, assuring them he'd heard no details on the subject matter.

"Laws called this one," West claimed. "I guess we'll find out what it's about when he gets in here."

Biding his time in the back bedroom, the door cracked just enough to let light glow into the long hallway, Laws stood beside a nervous Annabelle Frost. He whispered at her ear, "Look closely. Any faces look familiar?"

"I don't know if I can do this, Laws."

"Tell me. Point 'em out."

"What are you going to do? If I show you which one did it, what will happen?"

"I'm gonna talk to them, Annabelle. Get my point across that if anybody here ever stops you on the road, there will be consequences. Simple as that."

"You're going to hurt those men, aren't you?" she asked, her voice quivering.

"All the men here are friends of mine. Tell me which friend stopped you," he said, ignoring her question. "And I'll talk some sense to him."

Annabelle breathed deeply, let out a bothered sigh. Pointed a delicate finger. "That one . . . sitting in the chair by the window. He took me to the woods."

Clyde Judkins.

"Who else?"

"I don't see the other one," she said.

"Here's what I want you to do. See those men out on the porch?"

"Yes."

"When I go out, I'm gonna stand by each one of 'em. Make conversation for awhile. When you see me standin' by the other rider that stopped you on the road,"—he pointed to the only lantern in the room— "you blow out that light."

"Okay."

"Stay in this room 'til I clear everybody out."

Annabelle nodded.

Laws kissed the top of her head, turned away and buckled on his heavy gun belt.

A half hour of drinking and conversation went on among the men before Laws came out of the back room, comfortably dressed in his black trousers, boots, and a white shirt dented by thin gray suspenders.

He took West aside, whispered in his ear. West nodded.

Then Laws walked out into the cool air, lit a cigarette, and stood by Ab Martin. He looked back through the wide windows at the bedroom and talked awhile about nothing pressing. The bedroom light remained aglow, so he casually stepped over to Darren Forte. The rider looked pale and sickly in the lamplights hanging from the support corners of the porch, sipping whiskey from a metal flask.

"Doin' alright Darren?" Laws asked.

"Yep. Sure am."

"Did y'all get that buggy repainted last Friday?"

"Sure did. Sold it to a banker gent down in Lafayette."

"Look inside real quick, Darren. I want your opinion on somethin'."

The man got up and faced the window. "What is it Laws?"

"Thinkin' about movin' that woodstove there to my barn, get me another. Thing's old and cranky. Can you locate me a new one?"

Darren moved into the light. "Oh, yeah. I know a guy over in Quitman who'll grant you a fair deal for one."

Laws saw the lights of the back bedroom fall dark. "Call on him next day or so, will ya?"

"Yep."

Laws stepped to the opened front door and yelled over the chatter. "Alright! Everybody come on out here! I want to show y'all somethin'."

The rest of the riders filed out of the comforts of the house and gathered on the porch, wondering what Laws had in store.

Laws reached into his pocket and unrolled a red sash, handed it to Lec Ingram. "What's this thing?"

Known by his familiar gravel-rough voice, Lec replied, "It's a sash."

"What'd I say about this sash at our last meeting, Lec?"

"You said if we saw this here sash on a lady's horse we oughta let her pass by."

"Right. What warning did I give at that meeting?"

"You said if she got stopped you'd find the scoundrel done it and give 'em a what-for."

"Right again, old friend. Well, somebody at the last meeting did not hear my words, or if they did, they did not *respect* my warning. There's a man in our presence that stopped my lady friend the other evening, and I want that man to fess up! Don't be a coward, now. Step forward. Admit your mistake." Nobody moved. He breathed hard through his nose, agitated. "Let me put this another way: if you confess your crime in front of every rider present, I'll spare your life. On that, you have my word. But if you force my hand . . . if you make me hunt you down, what I got in mind won't be pleasant," Laws said, pacing the length of the porch. He searched faces for a twitch in expression, scared eyes, general disinterest, then stepped to Gus Rivers. "Gus, you didn't do it, didja?"

"Shoot no! C'mon, Laws, you know me better than that. I ain't never showed you no disrespect."

Laws stepped to the next man: Copeland Yates. "Copeland?"

"Laws, you know dang well I've always been loyal to this bunch. You give the orders, I do it. You say not to, I don't. That's that."

Laws stepped in front of Darren Forte.

Darren's eyes went wild with thought.

"Somethin' on your mind, Darren?"

"Just listenin', Laws."

"Have somethin' ya might wanna tell me?"

"Nothing in particular, no."

"Where were you Saturday last?"

"I—I don't rightly remember," Darren stammered.

"Do you remember stopping a lady had that red sash hanging off her saddle?"

Darren felt the eyes of surrounding nightriders focus in on him. A bead of sweat fell from his scalp and curved around his bottom lip. He knocked back a swig of whiskey, his breathing coming short. He knew if he did not speak up while given the chance of mild punishment (as Laws promised), the gang leader would ultimately discover his lie and deal him a bad hand. So he relented.

"It was a mistake, Laws!" Darren blurted out. "I didn't see the sash 'til later!"

"What did you do to her?"

"Not a damn thang! I held the reins when she stopped, that's it. We were on the hunt for gold!"

"Who was with ya?"

"I can't say," Darren replied. "It's against the rider code to give up a member for any kind of offense, and I won't do it."

Laws pulled his gun, put the barrel to Darren's throat. "It'd be in your best interest to make an exception to that code. Who was it!"

"I—Laws, don't make me do this."

"West?" Laws said.

John West grabbed Clyde Judkins and pushed him into the lamplight, a foot away from the top porch step.

Laws turned the gun on Clyde and shot him in the head, the impact launching the poor bastard down the steps and into the yard. Laws turned back. "He took her in the woods that night, didn't he?"

Shaking terribly at the sight of his dead running buddy, Darren nodded. "Yes! When I saw the sash, I knew we'd made a mistake. Clyde, yeah, he took her out in the woods but I never touched her! I swear to you by my mother's grave, I swear I didn't touch her. I saved her from Clyde, gave the missus my respects and sent her on her way. That's how it played out. Please Laws . . . have mercy."

The other nightriders watched intently. In that instance Laws Kimbrell reasserted his position among the gang as the most ruthless killer among them. If the urge moved him he'd waste any man in sight, just to prove the point. And if respect for Laws had declined for whatever reason during the past few years, after this meeting he'd regained that respect ten-fold.

Laws holstered his revolver, the steel hot against leather. He drew back and punched Darren in the stomach with such brute strength the rider fell against the window and dropped hard to his knees.

John West stepped over and handed Laws a long, curved hunting knife.

Holding Darren's head against his thigh, Laws slid the blade against the backside of the rider's ear. Dealing with strong resistance, he moved the blade through the tightly wound cartilage and sliced off the man's ear like a bothersome wart.

Darren covered the bloody wound with his hand, gritting his teeth against sharp, hot pain. Tears filming his eyes, he gazed up at Kimbrell.

Laws held the ear in his palm. "This is to remind you that I'm a fair man. You didn't give up Clyde when I asked you, so you're somewhat trustworthy. That goes a long way with me. But I had to give you a what-for anyways because you did stop my lady friend." Laws handed Darren his severed ear. "Now you get to go home alive." He grabbed the sash from Lec Ingram and looked around the porch. "This goes for any of you out there! If you see a lady on a horse with this fuckin' red sash hanging off the saddle you'd better let her pass by, or you will get the same medicine. We clear?"

They answered in their own way by nodding or saying, "yeah!", and waited for Laws to continue.

"Let's all get this straight right goddamn now. Me and John West are the leaders of this gang. If you go out on your own without us knowin' what you're up to like these fools did, then God help you . . . 'cause if we hear you're robbin' and not sharin', you'll land face first at the bottom of a well!"

Laws looked inside the empty house.

Behind the walls of the darkened bedroom at the end of the hall, he saw lamplight flicker across a set of beautiful blue eyes now glistening with fresh tears.

Chapter 24

Wydell Phillips and his wife, Flora, crossed the Mississippi River by ferry on a Tuesday morning. By mid-day, the Louisiana humidity welcomed them like a wave from a flame.

They had stopped in Monroe to shop for gear and necessities for the trip ahead, well-aware they had many miles of unfamiliar land to cover.

Mrs. Flora Phillips, a country girl from Georgia, persuaded her husband to buy her a new sun hat, a lavender colored thing that sat slanted on her head and only revealed half her beautiful face. Their daughter, Shay, using her youthful charm, persuaded her father to purchase her a vest that had frilly edges and paisley imprints stamped into the leather.

Wydell wasn't one to purchase such things on the spur of the moment. But he figured since he'd uprooted his family for life in another state (Shay hadn't been too happy about it anyway), that buying a few gifts to satisfy just might keep him from tearing out what was left of his hair during the journey.

Instead of setting their sights on the great land of Texas, as most folks traveling the Natchez Trace were apt to do, Mr. Phillips and his family were on their way to Lake Charles, where his cousin had secured him a job working as a clerk at a Citizens Bank of Louisiana.

Flora sat high in the bench seat, her newborn son, Luke, cradled in her arms. Shay, a pretty brunette blessed with her mother's almond-brown eyes and petite figure, sat behind her parents eating slices of apples on thin crackers. They passed around a canteen of fresh water, being careful to reserve it before they stopped at a spring or river to set camp for the evening—which wouldn't be too long now. The sun had slid behind the treetops, and the once narrow shadows now stretched wide across the dusty road.

The family had grown tired from all-day travel. The sooner Wydell found a spot to settle in, the sooner they could all eat supper and rest for the night. Nearly every five miles they traveled since Jackson the foursome passed a variety of waterways, so it wouldn't be long before they set camp.

At last, Wydell steered the horse off the main road to a clearing near a running bayou.

Except for the newborn, each family member tended to their duties. Wydell chopped small timber to start a fire for cooking. Shay fetched water in a metal milk pail. Flora put her sleeping son in the buggy and drew a quilt over him. She then managed the food items in preparation for this evening's supper of red beans and rice and chunks of fresh tomato. Dessert was Shay's favorite—thick slices of homemade pound cake topped with strawberry preserves.

Wydell fed and watered his horse and tied her to a pine tree. He then boiled the bayou water to purify it for consumption.

When night fell in a dark blanket, firelight snapping around them, Wydell asked his daughter if she was looking forward to making new friends in their adopted town.

"Yes, daddy," she said. "But I miss my friends in Georgia."

"Shay, you can write them a letter. They'll stay in touch, too."

"I hope so," she said, dipping a wooden spoon into her bowl of rice and beans.

Wydell looked up at his wife, whose face glowed in the firelight. "Your mother here says she'll continue her quilt-making in Lake Charles. After school you can help her. When she sells one, she'll give you some of the profits. That way you'll have an allowance so the next time you see a nice lacy vest in a store somewhere you can purchase it yourself."

Shay smiled and ran the tips of her fingers over the frills. "Thank you for the vest, daddy. I like wearing it."

"You're welcome, darlin'."

Holding the baby, Flora smiled, too. Waking up from a long-overdue nap, Luke wrinkled up his face and cried out gently. "Oh, he's hungry," Flora said. She slipped her blouse to the side, freeing her left breast. Luke honed in on the erect nipple and started suckling.

After supper, the family slept the night away in the covered buggy.

Well, at least her mother, father, and baby brother rested easily. But Shay could not reach the comforts of sleep. Breezes shook the trees, creating high whistling sounds that gave her a lonely feeling. She watched the campfire embers blink and glow in the darkness and finally fade out, the whole time wondering just how long it'd be before she could restart her life.

Yes, she was looking forward to making friends in a new town, but she wasn't at all excited about getting there.

*****

From out of the silence a blue dawn drew in on the forest.

Shay was awakened abruptly by the sound of a hushed voice.

"*Three*," the voice said.

Then Shay saw the rear canvas flaps of their covered buggy sway back against morning's light.

"There's three."

A man's voice.

Shay looked at her father lying still, snoring deeply; her mother, fast asleep, held Luke under the homemade quilts.

Who was out there?

Were they in danger?

Her mouth gone dry, Shay leaned forward and moved the canvas fabric barely an inch.

A tall man with a scruffy beard and black eyes stood there talking to a fat man who had red hair and a red beard.

"The horse might bring in a few coins, but I can sell the buggy in Tyler by Wednesday for sure," the skinny man said.

The fat man nodded.

"The man's got a gold chain watch hangin' outta his suit vest. Woman beside him's surely his wife. She ain't got no necklace on, but she's got a silver bracelet looks like it might fetch a bundle."

"You said there was three of 'em."

"Young girl in there, too," the tall man confirmed. "Pretty little thing. And they got some trunks."

Shay could hardly breathe. These men were going to rob them! She wanted to wake her father in a hurry but thought better of it. The strangers believed the family was asleep, numb to any action happening outside the buggy. Taking advantage of this assumption, Shay reached over by the back of the bench and felt the cool steel of her father's Liege rifle. She shouldered the heavy gun, aimed at the canvas.

First sight of a face, she thought, *boom.*

Her heart leapt in her chest. Wydell had taught her how to fire a gun when she was seven years old. She was a decent shot, but up until now it was all fun and games—taking aim at squirrels and birds and tin cans, helpless things that posed no threat. Did she possess the courage to fire a bullet into the heart of another human being?

She swallowed a hard knot down her throat, wished for a sip of clean water, her arms pounding with just enough adrenaline to steady her finger on the trigger guard and give her the strength to blast away.

A couple minutes ticked by. She tried making out the intruders' muffled conversation to no avail. She reached over and tapped her father on his belly, whispered: "Daddy, wake up."

"Inghhh, huh?"

"Shhhh!"

He opened his eyes. "Shay? What're you doin' with that gun?"

The canvas slit opened wide.

The skinny man peered inside, his face punctured by acne scars. "Lookey here! We got us a feisty one!" the man said, reaching in. "Come here, girl, gimme that gun before you hurtcher self!" He wrapped his knobby fingers around the end of the barrel, tried wrestling the weapon out of her grip.

Shay pulled the trigger, creating a blast so incredibly loud her ears rang out in protest.

The tall man was flung on his back in a cloud of gun smoke, the side of his face opened up like a busted melon.

Shay's perception altered into slow-motion—her surroundings a barrage of ringing silence and shifting images.

Her parents scrambled out from under quilts. Little Luke cried out. But Shay couldn't hear her brother's cries or her mother's screams. Her father was yelling at her, wrenched the rifle out of her hands.

Flora held Luke. "Shhh, baby. *Hush!*"

Wydell suddenly felt steel nudge the back of his head.

"Come on outta there, fella," the stranger demanded. "Else I'll send you to your Heavenly reward."

Wydell met his daughter's pleading eyes . . . lowered the rifle.

When the canvas swung open this time, the fat man glared at Shay. "Keep that gun on him, Laws!" He grabbed Shay's ankle. Pulled her out. "Come here you pretty thang!"

Shay tried resisting but the man was too powerful. He wrapped her up in the crook of his arm and kept her close to his chest, his pistol aimed at her parents. "Come on out, now, the both of ya! Or I'll let loose six bullets in her head."

Flora looked to her husband, who only nodded in shame. She lifted the blankets. Still crying, Luke clung tightly to her blouse. "Shhhh, baby. Keep quiet," she whispered. "You're gonna be okay."

Shay saw that there were actually four men, not two—three standing around the buggy and a lone gunman lying spread-eagle, bleeding out on the naked earth. The one the fat man called Laws had a look in his eyes that could paralyze a rattlesnake. The other, a devilish grin on his dirty face, was of medium height and wide-eyed, pacing impatiently, as though awaiting instruction.

"Jurd? Check the trunks. See what kinda goods they're haulin'," the fat man ordered.

Shay was repulsed by the odor of the fat man's unclean breath near her face. She winced. "Let me go!"

"Simmer down, darlin'. This won't take long. Whatcha got there, Jurd? Anything worth all this trouble?"

Jurd Vines, one of the more psychotic nightriders within the inner circle (if there ever existed such an animal), pitched articles of clothing over his shoulder, dug deeper, came up with a jewelry box. Opened it. "Got a few rings here." He picked out a long pearl necklace. "Now, this's mighty fine!"

"Keep lookin," the fat man ordered.

Wydell stood by his trembling wife, barely containing his strained nerves. These men were no good, and he was now unarmed against them. The only weapon at his disposal was common sense and logical thinking, as there was no telling what these rogues might do if he tried to be the hero.

"Mister?" Wydell raised his hands in a peaceful gesture. "Please, we mean no harm. Me and my family are passing through these parts." He looked over at the man lying in a pool of blood trying to catch a full breath. "I'm sorry about your friend there."

The fat one turned his pistol on the dying man and shot him in the throat. "What friend?"

"Oh my Dear Lord," Wydell said.

"Now, if you ain't from here, and I 'spect you ain't, then you must have coins to get along the trails. Money for food and fancy things like pearl necklaces?" Shay struggled in the fat man's grip, couldn't break away. "We'll let y'all alone if you got gold. Short of that, ya see . . . ."

"Gold? Yes, of course!" Wydell left his wife's side.

Luke had calmed down a bit, but still whined in gentle tones, somehow knowing even in infancy that something here was terribly wrong.

Wydell reached for a bedroll that he kept near the backend of the buggy. He pulled out a canvas bag . . . three . . . four bags, dropped them at the thief's boots. He knelt, opened a bag, revealing dull gold coins in the rising sunlight. "That's all I have. Over two thousand, my life's savings. Take it, please. Let us pass by. That's all I ask, mister."

The fat man smiled and freed Shay.

The girl hurried to her mother.

"Call me John West." He secured the string on the bag and collected the others, handing them over to the man he called Laws. "This here's Laws Kimbrell. We head up the West Clan."

"The West Clan?" Wydell asked, confused.

"And that there's Jurd Vines," West said, motioning to the excited man standing near the family's horse. "The fella your lovely daughter used for target practice, that's Zeek Crutchfield. What's your name, sir?"

"Wydell Phillips."

"Well, Mr. Phillips, it is certainly nice to make your acquaintance." West put his gun against Wydell's chest and blew his heart's blood out his back.

Wydell fell hard to the ground, his face slamming against the metal frame of the buggy, knocking out teeth.

Luke cried louder, the sound penetrating the calm forest.

West knew by experience that early morning hijinks similar to this incident near the main thoroughfare might summon unwanted attention. The Natchez Trace would soon be busy with travelers and he could not risk the chance someone may hear and investigate such commotion.

"Shut that thing up!" West yelled.

Flora kicked John West in the knee. "You bastard!"

"Mother! Stop!"

But Flora ignored her daughter's pleas and did not back down. "Oh, the courage it takes to be such cowards! Take on a defenseless man and his family? I pray God Almighty strikes you down! I pray for your *death!*"

Luke kept screaming, the high-pitched squeals getting on West's nerves.

"You need to shut that baby's mouth, or—"

Just then Laws Kimbrell snatched the infant out of its mother's arms and pitched the little one in the air. He pulled out his hunting knife, quickly turned the sharpened tip upwards. The infant struck the blade sideways, shook violently, went silent.

"Augh! Oh my God!" Flora ran to Laws, fists swinging.

West tugged her away.

Laws pulled the knife across the baby's spine and out of its stomach, cutting through pink meat and fragile bone. He dropped little Luke on the grass in a heap of broken flesh and bright blood.

Flora punched John West in the face as hard as she could, smashing his nose, the action loosening his hold on her. She squirmed away, landed on her knees in a quiver, and cried over her son's body.

"No, no, God please no! My baby! Not my *baby!*"

John West pulled his gun and shot the kneeling mother in the back of the head, showcasing the same amount of emotion had he slaughtered a hog.

Flora fell over Luke, dark blood spurting out of her skull, coloring the grass.

With her entire family lying dead before her, Shay wanted to die then and there. Crying would not bring them back. Screaming her energy out in hateful words had obviously done no good. Shay knew that within a matter of seconds she'd join her family in the afterlife . . . and all she could do was wait for that moment to come.

West stepped over Zeek Crutchfield's body. "Jurd? Throw Zeek in the bayou, along with those three." He turned to Laws. "What about this pretty thang here?"

"I'll send her on her way," Laws said, flinging blood off his fingers.

Before Jurd Vines dragged his fellow nightrider to the bayou for the delight of reptilian creatures, the rider proposed an unusual idea.

"Hold on a minute there, Laws. Don't be so hasty with this one. Why, she's pretty and fresh. How about I take care of her?"

"By what means?" Laws asked, although he had an idea what the crazy bastard meant.

Jurd Vines grinned, his eyes alight with wild thoughts. "Say I take her back there behind the trees for a spell? Then we can finish this business?"

"Don't lollygag. Make it fast. Then come back and throw them bodies in the bayou. That includes your sweetheart there."

"I'll complete my duties, that's for sure!" Jurd replied, the grin morphing into a dirty smile. "More than one." He approached the frightened girl, his palm sliding across the pistol grip of his firearm, attention focused on her youthfully toned legs and what fleshy treasure lay between them.

"Walk on back that way, gal," he ordered.

Shay obeyed.

"Past them trees. Quickly now, time's a wastin'."

They disappeared into the forest.

West positioned the family's horse in front of the buggy and secured the bridles for transport.

Laws unhooked a silver bracelet from Flora's wrist, shoved it in his vest pocket. He continued searching for valuables on her limp body but found nothing else worth stealing. While Jurd busied himself exploring a teenager's body, Laws turned up a flask of whiskey, swallowed hard. Passed it to West.

Eight minutes later, Jurd Vines came running through the forest, holding up his pants with one hand, the sheath that held his knife vacant and thumping at his hip.

"She cut me! She cut me! Mother Mary—augh! Bitch *cut* me!"

Upon closer inspection, Laws and West saw that Jurd's other hand was holding his blood-soaked, semi-stiff penis.

Paying no attention to Jurd's apparent pain, West hit his jaw. "Where is she!"

"She ran away! I was, I had her where I wanted, and the witch stole my knife and she sliced me!" Jurd thrust his hips forward. "Look!"

West backhanded his face. "Goddamn it, you crazy fool! She's loose!"

*****

Shay made her way through the woods, her grip around the knife so tight it hurt. She rushed by pine trees and jumped fallen limbs, using every spark of energy to escape the robbers. She made noise stamping through scattered leaves but didn't chance looking back.

If she faltered, they'd find her. If she stopped, they'd kidnap her. If she didn't run until her breath gave, providing her a safe enough distance, she'd join her family.

Finally she stopped and caught her breath, hands on knees, her backside against a tree. She observed the forest and was relieved to see the wondrous, natural movement of swaying trees and limb-hopping squirrels instead of outlaws in pursuit.

Through sunlight filtering through the treetops she noticed men on horses . . . a couple of carriages . . . people traveling the main road.

Shay pushed herself away from the tree and made her way onto the red dirt road, waved her arms in a signal of distress.

A man pulled the reins to his horse. "What's your rush young lady?"

Shay touched the bench seat. "Please, mister, you've got to help me! I need to find the sheriff around here! There's a gang in these parts that robbed my family . . . they killed my momma and my daddy and my little brother! Please take me to the sheriff!"

"Get yourself on up here, gal."

She did.

"Now, what kind of story is that to tell a stranger?"

"Mister, please! Make time! They're right around the corner."

The man, an older gentleman with a white beard and narrow, sneaky eyes, slapped the reins across the horse's back, and off they went.

For the next half-hour Shay did not explain in much detail about witnessing the death of her family. She did not bring up the fact that she'd been stolen away into the woods by that maniac named Jurd Vines, who stopped well beyond the other bandits' view and kissed her neck and groped her small breasts and pushed her to the ground . . . then lifted her dress, breath hard across her face, while he released his belt buckle and shucked his trousers . . . freed his penis.

She did not tell her kind host that she reached for Jurd's knife, jerked it out of the sheath strapped to his hip and swung the blade across his erection, cutting deep into muscle. She did not recall how the outlaw fell about in excruciating pain, cupping his hands over the wound to stem blood.

Up until they arrived in a town called Winnfield, all Shay told the gentleman was that she'd escaped the claws of brutal bandits, and now owned an outlaw's knife. She did not care whether this satisfied the gentleman's curiosity; Shay was simply grateful for the ride.

At the sheriff's station Shay told Sheriff Hayden Rose what had happened to her and her family, recalling to him descriptions of the men (as best she remembered) and the exact location of the murders. She mentioned the names "Laws" and "West" and "Jurd" and described a skinny fellow with a mustache whose name she did not recall, but noted that "he was shot dead."

Sheriff Rose listened to her story and ordered his men to saddle up, they were going to investigate. He asked that she hand over the knife—for evidence, he explained, and allowed her to wash her face and hands with fresh water before heading out again.

The sheriff seemed to believe her encounter actually happened. Counted that as a blessing. She hoped they'd find the outlaws and kill them, effectively avenge her family's senseless deaths.

A short time later Shay and the sheriff's posse of two deputies arrived at the clearing near the bayou.

"Is this where it happened?" he asked.

Shay climbed down from his horse. The look of shock on her face quickly changed to utter disbelief.

Nothing was there.

The clearing looked as it had the evening they set camp. The bodies of her parents and little brother and that scoundrel she'd shot in the face had disappeared. The grassy areas were clean of blood. No tracks from the wheels of the buggy . . . no hoof prints . . . no boot prints . . . no ashes from the fire that heated their supper of rice and beans. There was absolutely no visible evidence of any busywork to lend her story credit.

"They cleared everything," Shay said. "They cleaned up."

"Ma'am? Maybe you ain't in the right place," suggested one of the deputies.

"No! I'm tellin' you, my parents were shot and killed right here! My little brother, one of those devils stabbed him like a pumpkin! We had a fire. We cooked rice and beans over there. See? Right there! Do you think I walked all the way from Georgia to this God-awful place? Our buggy was *here*. We slept in it and that gang robbed us and . . . and . . . oh Lord, why is this happening? You must believe me!"

Sheriff Rose believed Shay Phillips' story, but he also knew that the nightriders were extremely competent at covering their tracks. Even if he wanted to catch these demons the gang would get to him before he apprehended the first one of the bunch.

Based on her claims of robbery and murder, presenting this case to a grand jury would be unsuccessful. This girl was not from the area and since there were no known next of kin to befriend her, Sheriff Rose decided transporting Shay Phillips into the City of

Natchitoches, accompanied by his deputies, was her best chance to escape the outlaws. She would stay with a Christian family for safekeeping until she was taken to Cane City. From there, his associates would see to it that she returned safely by train to her grandmother's house in Americus, Georgia.

This plan was the only way he knew how to keep her alive.

Before they left the scene, Shay sat behind Sheriff Rose on his black horse, drained of energy and feeling defeated in her plight to seek justice for the senseless murders of her loved ones.

The sheriff glanced across the bayou, into the woods . . . and saw a man wearing a tanned shirt and black hat, staring back at him.

If he so desired, Laws Kimbrell could dispatch all four of them in a mad rush.

But Sheriff Hayden Rose wasn't about to give the nightrider the satisfaction.

"Let's go, men," he ordered. "We've got to get this young lady out of town."

Chapter 25

Contessa felt like she was wearing a drape. It was too frumpy and swallowed her body whole. She looked in the mirror at Dan standing behind her. "It's pretty, but it's a bit large."

Dan factored in her resistance when he asked that Contessa try on one of Ezona's dresses she'd left behind in the hall closet.

"It's clean," he admitted.

"I'd rather wear mine."

"Then I'll make arrangements to buy you a new one," he said. "But I'll have to take your old dress to the tailor. They'll need the correct measurements."

"Why go through that trouble? I'll ride with you."

"It's best you stay hid away for now. If those men saw you with me, they'd come after us."

Contessa turned around, a look of disapproval on her lovely face. "I appreciate your hospitality, Dan, but I will not live as a ghost. How would you like it if someone told you you couldn't leave your house? Or go to the market? Step out and enjoy a beautiful day like this?"

"I'm taking precautions to ensure your safety," he replied. "You should be thankful."

She exhaled, bothered by the idea that she felt like a prisoner behind these walls. "Fine. Please leave the room while I change."

"Might as well keep that big dress on."

"Give me a minute to collect my thoughts, please. I'd like to be alone."

Dan closed the door on his way out.

Since the first night she spent at his farmhouse Dan had offered Contessa the comforts of his bed under thick quilts, while he took the cot in the loft. She declined his kind offer, though, instead opting for the front room fainting couch to watch the moon glow until she faded off to dream.

The past week had been a struggle for Contessa because of several reasons, and she had leaned on a stranger to get her through.

She felt safe with Dan Dean. She wanted to believe with all her heart that he was the gentleman he claimed to be . . . not a sly bandit going through the motions of hospitality just so he could give her up to that red-bearded bastard John West. For money. Pride. Had to be something devilish.

Surely Dan wouldn't do such a thing, she thought.

She walked in the den and threw her dirty dress across the couch.

Dan was hunkered down at the cavity of the wood burning stove, breaking sticks for a fire.

"I'm going to town with you," she said adamantly. "I'll wear this awful dress to hide my face if that satisfies you, but I refuse to stay here like a prisoner. Do you understand, or should we debate this issue further?"

Dan snapped a stick and placed it in the pit. "I'm grilling duck breast tonight. Do you like duck meat?" he asked.

"Are you listening to me?"

"I'm listening. And I think you're not thinking right."

She folded her arms over her chest. "So, what *are* you thinking? That I should stay inside this house all the time? With you? Forever?"

Dan lit a match and watched the flame lick the bark of brittle wood. He stood and faced her. "I think it's in your best interest to stay out of sight for awhile . . . nothing more. Let the memory of that tragic day at West's field, and the fact you escaped, lose its urgency."

"And just how do you suggest I do that, Mr. Dan Dean? Forgive me for holding on to lasting images, but that monster murdered my parents!"

"I'm referring to John West and his nightriders. When they feel enough time's gone by seeing no hair of you, they'll forget about tracking you. That's when I'll move you out of here under the cover of darkness. We'll hitch a train over to the Delta bottoms and take a ferry across the Mississippi, then ride to Jackson. I have some friends up that way who owe me a favor. They'll see that you get back to North Carolina in a safe manner."

His reply pacified her.

She was still scared.

She approached the window, took in the sunny day. Dan's idea made sense. She would be safe for the time being. Return home to

Charlotte. After a silent minute, she asked what she could do to help with supper.

Not used to having help around the cooking area since Ezona lived here (she had done most of the cooking, anyhow), Dan brought out a large bowl and a half bushel of purple hull peas.

"You can shell them peas while I go to town," he said.

A smile played on Contessa's lips. "I'd be glad to."

Dan picked up her dress from the couch and folded it into a bundle. He grabbed his canteen, some sugar cubes for the trip, and opened the front door. "If anybody shows up, you hide."

She nodded.

"I'll be a couple of hours. Boil the peas while I'm gone, and we'll have us a real nice supper when I get back. Lock this door behind me."

She did. Then Contessa sat back in a rocking chair, the bowl in her lap, and swayed gently, the chair's curved legs creaking across the floor. She tossed pea skins out the opened window, saw Dan stuff the sundress in his bag. She watched him step up in the foot support and head down the road, lost sight of him around the curve.

Now alone in the big house, Contessa wondered just how long it would take for a gang called the nightriders to lose the emotional urgency to track her down.

Chapter 26

That afternoon West called on Laws Kimbrell, Ike Hicks, and Jurd Vines to meet him at the Prescott Gin, where already the stench of rotted flesh and dried blood had climbed the depths of the well, permeating the area with death.

The four men left their horses to graze in the field while they discussed their most recent heist. West passed around a whiskey flask. Everyone thought the actual robbery went fine, as there were plenty of coins to share among them.

The single incident that nearly jeopardized a clean get-away needed no mention. They were in agreement that Jurd Vines' lust for flesh had now put them at great risk. Losing that girl posed a serious threat. Other than the sheriff there was no telling who she'd talked to by now.

They took reassurance in having cleared the area with the efficiency that several years of experience in waylaying unsuspecting people afforded them. Instead of hiding the bodies in the bayou, as originally planned, West and Jurd loaded the deceased into the covered wagon. The riders drove the wagon on a trail behind the Natchez Trace to keep from running into folks on the main road.

Laws stayed behind to eliminate the previous night's campfire, flinging leftover pieces of burnt firewood into the bayou. He dug the earth inside out to hide patches of blackened ashes and pitched handfuls of dirt over the surface. Smoothed it out with the edge of his boots so that no visible evidence of a fire was discernible by the naked eye. He used a large piece of cloth to soak up still-warm blood stains where bodies had been removed. He shuffled a two-step over the wagon's wheel imprints to make the ground appear partly disrupted from the rush of wind, and not marked by boot impressions or wheel ruts.

Then he waited to see if the girl, or anyone, might show.

When he met Sheriff Rose's eyes, he knew he was in the clear.

Sheriff Rose knew his place. Stepping out of line would cost him dearly.

Meanwhile, West dumped the bodies in a well near the narrow trail that led up to Horsehead Rock, then unhitched the wagon at a Blacksmith's shop along the Trace where it would undergo a variety of cosmetic alterations, including a new paint job and new seat cushioning.

The Blacksmith, Pete Emerson, was a longtime friend of West's. Much like Will Drake, Pete wasn't a nightrider, only an important associate behind the scenes. He assisted the gang without question, and was paid generously for his handiwork to ready wagons for profitable sale. He had connections to livery stables, gulf ports, and scores of wealthy businessmen willing to spend money on inexpensive, quality products. The family horse that belonged to Wydell Phillips, an older animal than the gang had anticipated, was not prepared for sale and left to rot deep in the woods behind the shop.

Now that they were gathered in West's cotton field near Iatt Creek the next logical step was to divvy up the bags of gold, then separate for a few days.

"Well, fellas, we sure caught us one helluva haul back there," West announced.

Laws produced three bags of gold. He handed one bag to Ike Hicks, another to Jurd Vines.

Jurd's eyes lit up in excitement. A stranger's blood spatter stained his collar, the pain of his private parts were still reeling from mutilation underneath ugly bandages, but all that didn't matter now. He had his bag of gold. "Aww, mercy me, West. I ain't never touched this much gold in all my days." He shook his head in disbelief. "Ha! First chance I get, I'm gonna blow through Nackatish and get me some whiskey and a late-night gal! Steak, too. A rich steak that'll fill my gut for two days!"

"West?" Ike said.

"Yeah?"

Ike eyed the bag of gold in his meaty hands. "I don't mean to sound ungrateful . . . I do appreciate this bag and all, but I ain't so sure why I'm here. I wasn't on that venture with y'all this morning. Still, you gave me gold."

West grinned. "Ike, don't you know? You're here to earn your *share* of that gold."

Confused, Ike looked at Laws then Jurd, and back to West. He swallowed hard. "What do you mean by that?"

West took off his curved, wide-brimmed hat and combed his fingers through sweaty hair. He situated the hat on his head and bent it down, shading his eyes from the sun. He took his own bag of gold off the ground and stepped near Jurd, who was still salivating on how to spend so many coins.

"What I mean by that, Ike, is you're about to do the whole gang of nightriders a favor."

West swung the bag, striking Jurd across the face.

The blow knocked him to the ground.

Jurd's bag fell. Coins scattered.

Blood seeped between the spaces of his teeth. Jurd looked up. "West! What's gotten into—?"

"Close your mouth!" Laws yelled.

West stood over him. "Ike, gather up Jurd's coins. Tie 'em and set 'em over there by my satchel."

Ike went to work plucking coins off the ground.

Even with his mouth busted, Jurd Vines could not keep quiet. "Hey! This's about that girl that got away ain't it?"

"Not chiefly," West replied.

"She pulled the knife outta my scabbard, I tell ya! She cut the tip of my rod then took off a runnin'. I couldn't chase after her, West! What with sufferin' that kinda pain—it smarted so bad!"

"That very well might be, but the outcome was the same. The little lady got free. Oh, her gettin' away ain't the heart of the matter. I'm sure she's long gone by now."

"Then what gives?" Jurd asked. "Why the scorned treatment all a sudden?"

West took a swig from the flask, smacking his lips as whiskey burned his throat. "Me and Laws've been hearin' quite a few rumors that concern you, Jurd. As a rule the nightriders take to the forests around here to remain hidden from folks in our quaint network of towns. When someone gets to shootin' off their mouth about what the riders are doing, that person gets dealt with."

"What? You sayin' I been runnin' my mouth about the gang? West, I wouldn't . . . I swear that ain't true! You heard lies!"

"You're tellin' me you didn't get soused one evening at a dance over in Olla and talk about the night last Christmas when we bushwhacked a man and his daughter on the Old Sparta Road? Remember? We got about two hunnerd coins outta that take. I shot the man in the face and you stabbed the girl in the stomach seven times." West thumbed at Ike Hicks. "That was Ike's cousin Tatum Joshlin you were yappin' to about it."

"I remember that night, yeah! Got soused at the dance. But West, I didn't talk to nobody about that. I never talk about the riders!"

"Last October. Me, you, Laws, and Copeland Yates took out a father, his wife, and three kids. Didn't get much outta that, but what a fine couple of horses we netted for our trouble. Then we heard through the grapevine you were in Will Drake's saloon offering details of that evening to a weary traveler. It was as though you were warning him about what might become of him. We allowed you to walk free because we didn't believe the chatter. But then we got wind you told one of our Blacksmiths, ol' Mitch Morris, how many coins you got in a haul when you and the Frame boys killed that barber in a skiff on the Red River for a satchel of foldin' money."

"John, please listen to me! I might've said a couple of things was out of line. I didn't do none of that to bring attention to us riders! I never spoke your name. Never spoke of Kimbrell, either. I was probably drunk as a skunk those times and got to talkin' out of foolishness. I won't do it again. I swear by my mother's grave, I won't do it again!"

"You're damn right you won't do it again," West said. He looked over at Ike Hicks. "Ike? You ready to earn a bag of gold?"

"Whatever you say."

"Keep that peacemaker trained on him, Laws."

A newfound fear rose in Jurd's eyes as he realized this was not going to end the way he'd expected. "West, please, I'll do whatever it takes to gain back your trust. Don't—don't kill me."

"I ain't gonna kill ya," West said. "Let's call this a firm lesson. Now get face down on your stomach.

Jurd turned slowly, keeping his eyes on the three men. If he disobeyed West's orders, he knew they'd kill him. His breath came in short, labored gasps as fear of the unexpected gripped his pounding heart.

West stepped on his back.

"Ugh! Augh!"

Frozen in place Jurd could not—*dared not*—move under West's hefty weight.

Ike Hicks looked on curiously. Ike was stocky, had big hands and biceps, one of the more physically intimidating men West and Laws knew of in the gang, which is why he'd been called here today.

"Jurd, have you ever heard the sayin' 'dead men tell no tales'? It's a reliable way to keep things secret. Ike! Get over there. Grab his head."

Ike bent down, took hold of the sides of Jurd's head.

"Make his face look at the sky. Do it slow, now. Let's hear his bones *crack*."

"No, Ike. I'll give you more gold!" Jurd pleaded, his face covered in dirt. "All the gold I got stashed, it's yours. Let me live!"

West applied pressure to the man's back, keeping him in place.

Ike turned Jurd's neck. Muscles twisted and veins burst and bones broke clean until finally Jurd's chin rested on the nape of his neck and his eyes were staring up at John West's grinning face.

West stepped off. "See that you don't say what happened here, Ike."

Still perplexed at his current part in West's plan to kill Jurd Vines, Ike ignored asking further questions, took the bag and stood. "You know I won't."

John West regarded the dead nightrider in disgust, gave a dismissive wave of his hand. "Toss him in the well. My Sara's cooked a roast so I don't wanna be late for lunch. Y'all're welcome to come along if ya ain't got nothin' pressin'."

Chapter 27

Gilley's Dress Shop on Main Street wasn't the type of establishment that Dan Dean typically patronized. But here he was asking the owner's wife, Mrs. Fara Gilley herself, about measurements for a dress he explained away as a gift for a friend.

"How nice," she said, studying the dirty rag of a dress on the hanger. She measured the neck, waist, and body length with tailor's tape and penciled the information on a paper ledger. "What color does your lady friend favor, Mr. Dean? We offer a variety of colors. Commonly white, blue, some yellow hues. We have exquisite pinks."

"Um . . . blue is fine."

"Absolutely. Ruffled sleeves?"

"Nothing fancy, just a day-to-day dress she might wear about town or wherever."

"A day dress, okay. No bustle?"

Dan looked out the window at a horse and buggy rolling along the bricked street, entertaining a loving couple nudged up against one another. "Something pleasant is fine. She's a slender gal, not so choosy. Long as it fits her squarely it'll be suitable."

Mrs. Gilley tapped the tip of a pencil on her tongue and started scribbling notes. "All right. What is her bust size?"

"Her what?"

"Her breast size, Mr. Dean. We have here her waist and length, but I cannot surely measure a lady's bust without her inside the dress to fill it out."

Feeling slightly embarrassed, Dan held up his fist. "This size." He looked out the window again.

"I don't mean to pry, Mr. Dean, but you seem to be preoccupied. Would you rather we do this at another time?"

Dan kept watch on the road for reasons he'd rather not explain aloud to anyone in his presence. He did not need the heated curiosity of a random nightrider catching a glimpse in his direction, then brainstorming questions about why ex-nightrider Dan Dean was buying a lady's dress in broad daylight. Those men knew he was without a wife, or lady friend, or even a mother . . . so just why was he patronizing a women's dress shop in downtown Natchitoches on a good day for fishing?

"Pack that one up," he said, taking out a coin purse.

"Excellent choice, Mr. Dean. I'll slip it in a covering and wrap a colorful bow around the box so when she—"

"No ribbon. A plain box'll do."

"Whatever you'd like," she said, a little miffed, and disappeared into the back room.

After paying more than he expected for a simple dress, Dan crossed the bricked street with a bulky brown box under his arm. He untied the horse's reins from a post. Looked up and down the street. Folks strolled along, going in and out of shops and restaurants, carrying on with their day.

He noticed no familiar faces. Saddled up.

Across the Cane River astride a black horse, hat tipped low to shade his eyes, was Copeland Yates, a member of the nightriders' special group of men.

Copeland gave a two-finger wave.

Dan turned his horse towards Winnfield and got lost in the bustling crowd.

He'd been followed . . . but why? Dan had been careful; Contessa obedient. The nightriders did not know he was harboring an escapee. Why would Copeland track Dan into Natchitoches? What did the fellow want?

Passing wind-blown fields of cotton Dan joined up alongside Jim Maybin, Fred Boss, and Jess Cady on the Trace, neighboring men with whom he had a trusting friendship.

Maybin explained they were heading into Winnfield to bid on the price of a mule for Cady's farm. "Afterwards, we'll grab a bite at the hotel. You're welcome to join us."

"I appreciate the invite, Jim. I've got other plans." Dan checked over his shoulder to see a lone buggy creaking along in the distance. The nightrider Copeland Yates hadn't found his trail.

In his mid-thirties, Jim Maybin was a tall, headstrong man who wore the finest threads and kept his hair parted neatly on the left side, shiny with pomade. He'd known Dan for years. "So, did ya hear what happened in Goldonna at the Bingham farm?"

"No."

Jim thumbed in Jess Cady's direction. "Cady here went lookin' for a couple of his ponies went missing. Him and Luke Gibbs trailed them to the Bingham place and met up with three nightriders. They led Cady to believe those horses weren't on the property, but the old man here wasn't havin' it. They clashed pretty good."

Dan looked at Jess Cady in the saddle of a healthy horse, his eyes drawn to the dull gray guns on either side of the man's waist.

"Ain't a soul outta that bunch alive to tell about it," Jim said. "I have to say, though, there's more 'n three of 'em I'd blast away."

"I agree," Jess Cady said.

"I'm of the same idea," Dan said. "If the inner circle was broken up, then the rest of them rascals might skid on out of the territory. They'd have no leadership to hijack folks on the Trace."

"Such an idea to stop them might be feasible if we knew the man in charge of the goddamn circle," said Fred Boss.

"I ain't for certain, but I believe the leader is John West," Jim Maybin replied. "There's been several instances when he's been a topic of conversation in regards to the nightriders. He sure leads the high life for a farmer and constable."

Dan could have spoken up about his knowledge of Laws Kimbrell, but something held him back. Maybe it was his level of loyalty to Laws; his vow to never reveal his old friend's identity within the gang. Or maybe Dan wanted to be certain (should the opportunity come about) that these good men would take necessary action to destroy the nightriders. At any rate, Jim Maybin was thinking on the same wavelength as Dan.

"It'd be a grand undertaking. The riders have ears everywhere," Jess Cady said. "I've found in my God-given years that anything can be done if you've got enough folks backing you."

Dan waved farewell and veered off the path, headed for Atlanta.

He had a feeling he'd be speaking to them sooner rather than later.

Chapter 28

When he arrived home Contessa was nowhere to be found.

Dan's heart skipped rhythm as fear rose in his veins, violent thoughts terrorizing his mind. Corn cobs and peas boiled in an iron pot atop the stove, filling the room with salty steam. Paying no attention, he searched the house, calling out her name.

God help me, did the nightriders find her?

"Contessa?" He stepped onto the back porch. "Contess—?"

She was picking figs off the ground. "Hey Dan."

"What're you doing? I told you to stay inside."

"You said nothing of the sort. You said if somebody came by, I go and hide." She popped a fig in her mouth.

She's here. She's safe.

"Come inside, I got something to show you."

As they walked she explained she had gotten hungry—"So I went looking for fruit. Same things I got by on before you caught me in that old barn."

In his bedroom he showed her a large box.

She opened it. "Oh, Dan, it's beautiful. Thank you!" Holding the dress over her arm, she hugged him and stayed pressed against his body a bit longer than either of them anticipated. "I can't thank you enough."

He realized that Contessa would not be comfortable wearing anything belonging to Ezona, so this time he rummaged through another chest of drawers. He pulled out an old pair of brown trousers with laces along the outer thighs, a beige blouse, and a thin leather jacket. These articles of clothing belonged to his onetime girlfriend, Miss Pencie Vines, who possessed the same thin, curvy body as Contessa.

"When you're finished trying on the dress, change into that get-up."

"Why?"

"Because if you're going to stay here for however long, you shouldn't go about your days in a fancy dress."

She insisted on wearing the new dress at supper time. "I'll change into those God-awful trousers afterwards."

"Jacket, too," he said.

Dan seasoned the duck breasts with salt, black pepper, and pickled cucumber juice. He set the twin breasts in a cast-iron skillet on the stove along with chunks of onions and bell pepper.

Still in the early stages of getting to know one another, they barely spoke as they dined on pan-seared duck, peas, corn, and slices of tomato at the table. He was impressed by her intelligence. Admired her youth. At ten years her senior he'd met several mature women—most of them not as worldly, nor outspoken, as she.

Then Contessa said that while he was away, two men on horses showed up for a visit.

"What did you do?"

"I hid in the loft so I could see them. One got off his horse. The other didn't. The man knocked on the door, called out your name. Put his face up to the windows to look in. They talked a little bit, then they left."

"What did these men look like?"

"One was tall in the saddle. Black hair, a mustache. The one knockin' on the door, he was short, had big arms. Just ugly as sin."

Dan had a strong feeling his visitors were nightriders. Not neighbors stopping by for a friendly visit.

Friends of his did not scope out his house and peer through windows for any signs of life. He processed possible descriptions throughout a list of nightriders in his mind and came to the conclusion that the tall one may have been Laws Kimbrell or Arthur Collins, the shorter one either Gus Rivers, maybe Lec Ingram.

He wasn't certain. Right now he was content that Contessa had gone unnoticed.

Dan set his knife on the plate, aggravated. "If somebody paid me a visit, why did you decide it was a good time to go picking figs? Why put yourself in harm's way? They could've switched back."

"Dan, I'm no fool. I waited a long while before making the decision to go outside. Besides, they can't see your back property."

"Can't see my back property? Those men know this territory like they know whiskey and whores! You're lucky you're not out there lying on the ground with them goddamn figs!"

Contessa slapped her palm on the table, jarring the plates and jug of tea. "Then do something! If all those boogeymen are out there, then why don't you put a bullet in *them?* I cannot—*live* like this."

Easy to say, harder to do, Dan thought. He'd have no chance in fighting off an entire gang of outlaws. Not only did they outnumber him, but they were more resourceful in weaponry, and their reach throughout the entire State of Louisiana also stretched far into Texas.

"Contessa, I am not asking you to form a life around this method of survival. But you've got to understand the gravity of what those monsters are capable of. They do not value human life the way you and I do. They don't love. They don't care. They don't feel *anything* but greed . . . and hate. I'm asking you as someone who does care for you—stay inside 'til I get you out of here."

She sipped her tea. "And when will that be?"

"When they forget about looking for you."

"When will that be?" she repeated.

"Whenever John West has something else to occupy his mind. Right now you're in his crosshairs, so you shouldn't make it easy for him. Do what I ask, and I'll make sure no one harms you . . . then you can move on."

Chapter 29

After dining with John West, Laws rode into Winnfield and called on Annabelle Frost at her father's house.

He found her in the side yard under a Sweetgum tree eating strawberries, legs stretched out, her lips red from the sweet fruit.

Laws stood above her, his shadow drawn out over her body. "Looks to me like you get prettier every time I lay eyes on you."

She looked up at him, expressionless. "My foot still hurts. It sprained good."

"You didn't have to go and jump out the window," he admonished.

"Well? I was afraid. It's not as though you served them tea and crumpets and had a nice little chat. I heard a gunshot, then I saw you cut a man's ear off!"

"I was taking care of a personal matter because I care for you, Annabelle. Those men won't bother you anymore. That was my goal, and I accomplished that."

"You're quite the gentleman, Laws, to protect me so. I just wish you'd've been truthful with me. You said you were gonna talk to those men that stopped me. You didn't say anything about hurting them. I believed you. I believed what you said!" She threw a strawberry at his chest.

He caught it. Bit it. "Wasn't my intention to scare you. I have a great deal of affection for you. I would never jeopardize our courtship."

He remembered her yelling out in pain the night she tumbled out that bedroom window and wrenched her ankle in his tomato garden. She sobbed, had asked him to escort her home. Laws obliged while the gang smoked and drank and cleaned up the mess that had become of Clyde Judkins. Laws wrapped his undershirt around her bruised ankle to lessen the swelling, then helped her onto his horse. She situated herself into the V of his lap as he guided his black horse through the night, steadying one hand on Annabelle's thigh to control her balance. Annabelle made the trip home without so much as a comment on the stars above, or the fact he'd blasted the life out of Clyde Judkins, but her moans of pain told the story of her busted ankle.

This conversation was not only inevitable, the subject matter served as a test to prove she could be trusted.

Would she tell her father? Call on Sheriff Rose? Could she love a man engineered by violent tendencies?

And for all the affection he bestowed upon her, did Annabelle believe that Lawson Kimbrell might someday, somehow, hurt *her*?

"I needed you there for a reason, to show me who attacked you." Laws knelt, put his hand gently at her bandaged ankle. "I'm not a mean man, darlin' . . . I'm a persuasive *leader*."

"So you wouldn't ever . . . ?"

"Ever what?"

"Laws, I'm afraid someday you . . . if you got mad, you could—"

"Hurt you? Annabelle, I adore you. I'd do anything for you. If you'll recall the essence of poems of yesteryear, I need that something precious . . . soft and welcoming, willing to shine meaning on my existence. Your smile every day, your heart in my hands. Mine in yours." He hugged her. "I am a gentleman. I believe in romance. But when somebody bulldozes the one thing I hold dear, a different breed finds its way . . . to make me make things calm again."

Laws left her sitting there.

She sniffed. "Where're you going?"

"Hold your chin up, darlin'. I've got you a surprise."

Annabelle turned the silver necklace between her thumb and forefinger, wondering if he was about to bring her another piece of jewelry—not that she expected such a gift. Annabelle was quite happy with Laws Kimbrell's affection for her. He needn't give her shiny things to afford her love. Even though he'd been courting her for some time now, Laws still held a shadow of mystery about him. There was something about the man that both intrigued and troubled her, and for the life of her she couldn't figure it out.

He turned the corner of the house leading a beautiful brown and white horse by the bridle, its long mane brushed clean and straight.

"Say hello to Miss Jolly," Laws said.

The horse probed its stout around Annabelle's thighs and face, sniffing at the airy scent of strawberries.

"Oh Laws, she's lovely! And so friendly."

She patted its nose and held out three strawberries.

The animal lapped them up at once.

"That's why I call her Miss Jolly. She always seems to be in a good mood."

"Where did you find her?"

"Friend of mine from El Dorado, Arkansas sold her to me," Laws lied.

Miss Jolly actually belonged to the nightrider Clyde Judkins. But Clyde no longer needed use of the animal, and Laws felt no need to explain this truth to his sweetheart.

"What about Hank?" she asked.

"Hank is my steed. Miss Jolly here, she's yours."

"A new horse?"

"Well, I figured you could use a new mare. Yours is looking long in the tooth."

She smiled up at him again, showing her whites. "Thank you, Laws. You're so good to me. Now I'll have two!"

"Take care of Miss Jolly. She's special."

"Oh, I'll take good care of her."

"Careful when you mount her, too. She's awful fast. One swift kick and you'll land in Shreve City before you blink a lash."

"I'm not able to ride any horse right now." Annabelle reached out her hand. "Pass me that crutch please?"

Laws helped her to her feet and situated the crutch's shoulder rest under her armpit.

"I've got chores to tend to. You're welcome to stay for supper if you'd like. Momma cooked a big pot roast with potatoes and okra."

"Another time. I'll put Miss Jolly in the barn. She oughta get along just fine."

Annabelle kissed Laws on the cheek. "This is a nice surprise, Laws. But it doesn't erase the memory of seeing what you did to those men. I can't ignore what happened. It's haunted my sleep." She curled her petite fingers under his leather vest. "Promise me you'll never do something like that again."

Laws kissed the top of her head. "I assure you that won't happen again."

He opened the back door for her, said he'd see her soon, and returned to Miss Jolly.

As he led the animal to the barn he whispered in Miss Jolly's ear: "Settle in, ol' girl. You've got a brand new life."

Chapter 30

Dan Dean watched indifferently as flames demolished the painted pieces of the family barn, burning wood to a blackened crisp and destroying memories of his childhood, sending tunnels of smoke through the treetops.

From the field he could see Contessa sitting on the back porch, crocheting the corner of a blue quilt, her long hair lifting on the breeze. A glass of tea sat beside her, sweating in the fading sunlight.

She'd been stubborn, defying his requests not to leave the boundaries of his house. He soon discovered that Contessa Menifee would go outside whenever she felt like it, and that was that.

He understood her perception of freedom. He had fought his Northern brothers in the name of this beautiful, far-reaching concept. As long as he was around to keep watch, Contessa Menifee could enjoy all the freedom she wanted.

For the first few days of knowing Contessa, Dan had formed a plan to see that she arrived safely from Morgan's train station in Monroe to a depot in Jackson, Mississippi.

But as the days melded into weeks it appeared as though Contessa was in no rush to return home to North Carolina.

And if he should be honest with himself, Dan did not want to see her go so soon, either.

Since her parents' murder, spring brought forth showers at the tip of another blistering humid Louisiana summer. Contessa still resented being penned up but understood that the passage of time was a blessing. There was a great chance the men who wanted her head just might forget to sniff her out. *"Out of sight, out of mind,"* Dan told her, which comforted her incessant need for reassurance that everything would turn out fine.

Dan backed away from intense heat of roaring flames and joined Contessa on the porch steps.

She asked if he wanted a drink.

He shook his head.

"Is this all there is? Me and you hiding from monsters?"

"You're the one hiding, Tess. The clan knows where I live. They could drag up any time, although it wouldn't be in their best interest to do so. I'd make damn sure they didn't get to you. As of now the bastards don't have a clue you're here."

It sounded like a lie, and indeed it was. Dan remembered when he'd been tracked into Natchitoches and was seen by a nightrider while exiting Gilley's Dress Shop. He didn't offer this information for fear he'd rattle Contessa's nerves, and Lord knows she'd already been through a tragic time. No sense in making the situation worse.

Ember sparks rose in a fast flurry to the sky. "That fire reminds me of the torches set up at the dances back home," she claimed. "We used to go to dances, me and Garrett."

"Garrett?"

"He lived down the road, on his father's farm. He'd court me to dances . . . ." she trailed off. "We'd have picnics by the lake."

Dan thought it odd that Contessa was just now recalling in detail a boy she favored. After her run-in with the West Clan, if not for her grandmother, why wouldn't she return home and visit this fella Garrett? He felt compelled to ask if she had serious feelings for the boy, or were they simply a summer romance now lost in memory?

This amorous detail should not have been a concern, of course, but Dan had taken a liking to her, and he felt a pang of jealousy at the mention of this Garrett character.

"Do you miss him?" he asked.

"I did. He didn't want me to leave. Now it doesn't matter if I go back or not."

"If your heart's in North Carolina, you should go."

"My heart's broken, Dan. If I went back I'd stay with my grandmother, and she'll be a mess once she hears about mom and dad. Garrett will want to take me to a dance, but I don't feel like dancing. Not just yet. I just—sometimes I don't want to go on at all. It's scary. It's wrong. It's how I feel, though."

Dan put his arm around her. "Listen, Tess, I understand you've been through something so dreadful most folks can't imagine. Hope is not lost. Your grandmother would love to hear from you. This Garrett boy, he'd like to see you again I'm sure. Any man would miss you."

Contessa looked at him then, her eyes searching his face for sincerity. "Are you saying this to make me feel needed?"

"I say it because it's true. You're a gem, Tess." He kissed her temple. "What say we fix some squirrel mulligan tonight?"

"Okay. Dan?"

"Yes?"

"You said that any man would miss a girl like me. When I leave, will you miss me?"

He faced her. "I already miss you, darling."

Contessa lifted his hat off his head. She rose on the tips of her toes, kissed him full on the lips, her fingers digging into the hat's curved crown.

He cupped her face in his hands and kissed her easy, their lips wanting more of each other.

Dan pulled back, eyes drunk with lust. "If you ever feel like dancing again, I know a great place to take you over in Olla."

"Maybe one day, Dan. Tonight I want to dance right here . . . with you."

*****

Dan lay awake in his bed eyeing the moonlight shining across the floor through the living area. Contessa was in a deep sleep on the cushioned couch, snoring lightly. He was pleased she enjoyed their supper. She even offered to clean the dishes. In a short time she had grown on him in positive ways.

She possessed attributes he found endearing, like how she prayed before each meal; shooed away raccoons on the front porch, calling them 'darlin', (when Dan just scared the piss out of them); how resolved she was in getting her ragged dress cleaned instead of him buying the new one.

These simple actions showed her true self: a kind, humble soul behind a strong mind and pretty face who felt safe in the presence of an honest man.

Dan Dean vowed that no matter what happened during the coming days, he would protect Contessa Menifee. Not only from the West Clan, but also from being alone in this life.

Chapter 31

Lawson Kimbrell was not the type to dwell on the death of someone he sent to the grave, rarely thinking of his kills as trophies to brag about. The outlaw instead focused on ill-gotten gains he routinely stashed away at Horsehead Rock, at the expense of other greedy men.

Greedy men didn't matter. They never mattered.

But night after night for weeks on end the gruesome image of that baby impaled on his knife haunted his dreams in a wicked vein. He'd wake with a start, skin dampened in sweat, turn to the window to see the slow, starry night, and wish he'd stay awake forever—all the while dreading another wink of sleep. Once he shut his eyes, he knew he'd see the infant's body split jaggedly along that shiny steel blade . . . .

Finally he'd return to dream in peace the remainder of the night. But receiving prolonged peace was a laughable ruse. Each morning refreshed his memory of that death, as he recalled in vivid detail the cruelness of his actions.

As rough as Laws Kimbrell lived his days, he shook it off as a scene in his life he'd never repeat; a memory that would gratefully fade with time.

Still, a heavy sense of guilt that weighed on his mind like a rot-gut whiskey hangover he couldn't shake kept coming back for colorful engagements—all at once jerking him awake at the Witching Hour, and lingering far too long during sunny days that shined on his face as though a spotlight from God.

If no one else, that little baby mattered.

One evening around the time Dan Dean and Contessa Menifee were showing their affection for each other, Laws sat drunk in a rocking chair on his front porch, wondering when his eyes might remain closed without the image of that baby replaying its death on the backside of his eyelids.

The sound of John West's bullhorn brought him crashing back to reality. The bullhorn meant either one of two things: West had bagged a "Big Buck" (a man with money), or riders had been called on for an urgent meeting.

Even in his wavy, inebriated mind, Laws knew he had to show up.

He belted on his guns and strapped a water canteen to his chest. With heavy footsteps he found his horse roaming around the side yard. Laws heard the call again, coming from the direction of China Grove Cemetery, near Moss Hill.

John West, Copeland Yates, Lec Ingram, Hank Wright, and some new fellow Laws had never met were grouped outside the cemetery gates. The evening sky was bruised purple, the setting sun flashing the last flames of deep orange over the graveyard.

"Where's the fire?" Laws asked. He looked around for a horse and buggy, for any stranger that they may have held up, and saw only the six of them in the middle of the forest by this creepy resting place.

In his usual merry spirit John West smiled and took off his white hat. "How ya doin', Laws?"

"Gettin' by fairly well. Who's the new gun?"

West motioned to the man on his left. "This here's Jake Shaw, friend of mine from Georgia. Used to ride with him in John Murrell's Clan. He's a good hand and a mighty fine shot. Let's say he's replacing Clyde Judkins, for the simple reason I need a certain amount of men in the circle. Seeing as how Dan Dean don't want to cooperate, I had to stretch the invite to another hardass. And as you know, Laws, our circle is only as strong as the men in it."

"What're we doin' out here?" Laws asked.

"Well, the other day when I came through this way I got to thinkin' about our setback with your old friend Dan. He's a stubborn one, that ol' boy."

"You still want him to be part of the circle, don'tcha?"

"By all means," West answered. "If he ain't on our side, then he's against us. Man's too good a gun thrower to just up and kill."

"If you can get close enough *to* kill him," Laws said in Dan's defense.

"I say it's up to you to get him on our side. He's a nightrider from the old days and never was part of the circle. Dan never knew what we did specifically . . . not 'til he saw us put down that couple. Think you can persuade him to see things our way?"

"I'll give it a try, West, but Dan . . . he's not like us."

West took a cigar from his vest pocket and bit off the end, stuck it between his lips. He lit a match and puffed the cigar tip at the flame, making smoke leap out of his mouth.

"He may not be like us, but he's got grit. A man like Dan Dean would be indispensable to our group. You know that as well as I do!" West looked at Laws, his eyes burning with sincerity. "If he doesn't become a member, Dan's days are numbered. He's a risk. He could get up a posse of Aces High from across the land. Then we'd have a real fight on our hands. The goddamn fool wouldn't listen to my reasoning, so I figured he'd listen to one of his old pals. How about it, Laws? Make him see things our way."

"Look, West, I'll do what I can, but say Dan doesn't go along? What's your plan?"

"Then I take matters into my own hands. You ain't even got to be a part of it." West motioned to the other four men. "He can't whoop us all!"

"Hey West, how about we go over to Mr. Dean's house and put a gun to his face? If he refuses you again, we'll just shoot him down. There, no more problem."

Laws regarded this new prospect with contempt. "Who are you to suggest that course of action?"

West held up his hand. "Now, hold on, Jake. I done told you before. Dan Dean is Lawson's friend. This is what you might call a *delicate* matter."

Jake Shaw raised his palms from the horse's bridles. "My sincere apologies, Laws. I spoke out of place."

"Out of place? In this outfit you don't speak *out of place*. You listen. You don't come up with half-assed ideas, because your opinions mean nothing to us. You have absolutely no say in anything we do."

Jake Shaw displayed a set of bent, tobacco-stained teeth behind chapped lips. "I understand fully. Accept my apology." He backhanded West's shoulder as though making a joke of the issue. "Guess I'm used to the good ol' days when me and West rushed in blind and came out shining like rubies."

The other three nightriders on either side of John West could not believe the new member's behavior in front of Laws Kimbrell—who, they knew, was all day long meaner than West.

Apparently, West had not informed his friend about the gang's hierarchy of power.

"Jake, that's enough," West said. "I told you, Laws is co-leader of the riders. Treat him with the same respect you show me. Got it?"

"I'll try," Jake said. He pulled out a flask of whiskey and took a long swig. "But I have always held the belief a man's got to earn my respect!"

In an effort to change the subject and calm Kimbrell's fury, West said, "Come now, it's time we get on with the evening's festivities."

Laws cocked the hammer of his pistol and aimed the long barrel at Jake Shaw's face. "You need a reason to respect me? Sass me again boy, and you won't live to show it."

Jake turned to West. "John, is he serious?"

"Laws, give the man some slack. He's been drinkin'. He'll come around."

"Drinkin' gives the weak among us courage to do things they wouldn't do sober. Your friend isn't one of us."

"You callin' me weak?" Jake said.

"Just what is on tonight's agenda?" Laws asked, ignoring the newcomer.

West piped up: "We're gonna set fire to the Winnfield courthouse! They got written records of crimes that could damn well lead back to us, if the right man pieced it all together . . . namely your war buddy, Mr. Dan Dean. Now that he's seen us in action, he knows way too much. And because of his stubbornness, our livelihood is in jeopardy. Arthur Collins, Copeland Yates, Lec Ingram, the Frame brothers. You. Me. All of us run the risk of gettin' locked up in the hoosegow!

"Now, I want to see that dag-blame building in flames before our dear Dan Dean shares his knowledge and sends us up before a grand jury."

"Fine with me. Lec, Hank, and Copeland will go. This horse's ass of a friend you got here ain't followin'. That fool's out."

"Whaddaya mean I'm out?" Jake asked. "Out of the clan?"

"You ain't *in* the clan!" Laws said.

"West! Tell him I'm trustworthy. I want to make some easy money, ya know, like the rest of y'all."

"Let's head out," Laws ordered.

Copeland Yates, Lec Ingram, and Hank Wright gently prodded their horses into motion.

West and Jake stayed behind.

West grabbed Jake's shoulder, pushed him in the saddle. "Close your goddamn mouth! Laws Kimbrell will butcher you where you sit and there ain't a damn thing I'll do to stop him. I been baby-sittin' you for twenty fuckin' minutes and already you've jeopardized your place in the clan. Do you have any idea what that means?"

"Wait, John, now listen! . . . You brought me on. Ain't it your decision to have the say so either way?"

"Most times, yeah! Something like this though? This has to be mutual. To be honest, I can't believe you're still breathing. I've seen Laws put down folks for much less than what you said to him. The only reason you're not on the ground bleeding out of your skull is because he understands you're a pal of mine."

"Let's be clear, Jake. Being my pal is the kind of metaphorical shield that's bull strong for just so long. The more you agitate Laws Kimbrell, the more transparent that protection gets. If ya keep acting like a jackass there will come a time when I'm not able to protect you using the whole '*he's my friend*' excuse."

"I can take care of myself," Jake said. "We goin' to town or what?"

"You stay behind me," West ordered. "I'll try to smooth this over, but I ain't promisin' nothin'."

*****

When the riders arrived, the town square was abandoned under a pitch black night. The red-bricked courthouse stood mighty in the shadows, lording over businesses that lined wide, dusty paths.

West and Lec Ingram tossed flaming torches though the side windows.

Laws and Hank Wright torched the entrance.

Copeland Yates and newcomer Jake Shaw kept watch at opposite corners of the building.

The entire affair lasted less than five minutes. Flames burned through court documents and wooden flooring and paneling. It didn't take long for the flames to reach the drapes and ceiling, destroying the ancient wood.

West nodded at Laws as if to say *it's done, let's get gone.*

Laws aimed his pistol at Jake Shaw, his eyes glowing in the reflection of the flames. "You don't listen, do ya?"

Jake looked over at West, who had backed into the streets of the square.

"Face me, boy."

"West said I could tag along. He's got a say in the decision-makin' too, right? I listen to him! Not you."

Laws dismounted his horse, holstered his gun, and kicked Jake Shaw in his left leg, easily snapping his kneecap.

Jake went down screaming, clutching at his thigh.

Laws grabbed Jake's weakened leg and dragged him across the street to an opened window bursting with fire. Then he yanked him up by the collar, got nose-to-nose. "Do you respect me now?"

"Goddamn you, ya crazy bastard! Rot in hell!"

Laws threw him through the window. Watched him roll along the burning floors.

Unable to run away, Jake Shaw gasped for breath. Flames overtook his clothes and burned him alive before their eyes.

West turned back. "Let's get gone Laws! For all this commotion, ever-body in town'll be stormin' through here!"

Chapter 32

News of the burned courthouse spread throughout the towns, eventually gaining the attention of the Mayor of Natchitoches and high-ranking politicians in New Orleans (including Governor Henry Clay Warmoth).

City officials of Winn Parish explained by telegraph to the Governor's mansion that a thorough investigation was underway. In three days' hence, however, authorities had no leads in locating those responsible for causing the massive fire.

The east side of the courthouse received the most severe damage. The fire had completely destroyed the records archive, which is exactly what John West and his riders intended—get rid of any and all documentation that could possibly link local crimes to the clan.

I'd never witnessed such a blatant disrespect for authority than the night the West Clan torched the civil courthouse of Winn Parish. I watched clean-up crews cart away smoldering brick and twisted metal, salvaging what little they could of the building's functional remains.

Mayor Montrose Henratty of the City of Natchitoches agreed that the clan had carried out this violent affair. He'd heard the concerns of several folks in the area who suspected the clan of this destruction, and now Henratty wanted the whole lot to hang.

Authorities proposed keeping a closer eye on select men rumored to be part of this bunch of gunslingers, most notably John West, Lec Ingram, Copeland Yates, and especially Lawson Kimbrell, a hot tempered, ruthless soul behind a gun.

During the reconstruction of the courthouse Mayor Henratty ordered Sheriff Rose and his deputies to find the responsible party.

The sheriff did not feel comfortable approaching the presumed leader of the notorious nightriders regarding his suspicions. Still, orders had been handed down on high, and as a sworn lawman, he had to carry them out.

I didn't run to the authorities with any information. They wouldn't listen to a snot-nosed kid like me. I'd just be in their way.

So I stood by and watched this unfold—the whole time wishing I was fishing Saline Lake for large-mouth blue gill.

Chapter 33

Monday morning Sheriff Rose rode out to West's place on Iatt Creek, accompanied by deputies John Harwick and Mitchell Carpenter.

West stood on a ladder hammering a piece of wood into the side of his house.

Sheriff Rose reined in his horse. "Termite problems, John?"

He plucked a nail out of his mouth, poked it in his shirt pocket. "Hackberry branch snapped, busted a hole. I'm fixin' it. You know, mindin' my business and all. What can I help you gentlemen with?"

"I'm sure by now you heard about the courthouse in Winnfield."

"Ain't nobody within a country-mile stretch that didn't. Why are you askin' me?"

"Have any idea who might be responsible?"

"I guess somebody that wanted the son of a bitch burnt down."

"Did any of your acquaintances have anything to do with it?"

"Not that I'm aware of."

"Do you know how it happened?"

"Hayden, I'm appalled you'd think I had a hand in such a senseless crime. Whoever you heard this from has bullshit in their mouth. That night I was right here, ask Sara. She'll vouch."

"That won't be necessary," the sheriff said.

West slid the hammer into his work belt and climbed down. "Come on inside, Hayden. I got some tea on the stove should be steeped now. We can discuss this in comfort without me puttin' a crick in my neck."

"That's quite all right, John."

"Your friends stay out here."

Hayden handed the horse's reins to Deputy John Ray Harwick, then dismounted and stepped inside the farmhouse.

At the long, clean counter, West picked up a teapot and poured two cups of steeped black leaf tea.

Sheriff Rose took a cup. He looked around the large room; noticed a child's wooden toy in the corner, a woman's coat on a coat rack, and his host's gun belt hanging from a nail—well within reach.

"Where's Mrs. Sara at?"

"She took the girls to their grandma's," West replied.

Hayden stood by the windows, admiring the lavish spread of land. "John, you've got to understand the mayor asked that I follow on all possible suspects. Your name came up. That's the only reason I'm here."

"Why didn't you come alone?"

"Let's just say that I wasn't taking any chances."

Cheeks reddened by the sun, West lifted his drink and grinned that alligator's smile.

"I trust I'm not much of a threat holding a hot drink in my hand. You know, Hayden, I resent being suspect in sensational crimes that happen on your watch. I'm a family man. A church member. I'm a civil servant for Christ's sake! Folks in this town have only good things to say about me and mine, and you know that to be true."

"Look, John, I'm not out to cause trouble. I know you head up the nightriders."

West regarded his guest with contempt. "The very reason you keep your official position is because *I allow it*. You're still alive because I've pulled back the reins on Laws Kimbrell. If I gave the say-so, he'd get the bulge on you in broad daylight. But I've made it clear to that mad dog that you stand for community peace and regulation. The people in this region need someone to look to for protection, ya see. Ease their fears about the riders.

"So I gave them you. And if you cross me, I'll stir up trouble you cannot comprehend."

Seeing that West was getting riled up, Sheriff Rose backed off. "John, the last thing I want to do is ruffle feathers. With you, Kimbrell, or any rider. Understand, though, when the powers that be send orders to investigate this case, I have an obligation to satisfy those orders."

"Do you have proof I did it?"

The sheriff shook his head.

"What if I admitted to the crime? What then? You're gonna arrest me?"

"Well, I—"

West nodded toward the window. "Those deputies out there, Harwick and Carpenter? I say the word, and they'll shoot you down like a fucking rabbit."

Sheriff Rose wasn't surprised to hear this threat. West had many in his gang, some of whom held high-ranking posts—evident in Hayden's long-time deputies.

"No, John. I wouldn't arrest you."

"Then I suggest the next time you ask if I've committed a crime, you'd better make damn sure it's my blood on the body."

"Speaking of a body, we found the skeletal remains of a man in the ashes of the courthouse. Not sure who it is, nor do I believe we'll ever find out."

"Might be the suspect you're searching for," West said. "Maybe the fool lit it and the smoke got to him."

"That's a possibility."

"Then you should explore that possibility instead of sniffing around my house." West set the tea cup on the counter, walked over to the wall, retrieved his gun belt and buckled it around his wide waist. He touched two fingers to his red beard, a thoughtful look forming in his eyes. "I've things to get done, so if you're through asking questions . . . ."

"Surely, John. I did not mean to monopolize your time. Enjoy the day."

In the side yard Hayden took the reins from Harwick and swung himself onto his horse. This search was not going as well as he'd imagined, and he left feeling uneasy that catching justice was next to impossible.

Hayden needed substantial proof to bring the outlaws before the court, but these outlaws weren't talking.

The nightriders roamed free.

And there wasn't a damn thing anyone could do about it.

Chapter 34

"Yes, I definitely feel it in my bones," Contessa said. "It's gonna rain tomorrow."

"Ha! You're too young to feel the weather in your bones," Dan said.

"That's what my grandmother always told me. I'm almost always right about it, though. What do you think about them apples?"

"Well, I was planning to go to town in the morning and get some essentials. If it rains I'll have to postpone."

Sitting in a cushioned chair, she smiled and said, "If that's the case, you might as well plan your day with me."

Dan was in the kitchen adding spices to a pot of chicken stew. He wiped his hands on a rag and approached her, bent down inches from her face. "Let it rain, then." He kissed her.

Contessa allowed his lips to remain on her skin, enjoying the tenderness of his touch.

Besides the touchy-feely affairs spent with Garrett on summer evenings while watching the sun pass behind strips of gray cloud, Contessa had never been intimate with anyone else. Geographically convenient, Garrett had served as a conduit that moved her through silly adolescent puppy-love towards becoming a young woman searching for another spark. A likeable farm boy, Garrett was cute, Garrett was nice, but Contessa knew that Garrett was not the boy for her. Even though she missed him as a close friend, when she and her family left on their westward journey, her mind condemned him as a love-sick fool who often held wandering eyes for other women's affections, while her heart was on the hunt for unfailing adoration.

Until she met Dan Dean, Contessa never knew the excitement of a man's love. Dan was not cute, but handsome. He was not adorable, like Garett, but stubborn—like a bull. He was assertive and physically strong. After suffering the nightmares of a dark past, Dan remained mentally stable and in control. He continuously looked at Contessa with loving eyes, as though she had always been there for him, giving him the emotional strength to be the man she desired.

And with every kiss she fell more in love with the mystery that was Daniel Arron Dean.

She broke the kiss. "Dan? I have to know something. How much do you love me?"

"What kind of question is that? I love you. You must know that by now."

"Do you love me enough to take me away from this place?"

"I do."

"Then why are we still here?"

Dan stepped away. Instead of returning to spice up the stew, he decided to spice up his soul. He downed a shot of bourbon.

"Truth is . . . I enjoy living here. I'm familiar with the area. I know the people. And maybe I'd like you to enjoy it, too. I've had high hopes the clan would forget about you, give us room to have a real courtship. Go to town together, hold your hand in church, enjoy a dance on the riverfront . . . so we could live without this fear, like normal folks.

"The more I thought of such fantasies, the more I realized it might never happen . . . and that you'd someday return to the Carolinas. Ever since . . . ." He trailed off, thinking of Ezona, the only woman before Contessa who had once made this house a home.

Dan needed the comfort of Contessa Menifee waiting for him at the end of the day. He needed to kiss her. Touch and smell her, lie in her arms every evening. Sending Contessa away on an eastbound train would have been fine had he acted within three or four days of meeting her. But the longer Contessa stayed, the more the need for her set hard in his heart.

"Ever since what?" she asked.

"Since the day I found you I knew you were something special. After awhile I didn't want to see you leave." He touched her cheek, moved a strand of hair over her ear. "If keeping you close means leaving Louisiana, so be it. I love this place, but I love you more, Tess, and I want us to be happy. Together. Will you do me the honor?" he asked. "Will you be my wife?"

"Oh, Dan, I love you, too. Yes. Yes, *please*."

"It's settled then. We'll move away and wed. How's Alabama?"

Contessa gushed. "Alabama sounds wonderful!"

"Get us a parcel of land, start fresh. Dance all night if we want to!"

She kissed him again. "Dan Dean, I can't wait to share my life with you. Tell me, when do we leave?"

"In a few days. I need to get some supplies for our trip, then we'll make tracks."

Dan hugged her, staring at evening shadows splayed across the back windows. He kissed her soft neck, relieved that their lives would soon change for the better.

Chapter 35

Dan opened his eyes from a restful night's sleep, feeling the warmth of Contessa's body wrapped around him, her hair tickling his chin. He smiled in the early dawn, thankful she was still here.

In months prior she could have struck out alone at any time, but she'd decided to give their relationship a chance. He kissed her forehead, tasting her salty skin on his lips. Before long, they'd board an eastbound train on their way to spend a new life together.

So many thoughts rushed through his mind that his joyous smile slowly faded to a concerned line. Leaving meant giving up his homestead, the very place he spent years dreaming of returning to. If he stayed, John West would continually seek Dan's allegiance to the nightriders. That madman would only ask him politely for so long. Having an intimate knowledge of the clan, Dan Dean was a liability. West would hound him until he either joined up, or died trying to defend Contessa—day after day.

He'd coexist among monsters, always looking over his shoulder, always in constant danger.

Straying clear of the gang to protect Contessa was a noble undertaking, but no way in which to live. They had to get away.

Careful not to wake Contessa, he slipped out from under the colorful patch quilt and pulled on his black trousers. He buttoned down his tanned shirt and crept into the kitchen to make coffee.

Today was the day. The trip to Monroe would take around four hours. They'd pack their clothes and carry only the essentials, probably go around noon. He'd get the train schedule when they arrived. If they missed the last train, his cousins in Sterlington would put them up for the night before the morning train departed.

Whatever the case, they'd be away from the immediate threat of the nightriders.

As the sun rose over the pines he rode the two miles into town for some last minute supplies: beef jerky, another canteen, a case of bullets for his Navy Colt .44s, and a bag of sugar cubes for Quaid.

Inside Will Drake's General Store, Dan exchanged brief pleasantries with Ms. Permilia Bordeaux, nodding in agreement as she recounted how the town just wasn't the same when all them boys went off to fight in that "God-awful war."

"It's been so wonderful having you back home, Dan. I know your mother was sure proud of you. She called on me every time she received your letters. Your mother was a very special woman. Church simply isn't the same without her."

"She sure was a special woman, Ms. Bordeaux. I still miss her terribly."

"God will make things right, darling, don't you worry," she said. "Speaking of church, I'm sure I'll see you at Easter services. Do stay after for fellowship, Dan. I'm making homemade cherry pies and a cream topping."

He smiled. "I wouldn't miss it for a hundred apple pies, Ms. Bordeaux."

"Have a lovely day."

Dan watched her walk across the dusty street, holding a sun umbrella over her head to provide shade. He opened his coin purse to pay, when suddenly the intrusive shrill of a bullhorn echoed across the land.

He stepped onto the store's front walk, his satchel slung over his shoulder, and looked around for John West. He just knew the call meant West was gathering his troops for another venture into the dark heart of sin. Seeing no sign of the redheaded thief, only townspeople going about their business, he brushed Quaid's black mane and fed the animal three sugar cubes.

"Didja hear that horn ol' boy? Sounds like trouble to me. Mind you, if these folks around here think anything of it, it's nothing more than a huntin' call. But me and you know what kind of hunting trips West favors."

"Dan Dean!"

Dan turned to the voice.

The nightrider Copeland Yates approached, all six foot three of him, and tipped his hat. "Nice day for a drink don't ya think?"

"I reckon."

"Why don't we go upstairs and get us a few?"

"Last time I did that I . . . well, let's just say I'm not interested. How're things?"

"Oh, I don't know. Things might be better if you'd take West's offer and support our outfit. To be honest I'm tired of hearin' him yappin' about how good you are behind a pistol."

"Then I suggest you stuff some cotton in your ears 'cause I ain't gettin' involved with the nightriders."

Copeland lit a cigarette, the smoke rising above his shadowed eyes. "Dan, let me tell you what John West wants."

"I couldn't give a damn what West—"

"Hear me out. Then we'll part ways."

"I'm listenin'."

"If you're in the circle, your duty is simple and matter-of-fact. Ya see, you won't have to kill an innocent, outright. Your only response is to make sure we are protected during the robberies. When you were in the war and made sure your fellow soldier was safe, it's the same response—watch out for us. That's all he's asking. Say a green gun with more confidence than skill thinks he can brush up on us during a take. If he reaches for steel, before he fires that first shot, we want you to take him down. That's all West wants—a killer for the riders."

Dan smiled a little. The fact that a nightrider was asking him to protect a couple of men during a heist showed proof that West was reaching, absolutely bull-headed in his objective to gain Dan Dean's loyalty.

"If West has enough devils to take down innocent men, women, and children, then he can find a snake to guard him while he does it. He doesn't need me for that. He wants me to kill so he'll have evidence of a murder to hold over my head . . . in an attempt to control me in some capacity. Perhaps buy my silence about crimes I'm privy to." Dan got on his horse. "I'm tired of West thinking that I'll have anything to do with the riders. I left my fighting back in the war. I didn't expect to be fighting for peace when I got home, but it looks like he won't let up."

"How can you pass up all that money?" Copeland asked.

"Blood money? Simple. I don't kill people that don't deserve it."

"Nothin' can change your mind?"

"I heard West's bullhorn when I was in the store," Dan said. "Aren't you late for a meeting?"

"I'm not the man runnin' late to meet up with West. You are."

"The hell I am. I'm not one of his yes-men."

Copeland pulled John West's jewel-encrusted bullhorn from inside his jacket pocket. "This is what you heard."

"Why are you doing this?"

"Well, I had to use some form of communication to let the others know you were in town. How else would they know?"

"I'm done talkin' to you, Copeland."

"That's right, it's probably time you make another trip to Natchitoches. Pick out another dress for your little sweetheart."

Dan pulled the reins. "What'd you say?"

"Don't you know Dan? I've been trailing you ever since that day you stepped out of Gilley's Dress Shop. I was in town to pick up a satchel for John West—a gambler owed him loan money, things didn't go as planned, and well, that's none of your business. Anyhow, I was counting the coins right there across the river to make sure the amount added up, else he'd have got the shit knocked out of him, and whaddaya know? I saw you.

"I figured it odd you visiting a lady's dress shop. Ezona left you awhile back, and there wasn't no reason you should be there. Sheer curiosity got to me, I guess. Because I started keeping a close eye on your place.

"Then one day a couple weeks later I saw that beauty sittin' on your back porch. Girl fit the description of a little whore that run off from a robbery we got caught up in. We offed her parents, see, but she escaped. Evidently she made it to your house seeking shelter, and you took her in. Protected her. The uninhibited things I've seen, *ha!* All from the edge of your property. Looks to me like you two've become mighty close." Copeland breathed in another drag and shot smoke out of his nostrils. "Now, before you reach for those guns, know that I didn't go and tell West quick-like. I wanted to see what you'd do with the girl. Would you set her free? Or go on seeing after her. In time I got my answer."

"You low-down, evil bastard. If I'd've caught you on my property, you'd be dead. What's keeping me from doing that now?"

"Daylight. People. Fact that there's more of me than you around here. The riders wouldn't think twice about torchin' your place with you and that girl in it, just to shut y'all up. But because you're Kimbrell's old friend, you have a ticket out." Copeland turned toward the street. "Look, that girl you got, she's seen our faces, and as you know we don't need unwanted attention directed at the circle. It'd be bad for a lot of folks."

"If a rider touches her, I will annihilate the whole gang. Bet against that and you *will* lose."

"Speaking of betting, I'll bet the family farm she's a cutie-pie without all them bothersome clothes huggin' her curves. Hell, I bet she has firm breasts and strong legs that could grip a man like a vise! Haha! Of course, I wouldn't know—not now anyhow. Maybe in a couple of hours, after some of the boys've had their fill."

Repressing the urge to put a bullet in the nightrider's head, Dan rode out of town.

Copeland Yates just stood there, laughing in the sunshine.

Chapter 36

Dan pushed Quaid into full sprint over the Natchez Trace in a rush to get home, unrelenting fear of the unknown stressing his nerves, making him anxious. He rounded the curve at his property and came to a stop in his front yard. He hopped off Quaid, instinctively drew his pistol.

The main door was bashed in, top hinges busted loose. He wanted to scream out Contessa's name, but held his tongue as he walked inside, the scent of fresh blood attacking his nose. A large mirror in the living area had been cracked by brute force and beside it fluttered a piece of paper impaled on a nail. He drew closer, his face becoming distorted in the spider-webbed glass.

Written in bright crimson, the crude note read: "P Gin Alon".

He yanked the paper off the nail.

Immediately deciphered the meaning.

Dan did not know exactly whose blood had crafted the letters, but he was afraid it might be Contessa's.

"Goddamn it!"

He crumpled the paper, threw the wad across the room. Removed his father's Liege rifle from the gun rack.

He lit out towards the Four Oaks Road, then on to Little Hill Bayou, where he believed John West was currently awaiting his arrival at the Prescott Gin.

*****

Trapped like an animal in the dry well, Contessa looked up at the circle of white sky. She held the tip of her finger tightly in the folds of her dress to stem the bleeding. Taking in sharp, quick breaths she dared not move or make noise. She believed the man's threat—*"stay quiet, or we'll leave ya down there"*—and that he might make good on it.

Contessa remembered hearing the husband say "we're the Tarltons, sir," before a bullet ripped through his eyeball.

Unwilling to hand over her newborn baby, the wife lashed out at the men.

Another shot stung the air, and then the tangled legs of the dead wife broke against the downward spiral of stone, her petite body landing hard on Contessa's back.

Now the concentrated smell of the murdered husband and wife made her retch up today's lunch of black-eyed peas and buttered cornbread. Barefoot and frantic, Contessa stood on broken skeletal remains of victims from long ago, trying to avoid the warmth of blood pooling over her feet from the fresh, twisted bodies.

Gunshots still rang in her ears, numbing her brain, but the ringing did not prevent the high-pitched whine of the couple's newborn baby wrapped in swaddling clothes from penetrating her eardrums, the little one still lying on the grass just above her, under that bright sky.

Her heart sank when she overheard the men debating just how they would silence the "gosh-darn thing".

She wished she could help the little baby, save it from immediate danger, but being held captive ten feet deep in a well left her very few options. Helpless, afraid, seeing no way of escape, Contessa bowed her head and prayed for the infant's soul in the midst of Hell's demons.

Chapter 37

Copeland Yates, Dave Frame, Royce Greene, Laws Kimbrell and John West stood around the Prescott Gin smoking cigars and sharing flasks of whiskey.

Dan rode up about ten yards from the men, his rifle pointed skyward. After finding the blood-written note the sight of so many crazy bastards engaged in idle conversation was surreal and off-putting.

Definitely concerned about fighting four nightriders, what really disturbed Dan was the sight of a baby lying on its back, wriggling its tiny arms and feet and crying out for its mother's touch.

"What on earth have you done, West?" he said, disgusted at the sight.

John West stepped out from underneath the gin's tin overhang, the sunlight turning his cheeks a deep pink.

"Just so happens we met up with a man and his wife down by the Four Oaks Road. She had some pretty jewelry around her neck, so I asked Dave here to get it. The problem we experienced stemmed from another source. See, that husband of hers tried to save the day. Kept on and on, beggin' me to set her free. I laid a bullet in his head to shut him up.

"Now, this tiny tit-sucker here? We weren't expectin' a tit-sucker. Damn thing's been cryin' to high Heaven for about an hour now and we've been wonderin' when you'd show up to make it stop." He grinned, fire in his eyes. "That's the deal, Dan."

"What deal?"

"Do away with that baby and we'll release your girl."

"You're a sick man, West. A rotted soul!"

"Sounds to me like you don't wanna save your purty little dove. What was her name again? Contessa Manyfeet? Yeah, couple months ago we put her parents in that well over yonder. Matter of fact, she's standing on their bones right now and don't even know it. Ain't that a shame?"

Dan dropped to the ground and hurried to the well, peered over the side of the brick formation. "Contessa?"

"Dan! They killed them! They're gonna hurt that precious baby! . . . I heard them talkin' about how, they're going to—!"

"Stay calm, Contessa! I'll get you out." Dan leaned his rifle against the well and returned to the gin. "Let her go."

"I must say I'm glad to see ya got my note, Dan. I trust you came alone? Trust is very important between men, as you know. Especially among us riders."

"I ain't part of the riders anymore."

West hocked and spit. "We had a time pennin' that letter, lemme tell ya. Your girl was fidgetin' like the dickens so I had a hard time spellin' out the "e" on that word *alone*. Tacked it up on the wall, concerned the wind might blow it away and all. Thank goodness nothing of the sort happened, else you'd be confused for the whereabouts of your sweetheart, now wouldn't ya?"

"Release her and give me the baby. We'll leave here peacefully."

"Well, shit, Dan. Seein' as how you won't agree to my proposal is unfortunate indeed. Your request guarantees nobody leaves here *peacefully*." West reached down, gently picked up the baby. He wrapped his big, freckled hands around the baby's legs and swung fast and hard, bashing its brains against a support post.

Dan pulled his gun and fired a shot at West's head.

West's hat flew off, and he immediately fell to his knees, returned fire—missed Dan's knee by inches. Convinced he'd been fatally shot by the sight of blood leaking from his scalp, West relaxed his trigger-finger.

Laws Kimbrell stood over West, telling the gang leader that it'd be best to let Dan go.

John West nodded.

Royce Greene did not provide so friendly a response. The tall man pulled his gun.

Before he got off the first round, Dan fired a bullet in his stomach. Then he shot Greene point-blank in the jaw.

Stepping back, Dan aimed at Copeland's face. "Guns! *Now*. Or I'll put you beside him."

Showing no emotion whatsoever, Copeland obliged, dropping his weapons at his boots.

Another problem walked slowly from his left, just out the corner of his vision, and Dan aimed true. "Get back! You don't want to die, do ya Dave? Over this senseless shit?"

"You'd better get yer girl and hit the road," Laws suggested. "When West gains his senses he'll want to take up the fight again."

"Goddamn it Dave, throw that rope down there and get her outta that well!" Dan demanded.

Freed within a minute, Contessa appeared out of the well with dirt and blood coloring her skin and lacy trousers. She seemed smaller than when he last saw her this morning, as though she'd lost weight from the terror she'd experienced.

"Get on the horse, Tess," Dan instructed.

"Which one is Dave Frame?" she asked.

Dan pointed at a stocky man with dark eyes and black hair. "Him. Why?

Contessa took the Liege rifle by the well, braced it at her shoulder, and aimed at the stocky man with dark eyes and black hair.

"Better calm your girl, Dan, or we're gonna have a whole lotta dead bodies layin' around here," Dave warned.

"Ease off, Contessa."

"This man killed my mother. I'll ease off when he's dead."

Dan recognized the intensity in her eyes and sidestepped out of her space.

Using her middle finger on the trigger, Contessa fired—the kickback a punch to her shoulder.

Dave Frame fell to his knees. Coughed up blood. Before turning black, the last images sliding through his mind was the daughter's face of the lady he murdered.

Dan got on his horse and pulled Contessa onto the saddle. He looked at the bodies of Royce Greene and Dave Frame.

Copeland stayed still, hands steady on his hips, eyes sharp with anger.

Laws stood over a fretful John West, assuring him that the bullet had only grazed his scalp. "You're not gonna die here, John," he said. "It's just a nick." Laws looked back to see Dan and Contessa ride away, and what passed for a grin played on his lips.

Chapter 38

In the side yard of Jim Maybin's farmhouse, brothers Andrew and Lynn played a fevered match of Mumblepeg—a knife-throwing skill game.

The tip of Lynn's pocketknife struck the side of Andrew's toe. Dropped in the dirt.

"Ow!"

"I lose!" Lynn yelled, bending down to retrieve his pocket knife.

Andrew shook off the pain. "Hush yer mouth, stupid ass. Look. Somebody's comin'."

Lynn followed his brother's gaze toward the end of the field.

A man and woman on horseback were coming their way.

Jim Maybin was in the backyard stacking wood between twin pines.

"Pa! There's a man here," Andrew said. "He's got a lady with him looks worse for wear. I think there's *blood* on her dress!"

"You boys get on in the house. Stay with your mother."

Andrew limped away, suffering the pain of a slashed toe.

"Want me to get your rifle, Pa?" Lynn asked.

"Goddamn it, stay indoors 'til I tell ya to come out!"

Because Jim wasn't expecting visitors. True, he'd never run into problems with the nightriders but was convinced of their overwhelming presence and political influence. With men like that scattered about, a family man could never be too careful in protecting his own.

He pulled the long-handled axe out of the tree stump. Walked around to the front of the house, the tool heavy in his hands.

At first sight of the man, Jim drew in a sigh of relief and relaxed his grip on the weapon. "Christ, Dan! I thought for sure you were one of the riders!"

"West and his gang are on the hunt for us *right* now! Get her inside. Need to hide Quaid too."

Holding back a curious line of questioning, Jim helped the girl off the horse and carried her up the front steps. "Put Quaid in the barn, last stall. Plenty of feed and clean water."

Dan led Quaid to the cool barn and secured the animal near Jim's black stallion, Curly. He then entered the house from the back porch and passed a bedroom housing a claw-foot tub.

Jim's wife, Rilla, undressed Contessa, careful of her wounded hand.

"It's bad, Dan," Rilla said. "But don't you worry yourself, I'll take care of her." She rubbed Contessa's cheek. "It's alright, darlin'. This is gonna sting for a quick second. Then you'll soak in a hot bath."

Rilla poured a shot of whiskey on what was left of Contessa's finger.

"Auuugh!"

*****

"Dan?" Jim called from the front room. "Rilla's gonna clean her up nice. Come on in here and let's talk."

Dan walked down the long hallway, mumbling, "I should've aimed lower. He was right there, right in front of me."

"Here, have a seat. What happened with West?"

"I shot him."

"Didja kill him?"

"Planned on it. Grazed his head. Didn't do him in, though. I'm a bit rusty nowadays. If I had aimed lower I'd've blew his brains out."

"Who's your lady-friend?"

"That's Contessa Menifee."

"How'd she come about?" Jim asked.

"West murdered her family. I found her hiding in my barn. Been seeing after her ever since."

Jim poured two tumblers of Old Crow. Handed one to his friend. "Drink up, ol boy. You need whiskey."

Dan sipped from the glass, the sting of the drink coursing down his throat like fire. It relaxed his nerves, and he wasn't usually nervous. More concerned for Contessa's immediate safety than his own, he avoided the Old Sparta Road leading home, suspicious that once West regained his bearings he'd probably send some men to finish the gun battle.

As much as he adored her, Dan couldn't bear to put Contessa anywhere near that type of danger. He decided that a detour to Jim's house would keep them both safe.

"The hell of it is that West found out I'd been hiding her at my house," Dan said. "She's a witness to his crimes, so he clearly wants her gone. I went to town this morning, came home . . . found a note tacked by my livin' room mirror. A message written in Contessa's blood. Told me where to meet him if I wanted to get her back. I killed Royce Greene to save her. Dave Frame, he's dead. Copeland Yates ain't. I took his guns, so he was no threat. And that bastard John West, he'd've been gone by now if I'd aimed lower."

"What can I do to help, Dan?"

"I've got to get Contessa out of Louisiana. That poor girl's been through enough, and I won't let them find her. We'll be no trouble. We'll stay 'til dusk, then disappear."

"I knew John West was involved!" Jim looked out the window at the bright day. "I say we get Jess Cady and Fred Boss and go down to New Orleans and contact the governor. Get the state militia up here. They'll wipe out the riders in one fell swoop!"

"Fine plan, Jim, but the governor don't give a piss about our problem. Even if he did, he's probably too busy shoving jambalaya in his fat mouth to get the state army movin' this way. Believe me, if I didn't have Contessa to look after I'd propose we get a posse together and kill 'em all. Every last son of a bitch in the inner circle!" Dan moved the tip of his finger around the rim of the tumbler. "I *would* do that . . . but me and Contessa . . . we're gettin' married. I'd rather settle down, live out a quiet life without all this goddamn nonsense. Jim, I have to leave."

"I understand. You're welcome to stay with us as long as you'd like. I'll try my damnedest to get the militia here. Aside from that? Shoot, I'm not sure what route to take."

Dan took down his whiskey.

"Another?" Jim asked.

After what he'd been through, Dan believed the bottle itself would do just fine.

Chapter 39

Lying naked in a steamy bath, Contessa explained in detail how that devil John West took a long-bladed knife, held her hand against the wooden railing, and sliced off her finger.

"Same as cuttin' the end of a carrot," she said. "Popped right off."

She studied what was left of her finger, the nub bound tightly in white bandages, nerves throbbing with distant pain. Any infection set to invade her body was long dead from the whiskey antiseptic Rilla had so freely dashed on the wound.

"One of his men brought my finger back to me and it had grass stuck to it. John West put his filthy hand over my mouth and warned me if I screamed again he'd shoot me between the eyes, so I calmed a little . . . but the pain, that *pain*, it hurt so bad I thought I'd faint. Then he took a piece of paper from his vest pocket and used my finger like a writing quill!"

"I'm sorry you hurt. You just forget about them, darling. They'll get their comeuppance, don't you worry."

"I suppose if Dan hadn't come along, I'd be in a well, too."

"Relax now, Contessa. You're safe as can be here."

She closed her eyes, feeling the warmth of water soothe her bones. "I feel safe, Rilla, I do. Thank you."

Rilla lent Contessa clean pants and dry shoes, as the women had similar body sizes, although Rilla was a bit broader in the hips. Such minute differences in measurement were irrelevant. The poor girl's trousers and thin leather jacket were mud-smudged, dotted by blood, and that was no way to travel. Stepping out of the bath, Contessa was blissfully unaware that she'd soon be in the saddle of a horse, her arms wrapped around Dan Dean.

Throughout the afternoon Contessa helped Rilla prepare food for their men. The result was a satisfying dinner of fried chickens, mashed potatoes smothered in onions and gravy, green beans and warm, sliced bread dripping with butter. Dessert was golden pound cake topped with blackberry preserves.

For a little over an hour, even Dan felt as though normalcy had crept back into his fight-or-flight existence. He believed Contessa felt the same way. They were having a nice time . . . enjoying the company and temporary shelter.

And like Dan, Contessa periodically peered out the windows at that fading sun to see if the shadows of deranged horsemen might fall across the ground.

After dinner, the women exchanged gossip and recipes in the front room.

The men stepped out to smoke cigars on the back porch and sip whiskey.

"I see why you feel the need to shin out. But I'm positive Fred Boss and Jess Cady would like to see you join us down New Orleans way and bring this issue to the governor's attention. You know more about those bastards than we ever will."

"I'm no longer a nightrider. At one time it was a thing of respect to be a rider. Protect community and all. Now the name itself conjures up pure evil . . . because West turned the gang into blood-thirsty robbers."

"I believe gettin' the militia involved is the only way we're gonna get rid of the clan."

"Or like I've been preaching to you—let's get up a posse and track 'em down, one by one," Dan retorted.

"Fine idea. If it'd work."

"Good luck to you, Jim. It'll be some time before I come back through."

"Godspeed, old friend. You've always been Aces High with me."

They clinked glasses and drank up, knowing by the falling darkness that Dan would disappear into the night.

Chapter 40

Dan and Contessa left Jim's house at ten o'clock.

"Are we going to the train station?" she asked.

"Too many riders up that way now, darlin'. They'll be expecting us to leave town that way. We're headed for Texas. My cousin'll put us up while I study our next move. It's just too risky to travel far in Louisiana."

For nearly an hour Contessa nodded off against Dan's shoulder, her lower back aching in the saddle, cheeks chapped red from the rushing wind in the chilly night. She wanted to stop and rest, but Dan was on a mission to get them out of the state as quickly as possible under the cover of darkness. A scarred, yellow moon helped them to see the ground speed by as Quaid gained full stride across the rough terrain.

She had a feeling that Dan was running on pure directional instinct towards Texas. He hadn't checked a compass or followed a well-beaten trail since bidding Jim Maybin farewell—crossing fields and shallow waterways with deft agility. "Stay quiet and hold tight" were the only words he'd spoken on their hour-long journey, and she'd obeyed, remaining silent throughout the ride.

Now Mother Nature stirred in her bladder, and Contessa needed to relieve herself.

"Dan, I need a rest."

"We'll stop later," Dan hollered back.

"I have to tend to personal business. Stop *now!*"

Dan pulled the reins.

She climbed down off the horse, walked behind pine trees and shucked her pants and squatted.

The tanned pants and chaps looked comical on her body. He was sure she'd rather be wearing her dress. Pants and chaps were practical for riding, though, and he figured once they reached his cousin's place, Contessa could shed those clothes and adorn her fancy new dress for as long as she cared.

When she returned, Dan was drinking fresh water from a canteen. He offered her a swig.

"Do you think they'll find us?" she asked, wiping drops of water from her lips.

"They won't find us where I'm taking you. My cousin, he's a good man. He'll see to our needs. And from what I've heard, his wife is a fine cook."

*****

As a banker in Hemphill, Texas, Nathaniel Artimus Dean made his living selling dreams to family men who wanted a slice of the American pie. He brokered real estate deals for upcoming businesses, secured loans for farm boys striking out on their own, and managed credit for all unpaid bills due the Hemphill City Bank. A gentleman in a suit with an easy smile, Nathan Dean was well-known and highly-respected in his adopted town. Ana, his wife of eight years and their two-year-old son, Elvin, lived in a large log home that overlooked thirty acres of fertile farmland and a bass pond.

Ana and Elvin were in the kitchen making flour tortillas when the stranger arrived on their property. She wiped flour dust across her pink and white apron, looked out the window, then back down the hallway for her husband. She set Elvin on the floor to play with scattered wooden blocks that had ABC's stamped into them.

"Nathan?" she asked. "Somebody's outside, Nathan."

He came downstairs buckling on his gun belt. Clean shaven and impeccably dressed, he was on his way to the local Masonic Lodge to attend their monthly meeting. "We have a visitor?" he said.

Ana pointed out the main window.

"Well, I'll be. Look who it is!" Nathan opened the door wide. "Cousin Dan!"

Dan tied Quaid to a post. "Hey, Nathan. Been a long time."

"Few years. You're damn right it's been a long time!" Nathan hugged him. "You're just as ugly as I remember you, old boy! Why, who's this pretty lady friend of yours?"

"This is Contessa," Dan said. "My fiancé."

"Lordy be, you're gettin' hitched! This is fantastic news. When's the big day?"

"You'll know."

"Nathan, you want tea for your friends?" Ana asked from the porch.

"Yes, thank you darling. Goodness, where are my manners? Y'all come on in. Ma'am," Nathan greeted, taking Contessa's hand and helping her to the ground. "Dan, you remember my dear wife Ana."

Dan tipped his hat over sweaty hair. "Pleasure to see you again, Ana. This is Contessa."

Ana nodded. "Very nice meeting you. Please, come in out of that heat."

Wearing dirty pants and muddy boots, a long night of travel etched into his face, Dan stood the polar opposite of Nathan's suit-and-tie, clean-cut appearance. "You look real spiffy, cousin. Hope we're not interrupting any plans y'all have."

"Oh, this is a blessing, Dan. No bother at all. I have a lodge meeting in town, but those boys can carry on without me. They don't need me around to record minutes and empty whiskey bottles. *Ha!*"

"Are you sure?"

"Let 'em tell tall tales without me. I'm excited you're here."

Ana returned with glasses of tea for her guests.

"Much obliged," Dan said.

Nathan bit off the end of a thin cigar, spat on the ground, and lit a match on the back of a matchbook. "So, Dan, what brings y'all to the Grand Land of Texas?"

Dan waited until Ana and Contessa were inside the house, well out of earshot, before he spoke. He first told his cousin how Contessa came into his life. Then went into detail about the West Clan, and how he was all but physically forced to leave Louisiana.

"Boy, that's some story! You know you can stay with us for as long as you'd like."

"That's mighty gracious of you, Nathan. It won't be long, though. I'll be looking for a house nearby. Buy a few heifers and a bull to get a farm up and runnin'. And to think I had it all right there back home . . . but that damned clan, they're just too intrusive. The threat of violence burned at my neck like the sun. The only thing I could think of was getting Contessa out of harm's way."

"Sounds like you made the right decision," Nathan said. "Look, if you're hungry, Ana's making some fresh beef wraps with tomato and onion. She's a swell cook, lemme tell ya."

"Contessa could use food in her belly. I need sleep."

"Just happen to have an extra bedroom reserved for special guests," Nathan said, patting Dan on the back. "It is really good to see you, cousin. You know you're always welcome here."

Chapter 41

"I want every available rider in a hunnerd-mile stretch lookin' out for that scoundrel! I want Dan Dean's head in a box!" John West slammed his fist on the table, the impact sending his bullhorn over the edge. "Som'bitch!"

At West's request, the riders of the inner circle were gathered in the back accounting room of Will Drake's store. Everyone was expected to attend, or face consequences. Everyone showed for the meeting.

West checked the emerald and rubies and ornate slivers of gold molded into his precious bullhorn for any cracks or chips, then strapped the bullhorn's string around his shoulder and ribs, letting it hang at his waist. He was still pissed off about the terrible gunfight at the Prescott Gin; pissed Dan Dean left a fresh red whelp across the side of his scalp—just an *inch* flying left, the lead would've shattered his skull. Pissed that little witch Contessa was still alive to run her mouth. Pissed that he had to drop two able-bodied nightriders down his well.

Laws spoke up, probably voicing the thoughts of several men in the room. "John, I understand why you want Dan dead, but he's got to be long gone by now. He's not foolish enough to stay around town with *this* outfit on his trail. He could be anywhere."

"And that's where the danger lies, Kimbrell. That man could come by night and wipe us out. He's the best gun thrower I ever seen. Better than you!"

"He's not stupid enough. I'm tellin' ya, he's gone. I highly doubt he'll be back. The Dan Dean I know wouldn't put himself in that kind of a pickle."

"Regardless, I want the message out," West continued. "If any y'all see him, kill him. Don't lose sight of him by knockin' at my door seeking further instruction. He's a threat like no other. Just shoot him 'til he's dead, then let me know. You men understand?"

"Yeah, West."

"You got it, West."

"Will do, Boss."

"What if he recognizes one of us?" asked Earl Gilcrease.

West looked at the back row of standing men, a scowl on his face. "Then you die."

There was silence among the group as his words sank in.

"Any more questions? Or are we all clear on this mission? Alright now, y'all leave us be."

Within seconds the room stood empty.

"You're overthinking this, John," Laws said.

"Perhaps. At least I got eyes peeled for him. If Dan Dean decides to show his face around here again, he'll wish he'd've stayed a ghost."

Chapter 42

Within three days of arriving at his cousin's home Dan and Contessa were married by Justice of the Peace, Tobias Threadcutt. Nathan and Ana attended this special occasion, along with a sleeping Elvin nestled in the comfort of his mother's arms.

For the first time in years, Dan was truly happy. He saw familiar emotion burst forth in Contessa's eyes as they danced to a band made up of Nathan's Masonic brothers.

She kept smiling the entire evening, a sense of wonder on her face, enjoying the peace that came from a good man who vowed to be there for her each passing day, to love her always.

Nathan hosted a pit barbecue at his house for the event, slow-cooking a whole pig on a metal grate over burning coals since early morn, the inviting, smoky smell permeating the yard. The newly-acquainted party of twenty-three visited, danced, and drank the night away in celebration of this joyous union, congratulating Dan and Contessa as though they were old friends.

By morning's light Dan was outside drinking coffee, looking out over the cool, calm waters of the bass pond. He touched the silver ring around his finger and realized he'd found a woman who would love him in return—come what may.

She'll always be with me, he thought. *This is real happiness.*

Nathan walked outside carrying his own steaming cup of black coffee and greeted his cousin. "Quite a time we had yesterday, huh Dan?"

"Oh yeah, it was quite the time."

"Pretty sunrise," Nathan said, sighing. "How I love Texas."

"It's some beautiful country out here," Dan said. "And that was a tasty pig you charred for everybody."

"Tried and true family recipe from our grandfather, Abel Dean. He showed me how to cook it slow on low heat. Really the only way to produce that kind of taste." Nathan sipped his coffee. "Ahhh. Boy, that wife of yours sure is a looker. Lucky you wedded her before some other lucky fella came along."

Having never been married it was strange to hear Contessa referred to as his 'wife'. "I feel very lucky to have her. Besides, any other man wouldn't've charmed her the way I charmed her."

"Ha! Yes sir, I can tell she's happy as all get out."

"She had a big night," Dan said.

"Well, I'm gonna mosey on to the bank. Need anything from town?" Nathan asked.

Dan pulled out a roll of bills. "Get me a few bags of dried beef jerky if ya don't mind."

Nathan waved off the offer. "Stash your money. I'll get 'em."

"You don't have to go and do that. I've got plenty of folding stuff."

"Let's just call it a wedding gift."

"Dried beef, ha! Now that's a *perfect* wedding gift!"

Dan drank the rest of his coffee, grateful for morning's peace. Last night's memory of becoming one with Contessa Jo Menifee would live on for many years in his mind. There had been cake and smoked pork and wine and whiskey and well-wishers galore. It had been so lovely. Everything seemed perfect. Not for his sake, really, but for Contessa's.

Visiting Nathan Dean only for a brief time, Dan witnessed how content and happy a man could be. His cousin had a steady job, a nice house, and most importantly a family waiting at home each and every day. Dan had yearned for the same life, and convinced himself that marrying Contessa was a step in the right direction—that they were safe from immediate danger.

But even here in the grand land of Texas, far from the Louisiana swamps, the West-Kimbrell clan's reach was undeniable.

During such an enchanted evening, great threats of violence shouldn't weigh on a man's mind. After the ceremony and on to the party, while he and Contessa fed each other pieces of iced white cake, smiling at each other, happy and finally feeling a sense of security, he noticed a familiar face . . . someone who could turn it all upside down.

The skinny man sported a trimmed beard and black hat and played fiddle in the band. Occasionally glanced over Dan's way for uncomfortably lengths of time. Dan recognized the player as Gil Pickett, a fellow nightrider. Gil was not a member of the circle. He was part of the chain that related information to the clan regarding probable heists or other illicit activities—merchandise being shipped down the Red River, or travelers passing through town—so that John West and his men could commit their crimes before opportunity escaped them.

The fact Gil Pickett was a member of the same Masonic lodge that Nathan Dean attended came as no surprise to Dan, as several members of the nightriders held authoritative and influencing positions in state and parish governments, including social alliances like the Masons.

Gil arrived with the band, played, and left, never once congratulating Dan and Contessa in celebration. It would take a fool to think Gil would merely let it go and say nothing to his fellow riders. If Gil recognized Dan (and Dan believed he did) then the fiddle-playin' nightrider would relay this message.

Dan also believed that in all probability John West had not forgotten their gunfight at the Prescott Gin and had sent out eyes on the search for miles.

Given Gil's inclination to speak of this event in order to gain John West's favor, the nightriders would locate Dan Dean and his new bride in no time.

Now enjoying himself on this beautiful Texas morning, feeling a gentle breeze kiss his skin, Dan realized that he had an unpleasant but necessary choice to make: either remain in Texas and witness his loved ones suffer senseless harm, or return to Louisiana and destroy the West-Kimbrell Clan.

He figured it was only a matter of time before the riders visited Nathan's nice, three bedroom log home, and brought with them the force of eighteen guns. The nightmare in his imagination previewed Contessa being injured in what was essentially Dan's fight against John West. Those cutthroats would bring trouble upon his cousin's family like no other violence imagined, and Dan Dean couldn't stop them alone. He needed help.

In the downstairs bedroom he found Contessa lying on a fluffy cot, hair fanned across the pillow, one toned leg draped over a soft quilt. Contessa was his everything. Yesterday he vowed to love her 'til 'death do us part,' and today he vowed he'd do anything within his power to keep her alive.

He followed the smells of breakfast to the kitchen, where Ana was frying sausage links on a greased skillet.

"Morning, Ana."

"Good morning, Dan. More coffee?"

"Sounds fine, thank you." He poured himself another cup and blew at the rising steam. "Smells good in here."

"Won't be long now and I'll have it ready."

Elvin sat on the floor in a diaper fastened by safety pins, rocking sideways on his butt, thrilled at the sight of the wooden alphabet blocks. He'd stack the blocks, knock them over, laugh with glee. Then repeat.

Dan knelt beside him. "Hey, son, looks like you're havin' a ball there."

Elvin looked up, eyes lit by intense curiosity. He stacked three more blocks, then slapped them down and giggled like crazy.

"He's a cute little fella," Dan said.

"Handful is what Elvin is. But we love him still," Ana said. "Fried eggs?"

"I love fried eggs."

Elvin watched spellbound while Dan gathered the blocks and took his time stacking them. He balanced eight in all, then pointed at the bottom block. "See that one? That one's holding the others up . . . now if I remove the strongest block, guess what? They all fall down."

Elvin giggled. "Faldun!"

Dan removed the bottom one, sending the blocks scattering across the floor.

Elvin clapped his hands, suddenly pleading for Cousin Dan to "Do agin! Do agin! Do agin!"

Chapter 43

April 1872

On a rainy Tuesday, Fred Boss, Jess Cady, Benny Bishop, Lucas Gibbs, and Landon Fulcher accompanied Jim Maybin to the Governor's mansion in New Orleans. They opposed sending a telegram to propose their idea; instead they left Atlanta without giving notice to anyone of their intentions or travel agenda, including their families.

When the men arrived in the city they were initially refused entry at the mansion gates. The guard explained that Governor Warmoth was occupied.

But Jim Maybin was adamant about his plight. He and his men did not endure riding through two days of rain to be turned away so casually.

Jim looked at the stubborn guard, stepped closer. "Listen here, son. I wore a uniform much like yours less than seven years ago. In that uniform I killed men for the sake of pride in a war that shouldn't have been. Now there's a war going on in my home region, in my home state—the very damn state I shed blood to protect! And it ain't navy blue petticoats runnin' around givin' the orders, either. The men I'm talkin' about fought for the south and now they're killin' the south. If me and my men are not granted the opportunity to speak to Governor Henry Clay Warmoth, the lives of many people will remain in jeopardy. Can you comprehend that urgency?"

The guard said, "If what you say is true, then I must seek the governor's permission. Be patient, gentlemen."

Ten long minutes ticked by, then a man wearing a gray coat rode up on a horse. He introduced himself as Mac Groves, the governor's assistant. He ushered the group through the gates and under the shade of Oak trees that bent crookedly out of the earth. Standing on the wide porch steps, Mr. Groves insisted the governor would see only three men.

Jim, Fred Boss, and Jess Cady got off their horses and followed Mr. Groves into the bricked mansion.

Upon entering the residence, they looked in awe around the spacious foyer. Exquisite oil paintings hanged on the walls, floor-sweeping burgundy drapes framed large windows, and a lit chandelier, directly above their heads, appeared to take up the entire ceiling. Twin grand staircases on opposite sides of the foyer led to a balcony and several rooms.

They paced about patiently, boots sounding out on polished hardwood floors.

"Good gracious alive," Fred Boss said. "This room alone is bigger than my whole house!"

Jess Cady took off his hat. "Sure would be nice to live like this. Don't think I'd grow tired of it."

"I'd say this here's proof politickin' pays off," Jim said.

"Somethin' swell alright," Fred Boss added.

Mac Groves returned. "Gentlemen? Governor Warmoth will see you now."

He led them down a hallway lined by tall windows, and through double-glass doors.

On the bricked patio Governor Henry Warmoth sat at a table overlooking the capitol's expansive acreage. He was dressed in a white suit and skinny bowtie, his large hat eased over his forehead to shield his face from the sinking sun. His goatee was as gray as the cigar ashes he repeatedly tipped at the rim of a bronze ashtray, eyes a cool blue. He stood and shook hands.

"Gentlemen."

"Governor Warmoth? My name's Jim Maybin. This here's Mr. Fred Boss and Mr. Jess Cady. Thank you for seeing us on such abrupt notice."

"Yes, of course. I've been informed of your urgency, Mr. Maybin. Please. Sit."

The men remained standing. "We won't take up much of your time, sir. If you will hear me out, hopefully you can assist us in a rather dire matter."

"Continue, Mr. Maybin. Explain your troubles."

"Well, we live up in the central part of the state. Around Winnfield and Atlanta, right there south of the City of Natchitoches. You see, there's a gang of men, about twenty or so, that've been robbin' travelers who pass through the area. Me and others believe it's the work of a gang called the West Clan. The clan is led by two ornery devils: John West and a Mr. Lawson Kimbrell. Brutal men to be sure. They rob and kill folks at night and leave no witnesses. Not a one. They've been at it for a long while. They even burned down the courthouse."

"Yes, I did get word about the courthouse," Warmoth said.

"Now we aim to get rid of them, but we need assistance. These men don't need to be run out of town like your average bushwhacker. They need killin', one and all, for the prosperity of residents struggling to live there peacefully. Nobody's safe around that place anymore, and it is imperative that we do something to end this madness. Governor, we have got to act!"

The governor dipped the damp end of his cigar into a glass of brandy, then stuck it in his mouth, puffed out a plume of smoke. "Gentlemen, I am keenly aware of the disorder sweeping this great state in several rabid forms. I am repulsed by the awful news you've brought to my attention this afternoon. Regrettably, I cannot assist in your quandary."

Fred Boss spoke up then. "Can't you just send in the state militia and make things right? You're the goddamn governor!

Governor Warmoth waved off the outburst and attempted to ease their frustrations by explaining his crippling influence on such grievant matters:

For a long while now the "Ku Klux Klan", along with "The Knights of the White Camellia," and an Italian organization called "The Innocents", had been patrolling the streets of New Orleans and rural byways to promote political advances in the face of racial tension. In an effort to discourage movements against their political position, the Democratic, white-sheeted Kluxers had destroyed Republican newspaper offices and disrupted Republican parades and meetings. Just before the election of 1868, to further tighten their grip on the state's political structure, sixteen influential Republicans were slain on Canal Street.

Following this horrific incident, Governor Warmoth wrote: *"The act of Congress prohibiting the organization of militia in this state strips me of all power to maintain extensive law and order . . . ."*

An appeal had to be made to restore political peace between the parties. The governor sent correspondence to Major General Lovell

H. Rousseau, U. S. Military Commandant of the Department of Louisiana, requesting aide in handling these political difficulties, "to make things right and restore order."

"Now here's that strange, sometimes bothersome thing called irony that makes life so damn curious," Warmoth said. "Rousseau was a *Democrat*. Politically, the man opposed every action I chose. I tell you, no matter what had taken place between those two groups, he was not interested in coming to my aide in resurrecting the Republican Party. Or even provide soldiers to patrol the city, by which their presence might lessen destruction. Nothing. I am sorry, gentlemen. My hands are tied. There is very little I can do to assist you at this juncture."

Jim Maybin was visibly disappointed. "Look here, governor. The West-Kimbrell outfit differs significantly from any other guerrilla band in the state. Some of their members were associated in sinful activities with Preacher John Murrell long before the North and South stirred up a fight.

"John West reorganized that gang, and now they do one thing, and they do it well: ride the Natchez Trace and murder honest citizens and travelers for their money, possessions, their *flesh!* They leave no trace of human existence or their handiwork." Jim slammed a fist against the huge white column. "Out of town folks making way to Texas for a better life are getting slaughtered on the side of the goddamn road! And you're telling me there's nothing you can do to stop it?"

Governor Warmoth agreed that Jim Maybin and his men needed military backing, but that kind of power was in the hands of the Commandant of the State who had sole authority to send in troops to maintain order and execute a mass cleanup.

It was doubtful Major General L. H. Rousseau would lend a helping hand in this matter, either.

Still, the governor realized that something had to be done. Throughout central Louisiana the buffer strip between Natchitoches and Winnfield had long been a lawless territory since the days of St. Denis.

"It's been slinging guns and tomahawk rule up that way for ages," Warmoth said. "I suggest, Mr. Maybin, that you gather a posse of your own and hunt down the men in this clan. Dispatch them like a pack of wild dogs. One by one, send them away."

"Sir, I respect your suggestion but I refuse to form a vigilante band of regulators for the purpose of eliminating the clan. Only a few trusted men I know might agree to join in a venture like that—Fred Boss and Jess Cady here among them. Most folks in that territory have a rational fear of well-to-do carpetbaggers, ex-union soldiers, and I'm sure they'd be extremely concerned about the various legal ramifications that might result in participating in mass murder," Jim explained. "Here's some irony for you, governor . . . the men of the West Clan represent some of the best people in Winn Parish. They are members of the church, loyal Masons, they profit in the farming community. Some of them are officers in local governments to boot!"

Governor Warmoth finished his brandy and set the empty glass on the table. "Well, if the issue is handled properly, maneuvering around those obstacles will not pose much resistance. Should you agree to track them, I will pardon every man who volunteers in the take-down. With that in mind, how many men do you think you'll need? Ten? Twenty? Name the number and I'll dip my quill."

Considering this plan of action might serve as the only way to bring about order back home, Maybin said, "Twenty-five."

"Very well, Mr. Maybin. Follow me inside and I'll fix up a pardon for every man."

Warmoth sat behind his Oak wood desk and, with pen in hand, signed 25 blank pardon slips prepared by his staff. He handed them to Jim Maybin.

"The blank spaces at the top, for names and dates, those can be filled in at a later time . . . when the deed is done," Warmoth explained. "You and your men will be in the clear. Officially, this is as close as I can come to sending in armed soldiers."

"Then it'll have to serve our interests," Jim replied. "We appreciate what you're doing, sir."

Warmoth stood, offered his hand. "Good luck, gentlemen. I wish you and your men victory. Understand that within my stifled powers I've done all I can. But *you* may go as far as necessary . . . you now hold complete executive clemency in your hands."

Chapter 44

Contessa sat on a stump near the pond enjoying morning's sunshine, her bare feet in the cool water, the hem of her dress waving at her ankles. The wine cork on her fishing line bobbed over shimmering currents while she waited for the next bite. Four good-sized bream lay in the pond, hooked to a stringer tied to a fallen limb.

Dan walked up behind her and put his hands on her shoulders. He was dressed in a collared shirt and vest, a bolo hanging from his neck, his boots waxed to a shiny black. Clean-shaven, hair slicked back and stiff with pomade, it appeared he was on his way to town.

"Any luck?" he asked.

"I caught a few for supper," she said, smiling up at him. "Where are you going looking that handsome, husband of mine?"

He leaned down and kissed her soft lips. "Good question, and I've got an answer for you."

At first, Contessa did not believe she heard him correctly. "You're doing what?"

"I'm goin' back to Louisiana," Dan said.

Confusion replaced the joy in her face. "Why in the world would you go back there? You said you wanted to make a new life here, with me."

"That's in the cards, but we're not safe here. Not for long. When the clan finds out where we are, we'll be in grave danger. You, Nathan, his family—all of us."

"How will they find us?" she asked, rather impatiently. "How do they know where to look!"

"On our wedding night I recognized the fiddle player in that band. He's a nightrider . . . one of several lookouts West has working under him. He saw me. He knows my name. Now my concern is he'll get word to the clan . . . then they'll track me here. So I'm headed to Louisiana. Gonna end this."

Contessa slapped him in the face. *Pap!* "Are you . . . ? You're serious, aren't you? Have you lost your ever-loving *mind*?"

"If I don't try something, the clan will go on hurting more people. I know what they're capable of. I won't have that on my conscience. *I* wouldn't be able to live with myself."

"Say something happens to you? They'll come after me!"

Dan took her in his arms, held her tightly. "Don't fret, Contessa. I won't let those bastards hurt you. I'm doing this to keep you safe."

She went silent.

"Contessa? Say it. Say you believe me."

"We should have gone on and made the trip to my hometown, in the Carolinas. We can still do it. Instead of Texas, let's go east. Negotiate a parcel of land. We'll start fresh! There's no trouble back home, not like what I've seen here."

He pulled back, eyes focused to narrow slits. "Say I'll keep you safe."

Tears dropped from her eyes. "Yes, I do . . . I believe you will, Dan . . . but I'm afraid for you, going at it alone. You can't fight them by yourself. You said so! There's too many of 'em!"

Dan held her face in his hands, feeling the warmth of her cheeks heat his palms, stared into her eyes. "I'm ridin' back to end their bandit rule for all time. Nothing will steer me clear of my objective."

She dropped the fishing pole and stood, wiped another tear off her cheek. "So what happens if you go to battle with those Godless devils and you get killed? What then? What about me?"

Dan grabbed his hat and threw it on the ground at her feet. "Dammit Tess! What the hell do you want from me? If I don't make the first move, they'll come here and finish us off! You know what kind of animals they are."

"That's what frightens me." She grabbed hold of his vest. "Dan, please listen to reason . . . God did not put us here to live in fear of savages like that. We can go far away. We're still alive, sweetheart, we're *married*. Let's enjoy the love that God gave us."

He pulled her body close. "You'll be fine with Nathan and Ana."

Contessa's eyes went glossy with fresh tears. She didn't want him to let go, but in her heart she knew he'd made his decision and that there was no turning back, no changing his mind.

"Whatever happens, you return to me, Dan Dean. I don't care how long it takes, you come back to me."

Dan kissed the top of her head and looked to the clouds. He prayed for Contessa. He prayed for Nathan's family. He prayed for strength and courage against his enemies.

Then he asked for God's blessing to commit calculated murder.

*****

That evening the Deans enjoyed a dinner of crunchy fish fillets and fire-roasted potatoes, slathered in slaw. Then to top it off, they had cinnamon-crusted apple turnovers covered in fresh cream.

His belly full and eyes heavy, little Elvin curled up on the floor under a homemade quilt.

Contessa helped Ana clean the kitchen while Nathan and Dan sipped brandy on the porch.

His cousin enlightened him on the simplicities of the banking business and the complexity of raising a family. They recalled entertaining stories from chapters of their childhood and laughed the evening away.

And Dan soon felt relaxed enough to explain his plans of retribution against the West Clan.

"I see they got your ire up, Dan. My concern is should you act on that idea? Sounds like there's a nest of vipers ready to strike out at your ankles. Just how in the hell're you gonna bypass all those eyes lookin' out for ya?"

"I've an idea brewin'. But to make it work, I'll have to devise a cover. If she'll allow I need to borrow one of Ana's dresses—a dim one, preferably, brown or similar shade. She's a good-sized woman, so I reckon it'd fit me."

"You want to wear a lady's dress?"

"If I wore my duster I'd resemble every other rider on the trails. I need to wear something entirely different. When daylight shines, a cover will be useful . . . else I chance an ambush, say a rider remembers my face."

Nathan drew in a breath, sighed slowly, and shook his head. "Are you sure there isn't another way you'd like to go about this?"

"Posing a disguise is the only way I'll make it to Jim Maybin's house without running into serious trouble."

"If that's the case I'll ask her. Anything else you might need?" Nathan asked. He elbowed Dan in the ribs. "Maybe some of her eye-shadow? Or that powder puff stuff she dabs on her cheeks before she's seen with me in public?"

"Ha! None of that. But if she's willing, I'll need locks of her hair."

"Her hair?"

"She's got black hair, I've got black hair," Dan said. "See if she'll snip off a few lengthy strips."

"You're serious?"

Dan nodded.

"Jumpin' jackrabbits! I can't promise she'll do that. Ha! Are you positive you want to do this?"

"Do what? Wear a dress and a homemade wig to make certain the riders don't spot me? *Yes*."

"No, no, I mean chase after the clan and all? By any means necessary?"

Dan finished off his brandy. "Nathan, if I don't do this there'll come a day I'll regret it. If I don't try, they'll find me . . . and if they find me, they'll find you. They'll find Ana, your son." He shook his head. "Your family should never face such a threat. Given the chance, I can stop 'em from the backside of a gun. I just hafta find them—one after the other."

"Listen, Cuz, I respect your decision. But this kind of thing, this is something you may not come back from. Beware your surroundings."

"If you see somebody you ain't sure of come up this stretch of land, get Grandfather Abel's rifle out of your gun case and take their head off."

"Your bride is safe with us, don't you worry," Nathan said, extinguishing his cigar. "Let's go inside. I'm sure she has something you can wear. After all, bless her heart, Ana is a good-sized woman."

Chapter 45

One last kiss and Contessa's soft lips touched his ear, breathed hard against his skin.

"I love you."

Dan mounted his horse, situated his brown hat over his head, looked down and welcomed her pleading eyes. "I'll be with you again, darling."

"Promise me that," she said.

"I promise."

Nathan stood on the porch, arm around Ana's shoulders. "God's strength, cousin."

Elvin popped his thumb out of his mouth. "Do agin!"

Dan couldn't help but smile at the little one.

Do again indeed.

As he drifted away in the bright moonlight he heard the sounds of Contessa's crying on the breeze, her hiccups and deep breaths reminding him that he was leaving something precious behind . . . something he had to protect . . . come back to.

He rode throughout the night eastbound on crisscrossing trails, stopping briefly near bayous to let Quaid rest. Dan sustained on fresh water and pork tortillas Ana prepared him. He fed Quaid slivers of dried beef, rolled oats, and sugar cubes (the ol' boy's favorite treat) as hours passed by with only the sound of rushing wind and the light of the moon providing company.

Road-weary and dragged out, getting in a few cat-naps on the way that reenergized his mind but failed to fully rejuvenate his working muscles, Dan finally recognized the lay of the land as he neared home.

At a creek he wet the blade of a shiny straight-razor and shaved smooth his mustache and sandpapered cheeks.

When daylight broke over the pink horizon in rays of brilliant gold, he decided this was a fine time to set his plan in motion. Determined to make it to Jim Maybin's without incident, Dan stopped short of the Four Oaks Road and opened the saddlebag's double flap. He removed the amber-colored, flower print dress Ana had so kindly provided him, and touched the slits.

Ana had not approved of the slits he cut into the dress. Against her wishes but given Nathan's permission, Dan took a pair of clothing shears to the fabric anyhow.

Dan unbuttoned his collared shirt and secured it in the bag. He spit on a handkerchief and cleaned the mud off his boots, then removed his hat and pulled on the dress to cover his trousers and pistols. Then he donned a different hat. This new hat was fitted with thick, lengthy curls of Ana's jet-black hair glued to the inner seam, so that he appeared, at a glance, to be a long-haired woman.

Dan thought if he caught a glimpse of his cloaked reflection in a mirror he'd laugh out loud. To further deceive prying eyes he fastened a long red scarf to the saddle horn, the cloth wavy in the wind.

The red sash seemed to be doing its job the closer he moved toward Winnfield. When a rider noticed the sash from a distance, they at once avoided all manner of communication—from conversation to eye contact, a reaction that offered the ex-nightrider considerable protection.

He traveled peacefully for awhile, head tucked, nodding at a few passersby, feeling that he was home free . . . . But the devil-may-care attitude of some men in the area soon nipped at his heels in the form of three nightriders.

The red sash swished along, a signal to clan members that the rider on *this* particular horse was definitely Annabelle Frost, and well, you know what would happen if you bothered Lawson Kimbrell's pretty lady-friend.

"Miss? Hello, Missus!" one of them called. "Are you from around these parts?"

Perhaps they didn't get the message, Dan thought.

"Looks like she's gone hard of hearin'," another exclaimed. "Pardon us, young lady! What's your hurry?"

Dan had the urge to outrun them but reconsidered that foolish idea. He'd risk a bullet in the back.

"It's mighty risky you being out and about all alone, ma'am," noted the third rider. "Me and my friends here, we can protect ya. For a favor or two."

The riders trotted up beside their prey.

Dan recognized the voices belonging to Otto Shrum, Gus Rivers, and Clifford Tingle. He'd known these cutthroats from his time spent participating in the nightriders' sweep of carpetbaggers, rough outlaws, and ruthless ex-Yankee soldiers—when things were settled with words and fists and moral integrity and the threat of a holstered gun, not from split-second, live-or-die actions in the art of drawing one.

Gus Rivers held a rifle pointed haphazardly in the woman's direction. "I sure would like to show you around if you'll oblige! There's a quiet place in the woods where we might get further acquainted," he announced. "Why don't ya go ahead and slow that pony to a walk?"

Dan kept his head down, shadowing his face. Eased Quaid to a gait.

"That's it, that's good. Slow her down . . . ."

Otto Shrum strolled up to Dan's left side.

Clifford moved right.

Gus went ahead of them all to block the trail.

Quaid stopped, carving hoof dents in the hard red dirt.

Appearing completely neutral to the outlaws, Dan slid his hands into the slits of the dress.

Gus dismounted his horse and approached the "woman". Patterns of off-white flowers swirled like teardrops in the dress's fabric, and he reached up to touch a flower. "Right purty dress you got there, gal. Come down off that animal and let's have us a time!" Gus Rivers placed his hand firmly on Dan's thigh. "When I get that dress on the ground, I'll make a woman out of ya!"

The others laughed out loud.

Dan looked down at the nightrider. Caught the surprise in his blood-shot eyes.

"Jesus *Christ* . . . it's—"

He kicked Gus in the face, cracking his nose.

Then Dan braced his thighs against the horse's sides, strong-legged the stirrups and came up off the saddle, the dress spreading out like a cape at his shoulders. Pulled guns from underneath swirling flowers.

Boom.

Clifford's head opened in a red explosion.

Otto Shrum was blasted clear off his scrambling horse.

Gus screamed: "Dan Dean! It's Dan Dean! We gotta get—!"

Managing both revolvers Dan blew holes through the front of the dress, breaking Gus Rivers down to a lifeless mess.

Chapter 46

Sure enough, word got back to West that Dan Dean had been spotted in Hemphill, Texas.

West looked up from his slice of apple pie and tongued a crumb off his lip. "You saw him?"

"Not personally," Vernon Beech said. "One of our lookouts over there identified him."

"Are you sure about that?"

"No reason to doubt Gil Pickett. Been knowin' him for years and he ain't never been one to talk out of his ear."

West put his fork on the plate and surveyed his land, wondering how he might use this newfound information. "If we know where Dan's holed up, I want some of our best trackers to investigate. Call on Hank Wright, Gus Rivers, and Otto Shrum and meet me at Drake's in two hours."

Vernon Beech left to do West's bidding, then stopped short of the door and turned to the gang leader. "What if we don't find Dean?"

"Then I'll track down Gil Pickett myself and tear out his tongue for wasting my time." West stood and buckled his guns around his wide waist. "If your looker is speaking the truth, and Dan Dean *is* there, I want you to shoot him dead and whoever else he's with."

*****

Will Drake shut the door to his office, walked to his desk and opened the bottom drawer. He withdrew a pint of whiskey and a .25 caliber Derringer pistol—the type "ladies of the night" kept strapped to their garters in case a customer refused to pay the pleasure tab.

Not long after marrying Rebecca he purchased the gun from a prostitute he'd occasionally visit. That was well over ten years ago, but the Derringer brought back memories of her black hair and bedroom eyes and large breasts bouncing in his face. Sometimes he wondered if he should reveal the affair to Rebecca, then immediately pushed that absurd idea out of his mind. Time may soften the blow, but he knew his wife would never forgive him for past indiscretions of that magnitude. Blurred memories of a Mexican prostitute and his willingness to lay down with her while tied to the bonds of marriage was not the problem making Will Drake drink heavily today. Other troubles perplexed his mind in a way that was currently causing him great pain and indecision.

He took a long sip, closed his eyes against the burn sending flames down his throat. Another sip and he pressed the barrel to his ear, touched the trigger.

He thought of his wife and daughters, his dear old mother . . . what would they think of him? A coward? Troubled soul?

Considering he'd be a dead man if he attempted his devious scheme, would his family believe that he made the correct decision?

Sweat beads slipped off his nose.

No doubt they'd kill him.

If they knew of his treachery, he'd be thrust in a well, eyes to the sky.

Either he went through with it and escaped town, or ended it here . . . because dying by his own hand, at least, there would be no torture. Just *bang*. Done. Let them find his cold body. Let them ask their questions. Let him go to the grave in relative peace.

But the temptation to get away with treachery was all too great. And besides, he had already initiated his plan. The clan leaders would soon discover someone they trusted had proven to be a snake in the grass . . . and that they had all been bitten.

By then, Will Drake would be a memory just like that big-breasted Mexican harlot.

Will took a handkerchief and dabbed his forehead, laid the pistol on the desk. He walked to the window and looked out at the town. He'd come this far. If he wasn't going to put a bullet through his brain, he might as well go on living as a successful thief.

He massaged the graying hairs on his chin. Thought of his family, his thriving business; the kickbacks he received in keeping the books on West and Kimbrell's activities.

The night he left, suspicion would certainly fall on his head. With the clan's reach, there was really no safe place to go. He'd have to settle in unfamiliar territory hundreds of miles away. Missouri or Arizona, where no one knew of the Louisiana nightriders. Stay the trails and rely on his guns and sheer luck to escape unscathed.

He believed it could be done, though. Once in motion there was no returning. He'd never again see his family or the town he loved.

Out the window he spied the heavy-set frame of John West maneuver his black horse through a bustling crowd on Main Street. Lec Ingram and Vernon Beech jotted alongside, horses kicking up dust.

They roped their horses in front of the store.

Will was not expecting John West and his men. Maybe they were thirsty for a drink. Or needed dry goods. They usually scheduled a meeting, but as Will can attest, John West was not a sane (nor predictable) man.

Feeling frantic, he faced the challenge of balancing fear while keeping his composure. Known as a gentleman, someone who did not talk much or wear his heart on his sleeve, the mere fact Will might show fear would raise flags among these outlaws that something wasn't right.

He kept calm.

Hid the pistol in the drawer.

Looked down at the beginning of his note: *Rebecca, I adore you. I wish for you only the sweetest life in these troubled times. May God bless my precious daughters, Hanna and Hailey, for I've tried to be a good father yet failed time and again. My sweet Rebecca, I trust you to help see them through this aberration. I beg you to find it in your heart to forgive my actions. I cannot—*

Someone rapped on the office door.

Will crumpled the piece of paper in his hands, shoved it in his pocket, and took in a deep breath, produced a smile.

"John," Will greeted. "I wasn't expecting you."

West strolled by him, his men in tow. He sat in Will's comfortable, high-backed chair, and propped his boots on the edge of the desk. "Won't take up mucha your time, Will. We simply need a private place to visit a private matter."

"I understand. Take all the time you need. I'll just—"

"Stay awhile," West said. "This concerns you as well."

Will felt like pissing his trousers. He did not question the clan leader. He nodded good-naturedly and leaned against the wall, crossed his arms at his chest. Listened.

West checked his pocket watch.

8:50 am.

He looked at Vernon Beech. "You told them nine o'clock, didn't ya?"

"Sharp," Vernon answered. "I went out to Hank Wright's farm and told him to contact the others."

"Well, we've got a few minutes to spare. Lec? Why don't you go up to the saloon and tell ol' Milt to fetch us some coffee? I'll take mine highfalutin!"

"Highfa-what?" Lec asked.

"Black, dashed with a couple shots of the finest whiskey our proprietor here has to offer."

"Stagecoach," Will said. "That's the finest I carry."

"Stagecoach it is," West affirmed.

"I'll take some biscuits n' gravy," Vernon said.

"Vernon? Drake don't sell hot food. Go to the hotel if you want breakfast—after the meeting," Lec said.

Will cleared his throat then and spoke up. "What is the purpose of this meeting, John?"

"Dan Dean."

Fifteen minutes later, Hank Wright showed up alone.

"Where's Gus and Shrum?" West asked.

"You don't know?"

"I know damn well they ain't here!"

Hank swallowed a hard knot down his throat. "Um, a couple hours ago they was found on the Four Oaks Road. Someone must've blindsided them. They're all dead as a doornail. Mr. Oliver Wilcox found Clifford Tingle's horse draggin' him down the road, foot caught tight in the stirrup."

"Shit! Tingle's dead?"

"Yeah, all three of 'em. I can't imagine who woulda done such a sorry thing. Gus Rivers, looks like he got the worst of it. Shot ten times in the legs and back."

"Who gave up this information?" West asked.

"Lanny Payridge. Said Wilcox went to his house right after seeing our men. Ol' Lanny came directly to me, told me of it. The sheriff's out there now with his deputies, clearin' the area. Rob Townes is across the way hammerin' down three coffins so they can bury them proper at the China Grove Cemetery. It's somethin' awful. Just a downright massacre!"

"You say someone came outta nowhere? From the woods?"

"That's what I was told," Hank said.

"You were told wrong." West knocked back his tin cup of highfalutin coffee. "Well, well, well . . . it looks as though we don't need a meeting after all. Those men weren't blindsided. They were fool enough to run into Dan Dean. He ain't one to hide out for the pounce. Dan fights when he's backed in a corner. Shit fire, man! Dan ain't in Texas. He's right here in good ol' Louisiana! Back home where he don't belong . . . and exactly where I want him."

Chapter 47

At day break Jim Maybin started clearing a section of his field to make way for a garden, working his old plow in the ground for rows of summer vegetables.

By mid-morning he took a break at his well. He pumped the handle and brought a gush of water into a tin cup, quenched his parched throat under the blazing sun. Then he removed his hat and drenched his graying head, the water cooling his scalp.

He dried his face with a rag.

Blinked to refocus vision.

Something moved between the spaces of pine trees outlining his back property, startling him. Whatever was back there was not small, but slow. Maybe a wild pig, panther, a deer? He wished he'd worn his guns, but rarely did he meet trouble in his own field.

Jim put the cup on the edge of the bricked well, shoved the rag in his pocket, and walked toward the corner of his property. On the way he picked up a fallen stick the length of a broom handle, crooked and blunt but heavy enough to do some damage if he had to defend himself.

His heart leapt in excited beats as he stepped closer to the unknown.

The thing moved again, spreading out a tall shadow.

Jim stepped into the foliage, leaves and acorns crunching under his boots.

"Jim?"

Jim raised the stick high. "Who's there!"

Dan Dean stepped out from behind a bush, holding the reins to his horse.

"Dan? What the devil are you doin' back here? You're supposed to be in Texas," Jim said.

"I'll fill you in later. First I need to hide Quaid."

"Of course. Come on out of there. You look like you could use a shave and a hot bath."

"Anything Rilla has on the stove will be mighty appreciated, too," Dan admitted.

"That we can do. Then you can tell me exactly what happened."

Jim hid Quaid in the barn with the other horses while Dan entered the house weary and hungry. Rilla prepared ham sandwiches on thick sliced bread bathed in mayonnaise and stacked with pickled cucumbers for her and Dan. Jim sat back on the couch, stomach still full from a breakfast of homemade biscuits n' gravy and scrambled eggs smothered in pink pig's brains.

Dan finished his sandwich.

"Would you like another, Dan? We have plenty, so eat you as much as you want."

"Much obliged, Rilla. This'll do."

Jim suggested they visit on the porch.

"I'd rather talk here if it's all the same to you."

Jim looked over at Rilla. She caught the unspoken message in his eyes, gathered her plate and excused herself from the table.

"Why aren't you in Texas with that girl?" Jim asked.

Dan watched Rilla walk outside and down the steps, making sure she was out of earshot before turning back to Jim. And when he did turn, the anger in his eyes glowed like wildfire.

"She is there, with my cousin and his family. The only reason I came back was to put John West in a grave," Dan said. "They're lookin' for me, I just know it. The evening me and Contessa were bonded in marriage, the eyes of our Lord weren't the only eyes looking at us.

"Gil Pickett, a rider I knew years ago, he was there accompanying fiddle in the ensemble. He left right after the last song, goin' east on his pony. I guess my suspicions got the best of me because I believed Gil was on his way to tell West where I'd been hiding out. I decided to come back and cut the head off the beast. Watch the body die."

"Was this Pickett fella part of the inner circle?"

"If that was the case he'd've picked a fight then and there. Gil is a shit-bird lookout on the edge of the circle. Like other scouts, he won't draw a gun on a man wanted by the clan . . . but that snitch'll inform the men who will."

Jim shook his head. "Jesus. They're connected to West from all sides!"

"Earlier I had a run-in with Otto Shrum, Cliff Tingle and Gus Rivers over on the Four Oaks Road."

"Did they make a move?" Jim asked.

"That's one way to put it."

"And you had to . . . ?"

"Wouldn't be here otherwise. I'm sure somebody's found them by now."

"Dan, no matter what, you cannot go at this alone. It's dangerous. You need assistance."

"Did you meet with the Governor? Is he sending out the militia to deal with the riders?"

"That particular meeting did not go as we expected," Jim said. "However, our visit was not in vain. I do have this." He pulled a slip of paper from his shirt pocket.

Dan stared at the seal of the Great State of Louisiana stamped on the paper and read the governor's signature: *Henry Clay Warmoth.*

"Pardons?"

"For each man." Jim uncorked a bottle of bourbon and filled twin tumblers. "I have more in my safe. Twenty-five in all. The governor's signature's on every one." He waved his hand. "I would've rather watched soldiers come in here and skewer those scoundrels, but as it stands politics played a large part in Warmoth thumbing down that suggestion."

"So I take it we're getting a posse up after all?"

"Shouldn't pose much of a problem. I've already sent word out to Jess Cady and Fred Boss to find some Aces High. In fact, we're meeting here tomorrow to see who'll be joining in the fight. Discuss a plan of attack on the whole dang gang!"

"I'm tellin' ya, it'd be more strategic to go after the circle one man at a time."

Jim slowly shook his head in disagreement. "Dan, those men have families. If we pin the devils at home they're liable to start a fight regardless. Put their wives and children in danger. They fire at me, by God, I'll unload on 'em. And I'm nervous innocent folks might end up collateral damage in the crossfire."

"Say we get 'em all in one place?" Dan suggested. "Then nobody else would perish."

"There's another hitch. How do we herd them to a single spot?"

"I'll think on it."

Jim drained the tumbler. "*Ahhh!* More whiskey?"

"Much obliged, no."

"I'll have another," Jim said, pouring a shot. He raised his glass. "To your new marriage! Congratulations, ol' boy."

Dan nodded, gave a weak smile.

Jim took note of Dan's blood-shot eyes and suggested he rest in the back room. "We'll eat us a good breakfast in the morning."

"Kind offer, thank you, but I cannot stay here longer than a solid nap. You've kids and Ms. Rilla in the house. As you stated, innocent people shouldn't stand in the way of our objective. Your family'd be in a fix if the clan tracked me here. I'll just go over and visit Clem Wilson. Lay low for a few days."

"We'll see you tomorrow evening then?"

"Come sundown," Dan said.

Chapter 48

Later in the day, Jim and Dan parted ways.

Well-rested and energized, Dan steered clear of the main roads, sensing that at any moment a clan member might approach him. He led Quaid along old Indian trails, getting lost in the thick woods as opposed to chancing worn out paths the riders used between towns.

Ever cautious, Dan crossed over Dugdomena Creek and rode to the backside of his own land. He and Contessa had left in such a radical rush for Texas that he'd forgotten to gather a few personal items he now wanted to retrieve—including his father's Liege rifle and mother's keepsake emerald brooch.

The last time he cried was when he heard the news of his mother's death. But to see what was left of his family home also brought on a sense of great loss, erupting within his heart emotions that he was not immediately prepared to deal with.

For quite some time he sat still in the saddle, blinking out tears, unable to fully accept the reality of what lay before him.

His childhood home had been reduced to fiery red embers flickering in heaps of gray ash. The only thing left standing was the old iron stove and a few long pieces of support timber, blackened and spinning off swirls of smoke.

"You Godless snakes," he muttered under his breath.

Whatever keepsake he wanted was now buried in the rubble, gone forever.

Dan turned his horse away and continued toward Clem Wilson's farm, infuriated by this unnecessary bullshit. He kept his head, determined to implement his plan. Negotiating a posse to seek and destroy the clan's inner circle had been his idea initially, but before that was carried out, Dan figured he could trim the herd by making one-stop visits.

He was near Earl Hargrove's house, so Dan decided he'd start with that trigger-happy bastard. Out of all the clan's members, Earl was quick to judge, quick to conclusions, quicker to shoot. Dan needed him out of the equation before the gang was brought together for a final confrontation. Given the chance, that maniac would blow the whole scheme shelling anything within arm's reach.

Earl lived with his wife and four kids on a ridge overlooking Rooster Cabin Creek in a brown clapboard house. At six-foot six he weighed over three hundred pounds, and had short, sandy blond hair and big brown eyes full of hate.

Dan had known him for years, and "Big Earl" had always been friendly.

But Earl Hargrove was as mean as they come. During train raids Earl always claimed a woman for himself, and that woman was usually a teenaged girl. He'd get his fix, then slit the child's throat, leave her wherever. As a family man carrying the weight of a horrendous past, living a double life as a Deacon at Mount Zion Baptist Church and executing the roles of loving husband and caring father, Earl Hargrove should've been made an example of long ago.

The setting sun formed a light blue evening around the house, sending shadows over lush green acreage. Dan heard Earl's kids playing in the back. Through a window he saw Earl's wife s peeling potatoes for a meal.

Earl was in the side yard, raking the last of September's leaves in a pile.

Dan tied Quaid to a skinny pine tree and crept out of the woods.

The closer he got, the angrier he became. It was men like Earl Hargrove giving this area a bad reputation. Earl might as well have been John West—a sad soul with no concern for human life, but who led a lifestyle convincing folks that he cared about God and his fellow brethren.

Bunch of horseshit, Dan thought. He eased up. "Earl?"

The man turned around, a look of surprise on his fat face. "Dan? What're you doing on my property?"

"I'm here to set you free."

Earl dropped the rake and pushed his hands out. "Now look here, Dan, I don't know what your story is but I ain't got no beef with you. You ain't supposed to be in these parts anyway. I heard you was . . . you been in Texas!"

Dan pulled his pistol, reached up and touched the barrel to Earl's jaw. "I'll ask you one question, and I expect the truth. Lie, and I'll spread your brains on that pile of leaves. Understand?"

Earl raised his hands.

"Drop your hands. Who torched my house?"

"It was West."

"Who else?"

"Um, a few more I believe . . . Maurice Washbow, Hank Wright, let's see . . . Darren Forte."

"What about Lawson Kimbrell?"

"It was just them."

"And you?"

"Yes, yes, I was there. But Dan, I was following direction. West is one crazed animal, you know that. I had to go along, or—or West would've—"

"You're a filthy, vile fool without a hint of decency. Say you're a family man then turn around and kidnap girls and boys for your perverted thrills. Your family deserves more from a protector than a sick-thinkin' beast that goes out and steals gold and murders children. I'm here to correct God's mistake."

"Hold on there, Dan." Earl stared at the barrel inches from his head. "If you wanna get personal, allow me to get my guns. We'll have us a stand-off duel, like General Andrew Jackson did! That's fair, ain't it?"

"You don't deserve a fair shake."

Earl closed his eyes, imagined a bullet tearing through his skull.

Dan secured his gun.

Earl opened his eyes. "Dan, I swear I—"

Dan unsheathed his blade and cut Earl's throat in one fluid motion, ending his plea.

"Gurgha! *Graagh*!" The big man fell against the house, blood spurting over his mighty chest.

When Dan reached the forest he could still hear Earl Hargrove's children playing in the back yard.

Chapter 49

Within an hour of leaving Earl's body lying in the grass, Dan visited the home of Hank Wright. As luck would have it, Darren Forte and Vince Sikes (two cowardly nightriders) were also present, smoking cigars and chatting in the front room.

Three against one was considered an unlucky ratio to most folks, but on this quiet evening these men were not expecting a fight. Dan could easily get the bulge on them.

He knocked.

When Hank opened the front door, Dan shot him in the stomach. Then he killed Darren and Vince in succession, both taking a bullet to the face.

He stepped over the bodies and searched the house for anyone else. He was willing to take on any nightrider—be it inner circle members or scouts.

Dan returned to Clem Wilson's house just before dusk.

Clem was an older gentleman who lived with his wife off the Old Harrisburg Road in nearby Montgomery. Having served as a three-term Sheriff of Winn Parish, Clem Wilson was well aware of the nightriders, especially during those early days when Uncle Dan Kimbrell and Aunt Polly occupied their house of horrors.

Dan rode up to the house, alerting three dogs into a yapping fit. A flock of chickens scattered.

Clem's wife, Pearl, stood on the porch sweeping spider webs out of the corners of the wooden supports.

"Well, I'll be. Dan Dean!" She set the broom aside. Held the hem of her dress from dragging as she stepped down into the yard. "For what do I owe the pleasure of your company on this lovely day?"

Dan got to his feet and gave her a hug. "I've just been dyin' to see my favorite girl. How've you been Miss Pearl?"

"Oh, I'm as swell as can be I suppose. Arthritis in my hand acts up every time the wind blows, of course, but other than that and this here gray in my hair I'm gettin' along fine and dandy." She held him by the arms, looked in his eyes. "How are you, Dan? Haven't seen you in church last couple of Sundays."

"I was out of town for a spell, Ms. Pearl. Is Clem about?"

"Yes, darlin', come on in. He'll be glad you're here."

Clem walked out of the back room holding a straight-razor, half his face clean and smooth. "Hey Dan. How ya been?"

"Do you have a minute, Clem?"

"Sure. Let me finish up. Pearl, get Dan some of that lemonade you made this morning."

"Have a seat and make yourself comfortable, Dan. I'll fetch you a glass," she said.

He sat in a Windsor chair and drank, looking around at immaculately cleaned floors and pretty decorations that colored the room. "Your house looks real nice, Pearl."

"Thank you, Dan. Ever since I resigned teaching those precious kids over in Calvin, I've had ample time on my hands. Cook more often, get more chores done, I make fancy drinks here and there. And well, seein' as how he's no longer politicking for votes to be sheriff, I visit with my dear husband more often." She lowered her voice and smiled. "Ha! Sometimes when I'm sweepin' the floors, I just want to sweep him on out the door, too!"

"I heard that!" Clem said, walking in. He leaned down and kissed her cheek. "I'd just come back to bother you."

She lightly swatted his belly with a hand rag, shook her head. "Silly man. I'll let you boys catch up. Dan, if you'd like more, we've plenty of lemonade and ice."

"Thank you."

Clem sat across from Dan. Opened a cigar box. He plucked one and struck a match. "Help yourself if you're so inclined, my friend. They're kinda sweet. Purchased three boxes in New Orleans at a quaint little shop on Canal."

Dan waved away the offer. "Not now."

Clem eased back in his seat and crossed one leg over the other. "Talked to Jim Maybin earlier in the day. I know why you're here, and the answer is yes. Stay here as long as need be."

"You know about the posse?"

"I do. And I'd be glad to participate. I'll be at the meeting at Jim's 'morrow night. You've got the right idea, son. Destroy that bunch of hypocritical lunatics as soon as possible. Way I look at it, every night that goes by they're on the move is another night somebody might fall prey to their diabolical designs."

"I'm relieved to hear this, Clem."

"Back when I's sheriff, I tried to catch the sonsofbitches in the act, had no luck. A grand jury won't convict any man without solid, substantial proof beyond a shadow of a doubt. Yet, when I was trying to capture any of those riders they kept piling up the bodies, gettin' away with untold evils. I found a well hid back in the woods up near Kotchee's Camp had close to fifteen bodies buried in it, stacked on top the next. Those men needed to be stopped *then*. God only knows the body count nowadays."

"They're still at it. West and his men burned my house. They're after me now."

"Not much happens within a twenty mile radius that don't get back to these ears, son. Damn shame."

"When we set the posse in motion, we'll stop most of 'em. Main ones, especially. I'm not so concerned about runners and lookouts. My aim is on John West and the men in the circle. Do you have a rifle handy?"

Pearl walked into the room. "Dan, I hope you're staying for supper. I'm fixin' goulash."

"He'll be around to put down a few suppers," Clem said. "As long as he pleases."

Dan smiled at his host. "Don't you worry none, Ms. Pearl. I won't be a bother like Clem here."

Chapter 50

"Sir, sir, please, I beg of you don't do this! I'm a father!"

Laws Kimbrell grabbed the man by the hair of his head and threw him down the well. The man's name was Joshua Lamar Mansfield, an eye doctor from Beaumont on his way to meet his extended family in Memphis, Tennessee.

His neck snapped on the ground like a twig.

Suspicious that gravity did not silence his witness, Laws Kimbrell dropped a lit lantern into the well. It burst in flames on impact, burning skeletal remains of past victims and the sweaty flesh of Mr. Mansfield. Ensuing screams of distress confirmed Laws's suspicion, as the fire extinguished the life of the family man.

Flames flickered across John West's red face as he approached the other side of the well. "Burnin' a man alive is a bit drastic, don't ya think?"

"Done it before," Laws replied.

"A bullet in the head would've served us just the same."

Laws turned to West, his eyes full of darkness in the firelight. "Perhaps maybe I should've impaled the sucker on my knife like that lil' baby. Remember the baby? The one kept screamin'?"

"There was no other way. Wiggly thing woulda brought on attention. You know we don't need attention during these operations. Actions like this here attracts attention."

"Damn it, West! That fire'll burn up evidence there was ever any bodies down there. What with Sheriff Rose investigating riders and the mayor in Natchitoches savvy to our *existence*—at this juncture, the best thing we can do is cover our tracks best we can. You should be grateful I'm settin' fire to this well."

Lec Ingram and Arthur Collins averted their gaze as the awkward exchange continued.

West was becoming more annoyed at his partner in crime. Instead of fueling their argument using loud, bone-cutting words, he calmed himself with a deep breath. "Laws, you need to use that aggression to help us find Dan Dean. I'm tellin' ya, he's back in the area!"

"Lec? You and Collins take Mr. Mansfield's horse to the livery," Laws ordered. "I'll stay 'til the fire burns out."

West handed Laws a bag of gold. "I'll run the rest of the loot to Horsehead Rock next hour or so. Just know your friend's back in town."

Laws would have traded the gold in his hands for a full night's rest. Several days had passed where sleep dipped in and out of consciousness as fleeting pleasure. He welcomed what little comfort he received but his muscles ached, eyes remained heavy, he forgot things. He'd been getting by on whiskey and catnaps and the occasional steak from Frost's Butcher's shop. Or some sloppy stew he juiced up with pickled peppers.

When he did close his eyes, if he *did* dream, only a singular image latched on.

And he was terrified of it.

The canvas of his mind displayed a pale, hollow-eyed baby grinning back at him, a grotesque black slit opening the middle of its belly. Its pink guts continuously spilled crimson over the knife's blade, covering the hand of its killer in lumpy, red warmth.

That baby could have lived on. It could've enjoyed life. Got an education, become a young man, created a family. Goddamn you, Lawson! Why did you kill it?

That wasn't all. His troubles in recent weeks had snowballed.

William confessed to his older brothers that he was ready for a quiet life, and so moved to Natchez, Mississippi, along with his longtime lady-friend. Laws hoped William stayed gone. If the young Kimbrell showed his face in the area, Laws could not protect him. Riders who left the ranks of the inner circle without unanimous permission from both clan leaders usually left in a nailed coffin.

Then there was his middle brother Shep—spending his days at the old house where Uncle Dan and Aunt Polly once practiced their dirty deeds. Shep regretted one particular night he joined his fellow riders on the Old Sparta Road. He thought it'd be another gain of easy money, but this robbery did not go as planned. The man they held up agreed to cooperate as requested, when suddenly the feisty brunette at his side wielded a pistol in their direction and fired. The shot shattered Shep's shin bone.

Now, like a horse with a broken leg, Shep was no longer an asset to the gang.

At least he's not a deserter, Laws thought.

Squinting through heavy smoke and the leaping, yellow flames of burning skeletons, Laws put a handkerchief to his nose, turned away from the stench. He thought of Dan Dean . . . had to warn him that West was on the search, as it was getting increasingly difficult to protect his old friend.

If Dan doesn't leave Louisiana, he'll be buried in Louisiana.

Rounding out these burdens, his lovely lady-friend Annabelle Frost was frustrated with him for some reason (there were plenty of reasons, he was sure), and had withheld opening her thighs—stating that she'd rather wait until they wed.

"Let's do it God's way," she said. "We'll enjoy relations again when we marry."

Laws initially took her suggestion in stride, but primal urges to take her body consumed him. Rejecting his advances was becoming a bit of a habit for her. He'd grown tired of her goody-two-shoes attitude towards intimacy. He missed kissing the softness of her neck . . . feeling hurried breaths hit his chest, the way she looked at him when it all felt so damn good.

Annabelle possessed pliable feminine magic that had started wars among men. Longing for that magic made him ill-tempered. Distracted. *Mad.*

Laws watched fire eat away at the clothes and flesh of his victim, his icy eyes giving off empty emotion, knowing in his sleep-deprived brain there'd be no pleasant dreams anytime soon.

Chapter 51

The next morning Earl Hargrove's wife, Katy, stormed into Sheriff Hayden Rose's office, her cheeks streaked white by dried tears, hair a mess, just all out flustered. She held the hands of her twin pig-tailed daughters while her six-year old son lagged behind, a tiny finger excitedly picking at his nose.

"Sheriff, my husband's dead!"

"Earl?" Hayden moved from behind his desk. "Goodness gracious, Katy. What happened?"

"I thought he'd gone off with his pals like he does, making a late night of it and all . . . but when I woke in bed, he wasn't beside me. So I went looking for him 'round dawn and found him lying in the side yard. I saw where they, it was so bad . . . somebody cut his throat."

Hayden shook his head at the ugly detail. "Do you have any idea who might've done this?"

"Why would I? My husband's a respectable member of the community. For Christ's sake, y'all go deer huntin' every fall. Why are you being callous like this?"

"Katy, I'm only trying to get some information here. Yes, I knew Earl, and yes he was respectable. I just need to know if you saw anyone else coming and going around your house in recent days."

"I did not see another soul at my house. I fed the children, ate supper, we all went to sleep for the night. Help me, Hayden. Please. Find the devil did this! Find him, and you *lynch* him."

"Mommy? What's a lynch?"

"Hush up, Angel."

"Mommy, can we get a sugar cane?" her son asked, blissfully unaware of the subject of conversation between his mother and the man wearing a silver star on his shirt.

"You ate a pear on the way here," she said. "Quiet now, or I'll give you another whoopin'."

Her son returned to digging in his nose.

Sheriff Rose donned his hat. "I understand you're angry and want something done quick, but a deadly crime may not be that simple to solve. I need to investigate further. When I do find the man who did this, I'll fashion a short rope."

Katy dabbed a polka-dot handkerchief across her forehead, frustrated by what would surely become a slow process in catching her husband's killer. She sighed deeply. "I guess that's that then. Come all this way to be turned away, told to wait. What happened to Earl is reprehensible. He was so good to us, he was . . . a good man, a hardworking man. My husband did not deserve to leave this world the way he did. I expect results, Hayden," Katy said firmly. "This is not right!"

"We'll look into it. In the meantime I'll send Grady Cobb out to retrieve the body before . . . ." he trailed off, thinking: *before rigor mortis sets in and insects start tearing at the fresh wound and crawl through orifices and create thousands of maggots*—but stopped short.

"Before what?" she asked.

"Before Earl starts to smell," Hayden said.

"Interesting choice of words for a fresh widow. I'll keep an eye out for the coroner."

Hayden watched Katy escort her kids across the dusty street. The sheriff knew of Earl's double-life as a family man by day and a nightrider the rest of the time. Earl was not respectable in Hayden's opinion, and he was only a good husband to his wife because he did not desire seeing his cover blown had he slipped up for acting an asshole.

Like West and Kimbrell (among other riders), Earl Hargrove was an exceptional liar living behind the beats of a cold heart.

Deputy Ty Ellis leaned against the door frame. Spat tobacco juice in a spittoon. "Who do ya think did this? West and his bunch?"

Ty was one of the few deputies Hayden trusted, so the sheriff did not see any harm voicing his opinion on the matter.

"John West comes to mind, sure. Perhaps one of the Kimbrells. Hell, it coulda been any of those jackasses. All I can figure is somehow Earl made an enemy of West, and West did away with him. Can't see otherwise why the leader of the riders would murder one of his own."

"Do ya think it mighta been someone else?" Ty asked.

"Other than a nightrider?"

"Yessir."

"Not likely. Who in their right mind would go after a nightrider in his own backyard? Use a knife, no less? Whoever pulled that stunt knew Earl on a personal level. The killer wanted to see his eyes when they cut him."

Ty put his hat on. "I'll hurry over to Ms. Katy's house and help Mr. Grady get the body."

The sheriff nodded approval. He had no proof that John West caused Earl's death. Hayden had already made the mistake of visiting West about the burned courthouse. Lacking substantial proof, he was not inclined to investigate a man of West's caliber regarding the death of several nightriders.

Hayden took his gun belt from the coat rack. Before he even stepped out of the office, Deputy Ty Ellis came rushing back inside.

"Sheriff, there's a lady out here just a hollerin' out God's good name and fallin' all about! Poor girl can't even make it up the steps."

Hayden went out to the front gallery.

Knees on the ground, hands shaky on the bottom step, the lady's normally pretty face was marked by dirt and tears. "Oh Lord Jesus! Please help me. Jesus Christ, please! I—I can't go on like this, not without him, *please!*"

Sheriff Rose immediately recognized the lady as Alicia Wright, Hank Wright's adolescent daughter. He knelt to help her up.

"Alicia, what's happened? Talk to me."

"Sheriff Rose, they killed him. They killed my father!"

"Who!"

"I—I don't know directly, I was at Auntie Mae's last night. Stayed with her 'cause she was feelin' under the weather and all, and when I got home this morning the door was flung wide open and my father was in the middle of the, he was on the floor in the front room . . . blood everywhere, and he, he's gone! Oh Jesus! Please save me from this!"

"Come with me, Alicia. Let's get you cleaned up. We'll figure this out." Sheriff Rose helped her into the office. "Ty, fetch her a wet rag."

"Yessir."

Alicia sat in a chair. Continued crying.

Hayden withdrew a handkerchief from his vest pocket. "Here, darlin'. Use this."

Alicia wiped her eyes, blew her nose, and twisted the slicked cloth in her lap. When she regained a hint of her composure she said, "There was two other men there."

"Did you see their faces? Can you tell me their names?" Hayden asked.

"No, I don't think so."

"If you give me a clue I might be able to catch them, Alicia. You do understand how important this is, don't you?"

"It would be important if they were *alive*. These men were dead, too. Right there close to my father."

"Did you know them?"

"Friends of my father, I'm sure," she said.

"No, no, what I mean is, can you tell me who they were?"

"I could tell you that, yeah, if their faces weren't shot off!"

"Please try to stay calm. I'm just tryin' to piece this thing together, find out who committed these crimes so they'll be captured and punished."

Deputy Ty returned carrying a dampened rag. "Here you are, Miss."

Alicia cleaned the dirt from her face and arms.

Hayden sat on the edge of his desk. "Ty, I want you to take Alicia to the hotel and tell Ms. Connie to get her something to eat. She looks hungry."

"What about Earl? Don't Grady need help movin' the body?"

Hayden grabbed the deputy by the arm and brought him into a side room, a safe distance from the girl. "Listen to me, son. Grady can take care of that sorry bag of shit Hargrove. Me and you, we're gonna go out and check up on John West."

"West? But I thought you said we shouldn't," the deputy said, fear evident in his voice.

"If my gut feeling's right, then it appears that West is killing off men who might know where his gold is buried."

"He has gold buried somewhere?" Ty asked.

"Oh, there's gold alright, but no one knows where to find it— except West. Sounds to me like some of his associates have inched too close to the location of that gold, and now West is putting down any member of the circle knows anything about it. Four bodies in one night? All of 'em nightriders? Only another rider would bring on hell like that. Go take care of Miss Alicia. Then saddle up."

Chapter 52

The sun's blinding heat scorched skin as Sheriff Rose and Deputy Ellis crossed the Dugdomena Creek on their way to the Four Oaks crossroads, a section of land where the nightriders had claimed untold lives.

Hayden was prepared to find out West's whereabouts the previous evening, but beyond a restricted line of basic investigative questioning his thoughts turned hazy.

If things got out of hand, did he have the guts to exchange firepower? Make an arrest?

Hayden was not frightened of his mission, merely concerned that a killer was walking free—be it John West, Laws Kimbrell, or any other nightrider in the clan. He took an oath to ensure the safety of his family and friends and the citizens who voted him to office, so he wanted to do right by the power given him. Although he'd never felt the need to track down a rider, this time was different. He felt an overwhelming urge to arrest the right man on the spot.

But another thing that bothered Hayden (if things spiraled out of control) was how many gunfighters John West would have at his disposal, ready to do the gang leader's bidding.

Hayden pictured an army of scoundrels set to waste him, staining the nice uniform his wife hung out to dry yesterday.

"So, what're we gonna do about Mr. West?" Deputy Ellis asked.

"Talk."

"That's it?"

"Yep."

"Say he don't wanna talk?"

"Then we arrest him."

"Why didn't you take West in that day you visited him? About the courthouse deal?" asked Ty.

Hayden slowed his horse. "Let me ask you something, Ty. Would you grab a snake by its head?"

"A snake?"

"Yeah."

"No way, Sheriff!"

"Then I'm sure you wouldn't fight *three* snakes, would ya?"

"Hell's Bells! Not me."

"What I'm about to reveal, you keep this quiet."

"Yes sir."

"The day I visited John West . . . that was the day I figured on catching him. Do the right thing and haul his ass in. Then watch a group of folks fed up with his gang strap a rope around his no-good neck and rip his head right off his shoulders." The sheriff lined his jaw with a plug of chewing tobacco. "Ya see, when I went out to West's house that afternoon, even though I had strong suspicion that West burned down the courthouse, there was simply no proof that he did so.

"I was performing my duties, investigating the matter as instructed by officials who've earned higher political rank than myself. The deputies who accompanied me there obey my orders so they'll stay on payroll. But they're mealy-mouthed backstabbers I never trusted. Shit, for all I know, when I spoke to West regarding his possible role in that crime those deputies could've had something to do with it just the same! Unlike you, Ty, Deputy Mitchell and Harwick are nothing more than yes-men for West.

"So I decided I wasn't going to fight three snakes. I held out. Thought there had to be another way to get to John West and his bunch . . . ha! Now that there're four dead riders, by God, that's all the proof I need to lock 'em up!"

"Why don't you get rid of Mitchell and Harwick? If they're not trustworthy and all," Ty asked.

"I'd need proof they're connected to the riders. Without proof, there's nothing to charge them for. They still maintain peace and order when other criminals come through town, so I can't dismiss them for doing their job. Only way to get rid of 'em is to get to West. Then the whole clan'll be washed out."

Deputy Ty pulled his horse to a stop, pointed through the woods. "Sheriff, *look.*"

Hayden turned swiftly.

Ty shouldered his shotgun.

The figure of a man silhouetted against the mid-morning sun came into view.

For a moment, no one spoke.

Hayden licked his lips to speak, reached for his gun, intent on accosting the stranger with lead-filled questions. But he retracted.

The silhouette clicked the hammer of a pistol currently aimed at Deputy Ty's head. "Tell your deputy we all got one life, sheriff. If he tugs on that shotgun, I'll end his. Tell him goddammit!"

"Back down, Ty. Don't try it."

The deputy gently dropped the shotgun on the grass, butt first.

The silhouette moved through the foliage and stepped into the grassy field. "It's good to see a familiar face."

"Dan? What're you doing out here?"

"Waiting."

"For what?"

"To kill John West."

"Well, that just might be the verdict when I get him in front of a grand jury. West's done killed four of his own men. If I were you I'd move on. Perhaps locate to another state."

"Someday, perhaps. Right now I won't leave Louisiana for any man's will or greed. Believe my words, Hayden. I am here to kill John West."

"I appreciate your interest. *However*. These dead riders don't concern you!"

"If you'll just step aside, I'll get him. Others too."

The sheriff nodded as though agreeing, even understanding, but Dan realized his words went unheard.

"Listen, Dan, as an elected official of Winn Parish I cannot allow vigilante activities in my town to trump my authority. It is high time someone answers for this violence, and as a man of your integrity and level of common sense, you might want to re-evaluate your stance here. To go after a living nightmare that is the West Clan will only result in bloodletting chaos of an ungodly nature. We don't want that, do we?"

Dan rubbed the pad of his thumb over the steel threads forged into the hammer of his pistol.

"I appreciate your concern, but in years past you have accomplished very little in stopping the clan from committing atrocities on folks passing through these woodlands. For that lack of diligence, many in town have scoffed at re-electing a man as weak as you to lead another term. They believe you'd allow the clan's rule to continue from here to Shreveport." Dan blew his nose on a handkerchief, folded and shoved it in his vest pocket. "Tell ya the truth, Hayden, I'm confounded to see you on this mission. You must've gone through a messy surgery."

"Surgery?" the sheriff said.

"Yeah, the surgery it took to replace your jelly spine with a steel one."

Deputy Ty stifled a laugh.

"Now see here, Dan . . . ."

"How else can you explain going after John West? After all these years, why now? Why all of a sudden do you see fit to take down West, or any member of the clan at this time?"

"Dan, look, I've always respected your opinion, but you've got it all wrong. I know the law, and the law states a grand jury cannot prosecute a man without *proof.* Substantial proof that points to the guilty party. Me? I've been helpless all these years. Most of my deputies are in cahoots with the clan besides, so when people are robbed on the Harrisburg Trail or Four Oaks Road, the blood dries up in the dirt and those bodies are gone before I hear of the incident. Burned, buried, shifted down river, who knows? To hell with your spine talk! Even when I look into a crime born of recent hearsay and *know* the clan is behind it, the very proof to bring these psychotics to justice simply doesn't exist!"

"Sheriff?"

Hayden turned to his deputy, eyes narrowed in anger. "What!"

"Why not give Mr. Dean a chance? He seems like he wants to go to battle. If we do it by law, we would have to go out and secure writs and a summons signed by Judge Obie Ryan, then gather up folks for a jury. Just a big hassle when you study on it. Shoot, I say let Mr. Dean go about his business and let's turn a blind eye of sorts. That's my two cents, anyhow."

Hayden gripped the leads, ready to kick his horse into action and forget this entire conversation. "Your opinion might hold water if not for the simple fact that I now have proof of death. Proof John West killed his own riders. Unlike the past, today I have witnesses who came across the bodies. The victims are there. The ladies who found them are alive and screaming for justice and it's now my job to see to it that John West receives the comeuppance he deserves."

"That explains your new spine," Dan said. "But how do you know West sent those riders to the grave?"

"Simple. Him and Laws Kimbrell are killers and it looks to me they're out for blood in their own gang. Those riders went and pissed them off somehow, that's what I think."

"It's all well and good you've a theory of how they were dealt with, but that's all you have—a theory. I'm the only nightrider with proof. I killed them, sheriff. Earl Hargrove, Otto Shrum, Cliff Tingle, Gus Rivers, Hank Wright, Darren Forte, even that squirrely Vince Sikes. And I'll finish off the rest soon enough. Clean up this area quick-like. So, I don't need interference from you, or any lawful force, because this has to be done my way . . . for what they've done."

Sheriff Rose considered Dan's confession and line of reasoning in destroying the clan. If he arrested Dan on threats of murder, others would come to the young man's defense, putting the sheriff in a difficult position at keeping law and order—all while the clan remained free of justice.

He spat on the ground. "What in the hell do you expect me to do, Dan? I have four dead nightriders, a grieving widow, and a hysterical daughter on my hands. More kin will likely come forward asking about the other men you dispatched . . . so what am I to do? Stay clear of it?"

"That's exactly what you do. Be content someone else is doing the job Winn Parish's sheriff and his three deputies couldn't accomplish. Besides, if you try to stop me, you'll be spitting on the fresh graves of those the clan murdered. Or will. As you know, folks around here get pretty unfriendly when their safety is threatened." Dan holstered his pistol. "Are we on level thinkin'?"

"Why is it all of a sudden you believe you've been granted this phantom power to surpass my authority? I'm the man with the badge, remember?"

"You got a badge, but I've got the pardon slips."

"Pardon slips?"

"You're damn right. It was sent down on high that this mission must be completed, no matter the odds. Armed with God's blessing and Governor Warmoth's signature, I've been granted the privilege to kill every last nightrider. You're welcome to join me if you still feel the need to use your brand new spine . . . . Failing that, stay out of my fuckin' way."

Chapter 53

Thursday.

"Let's go again!" Lynn demanded.

Andrew furrowed his eyebrows. He wasn't in the mood to give Lynn any hope of winning. "Why? I done beat ya both times!"

Lynn put his elbow on the edge of the desk. "Come on. One more and that's it."

They locked hands.

"Ready?"

Lynn nodded.

Andrew slammed the back of his brother's hand on the desk.

"Ow! You're mean, Drew!"

"I told you I'm stronger than you. You've got little baby arms."

"At school I beat Gary Sercy. He's bigger than *you*."

"That ain't sayin' much. Gary Sercy is a fat hog. Just because he's big don't mean he's strong. I'd beat him arm wrestling. Shoot, Sissy Ledbetter could whoop him down."

"Someday I'll be as strong as you, won't I?" Lynn asked.

Being the older brother had its advantages. At this moment, hearing that question, Andrew could either crush Lynn's spirit or give him hope that yes, some day he'd also be sixteen years old and those scrawny baby arms would be a thing of the past.

Andrew sat on the side of his bed. "The time'll come when you might get stronger than me. Just remember, dad says real strength is here." He tapped his heart with his fist. "You've already got that in spades, little brother."

Lynn smiled. "That's all fine and dandy but I can't wait 'til I get some dang muscle!"

"Shh! Hear that?" Andrew walked to the bedroom window, pulled back the drapes. "Look there. It's Gary's father, Mr. Sercy. He's talkin' to dad."

Out of the darkness of the back porch a curious group of men arrived carrying lanterns.

"What're they doin' here?" Lynn asked. "Is dad havin' a bash?"

"It don't look like everybody's happy-go-lucky, so my guess is no."

"Does mom know they're here? Think I oughta go get her?"

"No! Stay hushed."

*****

Twenty-five men were invited to join the posse.

Eight showed up.

Dan spread the pardons between his fingers as if showing off winning gambling cards. He searched the faces of men standing before him in the backyard and thought: *This is real. This is happening.*

"Friends, thank you for coming by this evening. You've all been given crucial information on the mission ahead and what you do for the posse in the next few days is entirely voluntary," Dan said. "Do not be concerned about a backlash of criminal charges. Jim and I have made certain that you will each remain innocent of any wrongdoing as we proceed.

"But know that what we have in mind requires courage and vigilance on your part, so I trust every man here is prepared to risk life and limb for this cause."

Silence.

The crowd seemed more interested in drinking whiskey while being away from the wife for a short time than discussing their future duties.

Taking this reaction as a willingness to attack their fellow man, Dan handed the pardon slips to Jim. "Your assistance in this venture is greatly appreciated and will not be forgotten. Now we need to find more hands."

Jim stepped into the light. "Dan, these are all we've got."

"It ain't enough."

"How many men you suspect are in the nightriders?" asked Landon Fulcher

"Several," Dan answered. "Around twenty or so."

"Ain't no way we'll beat that many assholes in a shoot-out," shouted John Wilcox.

"Who said there was gonna be a shoot-out?" Jim Maybin asked.

"Most of them are messengers for the gang. Our aim is to get the riders that make up the circle, the ones who commit the murders outright. Namely John West and Lawson Kimbrell. Used to be eight men in that outfit," Dan said. "They might have more in the circle these days, but I assure you West wouldn't operate with less."

"When do y'all 'spect we'll do this?" Wilcox asked.

"Sooner the better," Jim said.

"How's Sunday?"

"But Dan, this Sunday's *Easter* Sunday," Hiram Bertrand affirmed. "I wouldn't figure it a very righteous thing to do. Go hunt down them scoundrels on the day Mr. Jesus Christ left that cave."

Mumbles arose in agreement.

Dan raised his hands in a calming gesture. "Hold on, now, let's think on it. Most of the riders are family men. They take on family responsibilities. Make weekly visits to town. Attend church. Not every clan member will be available that day, but I bet the bulk of them'll be in town or at church." Dan took a shot of whiskey off the railing and peered into the amber-colored liquid. "If that doesn't assure victory, let's look at it another way. What better time to bury the devil than the day Christ rose from the dead?" He drank.

"Dean's got a point there, Hiram," said Fred Boss.

"Any objections?" Jim asked.

By the prevailing silence, everyone seemed to be in agreement. Not one man protested the day of reckoning that would be visited upon the West-Kimbrell Clan. Clem Wilson even agreed to shell out an abundance of firearms and ammunition for their proposed attack.

"Next Sunday it is then. I've got seventeen extra pardons, so we need to try and get seventeen more men to help round up as many nightriders as we can."

Fred Boss raised his glass. "Wait just a goddamn minute, Jim! How are we gonna get a concentration of the riders all in one place?"

Jim thumbed over at Dan. "Why, don't you fellas know? My old friend Mr. Dean here, he's an ex-nightrider. He knows their signals, passwords, hideouts, everything. He'll lure them right to our trap."

"Where's this trap gonna be set?" Jess Cady asked. "Out in a field somewheres?"

"No sir," Dan replied. "After Easter service, we'll meet up and search out the riders. Then get 'em where they least expect any kind of intrusion—smack dab in the middle of Atlanta, Louisiana!"

Chapter 54

Initially uncertain about the upcoming cleanup, the gang of men left the meeting feeling excitement lift their hearts, proud that they were doing right by the community.

Jim waited until most of the volunteers were out of earshot, then took Dan aside.

"Didja have any luck tracking West earlier?"

"He wasn't home. Saw a couple riders in back smoking a hog. Other than that, it was quiet. Thing is, my search got curious before I even arrived at West's property."

"How so? You meet up with some more of them crazy punks?"

"Ran into Sheriff Rose. Him and his deputy, some scrawny kid with a gap in his teeth, they were on the way to confront West about the riders found dead this morning. I explained to him that that was my work, and in so many words told him I was going to get rid of West."

"How'd he react?"

"He was against it. Claimed I didn't have the right to do such a thing. Didn't seem all that surprised, though. Then I told him we were gathering a posse of like-minded men to go after the clan's circle. And when I mentioned the pardons he closed his mouth. Matter of fact, there's a chance him and that deputy of his just might join us in this undertaking."

Jim patted Dan on the shoulder. "Good work. Can't wait to see how this'll pan out Sunday."

"Ready, Dan?" Clem Wilson called from the yard.

"You go on and head out. I'll be along later."

"Suit yourself. The door'll be open."

Dan retreated to the forest, believing it best not to be seen among the crowd leaving Jim Maybin's place. A couple miles later he came to West's property above Little Hill Bayou. The property was fenced on all sides, acre-to-acre, fronted by a ten-foot gate with the decorative letters JRW scrolled along the wrought ironwork. The large house was well-lit and guarded by several dogs.

Locating a perfect hiding spot in the thick, jungle-like woods, Clem Wilson's borrowed rifle at his feet, Dan noticed many nightriders arriving at the place.

He lay in the grass patiently, ready to send a bullet through the clan leader's brain.

Cut off the snake's head and the body will die . . . but getting a bead on the gang leader proved to be a difficult task.

For two solid hours Dan sat at the base of a tall, bushy pine tree, hidden behind the foliage, never once catching a glimpse of John Robert West.

Nowhere pressing to be, he waited patiently.

*****

Every nightrider of the inner circle had been summoned to West's house for a scheduled meeting to discuss recent activities. Especially damage control. The men sat around eating smoked hog meat with mashed potatoes, purple hull peas and cornbread, talking amongst themselves. They also enjoyed tin cups of whiskey and thick slices of pound cake courtesy of West's wife, Mrs. Sara.

At West's request, she had taken their girls into Natchitoches to see a Shakespearian play on the banks of the Cane River. She was given specific instructions to return around ten o'clock.

West sat in the corner holding court among Laws Kimbrell, Butch Hawkins, and Copeland Yates. When he'd cleaned his plate, West pulled a handkerchief from his vest pocket, wiped his mouth, and stood. "All right men, y'all lend me your ears."

The room fell quiet.

"Ever since the courthouse calamity, we've made solid progress in these last few weeks by not getting caught. Files detailing past activities that named certain members of the clan were burned to ash. We accomplished exactly what we set out to do!"

"Hell yeah!" one of the riders yelled.

"Now, because of this jolt to our local judicial system, you'd think there's nothing to fear, but you'd be wrong in thinking that. Folks around here've heard rumors about the clan and its members. Some of our names have sprouted up among those curious enough to go yappin' away to somebody else's ear. You see, the fact that we destroyed written information concerning robberies or other unlawful activities that could lead back to us does *not* mean we're in the clear. There are those out there who might try and convict us on sheer determination, on mixed up gossip. We can't be discovered. We must strike first!"

"Yes!"

"I suggest we move forward and get the bulge on District Prosecutor Jay Dungart. We do this before he puts together any remaining evidence, or relies on bullshit hearsay that points the finger at us for the courthouse burning . . . *before* that righteous bastard reaches out to his lawyer cronies in Natchitoches and has them sniffin' for proof we ain't been playin' fair. Raise your glass!"

Everyone did.

"I need two men for this operation," West said.

"I'm willin'," said Harold Basco.

"I'll go along," said James Frame.

"It's settled, then. Jay Dungart will find a new home in one of our wells before he fixes a case against us." West took a bite of pound cake and talked as he chewed, crumbs falling over his beard. "Now, as several of you may have heard, we lost some good riders recently. Otto Shrum, Tingle, and Gus Rivers were gunned down out at Four Oaks Road, just yesterday. Earl Hargrove was gutted like a pig soon after that. Heard his wife damn near tripped over him in the yard this mornin'.

"Hank Wright, Vince Sikes and Darren Forte were found in Hank's house, all of 'em shot point-blank range. I don't know who you think did this, but I believe it's the work of one man. And that man is Dan Dean!

"I want y'all to be on the lookout for this scoundrel, now. He's a pain in my red ass and a slippery son of a bitch, to be sure. If and when you do meet up with him, don't be deceived by his charm and handsome garb—he is a Confederate Infantry soldier and gun thrower who can and *will* put a hole in your head before you reach. I suggest y'all split in teams when ya can and hunt the area for him. The man knows too much, and if he talks we'll all be finished.

"Burned court documents or not, Dan Dean is that one loose string that could tie us all to crimes we've committed. Dean was a nightrider before me and Laws created the inner circle—and long before any of you came along searchin' for adventure and easy takes. He knows our secrets. He knows where the bodies are buried. The man knows how to destroy our livelihood!" West touched the scab above his ear, then pounded his fist on the countertop, knocking over an empty glass. "Have no mercy on him."

*****

Can't fight 'em all . . . not here . . . not alone . . . .

Growing disillusioned and increasingly frustrated that he would not get his kill-shot tonight, Dan rose to his feet, ready to leave. He might have been a sure shot, but Dan Dean was no dimwit. He realized that he was in no position to kill John West without creating an all-out battle on his hands. If they followed the sound of the blast, the nightriders would overpower him.

Just then several riders filed outside.

Dan noticed a familiar face in the crowd of men gathered on the wide walkway. The man removed his hat and drew his arm over his brow, giving Dan a good look at his rugged features under the lamplights.

"That goddamn . . . *traitor*," Dan whispered, recognizing Ridley Sercy among the other riders.

As one of the volunteers at Jim Maybin's meeting earlier this evening, what reason did Ridley Sercy have to fraternize with John West?

He came here to warn the clan of the cleanup! Dan suspected.

Sercy waved goodbye to a group of fellow nightriders and got on his horse.

Dan watched the man stride across the expansive front acreage and take a right on the Natchez Trace that curved around John West's land.

Dan led his horse through the trails to where it opened onto the road, then shoved his foot in the stirrup and swung up in the saddle.

Ridley was now about a half mile down the dirt path.

Dan kept a steady pace, careful not to cause a stir near West's place.

When he crossed the Four Oaks Road, far enough away that a gun blast might sound like a firecracker, Dan quickly gained on Ridley Sercy.

Dan rode up behind the man and clicked the hammer to his Colt .44.

Hearing that all-too-familiar sound, Ridley pulled the reins to his horse.

"Stay still, or I'll put a hole in your spine," Dan said.

Ridley faced straight ahead. "Who the hell are you?"

Dan remained silent.

"What do you want from me, stranger?"

Still silent.

"Mister? I ain't sure what you're after," Ridley said, confidently. "But it's not a polite thing to point a gun at a man's back. Furthermore, I will give you a gentleman's warning that should you harm me, you'll answer to the West-Kimbrell Clan. Ever heard of them? Because you're about to."

Dan kept his gun trained on Ridley's head, said, "The nightriders, huh? Oh, I ain't overly concerned about them."

Ridley licked his lips. "A careful man would be."

"Are you a nightrider, sir?"

"One of many," Ridley claimed with pride. "Stranger, if it's gold you want, I have a few coins you can take. We'll just agree this never took place, and you can move on down the road."

"You're not a nightrider. You're a liar."

"Beg pardon?"

"If they get buttonholed, a real nightrider wouldn't dare give up his gold," Dan said. "A real nightrider would fight to the death for his dignity, thieving pride, and worldly possessions. I believe you're a put-on. No matter how you try to sound sure of yourself, I can hear the fear in your voice. It's clear, because you know that any second now you might die."

Ridley sucked in a deep breath, looked to the stars. "All your observations aside, doesn't seem fair that I haven't seen your face, stranger."

"You want to discuss fairness? How is it fair that you attended Jim Maybin's call to arms for a posse that would likely rid this town of the riders, then the next thing you're in cahoots with John West himself?" Dan nudged his horse alongside Sercy's. "Didja warn him of our plan, Ridley?"

Ridley saw Dan's face in the bright moonlight and knew he'd made a terrible mistake going off at the mouth.

"Shit," Ridley huffed.

"Shit's right. You betrayed the trust of good men. Everyone at Jim's house this evening are men of their word—Aces High. I believed you to be of the same caliber, Sercy, but you proved me wrong. What did you tell John West?"

"Not a thing."

"Just how long *have* you been a nightrider?" Dan asked.

"Six months or so," Ridley answered.

"Long enough to know their agenda."

"Yeah, but I . . . ." Ridley moved the back of his arm over his sweaty forehead. "Look, West knew I was well-acquainted firsthand with men you and me both know. Some of those men even joined Maybin's posse this evening. In the beginning West offered me gold, a *great* amount of gold—the price is pumped up higher when blood's on it—to go out and get information about local folks here.

"Where they lived. How they made their money. Who they knew. Secrets, I guess, that West might use against 'em—threats and whatnot, if they ever found out he was the leader of the clan. It was insurance him and Lawson possessed, you see, in case any of 'em spoke up to authorities about the riders. Or sent correspondence to the governor's office, or whoever might set forth a plan of action to see to their arrests." Ridley smiled at Dan. "All in all, I'm a glorified news reporter in the outfit. I've never killed anybody. I been on a few robberies and saw a bunch of things I'd rather forget, that's for sure, the way they went about it and all. I mean, Laws Kimbrell, that man is one crazed monster when he wants to be. Him, West, and Ab Martin and Copeland Yates, they robbed a train up near Shreveport back in November. I saw that clear-eyed and sober. Realized pretty quick I was working for a ruthless crew.

"But me? I ain't never killed nobody. Extra money is what it is to me, nothing more."

"What did you tell West?" Dan repeated. "About our posse? Our plans?"

"Well, if it'll ease your nerves I didn't let on that you and Maybin and those Aces-High were plannin' a clean-up for Sunday. Tellin' West that story'd be a waste of his time. Y'all ain't a threat to us. Ain't got enough men anyhow. Shit, Dan, we'd massacre the likes of you and Fred Boss and Mr. Cady and the others by sheer force!

"And John West? Hell, he'd bust a gut laughin' at the very idea that you and six-er-seven men hounded a hunt for him. He's in charge of men who simply don't care about human lives." Ridley swallowed a heavy knot down his throat. "I might've said you were cooped up at Clem Wilson's house. Maybe not. What with all the whiskey I poured down my throat, I can't be too sure what I said. My mind's a little blurry."

Dan steadied his gun once again.

"Put that thumb-buster away, Dan Dean. I have a son. I'm married to a great gal that—she, she won't be able to make her way if! Not without me. I'm tellin' ya, if you pull that trigger the clan'll send a heap of riders after your hide. They'll make you pay in blood!"

"Ridley, you're a coward."

"Listen to reason, Dan. Just forget we crossed paths, and everything'll be fine."

"Do you even know the difference between a coward like you and a man like me?"

Ridley chuckled. "What Dan? What's the difference?"

"I'm the *real* nightrider."

Dan fired.

Ridley touched the bullet hole that had suddenly torn through his stomach and fell to the sun-baked ground, the hard hit snapping his neck.

Dan took the reins of the freed horse and moved on down the road.

Chapter 55

Biding his time at the Higher Learning School of Winn Parish, Andrew Maybin could hardly concentrate on his studies. A war had lit up in his mind. Nervous energy made him impatient, ready to burst apart. He and Lynn had vowed not to say a word about their father's plan to destroy the nightriders, but Andrew knew there was strength in numbers. Judging by his father's count, eight farmers with guns against sixteen or so outright killers was just as unlucky a fight as a cat jumping into a yard full of hungry dogs.

Andrew waited until all students left the English Studies class, then cinched the carry straps around his books and approached the desk.

Standing six-feet-two, his wavy brown hair streaked by lines of gray, Professor Kendrick George towered over his pupils. He kept trimmed a curled mustache, wore tailored suits and bifocals, and carried a sense of importance about himself usually reserved for elected officials and other assholes. Unlike some of those people, he was extremely intelligent.

"Professor George?"

"Yes, Mr. Maybin?"

"There's something you need to know. Say I tell ya, please don't go bother the sheriff about it. Mayor, neither. You must keep quiet. Don't even tell my father."

Professor George removed his eyeglasses and looked up from his sheaf of papers. "Is there something wrong? Are you in some sort of trouble?"

"Not yet. What I'm gonna tell you can get bad real quick, though."

Intrigued, Professor George closed the door to the classroom. "Have a seat, Mr. Maybin. Tell me what's on your mind."

"My name is Andrew. Call me Andrew. Now . . . if things pan out the way I hope they will, you'll end up in my father's gang."

Professor George smirked at his pupil's comment. He sat on the edge of the long wooden desk, folded his hands at his stomach. "Andrew. What are you trying to say?"

"What I'm about to tell you is a secret. Just a few folks know this information. So from here on out I need your word that you won't mention it, unless you're instructed otherwise."

"Goodness gracious, Mr. Mayb—Andrew. Your sincerity! I'm inclined to believe that this is a matter of life or death."

"It *is*."

"Then you have my promise of sworn secrecy."

"Ok. Ya see, last night me and Lynn—"

"Lynn and I—"

"—Lynn and *I* overheard my father outside talking to a group of men. Eight of 'em, in fact . . . ."

During the half an hour, Andrew explained that his father had gathered men for the sole purpose of destroying the nightriders once and for all. "Lynn started crying because he's afraid dad will get hurt. I'm worried for dad's safety, sure, although I am sympathetic to his mission. The only choice I have is to assist my father any way possible."

Professor George crossed his arms and touched a finger to his chin. "How do you propose you'll help your father by taking on this dangerous endeavor, Andrew?"

"Well, I was thinkin' that me and you can—"

"You and I—"

"Stop doing that! Just listen. Me and you and other students, we show up armed to the teeth and help get rid of those wicked bastards. That's what I propose, sir."

The professor looked at the floor. "I understand your concern for wanting to right a wrong. I do. These men, this clan, I've heard of them, and if a posse should go after them, don't you think that posse should be in the form of the armed military? Or, Peace Officers?"

"My father has already made a trip to N'awlins for that very reason, and the governor can't do a thing about it. The sheriff can't do nothing about it, either. Damned politics. That's what I heard dad say last night," Andrew said. "I can't very well stroll up to my father and say 'gimme a gun, I'll join your group.' He'll tell me no. You, I can tell, Professor George. You'll keep quiet about it because I trust you'll be part of this scheme."

"What, exactly, do you want me to do?" he asked Andrew.

"Governor Warmoth gave my dad signed pardon slips. So if any man in that posse kills a rider, he's granted clemency."

"When is Mr. Maybin planning this undercover assault?"

"He said something about this Sunday."

"Easter?"

"What better time to kill the devil than the day Lord Jesus Christ came back from the dead?"

Professor George gathered his papers and tucked them in his leather briefcase. "While I do not condone your father's method of execution in this venture, I understand he has a burning will to fight. I'll see if I can scare up the help you need. Until that time, let's keep this discussion between us."

Chapter 56

Pearl Wilson was thankful to have the house to herself this evening. She relaxed in a bath under the light of a glowing moon, feeling calm winds caress her skin through opened windows.

She entered the kitchen dressed in a nightgown that reached her toes and smelled the sweet scent of peaches in the air. She learned this recipe, among others, from her mother. Pearl covered a long dish of bubbling hot peach cobbler in a cotton towel and pulled the dessert off the stove, set it on the counter. The cobbler was like a pan of sweet, crusty lava now, so she waited for it to cool.

To pass the time she sat in a chair and continued crocheting an afghan she'd begun days ago.

She was suddenly distracted by the flash of lights shining across the front yard, moving around in the brush like fireflies, drawing closer to her property.

Put on guard, she set her needles and thread on the floor and strolled over to the long-barreled shotgun leaning against the front window. She checked the chamber, relieved it was loaded, then set it back in place.

Better safe than sorry, her father once advised her. Clem was out of town visiting family, and she was not expecting company this evening.

She stepped outside, keeping the door open in case she had to move in for the weapon.

Her dogs Oscar and Max went into a riled frenzy as three horsemen approached her house. She recognized the leader of the lot as John West, a deacon at her church (who was also rumored to be part of that nightriders outfit). She had a feeling he was here sniffing around.

"Quiet down!" she yelled.

The dogs hushed to a whisper.

"Mr. West?" she asked.

"Hello Miss Pearl! Glad you're home. Don't you look lovely this fine evening."

Skin dampened from bathing, her curly white hair tasseled and drying in the humid air, she smiled and said, "That's awfully nice of you to say so, Mr. West, but looks can be deceiving. I am actually feelin' worse for wear. It's been one heck of a day, and I was about to retire for the night."

West waved his hand dismissively. "Won't take but a moment of your time. I need to talk to Clem. Is he about?"

"He's visiting cousins, over in Montgomery."

"Then I shall catch up with him later. For now I have a simple question for you, Ms. Pearl, and a simple answer will suffice. Have you seen Mr. Dan Dean?"

"Dan Dean?" Pearl said. "Yes, I have."

"Whereabouts?"

"Oh, it's been a couple months now . . . that's right, it was in Olla I saw him last. At a barn dance."

"No," West said, getting evermore impatient. "Have you seen Dan Dean in the past *day* or so?"

"Why? Is something the matter?"

"I heard from a reliable source that Mr. Dean is here . . . settled at your house."

"You're mistaken. Mr. Dean is not on my property."

West moved forward. "I won't suffer liars, Ms. Pearl. If he's here, go on and fess up and we'll leave you be so you can get a good night's rest. We need to speak to the ol' boy."

"Well, as a curious citizen of this town who's married to the previous sheriff of this parish, I want to know why y'all are lookin' for that young man."

"Answer the question kindly, Ms. Pearl. Is Dean around?"

"If you're that danged determined, come on in and take a looksee. Ain't gonna find anything 'cept that peach cobbler coolin' on the counter. You gentlemen are welcome to it if you're hungry."

"We appreciate the offer," said West, dismounting. He slapped red dust off the thighs of his pants and walked up the steps, his big hands sliding along the railing, that sly, alligator grin forming over bright white teeth in the lamplight he held near his face. "We won't be but a minute or two. And we would sure love a corner piece of your fine cob—hey!"

West saw the shadow of a man drop from a rear window. The clan leader pulled his sidearm at his hip, peered down the breezeway, and aimed at wavering movements in the dimly lit darkness.

"Who's that there, Miss Pearl?" West yelled.

Pearl retreated inside, slammed the door.

West waved Maurice Washbow and Ab Martin into action.

The riders split off around either side of the house.

Seconds later a shot rang out.

West sidestepped into the wall, shocked to see Maurice Washbow's horse running free in the field, a lone saddle wobbling on its back.

Ab Martin quickly returned to the front steps. "Shit! Dean just put a hole in Washbow's head!"

West took in a deep breath, deadened fear in his bones coming alive. At the end of the breezeway the man moved into light. West fired six shots at the shadow until the trigger of his pistol lay flat under a mad finger. "God*dammit* Dean! Show yourself!"

Dan appeared around the corner of the house, pistols in both hands. "One down, West! Which would you care to be? Second? Third? I'll shoot Ab's knees out so you can reload."

"Oh no, no, no, Mr. Dean. *You* will perish tonight!" West pulled out his other pistol and resumed the fight.

Dan lunged backward and rolled along the grass, simultaneously firing lead at West and Martin.

Ab fell against the railing, arm limp at his hip.

West dove inside a window, shots sailing past his head. Kept low to the floor.

Just then, Ms. Pearl was upon him holding the tin dessert pan above her head. "Why do you want to hurt that nice! Young! Man!" She unloaded the entire pan of hot peach cobbler on his face. "Leave him be!"

"Augh—you crazy bird!" West yelled, slapping pieces of cinnamon crust and gelatinized peach off his face.

Pearl grabbed the shotgun and hurried outside. "Dan? Dan, are you okay? Oh my word!"

Ab Martin staggered toward her, holding his bleeding shoulder. "Please, Miss. Help me!"

Pearl searched the property but found no sign of Dan.

Then two other people emerged from the darkness.

Fearing that more riders had arrived to aide their leader, Pearl stepped to the front door.

"Ms. Pearl! What's happened? We heard shots."

The unexpected guests were her neighbors, Tillman Farrington and his gun-toting wife, Beth.

"My dear Lord, Mr. Farrington! It's John West . . . he's causing all this ruckus! Started shooting up the place, and I—"

"Everything's fine here, folks. No need to be alarmed." West stepped out onto the gallery, the side of his face reddened from the cobbler burn, vest colored in peach chunks. Roughed up from the gunfight, he shook it off and assumed the colorful persona he'd perfected over the years. "I was on the hunt for a fugitive in this area and had reason to search out the Wilson property here—me and my deputies." West looked at Martin. "Go get Maurice and his horse and we'll leave these nice folks alone," he said, turning his attention to the neighbors.

"Your soul is polluted by evil, John West! You tried to kill Dan Dean!"

"Kill? Oh no, Ms. Pearl. Your accusations are false. A man such as Dean needs to be stopped. I was only defending myself and my deputies from that devil."

"Dan's back in town?" asked Tillman.

Pearl said, "If not for West and his men, he'd still be here for sure."

"No need to get hostile, Ms. Pearl. Please point that shotgun elsewhere. We'll be on our way."

"You'd better speak the truth of what happened. Or me and my neighbors here are gonna make a citizen's arrest!" Pearl warned.

West's eyes burned with hatred. "Ms. Pearl, the truth is that you knew Dan Dean was on your property . . . and you flat-out lied and said different. *That* makes you an accomplice! You helped him hide. Dean's a fugitive of justice, and because you behaved like you weren't savvy to his whereabouts, then you're guilty as him."

"What did Dan Dean ever do to be deemed a fugitive? If anybody needs a hangin', it's *you*, John West! From the tallest pine in Louisiana. There's one in the backyard fit for swinging high a no-good coward like you!" Pearl yelled.

West again focused his attention toward the neighbors. "I should arrest all three of y'all!"

Tillman took his wife's free hand. "Now see here, West. We heard gunshots and felt the need to seek out the welfare of Ms. Pearl. That's the reason we're here. Ain't no wrongdoing in being a concerned neighbor."

"And seek you did, Mr. Farrington. But how do I know you weren't also rushin' over to assist Dan Dean escape? . . . or be party to our gunfight? Unless proven otherwise I've got to presume, as a Constable of the Law, that you might've had a hand in Dan hiding out with our dear Wilsons.

"Your pretty wife has a firearm aimed my way, and that alone is a threat to any peace officer. A threat for which she'd be punished. Furthermore, I could arrest you and your wife for the crime of aiding and abetting a fugitive like Dan Dean. Legally speaking, I could even have you both hanged."

"I saw what ya did," Pearl said. "Get the hell off my porch, or I'll put a bullet in your gullet."

West's predicament would give any man pause. If he kept at it and allowed deep-seated anger to overcome a cooler head, odds were he wouldn't survive an ensuing fight. He swallowed his pride, stepped off the porch.

Ms. Pearl kept the shotgun trained on John West as he walked to the side yard, where Maurice Washbow lay broken on the ground, his brain's blood splattered in an arc across the horse's rump.

Ab Martin affixed the rider crossways on the saddle of his horse. "What about them?" Ab asked, thumbing back to the neighbors and Ms. Pearl. "Me and you, we can waylay 'em right now!"

"Keep talkin' and you'll end up like Cliff Tingle holdin' your guts in your hands. Right now's not the time to claim more blood." West looked at Pearl and her neighbors, nodded, smiled. "When those three catch a bullet, so will Clem Wilson."

Chapter 57

That night Dan crossed the Dugdomena Creek and Old Harrisburg Road toward Atlanta, keeping to ancient Indian trails rarely utilized by the majority of riders. As he pressed on he watched throughout the tight panorama of tall, skinny pines for any horsemen on the main thoroughfare.

He stopped at Clear Spring to fill his canteen and let his horse drink. He'd rather doze off in the cool weather with his back against a fallen limb and his hat brim slanted over his tired eyes than move on, but Dan could not afford the luxury of sleep.

West probably had men searching the trails already. In this fight, an unconscious gunfighter was a dead gunfighter.

In need of a bath, a change of clothes, a fulfilling meal, and more ammunition, he washed his face of dirt and sweat in the cool creek. He continued traveling to the one place he felt safe; where West and his nightriders wouldn't find him: the home of Ms. Linda Youngblood.

It was well after midnight when he arrived at the small log cabin situated behind Drake's General Store. The properties were separated by a quarter acreage of land that bled into the forest. For added privacy, Ms. Youngblood kept a large, groomed hedge blossoming with honeysuckle. This natural fence barred her from seeing a bunch of locals habitually enter the back of the store and walk the stairs to the saloon, where they'd get soused on whiskey and lies.

He made his presence known by waking three sleeping coon dogs, their wails piercing his ears. Once they got a sniff of Dan's scent, though, they licked his palms and wagged their tails in anticipation of a belly rub.

He knocked on the door, peered through the window.

A light flickered on.

"Who's out there!"

"It's Dan," he whispered. He watched through the window as the lamplight floated toward him, then heard latches unlock.

Ms. Youngblood opened the door an inch and raised the light to see his face. "Well, my goodness Dan! What in blazes are you doing out there disturbin' JuJu and her brood? Come inside, son."

"I didn't mean to wake you, Aunt Linda."

"Of course you meant to wake me. How else would you have gotten in?" She turned back down the hall. In the front room she lit more candles, making shadows tremble over the walls. She sat beside him on a long couch and positioned her petticoat over her ankles.

"You're in trouble, son. I can see it in your eyes. Smell like gunpowder, too. What's happened?"

Dan gave her a brief summary of the evening that transpired at Clem Wilson's house, and how he'd narrowly escaped a vengeful firefight with West and his riders.

"I never did like that sorry excuse for a man. Low-down rascal if there ever was one! John West needs to meet his Devil's due far as I'm concerned. I've thought about bringin' the subject to the authorities but denied myself the pleasure. Who'd listen to a widow like me? His wife should know it, but Sara's such a fragile thing. You know Sara's a friend of mine, and those kids, they're just precious. I just can't see me breaking her heart by telling her the truth about her no-good husband." She patted Dan's leg and smiled. "I'm proud you're safe, son. Your mother would be proud, too."

"I'd hope so," he said, looking off. "I miss her terribly."

"We all do, darlin'."

"Aunt Linda, I must warn you that West has riders after me this very night. Answer the door for no one." Dan looked in her eyes. "In two days you'll notice a lot of unusual activity near the General Store. You see, me and a few other men are planning to gather up the nightriders and . . . *deal* with them. It'll happen Sunday, after church."

"When you say 'deal with them', you mean . . . ?"

"I'll put away your doubts and call it a cleanup."

"But, Dan, why? Why in the world would you put yourself in danger like that?"

"Because the clan's leveled their hand of evil far too long around here and it's high time the citizens of Winn Parish put an end to that madness. We have a posse. Fred Boss, Jess Cady, others, they're all in this with me. Come Sunday we're gonna make quite a scene on the other side of that honeysuckle hedge.

"It's only fair I make you aware of this. Men who got nothing to lose will be in close proximity to your house. If one of them somehow gets away and seeks shelter here, grab that 8-gauge shotgun Uncle William left you and shred their heart."

"Lordy be, this is chancy. But don't you fret, Dan. I'll open the door for you, not another soul. Now, go on and get in that back bedroom and lay down. You look like you're about to fall over asleep."

Chapter 58

Will Drake spent his Saturday morning eating breakfast in the company of his wife and daughters. They enjoyed buttermilk pancakes, sausage links, fig pie and fresh milk at a table fashioned from an Oak tree that he felled in his backyard the summer of 1868.

Looking at their cherubic faces, his heart full of sin, he felt sorrow for his loved ones, as it would take some time before they learned the truth guiding his actions. Whether they forgave him remained to be seen. Will Drake was about to carry out his plan— one he'd probably regret. There had been no coercion from outside influences. He based his decision solely on that green monster full of empty promises—pure greed.

The monster often whispered in his ear on quiet nights . . . saying that once he accomplished his plan, he'd cultivate a better life elsewhere. His store was not managing so well this year. Customers were seeking out new businesses in bigger towns. He was losing profits.

And in these times of economic hardship, without any skills beyond that of a merchant (and a damned good one at that he'd tell you), Will was unsure how he'd support his family.

He'd miss them. God, if there was anyone he'd miss, it would be his daughters, Hailey and Hanna. And his wife, of course.

Sweet Rebecca.

Will put these thoughts out of his mind and focused on their time at hand. He realized that this moment of peace marked the last breakfast they'd enjoy together before he intentionally split up the family.

Hailey poured a sticky line of homemade sorghum over two buttered pancakes. "Daddy?"

"Yes, pumpkin?"

"I wanna wear the blue dress, but Hanna says I can't wear the blue dress."

Will looked at his wife, perplexed.

"For Sunday services," she explained.

Hanna folded her arms across her tiny chest and frowned. "I said it already, you can wear the *white* one. Mom made the blue dress for me. Not you!"

"Okay, girls, that's enough squabbling. Hailey? I told Hanna she could wear it." Rebecca pointed her fork at Hailey. "You may wear the blue dress next Sunday."

"But *mother*," Hailey began.

Hanna smirked. "Ha, ha!"

"If you two keep it up, you'll spend this beautiful day in your room writing a two page report about what you'd like to be doing outside," Rebecca warned.

The girls, ages seven and eight, frowned at the thought of such creative work and bowed their heads, continued poking at their food.

I certainly won't miss the bickering, Will thought.

Rebecca wiped her lips with a cloth napkin. "Honey, what do you say we go into Natchitoches this evening and take in a nice dinner on the river? I heard a theatre troupe is passing through town to stage a play."

"Why, that sounds fine. The girls would enjoy that. Shakespeare?"

"Homer, I believe."

"I'm sure we'll have a grand time," Will said.

*****

Hailey and Hanna enjoyed a fun-filled day skipping rope, swimming in nearby Clear Creek, and playing hide-and-go-seek instead of jotting down on paper the things they'd like to be doing outside.

The afternoon tea party wasn't as pleasant, though. Their squirrel dog, Sparky, sat in the grass, tail swishing, staring at fat cat Rowdy. Sparky may have barked a few times, which enticed Rowdy to issue a deep, whiny growl, but the pets were relatively calm and attentive for nearly three minutes . . . when out of nowhere Rowdy charged Sparky in a fit of rage, jumping across the table and spilling the tea jug and fine china all over the ground.

While their guests gave chase into the woods, the girls were called inside the house for a stern talking-to about borrowing Momma's china tea cups and saucers.

"Maybe one day when you two have to pay for nice things, you'll understand the importance of taking care of something valuable. Not only did this dishware cost a pretty penny, it *is* special to me, and I expect it to stay in my cabinet! My Heavens, I have *told* you girls time and again these dishes are not to be used for tea parties. Use the tin cups for get-togethers with Sparky and Rowdy," Rebecca said in a huff. She pointed down the hallway. "Y'all go to your room. I'll boil water for your baths."

Hanna protested. "But mom, I don't wanna take a bath."

"Little lady, if you sass me again, come Sunday you won't be wearing that pretty dress you covet so, because you'll still be sitting on a sore butt. Now, your father is taking us into town tonight to see a performance on the river and we're leaving in one hour. Get on, now."

Hailey and Hanna smiled at the thought.

Although they had been given a what-for *and* a spanking, that punishment was a side note compared to visiting Natchitoches. Any type of outing served as a special time for the girls, but going to the "little town on the river" was always the best.

They couldn't wait to eat boiled crawfish paired with fists of cob corn and seasoned potatoes. Even the buggy ride into town was energized by the anticipation of good food and entertainment. They envisioned lights shimmering across the Cane River and people strolling along bricked streets in the fresh night air that smelled of jasmine and seasoned shrimp.

Around four o'clock, Rebecca finished putting up her hair for the evening. She walked into the guest bedroom to retrieve a pair of white dress gloves, and found Will lying on the bed. He had a pillow over his head, a cotton robe covering the lower half of his body.

"Will? The girls are dressed. Why aren't you ready? Are you okay?"

Will barely shifted the pillow, his hand moving to his stomach. "It's my stomach, darlin'. Maybe something I ate—whatever it is, it's making me vomit something awful. I cannot make the trip into town. You and the girls, if you're so inclined, can go on without me."

Disappointment fell across her face like a shadow. Rebecca understood that a stomach ache could really hinder one's motivation to leave the comforts of home.

"No, that's not necessary. We'll just stay here the night."

"Y'all go into town," Will urged. "Take the buggy and have a fun time."

Rebecca shook her head. "I won't travel with our daughters unaccompanied. Not with the nightriders about. Who knows what may happen?"

"Not a thing will happen if you just strap a red sash on the saddle horn. Any nightrider notices you, they'll turn the other direction, I promise you."

"Your daughters were looking forward to spending a nice evening with the two of us. What am I to tell them now?"

"Jesus Christ, Rebecca, tell them I'm sick. Sick as a dog!"

"I guess Mother Nature had her own plans for you." Rebecca sighed and turned away. "I'll steep some tea. You'll feel better."

"Dr. Tolli's Elixir would make me feel better," he quipped.

Rebecca left the room to inform Hailey and Hanna that they were not going into town after all.

When the door closed, Will took in a deep breath.

He'd planted a seed. His plan was in motion.

He was healthy as ever before.

Chapter 59

April 20, 1872
Easter Sunday

Thunderstorms rolled in early, painting the town gray and making mud of the trails.

In spite of dreary weather, folks arrived at church in good spirits, eager to enjoy fellowship and hearing the story of the Resurrection of Jesus Christ. As more folks arrived the rains gently dissipated, revealing clear skies.

A beautiful day abounded.

West escorted his wife and daughters inside the building, down the aisle, and to the front pew, all smiles and nods. Like many, the family was dressed impeccably for this special occasion. Pride swelled within him as West became aware of several nightriders in attendance—some of whom had never once stepped foot in a church.

When Brother Jimmy Skaggs sang the first note of the morning hymnals, the church came alive in vibrant harmony. The cheerful congregational choir sang a tribute to the power of Jesus Christ's love of man with such songs as Amazing Grace, How Great Thou Art, Rock of Ages, and He Leadeth Me.

Of all Sundays, Preacher James Weeks sent word to the deacons that he was suffering a severe head cold, and that services should continue accordingly.

West garnered little resistance from the other deacons when he took it upon himself to preach the Easter sermon.

His Bible in hand, he got behind the podium and adjusted his tie. Raised his hands toward the congregation. "Brothers and sisters, welcome to the House of the Lord on this fine Easter Sunday!"

"Amen!"

"Yessir, Amen!" West repeated. "Folks, I'm sorry to say Preacher Weeks is feeling under the weather this morning, so please send up a prayer of healing for our blessed brother. I will try and do my best in his stead." West asked the congregation to open their

Bibles to Luke 23:44-47. West read the verse verbatim, with enthusiasm:

"It was now about the sixth hour, and darkness came over the whole land until the ninth hour, for the sun stopped shining. And the curtain of the temple was torn in two. Jesus called out with a loud voice, 'Father, into your hands I commit my spirit.' When he had said this, he breathed his last. The centurion, seeing what had happened, praised God and said, 'Surely this was a righteous man!'"

"Surely a righteous man *indeed!*" West said. "For three days hence, the son of God would be risen from death and live eternally with our Heavenly Father!"

"Amen."

"What does Easter mean to you, folks? I can tell you in one breath, with absolute certainty, what this day means to me." He spread his arms on the podium, catching the ears of his audience. "Faith."

"Amen!"

"Faith that we will live another glorious day. Faith that Jesus Christ, our personal savior, will never leave us as we live out our days on this old earth. That a righteous man was not found in the burial tomb on that third day is a testament to God's wonders!

"I have faith, brothers and sisters, that we shall meet our God one day and sing his praises for all time." West slowly walked around the podium, his arms locked behind his back, a demure expression transforming his face. "Why faith? Because we were put here to recognize the fault of man, to see the sin in our own hearts, to send the devil's works back to hell using our *faith* in Christ. The *power* of Christ! Easter is not only about Christ returning to live again. Easter is about *us* living again."

"Amen brother!"

For the next hour, John West kept his audience captivated, citing scripture and personal testimonials of God's existence. He spoke of God's forgiveness to those willing to turn from their wicked ways; preached the love of Jesus Christ for those downtrodden souls who never gave Him a chance to be their spiritual protector; how the townsfolk should spend their days without fear—"because fear is having no faith!"

Jimmy Skaggs was asked to lead the closing hymn.

John West stepped down to join in, looking out over the congregation. "Thank you all for allowing me this wonderful opportunity to rejoice in the glory of our God, our savior. May Christ keep you, brothers and sisters!"

"Amen!"

Chapter 60

Soon after another rousing round of hymns praising the Son of Man, the congregation was dismissed.

As the crowd wandered into the mid-day heat, several folks passed by John West and remarked favorably on his sermon. Proud that he'd made an impression on the churchgoers, West thanked them, then made his way over the front lawn where Lec Ingram and James Frame awaited further instructions.

"Don't drag heel, now. Get 'em in there quick," West ordered. "Y'all got rope?"

"There's too many eyes around to do away with 'em," Lec said.

"Shit, ya crazy bastard, we ain't gonna put the four of 'em down right here. Tell them we're gonna take 'em to—"

"Brother West?"

West saw Mrs. Rebecca Drake holding her daughters' hands. She wore a light blue dress and had tucked her short blond hair under a white bonnet. She looked much younger than her age of twenty-eight.

"Sister Rebecca. My, don't you look lovely this fine day. And look at your daughters! They're pretty as peaches."

"What do you say, girls?"

"Thank you," they said in unison.

"We enjoyed your sermon. It's the best I've heard in a long time at this old gospel mill."

West tipped his hat to her. "My pleasure, Ms. Rebecca. Thank you for coming."

She patted his arm. "I won't keep you, Brother West. Have a wonderful afternoon."

"You do the same." He watched them walk away, then said, "Ms. Rebecca?"

"Yes?"

"I noticed your husband was not in attendance today."

"It's funny you spoke of Preacher Weeks earlier. You see, my husband fell ill last night and was feeling the same this morning, like our good preacher. Will said that we should attend services without him, for fear he'd pass on his symptoms. He asked me to open the store. Mr. Milt Hensley is managing the business today."

"I am sorry to hear of his complications. Tell Will we're praying he heals soon."

"Thank you." She moved a curl of hair over Hailey's dark brows. "Brother West, would you like to join me and my girls for lunch at the hotel?"

"That's a mighty kind offer, Ms. Rebecca, but my Sara has plans for Easter festivities at home. I believe there's a smoked ham, black-eyed peas, and a doomed pecan pie involved." He grinned.

"Have a blessed day," Mrs. Drake said, and escorted her girls down the dirt road to the hotel.

Dressed in black trousers, a cleaned white shirt, a silver pocket vest, and handsome black blazer, James Frame tapped West's shoulder.

Still grinning, West turned.

"They're leavin' the church lot," James said, pointing across the green lawn. "Want me to stop 'em?"

"James, that's exactly what I want you to do. Escort them to the saloon. Be casual about it. We mustn't breed attention our way over this little mishap."

Going about their day, Clem Wilson and his wife Pearl (along with their neighbors, Tillman and Beth Farrington) were accosted by West's men.

"Mr. Wilson? I have orders to take you into custody. You and your wife."

"What's the meaning of this, son?"

James nodded at Tillman. "That goes for you, too, Mr. Farrington. Mrs. Beth. Let's not make a scene, now. Come with me and we'll get this settled."

Clem put his finger in James Frame's face. "You listen to me, you stinkin' dog turd! We ain't goin' nowhere with you. Go on, step aside, or you'll get hurt."

Lec Ingram produced a length of twine. "Turn around, Mr. Wilson," he ordered, "before this gets serious."

"You're gonna tie my hands?" Clem asked, his face flushed a deeper shade of anger. "For what? What crime have I committed for you to take this action against me?"

The commotion brought on the attention of a small crowd.

West cringed. He was uneasy, thinking that his men may be regarded as doing wrong in their eyes, so he stepped over and said, "Folks! Folks! No need to be alarmed." Then motioned toward the four of them and searched the crowd's curious faces. "These people did a bad thing, y'all. As an active constable, I hereby arrest these folks for sheltering a fugitive from justice!"

"You bald-faced liar!" Clem Wilson addressed the crowd: "Friends, don't listen to this snake. John West, your constable, your bible studies teacher, the so-called deacon who gave us today's sermon about God's love, visited my house last night and *shot* up the place! Fell through my window like a fat drunk and broke it all to pieces. Pearl threw hot peach cobbler on him because he was such a nuisance—just look at the marks on his skin! That in itself is a waste, because you all know how good her cobbler is. And now? Now, Mr. West has the nerve to accuse me and mine of committing a crime? Our neighbors too?

"West, you know damn well Tillman and Beth came over last night to check on my wife, make sure she wasn't harmed—nothing more. This fugitive you speak of? It's Dan Dean." He turned back to the crowd. "A man who's never wronged any of us, least of all this heartless pig!"

Maddened by Clem's sudden outburst, West ordered his men into action.

"Get his guns! Tillman's too. March 'em over to the store."

Onlookers knew that Clem Wilson and Tillman Farrington were long-time residents of the community, salt-of-the-earth family men who obeyed the law. Arresting them seemed downright wrong.

Even so, not one person questioned John West's accusations on the matter. They simply looked on as James Frame and Lec Ingram removed the belts from the men's waists and escorted the four captives at gunpoint toward the store's back entrance.

Breaking away of the crowd, West walked beside Clem, a grin forming across his chapped skin. "Listen here, you mouthy fool, before you say another word or act out further, I must tell you with absolute certainty that I have no moral frame of mind that hinders me from shooting your wife in her heart." West patted Clem on the back like an old friend, pushed him gently forward.

As Clem passed by the townsfolk, he noticed Jim Maybin and Jess Cady staring back.

The two men nodded in Clem's direction as if to say, *go along, we'll take care of this.*

Holding Mrs. Pearl's hand, Clem whispered, "Don't cry, darlin'. We'll make it out alive. John West is a snake, no doubt about it . . . but snakes die all the time in Louisiana."

They were taken upstairs to Will Drake's saloon where scattered groups of men played poker at square tables and drank beer from clear glasses. The men glanced up briefly at the sight of the foursome, decided the matter was not theirs to question, and minded their cards.

As planned, Laws Kimbrell was waiting in the saloon for Clem Wilson. The rider licked the length of a rolled cigarette, tapered the paper ends and poked it between his lips. He sparked a match on the wood and sucked in a puff of gray smoke. "Tie 'em at the end of the bar. I'll keep watch 'til we ride 'em into Natchitoches."

"Natchitoches?" Clem asked. "Why Natchitoches?"

"Well, Mr. Wilson, it just so happens that some wildcats burnt down the Winnfield courthouse. We can't rightly prosecute you all without placing you in a proper setting, and the nearest courthouse is in Natchitoches across the Cane River. The hell of it is we'll need the use of another lawyer to see to your case. Troubling news, in fact. Last night Mr. Jay Dungart passed away." Laws turned to James Frame. "What happened to him, James? Suffer heart problems? Fell and hit his head?"

"He fell alright. On my *knife*." James tapped his chest. "Right here. Here . . . and over here." The detail James left out of the story was that Saturday evening Jay Dungart was nabbed from his home, stabbed several times, and pitched in the murky Bayou Rouge near the town of Beaux River.

"You boys don't know what you're doing taking on folks like us!" Clem yelled.

Laws slipped his gun out of its leather holster and touched the cold barrel to Clem's neck. "Calm yourself, old man. You and your friends sit over there and have a drink. West will be here to take y'all to the big town. Then we'll get this mess settled. Until then, close your mouth, drink up, and let's get along like jolly old pals."

Laws did not lie to Clem Wilson and Tillman Farrington about the upcoming trip.

Earlier in the day, after explaining to Laws the events of the shootout with Dan Dean at Wilson's farmhouse, West made it clear that after completing some pressing errands this afternoon that he'd return for the captives.

"Then we'll escort 'em out of town," he said.

John West informed Laws that at the very least they would travel The King's Highway *towards* the Town on the River, which would assure their prisoners that they were indeed traveling in the general direction of the parish courthouse. But should the prisoners meet an unfortunate "accident" along the way, well, that was out of his hands. "A man could get shot in the back," West told him. "That horse and buggy might get submerged in Saline Bayou and all them would die under water. Never can tell what'll happen out there on the trails."

Laws watched as James Frame and Lec Ingram secured the men and women to chairs at the end of the bar.

When he finished his duty, James approached Laws.

"Look here, Laws. I'd help guard these folks, but West wants me to go out and hunt a big buck with him."

"Better go meet up, then. You know how West is about delays. Me and Lec'll keep eyes on this group." He nodded at Clem Wilson and Tillman Farrington, crushed out his cigarette in a tin ashtray. "Go ahead and tell West that if any of these nice folks get feisty, y'all won't have to make Natchitoches after all."

Chapter 61

In the space of an hour John West had deserted the God-loving, sunny disposition he'd impressed upon church members and was now hidden in the forest beyond the Old Harrisburg Road, his dark side alive again, keeping watch for a Big Buck named Bryson Whitaker.

"Didja get that wild card Wilson settled down? Him and the others?" West asked.

"Yeah. Laws and Lec're with 'em," James answered.

"You did a fine job back there, son. Keep your wits about ya and you'll go far in this outfit. Be a shame to end up like your careless brother."

James did not respond to the comment. He only wished he could locate the woman who shot Dave Frame, make her pay with blood. West had advised him not to stress over ideas of retribution, because "her time'll come," he said.

James asked about their Buck.

West looked down and sighed as though bothered by the question. "Bryson Whitaker? Known him for years. Helluva business man. Radical, though. Got word he sold his land over in Cane City and he's making the trip to buy up some property in this locality. Anyhow, the man travels this way every Easter to visit his daughter and her husband, that 'ol Hughes boy has that crawfish farm up near the Rouge Bayou. Difference this time is, his visit'll be *permanent*."

West tugged at the reins of his horse.

"Stay here and keep an eye out, son. Bryson's a big man—bigger than me—so he'll be sittin' high on the bench. He's got big money, to boot. When you see him, strike up a conversation. Likes to chew your ear about fishin' and whatnot. Get him in the woods and I'll shut his mouth."

West turned his horse and disappeared between the trees.

It was odd, even a bit out of character, that West would abandon a stakeout (especially a proposed robbery of this scale), but James thought better of asking the gang leader why. As an underling who followed orders, he did what was requested of him, and waited patiently for the Big Buck from Cane City.

*****

John West led his horse deeper into the forest around sky-scraping pines and within minutes arrived at Horsehead Rock. The other evening had been a hurried affair when his gang intercepted a man with means. He suggested they shoot their victim in the head and get it over with, but Laws burned the poor soul alive in the Prescott Well.

West figured there was no talking sense to another madman, so he stowed away the gold in his saddlebag, intending to bury the treasure by the rock that same night. Instead, feeling tired and not so adventurous, West put off the task in favor of going home, where he scarfed down two slices of apple pie Sara prepared that morning, and finally drifted off to dream on her fainting couch.

Now was the perfect opportunity to add those heavy coins to his collection. While he was at it, West figured he'd grab some gold bullion for future use. A nice plot of land on the Cane River was up for sale, and he wanted to secure it before anyone else got wind of the deal and claimed the real estate. He planned building Sara a nice house on the spacious lot, somewhere else the couple could call their own during their golden years, after his daughters were married off.

West looked around Horsehead Rock. Alone in the ancient woods, he listened to chirping birds and felt calm winds lift tree boughs that splayed curvy shadows across his pink face.

He dried the sweat from his chin and cheeks using the collar of his brown shirt, then pulled a key from his pants pocket. Always in his possession, this key was one of only three created. The key was more important to West than his gold-plated, jewelry-encrusted bullhorn that currently resided on his nightstand at home.

This key opened the riches to the West Clan, revealing every stolen shiny piece of jewelry and every gold and silver coin—all of the bundled bricks of paper money and gold bullion stacked tightly in the wood-and-brass encasements. All here. All safe.

These ill-gotten gains were the result of blindsiding travelers, sure, but he'd admit to any of his victims that it wasn't personal. The only reason he robbed people was to get their means of wealth, nothing more. John Robert West was as sadistic and greedy as any land pirate, but on every single heist, he did not set out to harm. Killing for the sake of killing was not his driving force. He robbed people for their gold; killed them for their silence. Over the course of dark years, something as hateful as injuring another person simply served as part of his routine operation. This way he could satisfy his greed and flee undetected, assuring uninterrupted freedom—because John West thought absolutely nothing of taking a life. Murder, he once told Laws, was necessary in their line of work, and as simple as "smushin' a bug."

He unlocked one of three lockboxes. Lifted the top.

Blood instantly rushed his head, turning his face the color of blooming roses. Staring down in disbelief, he could hardly catch a breath.

The box was empty.

He went to work on the other two lockboxes.

Empty.

Nearly empty.

Pushed to one side of the third box lay four bags of gold, a bag of jewelry, and two gold bullion. These chests had not been pried open—whoever stole the loot had *unlocked them.*

West, Laws, and Will Drake each possessed a key. They were the only men who knew that the bulk of the clan's treasure was buried underground at Horsehead Rock in the middle of this vast forest. West did not suspect Laws Kimbrell of this hijacking. Laws wouldn't have done such a thing. Half the treasure was his anyway, and now almost three-fourths of the whole lot was missing. Had other thieves stumbled upon it? Long shot, but not impossible. A more plausible explanation was that somebody knew where to dig. Some lucky crook would have resorted to beating the locks in to gain access, and these boxes did not appear damaged.

Whoever committed this robbery used a *key.*

West figured he had the culprit fingered, but surely Will Drake was smarter than to pull something stupid like steal from the clan.

As the reality he'd been robbed blind sank in, West saw red and struck his fist on the side of the lockbox. "Back-stabbing, thieving horse's ass!" He transferred the remainder of the treasure to his saddlebag, then slammed down the lid and left Horsehead Rock in a rush of anger.

Will Drake understood the consequences that would emerge should he talk about the treasure, or dare try taking any of it. West, Laws, and Will had discussed this deal years ago in a secured room, over steaming bowls of jambalaya and warm beer. It was agreed that Will Drake would keep the books on the clan's finances, in exchange for compensation on each take. In addition to this responsibility, Will became the keeper of one of three keys for a single reason: if and when Laws and West were caught and sentenced to hang, Will was instructed to grease the palms of those in charge to secure their freedom.

If no amount of their stolen goods could save their heads, Will was then given the task of transporting the lion's share to the clan leaders' families so they may live a prosperous life at the absence of their protectors.

But West was not locked behind bars awaiting the hangman's gallows. He was alive and well and now ready to make Will Drake pay the ultimate price.

Why did Will Drake do this?

I warned the fool once, West remembered. *Once should have been enough.*

During that first meeting, when Will agreed to keep the clan's accounting and provide a safe meeting space at his store, West did not mince words or chase the devil around the bush. He came right out and said it.

"Now that you know where our stash is, if you speak a word about this to another person, I'll throw you in a well. Take any of that gold, and I'll bury you *and* your family." West gently pulled out his hunting knife. "With this."

Will raised his hands. "Yes, yes. I understand, John."

West pressed the blade to his skin and drew a straight slit down the center of his palm. Passed the knife to Will.

"Shake on it."

Will accepted the weapon and proceeded to puncture his hand.

They shook.

Circumstances now begged the question why Will Drake would put his wife and daughters in immediate danger.

The crazy bastard sealed the deal with blood. He went back on his word. He knew what I'd do.

*****

"Any luck?"

James turned to the sound of John West's voice. "Been a lot of traffic to and fro, but your buck ain't sauntered down this road."

"Forget it then. We've got hunting to do elsewhere. Move on south of Winnfield and put your ear to the ground for Will Drake. If you find him, bring him back to Atlanta. I'll meet you there in an hour or so. We still got to get Clem Wilson and his neighbors out of the saloon."

Not one to question an order from his superior, James nodded, and quietly stepped away. But after hearing the energetic hype about bushwhacking this Bryson Whitaker character for his big money, curiosity nagged at him. He had to know why they were deserting their previous plan.

Getting up the nerve, James said, "Is it more important trackin' Will Drake than to wait on this big buck you been tellin' me about?"

West grabbed James by the collar and nearly shook him off his horse. "Open your fucking ears, Frame! We're huntin' Will Drake right now because he's the biggest buck you'll ever sight in. Don't ask questions. Just get after the son of a bitch!"

Chapter 62

The town of Atlanta buzzed with foot traffic as several families enjoyed lunch at the hotel lobby, or picnicked by Clear Creek in the clear sunshine.

Through the window of his Aunt's house Dan Dean had witnessed Clem Wilson and his wife and neighbors be escorted upstairs to the second floor of Will Drake's General Store.

He did not know what John West had planned for them, but figured it wasn't good.

The ex-nightrider served as a crucial element in leading the posse to victory, but before any success was gained Dan Dean also needed to safeguard his identity. He knew that most (if not all) current clan members were probably following John West's direct orders to find him. He had to apply special caution in gathering riders because if someone outside the trusted posse recognized his face, their cleanup agenda would be devastated.

Dan covered his nose and mouth with a blue-and-white paisley handkerchief, then holstered his guns. He looked out the window, to the sky, and prayed:

"God Almighty, have mercy on the hearts of the innocent for what they're about to witness. Give me peace, strength, and focus . . . so that I can do what needs to be done."

Before leaving the security of the house, he once again reminded his Aunt Linda to only open the door for him.

Tears formed in her eyes as she hugged her nephew. She gently pulled back, touched his cheek, gave a sad smile. "You be careful out there, son. Those men're no good."

*****

At Maybin's request Fred Boss nonchalantly scoped out the saloon. He returned with interesting news: Clem Wilson and Tillman Farrington, along with their wives, were being held hostage at the end of the bar.

"Kimbrell's up there—him and Lec Ingram—watchin' over Clem and his bunch."

Jim considered this information. "Let us concentrate on the riders out here right now. We'll deal with Kimbrell later. Is Cady and the others ready?"

"Yes," Fred said. "Have you seen Dean?"

"Not since the other night. I'm sure he'll be along shortly."

Members of the nightriders roamed around going about their day without a care in the world—exiting the hotel lobby, picnicking under shade, walking along with their families. Some were part of the inner circle; others merely non-violent scouts—all of them a danger to Maybin's posse.

And Jim and his men vowed to put down as many as they rounded up.

From behind the General Store emerged a familiar figure with a swagger in his hips, wearing dark trousers, a black blazer and boots, face hidden by a bandana, his black Stetson shading steel blue eyes.

Jim Maybin recognized those eyes. He reached out and shook his hand. "Dan, it's good to see you."

"After that evening at Clem's, I'm sure glad to be here. Do you have our men in position?"

"Yep." Jim looked up at the saloon. "Careful now. Lawson and Lec Ingram are gettin' sideways on whiskey in there. If they sense we're wise to the whole mess it won't be nothin' for them to kill Clem's bunch."

"I saw James Frame take 'em up awhile ago," Dan said. "John West'll get his comeuppance today."

Fred Boss observed the crowd, noticing known nightriders among them, and relaxed his big hands on his guns. "So, Dan, tell me. How're we gonna get these riders together?"

Dan readily explained his method of execution. "They aren't all part of the circle, but they're worth getting. Approach every man you see as a friend. Catch him off-guard. Say 'the clover is blooming', then wait for them to answer. If they *don't* say 'spring is here' they're not a rider. Then go your own way and make it appear you're enjoying the afternoon."

He adjusted the mask over his nose.

"But if they respond by saying, 'spring is here,' then you're talking to a nightrider. Most important thing is to get on their level as a fellow gunfighter. Tell them John West wants to meet behind the store, that he has something big planned. Trust me, whoever says 'spring is here' will follow you."

Fred Boss and Jim Maybin informed five posse members on how they should snare the nightriders. "With words," Jim Maybin said, "not all-out force." The members split up and covered the town, approached every man, friend or stranger.

Dan passed by a couple of men and said under his breath, "The clover is blooming."

The men looked at him awkwardly, as though they'd never heard the phrase.

"Pardon?" one asked.

"The clover is blooming," Dan repeated.

"Yes, proper season for it." The man nudged his friend. "Good afternoon to you, sir." They walked on, minded their business.

It's like fishing, Dan thought, and moved on to a man standing with his wife and daughter.

"The clover is blooming," he stated.

The man looked over, seeing only Dan's eyes, and answered deliberately: "Spring is here."

Got one.

Dan stepped in closer so only the man heard his words. "West has something important brewing. He's callin' every available rider behind Drake's store. If you come across others on the way, tell 'em John West is waiting. Quick-like, now. There's gold to be had in this venture, and you know how he is about being on time."

The family man, Hal Weeks, nodded at the man behind the mask. He patted his daughter on the head, kissed his wife's cheek. "Go on home, darlin'. I'll be along later."

While making his way to the store, Hal gathered up three other riders, explaining that the clan leader needed their assistance. When pressed about details concerning the meeting, Hal claimed it was possibly another heist.

One fellow said, "Shoot, if he needs all us at once it must be a damn big buck!"

The very second those four riders stepped around the store, six armed men accosted them.

"Hands high!" Jess Cady ordered.

Caught off guard, the riders froze in place . . . slowly raised their arms.

"What's your intent here, old man?" Hal Weeks asked. "Where is John West?"

"Face away."

"Now, hold on now. Let's discuss this as gentlemen," Hal said. "I've done you no wrong, none t'all. For Christ's sake, I have a little girl!"

"Get their guns, Wes."

Wesley Xavier, a farmer from Olla, relieved each rider of their weapons.

"What in blazes do y'all have in mind we cain't fix over a drink?" Hal asked.

"First thing we're gonna do is take control," Cady said. "Stop your mouth."

Each man was bound at the wrists and ordered to press their noses against the brick wall.

In the course of twenty minutes the same procedure was initiated over and over again: a lone rider, or several, was instructed to show behind the store to assist in a heist, presumably at John West's request.

Instead of meeting John West they found themselves facing the steadied, long barrels of six shotguns.

At the end of his fishing expedition Dan counted sixteen riders, hands bound, guns at their backs. As far as Dan could surmise, John West, James Frame, Laws Kimbrell and Lec Ingram were the only outlaws unaccounted for.

"Well, we can't deal with the riders we got while there's two more up there," Jim said, nodding at the saloon. "He sees our activities, Kimbrell'll come apart and fire down on us out that window."

Dan and Jim Maybin then briefly discussed their plan of action to remove Laws Kimbrell and Lec Ingram from the saloon without endangering Mr. Clem Wilson, his wife, and their neighbor friends.

Dan knew Laws Kimbrell could make a bloody mess of his posse if the rider had enough bullets. He had to go about this in a calm, logical manner, go in and remove Laws without raising suspicions that something out of the ordinary (and very dangerous) awaited the outlaw behind the store.

"How do ya suppose we act on this?" Jim asked.

Dan removed his bandana and rubbed his eyes. "Well, I say we—"

Jim turned to see Professor Kendrick George coming down the dirt road, followed by a band of armed youngsters.

Gritty faces walking brave, the gang of boys were not properly dressed for an Easter Sunday in Atlanta, Louisiana, but for warfare—every one of them seemingly hungry for victory.

Their dark trousers and boots were caked in mud from trudging through the wet forest, and where fear should have fixed in their eyes, Dan saw undeniable courage.

Fred Boss stopped Professor George. "Kendrick, what in Sam Hill are you doing with all them young'uns in tow?"

The professor cleared his throat to reply, when Andrew Maybin stepped forward.

"We're here to help with the cleanup!" Andrew said.

Fred frowned. "Boy, does your father know about your involvement here? This here's a risky undertaking that's best left to men. Not kids with peach fuzz on their chins. Dang cat could lick that off."

Andrew stepped forward. "I respect you, Mr. Boss, but you and I both know my dad and Mr. Dean ain't got enough men for the cleanup. If my dad tans my hide after this, ain't nobody else's business anyhow. I have friends and guns ready, so make way and let us through."

Fred looked at the others, the youngest among them eleven-year old Caleb Cole, holding a rifle that made his shoulders droop.

Professor George took Fred Boss by the arm and said, "Fred, listen, there was no holding them back. I thought it best to have an adult accompany. You just tell us what to do and when to do it. They will follow my directive."

Fred scowled at the boys. "You hard-headed peach-fuzzers! Kendrick, if they refuse to listen to reason then it's your duty to protect these boys because there'll be enough blood floodin' this town come soon, lemme tell ya."

"I understand your concern for their safety. But these boys can shoot as straight as you, and they're just as vicious."

Dan Dean stepped in front of Fred Boss. "Professor George?"

"Yes?"

"If you and your crew of young bandits feel the need to assist, then we won't argue otherwise. But should one of them get hurt, don't place blame on our heads. Me and my acquaintances here aren't going to seek out these boys' mothers and fathers and explain why their child didn't come home today. That'd be your duty. So, you better pray that God takes care of any mishap, or you'll be the messenger who makes their mothers cry."

Dressed in a white shirt and brown pants and a shiny belt buckle, his usually spit-shined boots colored by mud and flecks of grass, Professor George touched his near-gray goatee thoughtfully. "Understood."

Upon hearing this agreement the courageous bunch of ten teenagers kept their steely eyes focused on the mission at hand—to fire their guns when instructed.

Dan took Professor George aside and explained to Fred Boss and Jim Maybin that under other circumstances, having these ignorant kids involved would be senseless. But the more available firepower they had at their disposal the better likelihood of celebrating a successful onslaught.

Fred said, "We got several of the goddamn punks back of the store. Can't tend to them 'til we get Laws. Him and that idiot loon Lec Ingram."

Jim Maybin told Professor George that those two nightriders were currently in the saloon. "If you wanna help, then you get them down here. Clem Wilson's up there, too, with his wife. We've got to make sure they aren't harmed. That's key."

Professor George regarded his band of hard-scrabble boys. "All right men, follow me to the saloon and let's capture a couple of bad guys."

"Let me go ahead of y'all."

The professor turned around. "Who spoke just now?"

"Me," the boy answered. "Caleb Cole."

"Son, this is dicey enough without you leading the pack. What's your reasoning for going through that door before me? Or Sebastian? He's bigger than you."

Caleb looked back at Sebastian Henratty, the mayor's son, a big-boned sixteen-year-old with arms grooved with muscle. "Well, Professor George, I figure them nightriders will make quick work of a man like yourself the second they lay eyes on ya. And Henratty's such a scattered klutz he'd fall and knock himself out on the way up. Then they'd hear us and start blastin'!"

"You little turd!" Henratty said, breaking his way through the pack. "I oughta—"

"Hey, hey, hey! Calm your nerves, Sebastian."

Henratty relented.

Hands on knees, Professor George stooped and said in a fatherly tone: "Caleb, these men are monsters. They'll shoot you just the same. We must outnumber our opposition—go in together as a group. It's the best way to beat the bad guys. Do you follow, Caleb?"

"Have you ever done something like this before?" Caleb asked.

"Don't be foolish," said the professor.

"Then how do you know going in like that's safer? Maybe they've got more men up there, ever thought of that? A group of gunslingers comes through that door and then *pow!* They'd fire on us! Say it's just me—at first—then they might take their time aiming down when they see a kid bust in with a big ol' rifle. Action like that'll catch 'em off guard. *Then* y'all can come up behind."

Professor George considered this strategy. "Boys? What do you think?"

They nodded in agreement.

"We'll back him up," said Andrew Maybin.

"Yeah, we can protect him," Paul Higgins affirmed.

"Caleb's a little turd, but he's got a clever idea," Henratty admitted. "Let's get them scoundrels!"

Professor George gazed up at the second-story windows of the saloon and saw shadows of men in the sunlight. He brought his attention back to the pint-sized, outspoken soldier in muddy boots, the boy's expression full of determination, holding a rifle that kept off-putting his balance.

"Alright, Caleb. Lead the way."

Chapter 63

Mrs. Rebecca Drake escorted her daughters out of the hotel lobby and onto the bench seat of their buggy. Flanked by her girls, she gently slapped the reins across the horse's leathery back, and off they went. They enjoyed a satisfying meal of smoked ham, green beans and mashed potatoes, candied yams and lemon custard. The girls were happy with full bellies, ready to play in the yard the minute they arrived home. Hailey wanted to play hide-n-seek; Hanna was in the mood for Hop-Scotch. Momma was ready for a nap.

All the morning Rebecca had feigned happiness, spending most of her time during today's church services fretting over her ailing husband. Will had welcomed this morning weak and sleepy, in coughing fits, suffering clogged sinuses and an aching head. He refused breakfast behind bloodshot eyes, but managed to swallow a few nips of Dr. Tolli's Miracle Healing Elixir, which quickly triggered unconsciousness.

Rebecca prayed her husband was feeling better. Lord knows his family needed him.

At home, the girls changed into their play clothes.

"Will?" Rebecca called, entering her bedroom. She laid her riding gloves on the side table. "We're home, darlin'."

Their bed was made up, nice and clean. *He must feel better,* she thought.

She was about to undress when she noticed a folded piece of paper lying atop the fat pillows. She picked up the paper and unfolded it, her blue eyes welling with tears.

My Dearest Rebecca,

I possess no words to describe the pain you must be feeling at this moment. Your feelings of anger and abandonment are rightfully placed in a heart I have loved since the day I met you, when we created our family's future. I believe you are understandably upset and for this I lay all blame on me. Nonetheless, I beg of you to save your tears for another day.

It is crucial that you take action without delay! The sake of our family is at hand. Collect our beautiful girls and see to their safety. You must travel north, to Barefoot, Louisiana. I shall await your arrival in the south section of town, near Honeysuckle Trail, on my Uncle Travis's homestead. At that time I will justify my abrupt absence and your questions will be answered completely.

Mister Frank Hines has equipped a horse and carriage at his livery in Winnfield. He has been paid generously for this favor and will assist you in getting out of town undetected. I have left for your aide a bag of gold coins under the bench. When the need arises, expend these coins on your journey.

My Love, I must express sincere caution that should you disobey my instructions, you and our precious daughters will be in serious danger! Burn this letter and leave now.

Forgive me,

Will Lewis Drake

"You goddamned coward," she whispered.
"Momma?"
Rebecca held back tears and clinched the paper in her hands. "Yes, darlin'?"
"There's a man out front. He says he wants to see the missus of the house."

Rebecca's heart grew heavy in its now icy cage. Her fingers trembled. She hated her husband for putting their family in jeopardy. She was so distraught over his sudden abandonment that she vowed once she met up with him she'd flat out strangle him for whatever misguided behavior forced the fool to pen such a ridiculous letter—then up and leave his loved ones.

What was he thinking?

"Momma?"

"Tell him I'll be a moment, Hailey," she said.

"Okay."

The girl turned away.

Rebecca stopped her. "Wait, where's your sister? Where's Hanna?"

"She's outside playin' with Rowdy."

Oh Lord.

"Listen to me carefully, sweetheart. Do not invite that man into our home. Do you understand? Let him wait on the porch. I'll be along."

"Yes ma'am."

Rebecca hurried to her daughter's room and packed articles of clothing in a single bag. She returned to her own bedroom, packed valuables in a purse and stuffed one change of clothes in another bag. When she caught her reflection in the wall mirror, seeing clear the stress of fear stenciled into her face, she felt like crying.

But she'd cry later. She had to save her children.

The devil was at the door.

*****

"That looks fine, darlin', just fine! I do believe you're skilled in the art of bandalore. Sure is pretty, see, when it turns and the light hits it."

Rebecca opened the door and saw John West standing near her daughter.

He watched as Hanna played with a yo-yo, making it drop, spin, and rush back to her tiny hand.

"Mr. West?" Rebecca said. She'd put on a white gown and a blue robe. At the sight of the burly man on her porch she feigned fatigue and crossed her arms over her breasts. Covered her mouth, yawned. "Oh, please pardon me. I was just about to lie down for a nap."

West tipped his hat. "Ah, Mrs. Drake. I apologize for interrupting your afternoon, but I was wondering if Will was feeling any better. I'd like to have a brief chat with him, if I may."

"He's uh, bathing in the tub," she said. "Hanna, put that play-pretty away and get in there to wash them dishes."

"What dishes? We cleaned up before chur—"

"Don't sass me, girl! Go on now."

Hanna eased by her mother, a bit confused. She looked back at the red-headed stranger in the big hat who had shiny guns belted to his sides. "Thank you for teaching me that yo-yo trick, Mister West. It's fun!"

Tugging at his hat again, West smiled. "My pleasure, darling. 'Til next time."

"If you'll wait a few minutes, I'll tell Will to get ready. He'll meet you out here."

John West needed to speak with Will Drake immediately, but controlled his stubborn impatience and leaned against the railing. Lit the end of a cigar. "Perfectly fine, Ms. Rebecca. Take your time."

Rebecca closed the door. Tried to remain calm. Will's written warning to get out now made her fearful of Mr. West . . . or maybe it was that look of something evil alive in his intense green eyes that caused her to second-guess his sincerity.

Whatever the reason, at this moment she did not trust Mr. John West.

She darted into the guts of the house and quickly ushered her girls out the back door, urging them to be quiet. Kept watch on the wrap-around porch for the big man with fiery red hair, unhooked the buggy's shaft from the horse's harness to set it free.

"Where're we goin' to go, momma?" asked Hanna.

"Shush!"

One at a time, Rebecca lifted them onto the horse.

She then sat between her girls in the saddle and gently nudged the horse toward a trail's opening at the forest.

"Hang on tight to me," she ordered.

Hailey rode at mommy's back, arms locked around her waist. Hanna was positioned backwards, hands gripping mommy's legs, her face buried against Rebecca's breasts. When they got to the trail

Rebecca slapped the ends of the reins across the animal's hide and high-tailed it out of there.

They would soon come out on the Old Harrisburg Road, where there was usually a fair amount of horse and buggy traffic pouring into Natchitoches.

From Winnfield they'd travel northeast to Coushatta, (and hopefully) to safety in a village called Barefoot, Louisiana.

*****

Luckily for Rebecca, West hadn't noticed she'd fled.

By now, though, his patience had worn thin.

Surely Will Drake was dressed and ready to meet face-to-face.

Or, she flat-out lied to me, he thought.

West pulled his pistol and tapped the steel barrel at the doorframe.

"Will? You in there ol' boy? Will Drake! Open up, now. Let's have us a talk." There was no sound, no movement. He tried the knob, pushed the door wide, and entered a quiet house. "Ms. Rebecca?"

He checked a bedroom on the right. Hurried down the hallway, found no one. He opened the back door to see a lone buggy stranded under shade.

"That conniving witch!" West yelled through gritted teeth, realizing too late that Mrs. Rebecca Drake knew more than she'd let on. He had to find her, and quick.

He broke a lamp across the floor and dropped his hot cigar in the spreading oil, determined that Rebecca and her daughters would never again find safe haven in this house.

Then John West walked out the door wearing a cape of flames at his back like a demon emerging from the depths of Hell.

Chapter 64

On any other day, Caleb Cole and his schoolmates would be enjoying the outdoors playing innocent games, or flicking pocket knives in a frightening round of Mumblepeg. They might be fishing the Red River, hunting raccoons, or slapping together a fort made of fallen branches and rusty nails until suppertime.

Today's afternoon activities were entirely different.

For better or for worse, today marked Caleb Cole's entrance into manhood.

Each step toward that saloon door made his heart beat faster. His hands gripped the gun tighter and his breathing came in hurried gasps. The long stairway stretched behind him, and when he looked down, thankfully, familiar faces stared back.

Professor George and the dirty bunch of teenagers had faith Caleb would do it. They had to believe he'd do it. This was their only chance to capture a monster who loomed on the other side of that ugly brown door.

Caleb shut his eyes and prayed for his soul, then he pushed the door wide.

Rushed in.

"Nobody move!" the boy yelled. "You there, Laws Kimbrell! Put yer pistols on the table!" He moved the gun's barrel toward Lec Ingram's head. "Both of ya!"

Laws swallowed his whiskey and slammed the empty glass on the counter. "What's the meaning of this, boy? Put that rifle down or I'll do it for ya!"

Caleb licked sweat from his lips. "You . . . you men're under arrest by the good citizens of Winnfield and Atlanta Louisiana! Y'all put yer guns on the table nice and slow, now . . . I mean it!" said the boy. "Or I'll—I'll *shoot!*"

Laws saw the fear in the boy's eyes and relished in it. He laughed out loud, as he was not to be taunted by a mere child.

Reaching slowly for his sidearm he knew what he had to do.

And the gunfighter had no problem in this world with his decision.

"Set that rifle down or I'll put a bullet in your tiny heart," he said.

Instead of obeying the rough outlaw, Caleb Cole steadied his aim, the intensity in his eyes growing stronger as he drew a bead on Kimbrell's chest.

The card players had stopped paying attention to their hands. They were now listening to the kid's every word.

"We're tired of the likes of you around here," Caleb said. "It's time you and your clan reap what you've sowed."

"Boy, with all the trees around here we ain't gonna waste time bustin' wood for your casket," Laws muttered. "I'll throw your worthless body to my dogs!"

Kimbrell pulled his gun from the holster, lifted it.

Shots rang out.

Whiskey bottles exploded. Glass flew overhead.

"Christ!" Lec Ingram yelled, covering his face.

In the chaos, Lawson saw Professor George rush inside waving a pistol, smoke curling off the end of the barrel.

"Set it down Laws!" the professor yelled, stepping around the boy. "Or you will die where you sit."

Suddenly, a crowd of armed teenagers stormed into the saloon.

Lec Ingram felt the urge to pull his guns in a foolish attempt to finish the fight, but thought better of that action and whispered, "God help me." Then he uncorked a small bottle of bourbon and drained it clear.

Four people, obviously in distress, sat at the far end of the bar, their hands tied behind their backs, rags shoved into their mouths.

Professor George ordered some of the boys to free Clem Wilson and his neighbors.

Caleb Cole kept his rifle trained on Lawson Kimbrell.

As he was being escorted past onlookers, Laws thought it interesting that after all he'd survived—all the blood and mayhem and killing in the name of greed—that he'd been captured by a bunch of kids.

The outlaw looked down at Caleb and said, "What're ya fixin' to do now, boy? Put a bullet in me?"

"No, Mr. Kimbrell," Caleb replied. "My dad'll do that."

Chapter 65

Pure fear beat hard against my breastbone as I stepped down from the saloon door. I felt disoriented, a bit dizzy, like I'd been hit upside the head with a dirt-filled stocking.

I held that rifle's barrel to Lawson Kimbrell's back, wondering just how long I could keep a steady pace and not crumble under wobbly knees.

Professor George and my schoolmates crept behind me, providing courage to my otherwise childish mentality. No matter how many firearms were aimed his way, I believed that any second Laws might turn and waylay the whole crowd of us for upending his good time. How that might actually happen was beyond me. There were too many of us, too much firepower to consider. I wouldn't be a bit surprised if he found a way, though . . . Laws Kimbrell personified walking, breathing evil of an ancient breed. I mean, who knew what he had hiding under that duster?

By the time we led him and Lec Ingram down those creaking steps and out into the bright sunshine, Mr. Maybin and Dan Dean already had a number of riders standing at the edge of the woods, right past Ms. Linda Youngblood's house. Sixteen riders, to be exact.

Seeing no way around it, Sheriff Hayden Rose and Deputy Ty Ellis had joined the posse to further assist in the cleanup. Their first unofficial task was ushering curious women and children from view of the execution area.

Once they were a safe distance away, it was time.

Jim Maybin gained the attention of his posse. "Alright men, listen now. We got lost souls here in front of us. Men who've gone against our Almighty God and the good folks of Louisiana. As citizens of Winn Parish, it is our rightful duty to clear the area of the nuisance that is the West Clan Nightriders!"

The riders stared at us juveniles holding them at gunpoint, sunlight heating their dirty, determined faces. I'm sure it was absurd to believe that a bunch of peach-fuzzers and Christian farmers were in charge of their fate. Tensions ran high. Tempers flared. Cursing fits lit up the afternoon in colorful detail as several riders swore revenge.

For men who were about to leave this earth, no fear flashed in their eyes.

They accepted their fate stubbornly, but accepted it nonetheless. There was absolutely nothing they could do to change the inevitable moment of their death.

Then Hiram Bertrand, a farmer and member of the posse, took Dan Dean aside, concern etched in his elderly face. "Look here, Dan, I can't speak for everybody present, but I do not believe I can fire down on a unarmed man and do him in. I reckon if he was raidin' my house, aimin' to hurt my family, I'd lay into him with all the firepower I could bring forth. But have that man stand there and wait like this, well I . . . I ain't the sort to go off and shoot the sorry sod! Neither is Bishop and Gordon and that feller Perry Vines over there," Hiram said, pointing to a few others in the group. "If I had my druthers I wouldn't do it. Just ain't Christian-like."

Dan realized that half of the men making up the posse were understandably apprehensive at the thought of committing murder on this Easter afternoon. Apparently at any time, for that matter. These men were not so hard of heart. Most of them did not have a military background, or the experience of running with the West Clan as Dan had. They lacked the sheer anger, the determination and quick trigger-fingers of Jim Maybin, Fred Boss, and Jess Cady.

He found the matter frustrating that some men who volunteered did not possess the grit to complete their ultimate goal . . . then again, this concern should have been addressed during those initial meetings. Keep the strong and pray whoever existed as a weak link be identified and excused.

What did this spineless bunch think we were gonna do? Give the nightriders a slap on the wrist? Ask them not to commit more crimes? Go on as though they've never shed the blood of families? I should—

Dan collected his thoughts, kept his cool. Looked Hiram Bertrand in the eye. "Do you realize the things these animals have done? Scores of travelers were killed because of them. Innocent families, Hiram. In coldhearted ways. Why is it they're allowed to get away with evil acts, and folks like yourself have to worry another day about your family's safety?" Dan rested his palm over the handle of his .44 caliber. "Now, you speak of what we're gonna do here today ain't Christian-like? The good book says, 'an eye for an eye and a tooth for a tooth'. *That* means these men must pay in blood for the wrong they did. And if you don't cinch up your boot strings and send them straight to Hell, then you're just as wrong as they are."

Hiram shook his head in dismay. "I've got a wife and a little boy, Dan. I ain't so sure I can go through with this and look them in the eye and be sure I done the right thing. What I figured we'd do today was go ahead and gather up the gang, but that it'd be different, all this. I really didn't expect this kind of attack."

"What's your suggestion, Hiram? If not this plan, what?"

"A trial. Judgment to hang," Hiram affirmed. "Proceed legal way."

"Legal way?" Dan said. "We're in possession of pardon slips signed by the goddamn governor! A pardon for every man in this lynch mob. The only work you've got to do is pull a trigger. So, if you and those squirrely men ain't up for it, I'll do it myself." He pulled his gun.

Jim Maybin hurried over. "What's causin' the ruckus, Dan? We've got an agenda!"

Dan holstered his pistol. "Mr. Bertrand and I have a bit of a disagreement on how to proceed here. But I just got an idea how we can move forward."

*****

"What's the fuckin' hold up?" Laws Kimbrell yelled. "Y'all get on with it if ya got the guts!"

Dan turned away from the riders. Taking Jim Maybin aside, he spent a few minutes discussing the reluctance of some of their volunteers to see to task.

"Now that it's time for the nut cuttin', they ain't so willing to draw blood," Dan said. "So I suggest we pair up our men with some of the school kids. Each pair will aim at one rider. Just one man in the pair will fire a fully loaded weapon. The other shoots blanks.

Assign this plan and men in Hiram's position won't feel guilty—seeing as how no one'll know who took the kill shot."

Jim agreed. "Just might work. We'll outfit the men firing blanks with muzzle powder and a cap. No lead."

"Let's get a handle on the firepower, then," Dan said, gathering his troops.

While the nightriders cursed aloud, awaiting their demise, Professor George and the school kids and members of the posse finally agreed on a paired-off firing squad.

Standing to the side of the large group Laws Kimbrell overheard Dan's idea in dealing with the riders. At once, the outlaw stepped out of the broken line of condemned men and approached Dan.

Sheriff Rose turned his gun on the outlaw. "Back up Kimbrell!"

"Fire away if you feel the need, sheriff, but allow me to speak before your kneejerk reaction puts me out of my misery." Laws looked over at Dan Dean. "If y'all're gonna pair off, so be it. But should a man fire down on me, I want that man to be Dan Dean!"

Fred Boss spat tobacco juice on Kimbrell's boot. "That's a fair request, I suppose. Whaddaya say, Dan?"

"I'm willin' to fulfill that request."

Laws walked by Dan, whispered: "Get . . . Gibbs."

"Back in line Kimbrell!" the sheriff ordered.

Dan caught the message in Kimbrell's eyes, immediately deciphered the meaning.

Laws returned to the grouping of the condemned.

Mr. Gibbs stood at the far end of the store, picking at his fingernails using the sharp tip of his pocket knife, awaiting Jim Maybin's direction. Much like Dan, Lucas Gibbs had always been a loyal friend to Laws Kimbrell.

"Lucas, me and you are gonna take aim at Laws. He thinks you owe him a favor?"

"Well, yes, I suppose I do. Happened last November. Me and my daughter was comin' back from town and three riders stopped us. One of them took her arm and pulled her right off my horse. Drunk fool was gonna hurt her. I knew it. I knew what he wanted to do to her." He shook his head, shame in his eyes. "But I couldn't help her. They had them guns."

That's when Laws showed up and witnessed the vile injustice forced upon his friend by members of the outlaw gang. Seeing red,

Laws dragged the rider out of the bushes gripping his throat, the man's trousers at his ankles, his stiff penis scraping across the rocky ground. Laws beat him senseless with heavy fists.

Lucas retrieved his daughter.

The leader of the West-Kimbrell Clan told the other riders that Lucas Gibbs was an old friend and that "if him or his family is ever harmed by you crazy animals, I'll leave you on the ground!" Laws pulled his thumb-buster, then turned to the rider who had raped his friend's daughter and said: "Just . . . like . . . *this*."

He shot the rider in the crotch.

After that incident, Lucas and his daughter had no further problems from the highwaymen.

Lucas realized then and there the outlaw Lawson Kimbrell would someday seek out some other form of appreciation . . . and that day of appreciation had arrived.

He nodded, shook Dan's hand. "That's what happened. If Laws needs me to pay back that favor, just tell me what to do."

Chapter 66

James Frame skirted the edges of Atlanta on the search for Will Drake and soon came upon a curious gathering of townsfolk near the General Store. He stopped his black horse in the mud, feeling increasingly uneasy.

Something was amiss. There were too many ordinary men bearing firearms.

Unusual behavior for simple town folk on a Sunday afternoon, he thought. *This ain't right.*

The outlaw dismounted and crept along the forest floor, masking himself behind a canopy of trees. From this vantage point he witnessed a troubling sight: several nightriders being held against their will.

"Maybin," he whispered to himself. "Mr. Cady. Fred Boss. Sheriff Rose." He squinted, caught sight of Mr. Clem Wilson and his wife standing near the hotel. "Shit. This ain't good at all."

James did not want to bring attention to his position, so he hopped on his horse and got ready to slip out. He chanced one more look at the gathering, at his fellow nightriders stripped of their firearms—trapped at the mercy of farmers and merchants and bankers and teenaged kids . . . then locked eyes with Dan Dean.

He directed his horse deep into the woods, feeling the distant sense of danger rush closer and envelope his hardened heart.

*****

Each nightrider was blindfolded and ordered to stand still against the backdrop of a thousand pine trees. Their eyes hidden from vibrant colors of the bright afternoon, some riders panicked through quickening breaths, fear finally taking hold of their hearts, knowing now they were breathing their last.

Jim Maybin directed each posse member on which nightrider to aim their guns.

"We've come this far, now it's time the devil got his due. I want you to look at these men and remember why they're standing in front of you. They've been accused of mass murder—that's why! They are a violent threat to our community and must perish for their sins. For some of you, especially you young men, this won't be a simple task. The memory of this day will weigh on your shoulders for a very long time.

"But right now be courageous. Your duty today is righteous and fair. It begs success."

One of the nightriders, Butch Hawkins, lifted his blindfold to see the firepower aimed his way and suddenly hightailed it through the woods in a fit of emotional urgency as quickly as his fat legs could carry three hundred pounds.

Before he made it six yards, a loud blast sounded out.

Butch fell.

Sheriff Hayden Rose aimed a smoking pistol to the sky.

"Helluva shot," Jim said, taking his position beside Jess Cady. "Find your target men!"

Dan Dean and Lucas Gibbs aimed their rifles at Laws Kimbrell.

No one spoke.

No one shot.

The hour got deathly quiet as the posse awaited Jim Maybin's command.

Nearly all nightriders stood shaken, disappointed that their double lives had led them to a backwoods execution without judge and jury.

Some men started praying aloud to Mother Mary.

Others decided they'd go down angry and remorseless.

Laws Kimbrell remained silent, perfectly still, hands resting at his sides, a hint of a grin curling into his cheek.

"Fire!"

Chapter 67

John West heard the echo of gun blasts rumble over the hills. He hurried along the Natchez Trace toward downtown Atlanta, wind slicing at his eyes, focused on hoofing it past the out-of-towners here for the holiday.

He arrived to see a crowd strolling through layers of gun smoke that had settled over the town like thick morning fog.

Alarmed by the chaos, West searched the crowd for James Frame, or any familiar face; any nightrider who might explain the explosive gunfire. Merchants and churchgoers and farmers roamed about, most of these regular, everyday folks armed with rifles and pistols and 12-gauge shotguns that propelled swift swirls of smoke over their hands.

West saw the bodies of several men lying in the overgrowth among blood-splattered trees. It took a solid minute for his brain to register how many nightriders had met such a disastrous end. It was surreal, as though he'd stepped into a waking nightmare.

I heard someone say, "It's him!", and looked over at a woman talking to her husband.

"It's John West!" her husband said. "He's the leader of them nightriders!"

"Get him!"

The crowd stared curiously at John West, waiting for him to either speak or draw his gun.

If he wanted to get out of here unharmed, West needed the sympathy of his fellow church members (and in the process hopefully gain the trust of other townsfolk).

The outlaw jumped on a tree stump and raised his hands, his tone geared for damage-control. "Folks! Folks! Lend me your ears and hear me out. These accusations, they're flat out lies! I ain't certain why some of my friends are layin' dead over yonder, but for some ungodly reason you all are bitin' at the bit to bring a dark cloud to this Easter Sunday!"

"Don't listen to his mouth!" someone yelled. "He's a criminal!"

West found the man who spoke. "Well, Dan Dean, that ain't such a nice thing to say to your old runnin' buddy."

"No buddy of mine murders people."

"I'm asking you, Dan, and all of you here today," he said, turning back to the crowd, "give me the chance and I'll show you the light! Brothers and sisters, each and every one of you will live out your days in much better financial shape. All you've got to do is give me the chance to make that happen. *That* is my guarantee to you as a man of God and civil servant to the people of Winn Parish!"

Those currently not serving as an acting member of Jim Maybin's posse were intrigued, even romantically taken by West's assurance of proposed wealth. Maybe, they thought, he wasn't the monster so many rumors had made him out to be. Could John Robert West be the man to make their financial concerns disappear? If so, was it not natural to give him the opportunity to do so? Shouldn't they hear him out?

"What do ya say folks? I'm tellin' y'all, I ain't never harmed a soul. Never even thought of doing such nonsense! I've got gold from my cotton gin profits in safe keeping up in a bank in Shreve City. Give me three days to retrieve it and I'll divvy up every last—"

The deafening gun blast exploded in the air.

Blood spewed forth over the stump. West fell on his side, body convulsing before the shocked crowd. Women cried out. Others looked around for the shooter. No one held a smoking gun.

Immediately after the shot rang out, Dan saw a long rifle barrel retract from the second-story window of the saloon—which had long been vacated.

He left the crowd, walked calmly past the broken line of still bodies and went inside the saloon, taking the back stairs two at a time.

Opening the door, Dan saw a man behind the long counter help himself to a bottle of whiskey.

The man raised his glass. "It's about time somebody killed that sack of pig shit, don'tcha think?" He filled another glass. "Have a drink, Mr. Dean. Far as I'm concerned, this is a celebration—not a tragedy. Join me."

Dan smiled. "It'd be my pleasure, sir."

"Did anyone else happened to see me?"

"Nobody, far as I could tell."

The man nodded. "That's good. I don't need any riders y'all missed in the roundup seekin' me out . . . how about we keep this here between us for the time being?"

Dan approached the window. The mumbling, nervous crowd stepped back, avoiding the black streaks in the red dirt as blood spread outward from under West's shoulders. Some of the womenfolk dabbed handkerchiefs at their eyes, holding tight to their men. Mothers led their kids away from the madness of the gruesome scene. The bullet had torn open the outlaw's throat, nearly taking his head off.

Happy Easter, Dan thought, and swallowed his whiskey.

John West, leader of the nightriders, was dead.

Chapter 68

I stared at West's green eyes, at the destruction that single bullet made of his neck, and felt sick to my stomach. Even in death his child-like eyes stared up at the heavens bearing the same focused wonderment as in life.

The whole damned thing was an awkward, terrifying scene that would continue to disturb my waking hours and haunt my nights for years down the road.

"Caleb?"

I turned to Dan Dean.

"Your father wants to see you," he said.

I walked away from the crowd.

My father relieved me of the heavy rifle and handed over his revolver. He knelt before me, gripped my shoulders. "Caleb, are you alright?"

"Yes sir, I think so."

"I'm proud of what you've done here today. You did what you had to do. Now that it's over, you get back to being a good boy."

"Yessir."

He patted my head and stood. "Me and the others need to discuss how we're gonna dispose of all this mess before the air starts stinkin' somethin' awful. Stay here and guard the bodies, son."

"Where're the bodies gonna go?" I asked.

"All you have to do is watch for wild animals bent on consuming still-warm flesh. If you see a panther or some wild dogs or any other critter come about, you fire down on 'em with that Colt." Wallace Cole paused. "Watch for anybody who might come up and try to rob these men, too. These bastards are sure to have in their possession gold coins or watches or walking-around money. Outright theft ain't right no matter who they are. They'll be stripped of valuables before we burn them, and that money will be useful for the town of Atlanta."

"You're gonna burn 'em?" I asked, surprised.

"We've got to get rid of them somehow. You just do as I say and pay no attention to further details in this matter."

"Yessir."

My father left.

I wish I was home standing guard over the last slice of pound cake instead of performing this unpleasant task. I could see Professor George talking to my classroom friends by the hotel. Deputy Ty Ellis instructed the majority of folks to go on home, that their presence here was no longer needed, nor desired.

A couple of members of Jim Maybin's posse dragged West's body around the store to join the deceased. I heard Mr. Maybin discuss with my father and others on how they should properly dispose of the bodies. It was all so bizarre. But so real.

I stood there alone surrounded by death and felt as though someone was watching me.

When I looked at John West I saw that his eyes were still open, the busted side of his neck leaking blood. I really wanted to shut his eyes, just close them with two quick swipes of my fingers, but even in his death I was scared of the man. I didn't want to touch him. Couldn't look away. So I waited for the posse to reconvene when suddenly John West's body shook, giving me a jolt.

He's still alive!

I shot John West in the leg, the arm, then steadied my shaky aim at his head. The blast tore his neck clean off his big shoulders.

A few people hurried up, asked what happened.

"He jerked!" I said. "I thought he was alive!"

"Ain't nothin' but nerves, son," said Jess Cady, watching the head of John West roll to a stop in the grass. "Dang, that was a cold shot, Caleb." Cady turned to the rest of the posse. "Alright y'all, let's get these bastards on that wagon!"

The head of John West lay sideways, eyes looking at the underside of fallen tree branches, his neck and part of his lower jaw ripped away from bone.

The posse started dragging riders out of the grass.

"Hold it! Count's off!" Fred Boss yelled. "One of 'em's missin'!"

Missing? I thought. *Ain't none of them got up and run off!*

Out of all the nightriders, Lawson Kimbrell was nowhere to be found. There was no trail of blood. No boot prints. It was as though he'd disappeared in plain sight.

"Where in hell's Kimbrell!" Fred yelled.

"I saw the sumbitch drop dead right there!" said Clem Wilson, pointing in the brush where flattened grass and a floor of pine needles formed the indentions of a fallen body.

"Then he should've stayed there!" Jim Maybin retorted. "I saw Dan and Lucas Gibbs fire down on him."

Dan Dean seldom missed an intended target, and the consensus among his peers caused several to wonder if he'd fired blanks.

Jim turned to him. "Lucas's was loaded, right?"

Dan did not care being questioned about his part in the firing squad. He owed Laws Kimbrell a favor for saving his own life, and he'd followed through. Jim didn't need that information. It'd just cause more trouble and confusion. "Maybe you oughta ask Lucas. The deal was two shooters. One loaded, one throwing blanks," Dan recalled.

Jim ordered some of the men to search the forest. "If Kimbrell's still breathin', then he's on foot. He might be hurt, movin' slow. Remember that you men have the governor's approval to shoot to kill. On! Sight! Y'all go on now. Bring him back!" Jim wiped a handkerchief over his sweaty face, then cupped his hand over his brow to shade his eyes from the sun.

Lucas Gibbs sat on a bench by the corner of the building, staring at two empty wagons, a still, emotionless expression on his face.

"Lucas?"

"Yes?"

"During the executions, was your rifle loaded? Or didja fire blanks?" Jim asked.

In shock by the death surrounding him, Lucas Gibbs did not feel the need to answer Maybin's question. But he'd overheard Dan and Jim's brief chat about which shooter had fired blanks, and who pulled back the hammer on a loaded gun, so felt a white lie would suit the situation better than fact.

"My rifle was loaded," Lucas lied. "I'm, well . . . you should know I am not as good a shot as others here, Jim. Must've hit a tree."

Disappointed by this news, Jim rested his hands on his hips and looked at the shadows of men roaming horseback throughout the forest. "Well, it'd be a shame to let loose that kind of evil when we were so close to gettin' him for good. If Kimbrell ain't caught this evening, stay alert. I suspect he'll come back with a vengeance in mind."

Chapter 69

Annabelle Frost was helping her mother wash dishes when she saw the dark figure of a man loitering around the stable. Full of thick-sliced ham, candied sweet potatoes, spiced greens, and hot-water cornbread, she thought maybe her brain was playing tricks on her; that the figure was nothing more than light sending shadows jumping along the ground.

But she knew better.

Someone was out there.

Her father lay sound asleep on the living room couch, snoring loudly.

"To be honest, Anna, I do not like what he might be, is all," her mother, Jean Frost, said. "I've heard from too many sources that Mr. Lawson Kimbrell is a member of that crazy night-people gang. You're too innocent a child to know what they've done to others coming through these parts, but hear me clear: if he is part of that gang then he ain't right in the head. I'd rather my only daughter avoid a man claims to be connected to *that* crazy bunch."

"Yes, momma," Annabelle responded. She wiped her delicate hands on a cloth, grabbed her crutch, and retreated to the back of the house.

"Where are you off to?" Jean asked.

"I've got to relieve myself." Annabelle turned down the hallway and exited the house.

She hobbled with a purpose past the outhouse toward the barn, keeping watch for a man in the shadows. Annabelle opened the stable doors and stepped over scattered hay. "Hello? Miss Jolly?"

The stall that held Miss Jolly was empty.

A hand clamped over her mouth, pushed her to the door, closing it hard.

"Mmph!"

"I've got to take her, Anna. They're after me."

Shaken, tears blurring her vision, Annabelle tried to speak as her tongue touched the salty skin of the man's palm.

"They're on their way. I wanted to see you before I cut out. Annabelle, I wished it could've been different, this life I've led. It would've been so fine, me and you together . . . my troubled heart won't allow it, but I had to see you one last time."

He removed his hand from her lips.

"Laws, who's after you?" she asked, facing him.

"Men with guns that have a lot more time than me. So I've got to head out."

"You're taking Miss Jolly?"

"She's the fastest horse I've ever ridden. I have to."

"Annabelle!"

She peered through the barn's stained window and saw her mother searching the yard.

"Girl, where are you!"

Laws kept his eyes on what might have been, then kissed her pink lips. He felt the curls of soft hair caress his calloused hands, pulled back. "I'll always remember you, darlin'."

"I love you," Annabelle whispered. "Go. You need to get movin'."

Laws hurried to the back of the stable and hopped on Miss Jolly.

Annabelle opened the barn door.

Miss Jolly broke into a run across the back field.

"What happened here?" her mother asked. "Who was that tore outta here like lightning?"

Annabelle touched her lips, feeling the wetness of Lawson's last kiss. "My husband . . . if things had been different."

Chapter 70

While some men searched for Laws Kimbrell, Jim Maybin and the rest of the posse loaded the bodies onto flatbed wagons for transport to the Prescott Gin.

I believe those who had suffered his murderous rage would agree this a fitting burial plot for John West and his fallen nightriders—at the bottom of a dry well.

Sara West was sweeping off her front porch when she saw the brigade of horsemen enter the opened gates and cross onto her property, trotting beside two wagons crammed full of broken bodies.

Confused, she raised her hand to her mouth.

Jim pointed to the back field. "Fred, you and Jess and Professor George take the wagons over yonder by those wells. We'll be there in a bit. C'mon, Dan."

Dan and Jim approached the house.

No one in their right mind simply strolled onto John West's property so nonchalantly, without invite, Sara thought. She held the broom nervously, twisting her hands at the knob of it, searching the men's eyes for apprehension, for any signs of weakness, and saw none.

"What's this all about, Mr. Maybin? If you're lookin' for John, he ain't here."

"Oh, your husband's here," Jim said. He pointed at the first uncovered wagon. "See there?"

Topping the pile, lying stomach down, lay the massive, headless body of John West. She recognized the brown shirt she'd washed and folded the previous day. Tears welled in her eyes, blurring her view of the twin gunmen at the bottom of the stairway. "You devils! You killed my husband! By God, you'll pay for this!" She swung the broom at Dan Dean, knocking his hat askew.

Dan straightened the hat.

Sara went wild, continued swinging at the men.

As the broom came his way once more, Dan grabbed the handle and pulled the woman off the porch.

She hit the steps knees first, rolled to the ground, her face bloodied and colored in dirt.

"What did you do to my precious husband?" she yelled, fighting to catch her breath. "Oh Lord, what did you *doooooo?*"

Dan tied her arms and legs with twine.

"No! *No!* Don't hurt me," she pleaded. "My young'uns are in the house. I'm all they got. Don't kill me, not like this. I haven't done anything to you!"

"We're not gonna hurt you, Ms. Sara," Dan said. "We can't perform our duty if you keep swingin' that thing at us. Or whatever else you get in your hands. I'm convinced there's a loaded gun in your house, and we can't take the chance of you using that on us either. We need you to remain calm."

"Leave her be," Jim said. "She ain't goin' nowhere." He hurried up the stairs and opened the door. West's daughters stood at the end of the long hallway. "Girls? Y'all come on in here and have a seat. Don't be afraid now."

The three girls took each other's hands and obeyed the stranger. They sat on the couch in the front room and silently watched as the men wandered through the house.

In West's bedroom, Jim and Dan found a cache of guns, six large green felt bags of gold coins they believed worth several thousand, and a surprise find in the top of the closet: twin burlap sacks weighted down by dried, gray, sliced-off human ears and tongues.

Dan and Jim realized that whatever grand treasure John West and his men had stolen over the years was not hidden at his home.

Upon exiting the bedroom Dan noticed something else of value indeed: West's jewel-encrusted bullhorn. Dan strung it around his neck as a personal souvenir.

Outside they stocked their saddlebags with pistols and ammunition and the bags of gold, now ready to light a fire.

Bound and motionless, Sara West's face tight with anger, she said, "Where're my babies? Don't you hurt my sweet babies!"

Jim knelt by Sara. "Look here, Miss Sara. You may or may not know what your husband has been up to, but I'm gonna say you did. There is no way you lived by that man's side for years and didn't once hear about his nightly affairs killing folks."

"Killing folks? What are you sayin'? John, why, he'd never harm any—"

"Stop your mouth!" Dan said. "You need to pack up your kids, get your things, and put some dust behind you. That buggy West has out back is sturdy and there're healthy horses in the stable to drive it. We'll fix it up while you get things together. It's in your best interest to leave this place and never return. Are we clear on what's going to happen next half-hour? Because if you don't comprehend the nature of our request, we can clear space in that well for one more body."

"Yes, yes, that's fine. I'll go, Dan. Untie me and I'll go."

Jim cut the rope.

Dan gave her a bag of gold for her travels.

Sara hurried back inside, telling the girls to pack their clothes.

They were taking a trip.

******

Jim and Dan met up with the others in the field.

Now that the boards were ruined by bloodstains for future transport, and it'd be a pain to remove fifteen lead-weight bodies, it was agreed the loaded wagons would be destroyed between the wells.

Only one body would see the bottom of a well.

"Grab his boots, Jim. I'll get his arms."

Jim and Dan moved John West off of the others and carried the heavy man to a well scarred by time, positioned the body over the top.

Let go.

The body fell and cracked upon itself at the bottom.

Within minutes the wagons were ablaze, sending smoke of a black bonfire over the treetops.

Jess Cady volunteered to hitch Ms. Sara's horse and buggy so she could get on the road while still daylight.

Inside the stable he found a fine black mare that fit the bill. Looking around at three more horses, he saw a stallion that had been stolen from his own stable months ago.

"Ringo!" he said. "Ringo, hey, it's me." Cady caressed the horse's mane lovingly. "Yes sir, that's right. I knew that sombitch West had something to do with you missing." He smiled, and Jess Cady didn't smile often. "You never went to Texas, didja? You was here all along, huh? C'mon, boss, I'm takin' you home."

*****

Sara and her girls loaded their belongings onto the buggy and got comfy on the large bench seat.

Her oldest daughter asked where they were going.

"To Hell if we don't get a move on. Now, hush up and hold tight to your sisters."

Chapter 71

Jim Maybin invited all the volunteers to his home.

"We'll have everyone sign off on their pardons and toast some bourbon to celebrate!" he exclaimed. "And my dear wife baked two cakes just for this occasion, so y'all eat up!"

The men of the posse rode out to Jim's place, relieved this fateful day had reached its anticipated end.

Professor George and some of the teenagers agreed to watch over the burning wagons.

"Thank you, Professor. You and those boys meet up with me tomorrow for your pardons, okay?"

"Will do, Jim," he said. "Although, I have to admit, since the governor granted you this awesome power, you must understand that an undertaking of this kind, for boys no older than sixteen, may offer them psychological and emotional struggles in days ahead."

"They'll cross that bridge when they get there. Those boys were hungry for blood, just like you said. They'll be fine. They're survivors. Hell, this's been a rough ride for all involved."

Professor George looked back at the gang of students in the firelight of burning bodies, wood and steel, enduring the repulsive stink, their faces mean and hard, tough beyond their years.

"Tomorrow it is, Jim. You go on. We'll watch the wagons 'till they flame out."

******

Dan Dean decided he'd catch up and celebrate later this evening. Ever since the scene behind the store, he had unfinished business in mind.

He made his way toward the Old Sparta Road and through a set of overgrown trails, seeing sights that reminded him of more peaceful times, and also one of his best friends. They used to play Army in those woods. Fish together on Saline Lake, laugh out loud at playful jokes, and fist fight in jest during stubborn arguments.

Throughout these years, another childhood friend Dan Dean once knew had molded into something else entirely—a beast Dan no longer recognized.

The setting sun painted the trees in fiery glow as he guided his horse through the Dugdemona Creek and onto the property of James Douglas Frame.

Aside from Laws Kimbrell (who was probably out of the state by now), James Frame was the last nightrider standing.

And he had to be dealt with.

The old house the Frame brothers once shared was a run-down, weather-beaten structure nestled in the woods far off the Sparta Road—nearly impossible to locate if a man did not know the land, or the temperament of the brothers' lack of hospitality. Dan had known them both well through the years. Witnessed firsthand how life's tragedies made these men meaner, mentally incapable of positive thoughts, and later absolutely psychotic in their dealings within the clan.

They had been the go-to bandits of John West's motley crew. When the leader needed someone dispatched in another area of Louisiana, or another state of the union entirely, the Frame brothers were called in to seek out and destroy. They always returned flush with valuables—gold, jewelry and what-not, but it was James Frame's idea to slice off the ears or tongues of their victims to further prove to West the job had been completed. A fan of this token, West applauded the brothers' skill in the art of hunting men. Every ear, every gold coin, every necklace brought to West's hands cemented the brothers' place in the clan as preferred members who completed each goal without question, and by brutal due diligence.

Dan made no effort to hide his face behind the bandanna that was now slack around his neck. He wanted James to know that this time, someone had tracked *him*.

A black horse grazed by the corner of the house. The saddlebags appeared full.

Dan fed James' horse dried beef and petted its longhaired mane. "That's a good girl," he said. "Where's James? Inside?" Hearing boots on wood, Dan looked up at the porch.

James had a thin cigar tucked between his lips. He wore a beard and wild hair underneath a black hat, his narrow eyes like sharp blue diamonds. "You got nerve comin' here, Dan. Just what in tarnation happened back in Atlanta?"

"A day of reckoning, James. We got rid of the clan today. But looks like you missed our get-together." Dan stepped away from the horse, his hand dangerously close to his polished pistol.

"Hey! You pull on that sidearm, you'd better kill me."

Dan relaxed his hand. "James, I was thinkin' about talkin' this out with you, seein' as how we've known one another since we were kids," Dan explained. "Or do you want to die right here?"

James Frame, a man whose eyes showed no hint of a soul, set his jaw and placed his sweaty palm on the handle of his holstered pistol.

"I heard y'all shootin' it up," he said, breathing in another puff of the cigar. "You and that gang of fools went about wholesale murder. Because of your actions there will be a day of reckoning for you, too, old friend. Now, your decision is simple. Leave me be to go my way, or I'll plug a hole in your—"

Dan drew, fired a merciless shot, the blow rocking Frame's head back like a sprung hinge. Blood sprayed a broken arc over the gray wood of the ramshackle house. The nightrider's body fell hard.

Startled, the horse reared up on hind legs.

Dan took the reins, held her steady. "*Shh. Shhh.* C'mere, ol' girl. Calm down, now. You're gonna be all right."

He led the horse east of Winnfield and Atlanta throughout forests that bled darkness and soon found an old, familiar trail that ended abruptly at the back field of Jim Maybin's house, where the posse had gathered to receive glasses of whiskey and thick slices of soft white cake.

Jim Maybin met Dan in the yard.

Dan handed over the reins. "Do you know where this fine animal might find a home?"

Jim recognized the horse as James Frame's sturdy mare. "Ha! I'll take good care of her, don't you worry. Come on in, Dan. You've got a pardon to sign."

Chapter 72

The day after Dan killed James Frame, he led members of the posse to Laws Kimbrell's house.

Jess Cady showed up guiding a horse and buggy. The old man sat on the bench seat with a rifle aimed at the large house. Two other men kept watch on the north and south corners.

Dan knocked on the large door, his gun ready.

Jim peeked through the opened windows.

"Here he comes," Jim said.

Shep Kimbrell answered the door dressed in long-johns, his tired eyes blinking away restless sleep. He was unaware of the trouble that had been brewing against the riders the last few weeks, and meeting Dan Dean at his front door caused him fear.

During a robbery back in March he'd been injured by a daring woman who had the grit to take her dead husband's pistol from its holster and shoot blindly at her predators. One bullet shattered Shep's shin bone and reduced the once hyper-active outlaw to hobbling around on a crutch.

To make matters worse, Shep had no one close to assist him in accomplishing the most routine things. Cooking meals, cleaning house, wiping his backside, all became obstacles of monumental proportion. He envied his younger brother William, who left the outlaw life months ago in hopes of finding peace in Mississippi. Shep's favorite brother, Lawson, hardly visited with him when home. It was as if Laws didn't even acknowledge his existence.

Coming to grips with being alone and confined, Shep did not often venture outside if he could help it. Pale skin and a long, scruffy beard offered further evidence of his reclusive lifestyle.

"Shep Kimbrell?" Jim called. "You are under arrest for lying in wait for the deliberate murder against your fellow man, grand larceny of their possessions, and horse thievery."

"Well, who says I did all those blasted things?" Shep yelled.

"Your brother told us, Shep," Dan lied. "Mr. Laws Kimbrell."

"Laws wouldn't turn on me like that!" Shep said.

Jim pulled his gun. "Either you come with us down to see Sheriff Rose, or I'll put a hole in your good leg."

"For God's sake, y'all need to understand I was bulldozed into doin' those horrible things! Laws woulda killed me himself if I hadn't been part of the clan. I'm tellin' ya, I did what I was told . . . it's the only reason I'm still alive. Lawson's a cruel bastard! Don't you fellas know that?"

"Consider yourself lucky, Shep. All the other riders are dead. Tell your side to a grand jury and you might get to walk away from this. Put up a fight, you'll fall right here," Dan warned.

Shep adjusted the crutch under his arm, spat the cigarette out of this mouth. "Fine then! Let's go see the sheriff."

They assisted Shep into the buggy.

The men searched the Kimbrell house for evidence of their crimes—mass amounts of gold or foreign clothing, but found nothing to connect Laws Kimbrell and his brothers to the robberies they'd been accused of.

Dan did not need physical evidence of the Kimbrell brothers' influence and participation in the West Clan's operations. He'd witnessed the evils of the Kimbrells up close, in the open, when no outside authority had been watching.

Walking through the kitchen, Dan and Jim stood on a large, blackened blood stain where years ago Mary (Aunt Polly) Kimbrell silenced the cries of screaming women.

The house was lit by torches at four corners, sending a whirling blaze of deep red flames and black smoke hurling through the evening sky.

At Dan's direction, most of the wells dotting the Natchez Trace were found and inspected.

Maybin's posse discovered over forty human skulls in John West's well alone.

Thirty-seven more in Kimbrell's well.

In all, ninety-three skulls were uncovered.

Chapter 73

I cannot live this life alone.

He must come back . . . please, God, bring him back to Texas.

Safe in the company of Dan's extended family, uncertainty haunted Contessa's nights as days passed without her lover to hold. Every morning when Nathan Dean journeyed into town for business she helped Ana clean house and feed Elvin, then gathered fruits and vegetables from the garden for that evening's supper. Not nearly as talkative as Ana, Contessa kept busy tending to whatever task at hand, all the while keeping Dan close to her heart and in her prayers.

She was sitting on the hickory stump fishing the bass pond when a shadow drew across the shimmering water.

"Contessa? There's no need to catch anything for tonight's supper. Nathan is making fresh barbecue beef. Why don't you come up to the house and we'll—"

"Thank you all the same, Ana, but I'm settled nicely here." Staring ahead, lost in the beauty of the scenery and her troubled thoughts, she adjusted the tip of her bonnet to hide teary eyes. "I'd like to be alone."

Ana walked back to the house.

Contessa was grateful she had the hospitality of kind people, plenty to eat, and shelter against the weather. But she'd grown lonesome since the time Dan left her in the front of that huge farmhouse. She needed to know something. Whether he was dead or alive, or if he'd moved on without her, Contessa needed to *know*.

"Any luck?"

Contessa turned around, her brain processing the sudden image of Dan Dean dressed in dirt-stained black trousers and a brown shirt, his cheeks shaded by a day's stubble. He looked worn out. She got up and stumbled, then ran to him.

"Oh my goodness, Dan! You're here." She held his waist, rose onto the tips of her toes and kissed his lips firmly.

Dan hugged her. "God, I've missed you, Tess. It's so good to see you."

"I worried you were . . . that you might've—"

"I'm here now, don't worry. We'll have plenty of time to discuss what happened. Though, I'm not inclined to go into much detail this minute. Let's just say that folks back home don't have to fear the clan any longer." Dan held her by the hips, felt the firm push of her breasts against his chest. "Ana told me you've been quite the helper around here."

"Idle hands . . . ." She kissed him again. "So, where are you going looking that handsome?"

"With you."

"Are we stayin' in Texas?"

"For the night," he said. "Come morning, me and you are gonna head out on a trip to Tennessee. When I was in the war, I passed through beautiful country up that way. Rolling hills, plenty of wildlife, a nice place to start over."

"Tennessee sounds wonderful!" she exclaimed.

Dan took her by the hand. "In the meantime, let's eat barbecue and drink some sweet tea."

As they walked back to the sprawling house, Contessa leaned her head against the man she loved, finally happy.

*****

In the summer of 1872, Dan and Contessa Dean settled in the small community of Watertown, Tennessee, forty miles outside Nashville. They had three children: Dan Dean Jr, and twins Vivian and Georgina Dean.

Dan and Jim Maybin had split six satchels full of the Clan gold (treasure they found searching John West's home), and Dan used this bounty to purchase farmland and thus construct a two-story A-frame house overlooking Gooseneck Creek. He used a rifle for hunting game, but still wore his six-guns in public. He became well-known in the area as an honorable, hard-working family man.

He did not mention the stories of the West Clan to his new friends or acquaintances, nor his involvement in the gang's demise, as it was a chapter in his life he'd rather let be.

Dan Dean soon discovered that married life provided peaks and valleys, joy and heartache, and habits he couldn't change to please his wife. But through it all, his love for Contessa and their children never wavered, and he found himself quite content living in the wilds of Tennessee.

Chapter 74

May 12, 1872

Skilled in the art of camouflage, Laws Kimbrell considered himself lucky to have escaped the posse's clutches. Led by Jim Maybin and Jess Cady—after well-deserved celebratory drinks—the posse searched into the morning. By noon the next day, they realized they had lost the pulse that might lead to the rider's capture.

Laws rode Miss Jolly fast through the swamplands that Easter evening, finally reaching the Texas line unscathed. He spent several nights sleeping under the stars, eating whatever fruits he scavenged and squirrel meat he cooked over a small fire pit. He did not know his next move, only that he must travel westward until the forests of East Texas rescinded into the open plains of Longhorn country.

Seeing as how the West-Kimbrell clan was a tight-knit and far-reaching bandit outfit, there was a possibility he might run into one of his extended cohorts. Laws kept a keen eye out for those who may recognize him, but also welcomed strangers, as they would not know his name, nor his current struggle in finding freedom.

His clean-shaven face was now a dark shadow, his hair longer and touching his neck under his field hat. To be safe, Laws gained coverage at night, expertly avoiding the detection of many outlaws intent on bushwhacking a stranger across these trails. He kept his six-guns loaded, ready for confrontation against any man or beast.

Consequently, within the two weeks he'd left Louisiana he was attacked by three different men on three different occasions. These wildcats found out too late that they were not of the same caliber as Laws Kimbrell, and ultimately fell dead at his feet.

He finally settled in the City of Austin, and it was here that his fate was sealed.

On a balmy afternoon as he rode back to his hotel room the horse's movement startled a rattlesnake, which sprung up and bit Miss Jolly's leg. Laws shot the reptile in the head, but could do nothing to save his horse. The poison spread quickly throughout the animal's body, and by nightfall clenched her big heart in a venomous fist, stopping it cold.

Laws was not accustomed to being on foot in unfamiliar territory. He needed the advantage a horse afforded him, in case he had to get away at a moment's notice.

Opportunity presented itself a day later when he ambushed a suited man traveling north of town.

The man's name was Shane Philpot, a local business owner. Mr. Philpot did not put up a fight, although he did try talking his way out of that dangerous meeting. "Stealing a horse around here is a serious offense, son. You'll be hanged, that's the truth. If I was you, I'd change my mind about doing so."

"Close your mouth and climb on down," Laws demanded.

Mr. Philpot obeyed.

Laws grabbed the bridles, stepped into the stirrup, and swung onto the saddle. "Now, give me your wallet and that shiny pocket watch ya got there."

Mr. Philpot reached into his vest for his leather wallet. "It's not wise to live your life in sin. There's a better way," he said, handing over both items.

Laws pulled the brim of his hat over his eyes. "Sir, with all due respect, that's the only life I recognize."

"Repent now, wayfaring stranger. And God will forgive you."

"Not for things I've done," Laws replied. Then he shot Mr. Philpot in the neck.

The old man fell to his knees.

The horse drew up on its hind legs. Laws took control of the animal and dashed away, leaving Mr. Philpot lying on the dusty trail.

His body was found hours later by two boys returning home from a fishing trip.

Next morning, news of the slain gentleman spread around town. Someone identified the horse strapped to the railing outside a local saloon as belonging to Mr. Shane Philpot, resulting in the dispatch of lawmen to apprehend the current owner.

No one recognized the stranger exiting the building. Dressed down in a long brown duster that swept the ground, challenged by a drunken mind, he made his way to the dead man's horse. According to locals, the man wearing a black hat over his bearded face looked upon the world behind wicked eyes that personified outright madness.

The sheriff's posse tracked this stranger a safe distance out of town before circling the rider under the midday sun. They were certain this was the man who murdered Shane Philpot. The tan and white mare was the only one of its kind in the area, and those who knew Mr. Philpot knew of his spotted horse, "Buck".

Jackson Lawson "Laws" Kimbrell was arrested for the murder of Shane Philpot and the crime of horse thievery—both offenses punishable by hanging. Laws did not put up a fight, nor did he argue why he was in possession of the animal. He'd been careless, got himself caught, and knew he'd face legal consequences.

After a prompt trial Laws was sentenced to hang in the town square in two days' time.

The night prior to his execution, shackled to a cot in a bricked jailhouse, he stared coldly out the window at a dark sky bruised by rainclouds. Condemned to die, Laws did not shed a tear for himself. He did not cry out for mercy. He did not search his soul in an effort to forgive a black heart of past actions that had continuously gained him profit while the bodies of his victims rotted away in wells . . . .

He found looming death comforting. No more madness, only peace from the life he led. His victims could now celebrate his death. If they could speak, he was certain they'd cheer on the hangman. But he couldn't care less what they might yell out at his execution. His victims didn't matter.

Throughout his criminal career Laws was burdened by only a single regret: the killing of that innocent baby. This disturbing vision had haunted him so profoundly that he welcomed the relief of an uninterrupted, endless sleep. All Laws wanted before he died was that God might see fit to forgive him for harming that little one.

At dawn, Laws was still sitting on the side of a cot that was suspended from the wall by two strong chains, looking around the room holding him captive.

The deputy of this Texas outfit set on the floor a shot of whiskey, a slice of stale bread, and a peeled, boiled egg sprinkled with salt.

"Last meal," the deputy said.

Laws downed the whiskey. Left the plate of "breakfast" on the dusty floor.

"Ain't you gonna eat that?" the deputy asked.

Laws stood, towering over the peace officer. "You eat it, fat face. Then take me to the gallows."

The outlaw was escorted out of the jailhouse in the back of a flatbed wagon to the erected crossbeams that had been constructed in the square.

Deputies led him up the stairs to a small platform, tied his hands at his back. The sheriff then spent a full minute explaining to the gathered crowd why this man, a mister Lawson Kimbrell, had been sentenced to hang.

"To that end, folks, this punishment is absolute, and it is fair, for the senseless murder of our good pastor, Reverend Shane Philpot!" the sheriff said.

Cheers erupted from the crowd.

Another man circled him.

Laws searched the eyes of the townsfolk gathered here to witness his pending death, and he saw curiosity, resentment, even plain old hatred alive in them.

Asked if he had any last words, Laws sucked in a deep breath and said, "I should've died in Louisiana."

The thick rope was secured around his neck. Laws looked down at the planks and saw bizarre movements in the sunlight, outlining his boots. Like snakes, the swirling, shape-shifting images of evil spirits grew more abundant . . . waiting to take him down.

Laws closed his eyes, heard his mother's haunting words as she'd lain on her deathbed: "*You can't see them now . . . the spirits . . . but you will, son. I'm sorry, but one sad day you will.*"

That's when real fear caught him. Within seconds the hinged door beneath his boots would drop into open air, and he'd be no more of this earth.

He gasped.

"I see them mother! Risin' up! I see . . . a-haha. Ha! I see *you!*"

The small door freed itself of weight, and when that long rope yanked back his neck and detached his spine, the light of the living escaped his eyes and his body trembled violently. Lawson "Laws" Kimbrell swung against the brilliant sun, turning and sending shadow over the vengeance-seeking crowd, his wild soul now condemned forever.

Epilogue

Rebecca Drake finally made the long trip to Barefoot, Louisiana, a community on the border of Arkansas. When she met up with her husband, she slapped "the fire out of him."

"Don't you *ever* do a foolish thing like that again! Leave your kids like that? Leave me? Selfish bastard, you should be ashamed of yourself!"

Will Drake had sorely regretted his actions and explained that greed played a major role in his decision-making. He apologized profusely, but Rebecca declared it would take more than words to repair this troublesome valley now weighing down their relationship.

He sat with her on the lawn of his Uncle Travis's house, held her hands and informed her of his fixture in the company of merciless outlaws called the nightriders. "I was their bookkeeper for years," he confessed. He detailed how after every robbery, after every single murder, that he was charged with hiding the bounty in lockboxes kept buried at Horsehead Rock. "There were three keys that opened those boxes," he added. "I had one." He admitted to Rebecca that his role in the Clan's operation was strategic, exceptionally dangerous, and necessary to avoid attracting the attention of authorities.

"I was warned that if I discussed the clan's activities to another human ear, those men would come lookin' for blood. They would've done away with us like so many travelers on the Natchez Trail." Will watched his daughters circle a small bush in the yard, singing "ring-a-round the rosie, a pocket full of posies, ashes, ashes," feeling satisfied that they were not as angry as his wife. He took a breath. "Truth is, I figured one day I'd be of no use to them. I'd been granted guarded information that could send them up in front of a judge. I guarantee you, they'd silence *me* before they got lynched.

"I wanted my family to be safe, sweetheart. That's why I took those valuables from Horsehead Rock. Gold bricks, gold coins, shiny jewelry—from rubies and sapphires to diamonds as big as your teeth. I betrayed the clan to assure us a new beginning somewhere else. Rebecca, darling, I did it for us . . . for our sweet girls."

"What do you plan doing with all that bounty?" she finally asked him.

He wanted to delve back into the trade business, perhaps build a mercantile store in this area, and told her so.

Rebecca wasn't having it.

On her four-day trip from Winnfield she noticed that the timber-cutting industry had exploded in the northern part of the state. And now the scenery of a town surrounded by tall, whispering pines gave her a gem of an idea. Rebecca suggested they invest the stolen treasure in the construction of a sawmill so they might compete with the up-and-coming timber industry.

And so, after months of drawing up business plans and bringing on like-minded investors (using the bulk of the West Clan's gold to make their vision a reality), Drake's Lumber Mill was born.

Many years later, the sawmill town of Barefoot would be renamed Springhill, Louisiana—home of the Springhill Lumberjacks varsity football team.

*****

July 1913

My name is Caleb "CS" Cole. At fifty-two, like most everybody, I've seen my share of horrors in life. I wish I'd never met the West Clan. But meet them I did.

I knew the names of the members of the murderous inner circle. I knew their codes and signals and I witnessed them carry out the most heinous crimes. I also know how they were taken down.

There it is. Shiny as ever.

Sun-bleached bone staring out at the world through empty sockets over a devil's grin.

I look at it often, John West's skull on that fencepost. Makes my stomach turn to look at it, but knowing how it got there gives me a measure of satisfaction that some form of justice was done.

The things I've seen, some folks will find hard to believe. And that's okay. But these eyes don't lie . . . .

Nightriders:

John West
Lawson Kimbrell
Zeek Crutchfield
Jurd Vines
Dave Frame
James Frame
Shep Kimbrell
William (Billy) Kimbrell
Abram (Ab) Martin
Gus Rivers
Otto Shrum
Clifford Tingle
Arthur Collins
Hank Wright
Clyde Judkins
Darren Forte
Maurice Washbow
Copeland Yates
Lec Ingram
Earl Gilcrease
Harold Basco
Raymond Hayes
Irvin Broussard
Vernon Beech
Mitchell Carpenter
Earl Hargrove
Ridley Sercy
Butch Hawkins
Ike Hicks
Emery Tango
Ed Mooney
Gil Pickett
Hal Weeks
Mickey Fontaine
Vince Sikes

Cleanup Posse:

Dan Dean
Fred Boss
Jim Maybin
Jess Cady
Antone Luke
Professor Kendrick George
Richard Veltrea
Benny Bishop
Hiram Bertrand
Ardell Gordon
Lucas Gibbs
Deputy Ty Ellis
Guy Dickeson
Landon Fulcher
Wesley Xavier
Perry Vines
John Wilcox
Paul Higgins (15)
Travis Caruthers (16)
Caleb "CS" Cole (11)
Frank Echols (13)
Charles Logan (16)
Andrew Maybin (16)
Lynn Maybin (12)
Sebastian Henratty (15)
Sheriff Hayden Rose
Ira Smith

Bill Carter
Wendell Riley
Royce Greene
Jake Dodson
John Harwick

* John Robert West is buried at the Atlanta Methodist Church Cemetery in Atlanta, Louisiana. His grave is far removed from other markers, standing alone near the honeycombed fence. He was 42 years old when shot dead by Jim Maybin's crew.

* Lawson Jackson Kimbrell is buried in Austin, Texas. He was 31 years old when hanged.

Just a note:

Every year I journey south to attend the Blake Family reunion at Yankee Springs Baptist Church near Goldonna, Louisiana, where my grandparents were raised.

Many of my ancestors, including my Gibbs and Peterson kinfolk, are buried in the church graveyard. The reunion is always a wonderful time. We set out flowers on graves, clean debris from tombstones, and remember the ones who've gone on before us. One of the main attractions is a long concrete table covered with tasty, homemade food, cooked in several different kitchens.

The church was named Yankee Springs because it was built near the exact location where Northern Lieutenant Simeon Butts had been gunned down at the cool spring by John West and Laws Kimbrell.

Another note:

One evening during those tumultuous times my great-great-grandfather Daniel Gibbs was actually accosted by the West Clan. They stole his horse and buggy, the only means of transportation he owned in which to accommodate his wife, Susannah, and their 11 children (one of which was my great-grandfather William Franklin Gibbs, who fathered Ezona Gibbs—my grandmother—in 1910). This story is hazy, of course, like most stories handed down through generations, so I do not have specific details.

But I was told that Grandfather Daniel Gibbs heard noises on his property, walked out with a rifle, and was met by four riders. They were in the process of taking his horse. They didn't want any fuss about it.

I'm not sure that my grandfather was a gunslinger—he could've been, for all I know, but if not, the man was smart enough to realize he wouldn't survive a firefight against these outlaws.

He had to protect his wife and their children, but I have to believe he was frightened, as smart men would be in his particular situation. He rested his rifle on the porch and watched the men leave without incident, taking away their property.

I'm proud of my grandfather. I believe if Daniel Gibbs hadn't used common sense and relented, many of us Blake's in Louisiana wouldn't be around.

A. Blake

Acknowledgments:

I'd like to extend special thanks to some amazing friends for their contribution to this long-running project:

Butch Baldridge for allowing the use of his authentic 1860 Navy Colt .44 revolver for the front cover. Without that photograph I believe the appeal of this book would not have been as inviting. Thank you, Butch. I hope you're doing well, old friend.

Scott Allison, my brother from *way* back, and Stevie Williams, my brother for times to come: many thanks for helping capture the ideal camera shots depicting members of the Nightriders. You guys are Aces High.

A very special thanks to my talented rock star of a sister, Julie Blake, for creating the layers of an intriguing cover, naturally giving it a genuine feel of the Old West in the Deep South. I love you Ju-Ju!

"There can be no doubt, John West and Laws Kimbrell were greater in outlawry than Frank and Jesse James. They killed more, robbed more, and terrorized more people. They were bolder, meaner, and more irritable, altogether more dangerous. Because of the confusion in the Deep South and the difference in methods used, West and Kimbrell failed to get the publicity the James brothers received. Where Frank and Jesse, with Cole Younger and their gang, rode into towns, robbed banks in daylight, and shot it out with officers and posse's on the spot, West and Kimbrell, with the Clan, moved about at night, robbing travelers and wagon trains, killing everyone they contacted in secrecy, under the cover of darkness. When the James boys struck, the newspapers told their story in great headlines; when West and Kimbrell robbed or killed, no newspaperman knew anything about it, or if one picked up such news he was afraid to say anything even to his friends, let alone run such material in his newspaper . . . ." —Quote by Hardware Store owner P.C. Lang of Montgomery, Louisiana, 1963.

Hijinks and Other Mischief

(As told by Caleb "Cold Shot" Cole)

The Crooked Cousin

Twenty-one year old Bill Carter hailed from a prominent family in Winnfield and was known around town as a nice, honest farm boy. But after inviting his cousin out for an evening of fun, trouble came that forever changed this projected image.

Bobby Carter didn't favor the idea of making the seven-mile trek to a barn dance on Caster Creek near the town of Olla, but Cousin Bill urged him to go.

"There'll be others there around our age. I'm tellin' ya, we'll have us a big time."

So Bobby agreed to attend the affair, thinking it'd be nice to meet some girls from another parish, and possibly make new friends.

When the afternoon arrived the young men dressed up in spiffy duds and saddled their horses. They crossed Dugdemona Bayou at Joyce Union, then headed eastward on Tullos Road, which led to the Castor Creek community

The further they traveled the more Bobby mentioned the dance, a sense of wonder in his voice. "I hope there'll be some pretty ladies willin' to kick up some sawdust. I'd love to feel that soft skin against me."

"Should be plenty, Cuz," Bill replied.

"And food. I had some cornbread and beans earlier. When we get there I'll be ready for some stew, or something filling."

Cousin Bill did not continue the small talk, which was odd. This morning he was going off at the mouth, claiming that given half a chance they'd dance with every lady within arm's reach, drink their fill, and enjoy themselves immensely.

Ever since they crossed the bayou, however, Bill had grown less interested in discussing the dance, or even the prospect of making lady friends.

At a crossroads they were approached by two other men their age who turned out to be friends of Bill's from the village of Possum Neck. They were also on their way to the dance.

The newcomers had dressed handsomely for the party, cleaned jackets and polished boots, their hair slicked back neatly. What seemed out of place were the Springfield rifles they carried across their laps.

As they rode on, Bill introduced his friends to his cousin Bobby. Once the pleasantries were out of the way the conversation lagged for quite some time, bouncing between the anticipation of mingling with girls and getting in a late night to hunting whitetail deer come October.

While Bobby listened, another strange thing happened: one of the men changed the course of conversation by drawing attention to the financial and economic conditions of their region—how the mess affected them personally, and that they should strike fast and hard to survive. The man explained that there was plenty of money to be had in the area, if such a brave soul were inclined to reach out and snag it.

The other man, tall and lanky in the saddle, leaned over the leather reins of his steed, the shaft of his rifle dull in the sunlight. He looked directly at Bobby, eyes burning with greed.

"Money, gold, jewels and other things of value, that's for sure," he announced. "A man with a spine and reliable trigger-finger could do right well for himself. I'd say he wouldn't have to go through much trouble to gain such prizes, either."

Talk of easy money continued for the next three miles, when the four men arrived at Big Brush Creek. The man with the long hair (who seemed to have taken over the conversation) suggested they stop and rest their horses. Empty a flask.

Bill Carter walked down to join the men.

And the three of them shuffled away.

Feeling left out, Bobby tied his horse to a tall pine and walked to the water, hanging back a little so not to disturb their private chat. He was not a big drinker, but on a late afternoon like this, going to a dance, a sip or two would surely relax him enough to approach the ladies.

The closer he got, he saw no bottle of whiskey being passed around. Bobby hadn't the slightest clue what this was all about; why the three of them decided to huddle and speak in hushed tones. Something nagged at him that this setup was all wrong.

There was another reason they'd stopped by the creek, and it had nothing to do with resting.

At this point, no matter what Bobby Carter thought of the affair, or the strange actions of these newcomers, he could do nothing but wait and see what Cousin Bill and his friends were scheming.

A few minutes passed. The huddle broke. The long-haired man leaned his rifle on his shoulder, then approached Bobby.

"Okay, boys, y'all wanna haul off some easy money? There's a man and his wife camped out over yonder, other side of the creek. I saw them sell fifteen bales of cotton in Winnfield this morning and you just know they got all that money in their possession. If we act with precision, that gold is as good as ours."

Just then Bobby Carter felt uneasy. He looked over at Cousin Bill.

Bill paid Bobby no mind. He was focused on Long Hair's plan.

"Now, considering the three of us are members of the West Clan, we've had experience in this kinda work," said Long Hair. "But seeing as how this evening Bill brought along a new prospect, he'll have to be initiated to a firm degree before we move along."

His fear rising, Bobby shook his head. "Wait, what's this all about? I . . . I thought we were goin' to a dance."

"That's still on the agenda," Cousin Bill replied.

The tall man grinned. "Business before pleasure, Bobby Carter."

"Right now, money is the most important thing," Long Hair announced.

Bobby spat on the ground. "Y'all're in the West Clan? I just knew something was wrong with this outfit!"

Long Hair continued: "You know, Bobby, in the clan we have a saying that insures our existence and furthers our prosperity: 'dead tongues tell no tales'. We abide by strict rule that no new prospect is considered a member until that prospect's dealt some serious history with us . . . until he's robbed for fortune . . . when he's killed another man for that fortune."

Young Bobby couldn't believe his ears. "Kill?"

Long Hair turned his attention to Bill. "You claimed your cousin was keen to adventure like this. Why do we have a problem all of a sudden?"

"He'll go along with it, just you wait. I vouch for him."

"Nobody'll vouch for me!" Bobby yelled. "If this is how it goes, then I don't want any part of your clan."

"You can't back out now," the tall man said. "You already know too much just being in our company."

"He's right," said Long Hair, pointing to young Bobby. "We'll wait here 'til dark, then you slip down there. My partner here'll be right behind. Doesn't matter if the campers resist or not—you shoot one of 'em. He'll do in the other."

Bobby thought the whole idea unreal, conjured from the evil hearts of greedy men, and wanted nothing to do with their plan. "This, it ain't right. I can't do this!"

"Don't too get excited, Bobby," Long Hair continued. "Follow instructions and you'll come out of this smelling like a spring rose. Then we can go to the dance with money lining our pockets and enjoy the rest of the evening!"

"No," Bobby said. "I work for my money. I don't go around killin' strangers for their possessions. You boys can't be serious."

"We're goddamn serious, Bobby Carter," the tall man said.

"So, you'd kill a man and his wife for a couple hundred dollars on the sale of cotton?" Bobby snapped his fingers, *pop!* "Just like that?"

"Shit, I'd use your ears for target practice," Long Hair replied. "Tonight, it'll be *you* doing the shootin'. And if you need something else to think about, think about this: you go over yonder and do them in, or you'll be the body someone finds in that bayou."

Bobby looked again to his cousin Bill for any assistance and was disappointed to see Bill totally immersed in the affair—ready to heed Long Hair's every command.

"You lying, *conniving* . . . son of a bitch of a cousin!" Bobby said. "How could you do this to me? Get me in this fix with these nightriders?"

"Quit complaining. You knew quite well what you were getting into from the start."

"How? How would I know you were a member of the West Clan if you didn't tell me? You invited me to a dance and all, and now look what you've got me up against! You tricked me, Bill! You swindling jackass, you *tricked* me!"

Bill grabbed Bobby's collar. "Look here, Cuz. I told them you'd be no trouble, and now you're acting like a little pigtail. Making me lose face like this? If you don't do what they say, I'll shoot you myself."

"Calm down the both of ya!" Long Hair took his rifle and offered it to Bobby. "Now . . . are you gonna get this gun and do what I said, or do I have to use it on you?"

Having no viable choice in the matter, Bobby decided to go along with their plan, insisting he use his own .38 pistol.

No longer perceived as an obstacle to the robbery's completion, Bobby understood the role he had to play. Kept quiet. As he listened to final instructions he fetched the pistol from his saddlebag.

He untied his horse, carefully slipped his foot in the stirrup and swung up on the saddle. He hurried in the opposite direction, taking off at high speed down the dirt path, bowing his head in case they took aim at him.

Oddly enough no shots sounded out. No one gave chase. Bobby figured the nightriders still planned to rob the wayfaring campers, and felt that making a scene by chasing after him might scare off their targets.

He believed someday they'd come after him to exact retribution and that he'd have to fight them off. As the tall man warned, *"You already know too much . . . ."*

Bobby arrived home in Winnfield, out of breath and red-eyed from traveling so quickly.

His father was on the back porch eating an apple and looking out at his crops. Bobby sat beside him and explained what transpired.

"That's it, Pa. I'm as good as dead. They'll come for me to shut me up. And my own flesh and blood's to blame for this terrible mess!"

His father was surprised by the story. He just couldn't believe his nephew would involve Bobby in the murder of innocent people. William "Bill" Carter hadn't been raised that way. The boy knew better.

"Tonight I'm ridin' back to Dugdemona Creek and settle the score for all time. He's gonna cross there at some point between now and dawn . . . depending on how long it takes to dispose of them campers and how much fun he has at the dance. But he'll come through. And I'll be waitin'."

"What do you mean 'settle the score', Bobby?" his father asked. "You're not going to—?"

"Yes. I'm gonna kill that stupid hothead. Then throw his sorry ass in the bayou. Fatten up some turtles and 'gators."

"Oh no, son. You can't go and do a thing like that. Bill's kinfolk."

"Kin or no kin, the man's pure evil. Evil like his nightrider friends! I'll do it quick-like. It's either him or me. If I chicken out and don't act first, those men'll find me, and my life'll be worth a bucket of coon piss."

The old man was proud of his son for his courage and determination to right a wrong, but felt deeply concerned for the boy's welfare. Bobby was living on the sharpened edge of sixteen, between childhood innocence and becoming a young man. No question he had a better head on his shoulders than Cousin Bill.

Still, such virtue didn't mean the boy couldn't get hurt.

After a lengthy discussion on the merits of Bobby's headstrong decision, his father relented and saw things from his perspective. Cousin Bill's scheming had placed his son's life in danger . . . and something drastic had to be done.

Bobby climbed on his horse, the .38 pistol strapped at his hip.

His father held the bridles, looked up at him with saddened eyes. "No matter what happens, son, know that I care a great deal for you. Come back to us."

"I will, Pa."

"Here . . . use this if he gets too close." He handed Bobby a Parker model 12-gauge, double-barreled shotgun. "It's full of lead."

Bobby rode back to Dugdemona Creek.

Sure enough, as dawn lit a blue/white haze through the trees, Cousin Bill came wandering through the forest, hungover after a night of gallivanting around.

Bill directed his horse down the incline and saw Bobby sitting on the bank.

"Bobby Carter! What the hell're you doin' here at this hour?"

"I'm here to kill you, cousin. Then I'm gonna throw your bones in the bayou."

"Settle down," Bill said. "You're talkin' crazy!"

"It's clear what you had in mind last night. You wanted me to kill those campers to get initiated in a gang that I couldn't walk away from. I'd be under your charge. Otherwise, them nightriders would've done away with me. As long as I know your secrets my life will be in constant danger, and I figure my nearest hope for survival is to take you out of this world." Bobby raised the shotgun, thumb-clicked both hammers. "Defend yourself."

"Hey! Don't be foolish! For Christ's sake, Bobby, I'm your cousin!"

Bill quickly realized his pleas wouldn't save his hide. He suddenly reached for his sidearm, and at the deafening sound of the shotgun blast went flying off his horse, his body hitting the ground and lying across the scattered bits of bone of what was left of his skull.

Gun smoke swirled in white curls over Bobby's arms, drifting away on a gentle breeze.

Bobby did not immediately feel satisfaction for his actions. He did not feel altogether guilty, either. He dragged the body of Bill Carter to the deep part of the creek and dumped him in, just as promised.

Bobby returned to his horse when movement caught his line of vision. He looked above the incline, felt blood pump harder through his veins.

A man and woman were staring down at him.

He recognized the pair of onlookers as poor relatives of the Waverly family—Mr. and Mrs. Randall Waverly.

Bobby believed they'd witnessed his crime, so he took in a deep breath to relax his rattled nerves and steady his words.

"Hello folks. Y'all're out mighty early."

The man held up a fishing pole. "Better bitin' at dawn." He looked at his wife, then back down at Bobby. "We've been here quite some time."

"Then you pretty much saw what happened?"

The man nodded. "Heard everything, too. It looked to me and Amy here that you had no choice in the matter."

Bobby led his horse across the bank and joined the couple. Recalled in detail why he'd killed his cousin, Bill Carter.

"They would have tried to find me in a matter of time. So, I attacked first."

"Well, from what we saw, you did the right thing. We won't say a word. I can promise you that."

Bobby left for home, vowing never to breathe another word of the crime, relieved in his act of defiance.

The Italian Fix

Born in Italy, Antone L. Radescich was shanghaied as a boy at an Italian seaport. For more than five years he was held against his will to undergo forced labor on shipping vessels, having no choice but to do what was asked of him or face near-fatal consequences.

One day, south of the City of New Orleans, Antone and another boy jumped overboard. They swam through choppy waters, headed for the distant Louisiana coast.

Halfway to freedom the other boy gave out and drowned.

But Antone Luke Radescich finally reached ashore, thus becoming a citizen of the New World. He first settled in New Orleans, getting accustomed to the draw and luxury of freedom before moving north.

He came up the Red River on a passenger boat and crossed the Montgomery Landing at St. Maurice, six miles from Winnfield. Beyond the Dugdemona Bayou he staked out farmland in the Tannehill Community, and by his Fortieth birthday Antone Luke had become a prosperous farmer in the central territory. He owned a nice home, two cotton gins, and three hundred head of cattle across acres of fertile land. When making a sale of cotton or cattle he always exchanged his paper money for gold. Rumored to be an eccentric miser, Antone watched his money with a hawk's eye.

Living in a rural area far from the convenience of a trustworthy bank, he kept his gold confined to compartments carved into the walls and floors of his home. This manner of securing personal treasure became a topic of conversation among those interested in rumors, and placed Antone Luke in the mental crosshairs of many robbers this side of the Mississippi.

At the request of John West, select nightriders performed keen surveillance on the house from time to time, waiting to catch the man alone. West was not interested in harming him or his family. He just wanted all those coins Antone had stashed away.

One day word got back to John West that Antone's wife and children were seen going out of town in a packed carriage, and so West saw his chance to act. On that full moon evening he gathered some of his men and surrounded Antone Luke's house. They announced their presence and asked that Mr. Luke let them in.

Antone Luke had bolted his doors and windows and refused the nightriders entry. He warned them all they should leave the premises, "so nobody gets hurt!" he yelled.

West said, "Open the door, old man! If you don't, I will not be held accountable for these men's actions. They just might ransack the whole place. Let's keep this simple. Unlock the *door!*"

In response, Antone Luke aimed a rifle out the front window and fired a shot over their heads.

"Jesus!" yelled Ed Mooney.

The gang of five men hurried back a safe distance, put on guard.

In another attempt to get Antone out of the house and into their sights, the nightriders set fire to the nearest cotton gin. By the light of the fire they started shooting, breaking apart glass and wood.

Defying the odds against him, including John West's incessant demands to throw out bags of gold, Antone Luke returned shot after shot, keeping the gang at bay like a black panther guarding a fresh kill.

Shortly thereafter, realizing they were wasting time, West and his men ceased fire. In the calm that fell around them the gang leader decided to talk sensibly to the man.

"Antone Luke! Throw out your gold and we'll go away. You won't ever hear from us again. That's a deal!"

"You come here to rob me my gold . . . then you come get gold!"

"I'll put it this way, Luke. If we come inside, you'll be done for. Do yourself a favor and be safe about this. Give up the gold so you won't get hurt!"

"Ha! Step foot in this house, *you* get hurt!" he replied, laughing at them.

As an ex-Confederate sharpshooter during the Civil War, Antone Luke had gone up against more desperate men than John West and his band of thieves. He had risen out of that bloodbath with an exceptional record of target shooting and was about to show these fools the accuracy of an angry marksman.

John West resumed the fight.

For more than two hours five men held Antone Luke hostage behind the walls of his home. When there came a significant pause in gunfire, the men again ordered the hardheaded farmer to surrender the goods and to "stop shootin' at us, goddamn it!"

Antone Luke ignored all demands. He returned fire from alternating windows with such energy and marksmanship that the nightriders never reached the front door. They couldn't even get close enough to torch the place.

When dawn broke and folks were starting their day in the settlement, West and his riders surrendered the fight and left Mr. Radescich alone.

Ed Mooney realized this come-to-Jesus volley of bullets could've ended rather violently. Having experienced such a close brush with death, feeling lead whiz past his head and puncture the ground at his foot, Mooney decided life as a clansman was exceedingly dangerous. He decided that very evening to exit the ranks of the West-Kimbrell Clan and journey to a more peaceful area of Louisiana. He took off alone and made his way eight miles east of Antone Luke's farm, where he stopped at C.W. Jones's house for food and water.

Mooney told Jones about the raid on Antone Luke's farmhouse as he led his horse to a water trough. "We were in a fix, alright. Burned the gin but couldn't reach his house with the force we had. There was just one man behind those walls, but that whole place was a verifiable arsenal! I'm tellin' ya, that fellow was tough to match. Come to realize that crazed life is too risky for my sensibilities, so I'm moving on to find a more civilized part of this country."

Antone Luke's stronghold on his property also impressed other nightriders. The gang was adept in their usual routine of striking the roads at night, then clearing out before things got heated. They were not as effective in besieging a victim at their home, waiting for surrender.

The riders never again set foot on Mr. Luke's property, nor did they seek any type of vindictive retribution against his family. Some think it was probably out of respect, but I believe it was mostly out of fear.

Antone Luke Radescich continued living peacefully for many years until the morning he died, surrounded by loved ones.

He is the ancestor of several politicians, doctors, lawyers, and school teachers in Winn Parish.

The Cotton Deal

September 1869

Laws rode to Will Drake's General Store around noon for a sack of feed, packages of dried beef, and some cigars. Once there, he met up with John West, Arthur Collins, Lec Ingram, Copeland Yates, and the Frame brothers—James and Dave.

Laws did not expect a meeting today. Curious, he pulled West aside for a briefing. "What's going on here? Me and Will went over accounts last week."

They stood on the front porch in the sunshine. West nodded at the windows. "See that man in there talkin' to Will? Name's Holt Reagan, a buyer from New Orleans. He drew up this morning on a steam packer off the Red, lookin' to purchase cotton bales. We're set to oblige him."

The cotton season was nearly over and prices had dropped low enough to prove financially advantageous for those who bought in bulk. Mr. Holt Reagan made it his mission to purchase every puffy bale of dirty white cotton he could get his hands on. The bales he secured would be transferred to a compress in New Orleans, then shipped to textile manufacturers in England and mills in South Carolina.

Mr. Reagan was pleasantly surprised while visiting Will Drake that day. Piled in an adjacent lot stood two hundred bales of quality Louisiana cotton ready for market—and he wanted them all.

Will Drake invited the buyer inside for brandy and cigars, eagerly awaiting his bid for the entire haul. A number of bales were cultivated at the Prescott and Peck gins by the nightriders themselves. Most of this haul had been stolen from victims on the Natchez Trace or the Old Sparta Road during peak season, but Mr. Reagan needn't know those details.

They haggled over cost, finally agreed on the amount, then walked outside.

"It's settled then, Mr. Reagan," Will said. "Twenty-five dollars a bale and they're all yours."

Mr. Reagan, a short man with a small mouth and clean-cut appearance, wearing a sharp gray suit, produced a bank draft.

Will took the document and said, quite firmly, "Mr. Reagan, I'm delighted to sell you our product. But I'm afraid we cannot accept a bank draft from New Orleans."

"Well, sir . . . for this amount of cotton, you understand I do not have that much cash on me. Now, my firm does have an account in Arcadia, at the home of Leon Brinks. If you send a rider up there, Mr. Brinks will honor this draft. You'll have money in hand before the boat departs tomorrow."

Will looked at John West.

West nodded.

Will said, "I have someone who might be interested in cashing that draft; my co-worker there, Jennings. Trustworthy, excellent rider, knows the trails. His brother lives near Arcadia. He can make it there in no time. Of course, that decision is yours to make, Mr. Reagan."

"Mr. Drake, if you trust him, perhaps we can work something out."

"I vouch for his honesty. As I've stated, this is your deal. Until that money is in our possession, we assume no responsibility in the matter. When Jennings returns, then we'll load those bales for a ride on the Red."

Mr. Reagan nodded. "Agreed. Get me paper and a pencil and I'll write out Mr. Leon's address."

Will called on his cousin, Henry Jennings.

The big man learned in detail the nature of his errand, well-aware that the sooner he returned the sooner their transaction would be finalized.

"You'll make good on this," Will told his cousin. "Just bring back the money."

So for his efforts, Jennings was promised a nice profit.

Bank draft in hand, Jennings moved north on the Old Sparta Road toward the trading center in Arcadia, ready to put miles behind him and money in his pocket.

*****

An hour later Jennings was making good time on the trails, immersed in fantasy of how he'd spend his coins. A new mule to plow the fields would be helpful. His sons needed books for school. His brother could use a younger horse. He'd escort his wife to a pleasant dinner in the city, and maybe she'd forgive him for staying out late playing cards. Warm jackets and leggings for more comfortable winter months, steaks as thick as his thumb, fine whiskey . . . but then he had to patch sections of his roof . . . replace a drainage pipe . . . the house was peeling paint . . . .

Shadows spread across the middle of the thoroughfare, interrupting his thoughts.

West swung out in front and rode alongside Jennings.

"Headed to Olla for some livestock, Mr. Jennings," West announced. "We'll be back in town by the time you return. Safe trip, now."

For several minutes the clansmen followed Jennings—saying little, if anything, among themselves. The thieves soon disappeared in the forest.

Seven miles away the gang reappeared. They kept pace behind Jennings for a short while, and then exited the main road once again.

Jennings did not see them for the remainder of the sixty-mile trip.

He trotted into Arcadia at sundown, sore from his journey. He went directly to the home of the man expected to cash the buyer's check. Leon Brinks worked for Mr. Reagan's firm and also knew Jennings' brother, so there was no hesitation in cashing the draft.

The man unlocked his safe and shelled out $2,000.00 in gold, placed the shiny coins in a canvas bag.

Grateful to rest a while, Jennings enjoyed a big bowl of crawfish Étouffée, then bid farewell.

But the horse was tired and weak and could not be ridden further this night. Not to be delayed, Jennings traveled to the home of his brother and explained the importance of his pressing errand. His brother allowed him to take a well-rested mare from the stable and continue on his way.

Jennings had worked with his cousin Will Drake for years, but was not a member of the West Clan. He also did not suspect his employer to be connected to that dangerous outfit, either. He'd heard rumors of atrocities committed on the Natchez Trace that led back to that gang, and steered clear of them at all costs.

Ever since encountering West and his men on this trip, Jennings realized the clan might still be following. A daunting journey lay ahead of the rider, one for which he held a fair amount of reservations. If the rumors he'd heard were true, Jennings would travel a lonely road infested by aggressive men and surely be robbed of the gold in his satchel. Given the chance, they'd literally destroy him.

The whole thing represented a looming premonition that the gang might waylay a messenger who, in good faith, was delivering funds to pay them for their *own* ill-gotten cotton.

Then again, it was the buyer's money, Mr. Reagan's—not Will Drake's. The brains of the clan were probably contemplating selling the cotton for a higher price to another competitive buyer. Keep Mr. Reagan's gold, plus gain a sizeable profit.

Just after midnight he approached the Sanders Chapel Road and tied his horse to a pine tree; quietly stepped toward the crossroads and knelt behind thick brush. For a while he heard no sounds, only his heated breath in the lonesome night. An hour later the noise of galloping horses stopped just short of his camouflage.

"He should be coming through here before too long, if my calculations are right," someone said.

Jennings thought the speaker sounded a lot like John West.

"Me and Lec will wait here," West said. "Lawson, you and the others head over to the Harrisonburg Road. He can't make it by us all!"

Jennings remained frozen in the woods, fearing the worst, and waited for the gang of seven to clear out. He carefully considered his next move. If he continued along this path, he'd be done for. He simply had to find another route.

The rider left Sanders Chapel Road behind and trekked westward to the Coldwater and Goldonna Roads. When he reached the Eberville and Monroe crossings he turned south, his eyes and ears tuned to every sound in the black night.

Dawn arrived when he reached the Red River below St. Maurice. Although the detour added ten miles to his trip, Jennings rode up to Will Drake's store as business was opening for the day, thankful to be alive. Hungry, sore, and ready to get this over with, he was deeply concerned about West and Kimbrell's deception. He wondered what they'd plan next. Until he consumed a fulfilling breakfast and thought it through, Jennings had no clue how he'd deal with those clever snakes.

West, Kimbrell, and others showed up later that morning, weary and ready for coffee and answers. They hitched their horses to the posts, shuffled into Will Drake's store and filed into the back office.

The buyer, Mr. Reagan, who knew nothing of the nightriders' scheme to rob Jennings, greeted them.

West opened his mouth to speak when Will Drake said, "My cousin's back with the money. We can load up that cotton for Mr. Reagan whenever you fellas are ready."

The leader eyed Will Drake humorously, as though he misunderstood. West couldn't believe Jennings had escaped their dragnet. Fellow bandits stood there hushed, equally surprised at the news.

They met Will Drake and the buyer on the other side of the large desk to complete the deal.

Jennings dropped the satchel of gold on the desk and left the room.

That evening he packed up his personal belongings and headed for the Appalachian mountains of West Virginia, never to return.

*****

One thing was certain in their thought pattern as thieves—West and Laws sought to gain more money from the cotton deal than Mr. Reagan had initially offered.

Following the business exchange, the riders returned outside to briefly discuss how they might still benefit.

West and other riders directed their horses southeast in a hurry.

Laws joined a crowd near the river, watching a group of men wheel cotton onto a huge steamer. Once the bales were settled for transport to Holt Reagan's hometown, the crew got busy loading a lighter freight of boxed vegetables.

That's when Laws made his move.

Carrying a two-inch auger he slipped aboard and went below, undetected. Using the handheld auger he bore a hole through the wooden hull, then climbed back on deck and assumed polite conversation among crew members, just before they set sail.

He returned ashore and headed down the road to meet up with the others.

The huge steamer cruised on, gradually taking on water. Three miles downstream the steamer lost its battle against the strength of the Red River and sunk to the bottom of the waterway—taking the produce down with it.

Very few bales were lost in the incident.

Each cotton bale the riders saved was transported by wagon train to Pineville, Louisiana.

A greedy West and Kimbrell went on to sell their catch at twenty-eight dollars apiece, in gold. This fee netted the gang three more dollars per bale than they'd received from the original sale to Mr. Reagan.

After hearing that John West and his men were present *after* the event, authorities conducted an investigation of alleged foul play.

These men lived in the hills far from where misfortune occurred. Officials thought it mighty convenient that they were in sight of the steamer when it sank.

Days later, while the river was low, authorities searched the vessel's depths and discovered the threaded auger hole.

John West and Lawson Kimbrell were under suspicion, sure, but authorities had insufficient evidence to convict them.

Word soon spread that West and the Kimbrells were probably highwaymen, which prompted folks to be more cautious of their surroundings while traveling the roads after dark.

Lost Horses

Goldonna, Louisiana
March 1872

As successful as they were in the art of banditry, the nightriders did not prevail in every fight.

Sometimes they failed.

A perfect example is when I witnessed one of the greatest gun battles in the South.

This interaction of gunplay did not gain far and wide attention, but it definitely rivaled Wild West legend. Like many colorful stories back then, folks picked it apart in interesting detail.

You see, it all came to pass when two beautiful horses were stolen from a farmer by the name of Jess Cady. Now, Jess was a tough old farmer who had been in the area for well over forty years, and he did not take kindly to thieves trespassing his property. The bunch he suspected of the crime were those cutthroats in the West Clan.

So the next sunny morning, Jess Cady and Mr. Lucas Gibbs went searching for his prized stallion and a mare he planned to breed.

They trotted onto John West's property but found no horses about. Then they ventured to the Kimbrell farm near Sandy Creek. There, Aunt Polly's daughter, Mattie, insisted that she was home alone.

The men searched the acreage to no avail.

Then they found their way to the Bingham farm, an expanse of gated land that held several fenced-in areas of livestock, including cattle and chickens and goats. The Bingham farm was ghost real estate, owned by Sarrett Bingham, a fictitious land owner from Gretna who existed only on the land deed. The true owners were John West and Lawson Kimbrell. They hardly ever showed up at the place, usually leaving this as a last ditch shelter for members on the run, or those who just wanted to get away from their wives. Either way, this location served as the property of choice whenever a rider needed to hide something valuable, as the layout provided privacy and thwarted any type of law enforcement.

The riders also kept a stable of stolen horses here.

One stable held seven horses.

Of those seven horses, a midnight black beauty named Chloe belonged to Mr. Jess Cady.

Two men Jess Cady did not recognize stood on the front porch smoking cigars and sipping from pints of amber-colored whiskey. A third was out in the corral brushing a steed's shiny dark mane.

The outlaws watched the men on horseback pass through the towering iron gates, curious as to why they were crossing onto the Bingham property.

I was in the woods sitting by the bayou, trying to catch a nice-sized fish for supper. I watched the scene unfold like something out of a storybook.

Mr. Cady and Mr. Gibbs stopped short of the farmhouse.

"We're lookin' for John West and Laws Kimbrell!" Cady announced. "They about?"

One of the men spat brown tobacco juice in the yard. "Naw, they ain't here. What's your business with them two anyways, old man?"

"I suspect they stole my horses. I aim to get 'em back."

"Ain't nobody here but us," the man said. "Them over there's all we have, and ain't none of 'em yours."

"That girl is," Cady said, pointing to the mare. "Y'all been on my farm and you took from me, so I'm bringin' her back. Where's the other one? My stallion?"

The third nightrider joined his partners on the porch. "You take anything from this farm and we'll shoot you to the ground like a pig!" He nodded to Mr. Gibbs. "Your friend'll get a barrel-load too."

Both Jess Cady and Lucas Gibbs surveyed the area and thought better of taking on three armed, drunken outlaws.

"Tell John West he's made a grave mistake," Mr. Cady warned.

The farmers retreated to the road, soon trotted out of sight.

"That old coot's a damned fool," said another rider. "We'll plan it proper and waylay him come nightfall. Laws won't like this, what with them riders tearin' in here like that. We'll deal out this trouble before he hears about it."

*****

As the hours passed by I overheard them clan members discuss when and where they would lie in wait for Jess Cady. It was decided they'd take him out at the Four Oaks Road, a well-beaten crossway where many people had met their demise.

"And if Jess Cady ain't out for the evening," one of them said, "we'll move on to his house. Get him, his wife, and whoever else might be there."

They figured while they were out it'd be to their advantage to locate Mr. Lucas Gibbs and dispatch him as well.

I sat and waited for them to take action, knowing that I could not (would not!) interfere with their affairs. I was deathly afraid of them. Even if I was fearless to the point of irrational decision-making and approached them with logical, death-free answers to their predicament, those men wouldn't hear my pleas. Outlaws in the West Clan lived by the skin of their teeth. They listened to their own heart's desire. They were downright wretched souls, void of all compassion for their fellow man, and I was in no position to change their free will. The riders acknowledged a collective fear among themselves that Mr. Cady, a powerful man with plenty of political connections, might bring this occurrence of horse thievery to the public's attention. For years, clan members had initiated great measures to insure they were not caught for their deeds, and I've seen them risk life and limb to keep things secret.

No, they wouldn't listen to reason—at least not from a kid like me. They'd pay no mind, just move right past me on their journey to spill blood.

The sun was bright in the late-afternoon sky, casting shadows throughout the forest. I watched the riders clean their hand-heavy guns on the expansive walkway of that farmhouse like they had not a care in the world. More whiskey was passed around, more cigarettes were rolled and smoked to delight, more talk continued about which bricked well they'd use to dispose of Mr. Cady's body. Prescott Gin? The Peck Gin? The one at Two Sweetgums farm?

John West and Laws Kimbrell were absent during this meeting of the minds, but I was positive that not only would the gang leaders agree to remove Mr. Cady from this earth, they would've happily participated in the undertaking.

While the clan members relaxed on the porch I watched it all unfold from the shaded woods, praying (for his sake) that Jess Cady wouldn't create a charge against these men.

It wasn't long after that I saw the farmer once again make his way up to the Bingham farmhouse, his face slightly hidden in shadow under his wide-brimmed hat.

The three nightriders, who all expressed surprise on their hardened faces, could not believe the "old coot" possessed such determination in reclaiming his property.

Mr. Jess Cady was brave to approach these men alone. Maybe he just wanted to discuss the issue further. Maybe he wanted to meet with John West and Laws Kimbrell and see to it that they stopped stealing from the locals. Maybe he realized he'd made a mistake speaking to these nightriders in a threatening manner and felt an apology, on his part, was in order.

But then again I reckoned the farmer had enough time to return home, think it over, and clean his pistol in accordance with his plan. No matter the consequences, it looked as though Jess Cady was getting ready to snag that pretty mare.

One rider got up out of his rocking chair. "You got grit, old man, I'll give ya that. Listen now, we already made our stance clear on this issue. Best thing you can do is make tracks outta here."

Cady looked up and said, "I'm tellin' you boys one more goddamn time. Give me my horse."

The riders searched the woods beyond Mr. Cady.

They were thinking the same thing I was. Maybe Mr. Lucas Gibbs, or another gunslinger, just might be hiding behind those trees below the iron gates, aiming the barrel of a long-range rifle at their heads.

Put on high alert, the riders were still stubborn, full of pride. Even if Mr. Cady's strategy was to position hidden weaponry on the periphery, he'd surely feel the pain of bullets penetrate the muscle of his heart, all before any of them suffered the first long-range shot.

"Simple words from a fool!" said the nightrider in charge. "Leave now, or we'll kill you where you sit. We'll take that horse you're ridin', too!"

Jess Cady eased off his horse and started toward the house. His eyes glowed with hatred for the three men. He did not slow his stride until he saw a rider reach.

Cady pulled his .44 and shot the man in the cheek, blowing the back of his skull across the front windows in a reddish/white splatter of blood and bone fragments.

The others went for their guns.

A quicker draw than these nightriders, Cady shot one man twice in the stomach. He leveled his gun on the third man's neck and fired, opening the man's wind pipe in an ugly, broken circle the size of a silver dollar.

Both men dropped heavily on the porch in a stretch of fresh red blood.

I sat bewildered. One man against three, and the farmer survived. Not even a nick.

Jess Cady stepped around pooling blood that stuck to the soles of his boots.

The rider holding tight to his stomach was still breathing.

Cady knelt down. "Where's my stallion, son? He goes by Ringo, and he ain't over there in the corral hounding my mare. Say where he's at."

The nightrider looked up, his eyes falling fast, lengths of purple intestines slipping over his hands.

"Texas!" the dying man answered. "Sold it morn—*aaack*—this mornin'!"

Mr. Cady spat on the man's forehead, then stepped on his throat, the weight pressing down so brutal I heard cartilage snapping. For a moment the farmer stood still, surveying the destruction lying at his feet.

And just like that, he retrieved his pretty mare and rode off.

I left the bayou without a decent catch, in awe of Mr. Cady's level of raw courage—secretly wishing I'd been blessed with a similar backbone.

Window Justice

As many of you have heard, over a period of six years, rumors drifted around the rural communities in Winn Parish that John West and Lawson Kimbrell operated a gang of predatory outlaws.

Some folks believed this was true and so steered clear of the duo. Yet others denied these accusations. Perhaps Laws Kimbrell was a member of the gang. He was, after all, a wild soul and as mean as a bull, his time in the infantry having instilled in his brain a war-like mentality.

But to believe that a respectable patriot and God-fearing churchgoer such as John West might even conceive of doing the outlandish things the nightriders were accused of, was not only hard to imagine, it was beyond absurd.

And if you believe that load of horse slurry, Wallace Cole would call you a damned fool.

Mr. Cole led a simple life in Winnfield with his wife, Olivia, a homemaker, and his son. They lived in a nice house on twenty acres of land. Like many in the area they raised their own crop of sustainable food. Other than a friendly dispute over the price of feed or a bale of hay, Wallace Cole had never been confronted with much trouble.

Then at church one particular Sunday, following a special rendition of "Bringing in the Sheaves," Preacher Weeks adjusted his tie and rose to deliver his sermon.

The piano stopped.

Laws Kimbrell strolled by in polished boots, his duster swaying at the hardwood floor, reserving no misgivings about disrupting services. He placed his hands on the edges of the podium and looked out over the curious crowd, catching the attention of some of the more humbled men in the area.

That sharp, threatening look in his eyes dared anyone to make an issue of the interruption.

"Friends and neighbors, I've heard disturbing things regarding my family and some of my closer acquaintances. There's word goin' around that me, my brothers, and other men of note are part of this nightrider outfit people keep talkin' about. I stand before you today and tell you that that is a flat-out lie. I don't care for hearin' this sort of nonsense when ain't none of it true!" Laws paused, then pointed out Wallace Cole, seated mid-section next to his wife and son. "Matter of fact, Mr. Cole, your name has risen on several occasions as being the ringleader of these rumors. I advise you to shut down that gossip mill you call a mouth."

Wallace Cole, a dignified, hard-working man of forty-two, was not to be hassled in any way, from anyone, *especially* in view of his religious family.

He stood and rested his hands on the pew.

"Lawson Kimbrell, I might add that your name, sir, has risen on a number of occasions in connection to that rowdy bunch of criminals . . . in wide circles, no doubt. So, it stands to reason that if you heard *my* name, that *I've* been the one spreading these rumors, you must have surely heard about others jawing on it. Now, I wonder why you would single me out in this fashion, in the presence of everyone here today. The only justification I can conjure is that you belong to that gang of wretched men. Why else bring up this subject with such energy and detail?"

I could tell Laws wanted to brandish his gun right then and there and shut my father's voice for good. But the outlaw kept his head under pressure. He was grossly outnumbered.

"My family's lived here all our lives! We've put stacks of money in this hard town. I'll be damned if I'm gonna stand here and be disrespected by you or anyone else concerning this nonsense."

Wallace lifted his head. "Are you finished, sir?"

"Why you ornery skunk!" Laws shouted. He left the podium and walked right up to my father, nose to nose. "Keep on with accusations and you'll find trouble you'll never see comin'."

Wallace said, "A threat? Sounds like the words of a true bandit, if you ask me."

Annabelle Frost touched Kimbrell's arm. "Come along, Laws. This is no way for men to behave in the Lord's House."

*****

It infuriated Lawson that Wallace Cole had shown him up in front of the congregation. The nightrider wasn't used to folks back-talking him or arguing a point, especially when it dealt with such a sensitive subject as being a member of the elusive, secretive clan of nightriders.

Laws vowed to do something about it. Pissed off about the issue, he couldn't just go and murder the fellow. Church attendance had reached its capacity that day, and if something wicked happened to Wallace Cole so soon after their unpleasant confrontation, then all eyes would be on the Kimbrell boys.

He couldn't risk it. That kind of pressure on his head might lead to an arrest, conviction, and a sentence to hang.

But sometimes even good news made its way to evil ears. A few days later, Laws received news that Wallace Cole had bought two new horses for his stable—a black stallion for breeding and a pony for his son.

That was it, he thought. If he couldn't kill Wallace Cole outright, then he'd take from him something of value. Wallace would put up a fuss over the exchange, maybe even try fighting him. Guided by his own warped logic, Laws figured if Cole decided to protect his property, the outlaw would then have a perfectly good reason to shoot the family man dead.

The next evening was a cool blue ocean of color when Laws and West rode up to the quaint farmhouse on the Old Harrisburg Road. The house was well-lit. The family of three was having supper.

"Let's get them horses," West said.

As they collected the stallion and pony, Laws aimed his pistol at the sky and fired off three shots.

The horses pulled back.

The outlaws held strong to their halters.

"Settle down!"

Mr. Wallace Cole walked out on the porch holding up a lantern in one hand and a rifle in the other.

"What's the commotion out here? Who's there!"

The riders moved closer toward light that now panned over the yard.

Recognizing West and Laws, Wallace said, "What's this all about, West? What're you doin' with my horses?"

"We're takin' your horses, matter of fact," West said. "It's the least you can do for Mr. Kimbrell here, since you felt it proper to accuse him of being a nightrider . . . in front of Sunday's congregation, no less."

"Well, I can see now it's more truth than rumor, John. I had a gut feeling you and Laws were in that Godforsaken gang."

"Rest that rifle on the floor or you're gonna have another feelin' in your gut," Laws warned, aiming his heated pistol at Mr. Cole.

Wallace leaned the rifle against the door frame. "Now, there's no reason for this situation to go any further. Take my property, if that's what you're here to do. Y'all leave me and my family alone!"

"Oh we're gonna do just that, don't you worry," West replied, smiling big. "I do want to make clear that if you keep runnin' your mouth about the nightriders, we won't come after you. We'll find your wife. Your son. See to them proper . . . do we have an understanding, or should I make my point now?"

Wallace swallowed, fearful that he may fall dead on the porch any second, leaving his family unprotected. "I won't say a word, John. Far as I'm concerned this evening never happened."

"That's what I want to hear, old friend!" John said, sliding his pistol into its holster. "Remember now, we see each other on occasion. Mostly at church. If you say something, then one of those trustworthy members of our God-loving congregation will pull me aside. They'll say, 'John, I just heard the strangest thing. Mr. Cole claimed that you're part of that nasty gang, the nightriders,' and I'll say, 'how rude that is for Mr. Cole to make up such a story . . . .'"

"Ha! I'm not *part* of the nightriders, Wallace. I *am* the nightriders! My say isn't questioned. Orders are obeyed, tasks completed. So, if word gets out we've been here tonight I'll tell one of my friends to find that lovely, big breasted wife of yours and have a good time at her expense. Then he'll follow my order to put a bullet between those big breasts. They'll bring me the boy and I'll bash his cute, little head in with a pole axe," West said, turning to Laws. "Uncle Dan style!"

"I said this never happened. I love my family more than trying to bring to light the injustice y'all are to this community," Wallace explained.

"As long as we have an understanding, you will have no further problems," West said. "Laws? Is there anything you'd like to say to Mr. Cole before we trade these ponies for gold?"

"Yeah. You're lucky John West came along tonight, Wallace . . . else I'd've fired down on you the second you stepped out."

The clansmen turned away with their prizes and rode on through the darkness.

*****

That episode in his life haunted Wallace Cole for days on end. He wanted so badly to reveal his story to someone in a position of authority, someone who could bring the clan to justice. But he feared that anyone he confided in might speak of it, and word would get back to the nightriders, thus putting the safety of his family in jeopardy.

From then on Wallace Cole was careful of his dealings with others in town. He'd had his suspicions about Laws Kimbrell being in that gang, but never once did he believe John West had anything to do with it. If he'd been so blind to this fact, Wallace assumed others whom he'd known well may also be a rider. Now during church services, Wallace observed in silent disgust how the majority of folks looked upon West as a righteous man.

A month later when he heard that Jim Maybin was in the process of creating a posse to possibly take down prominent members of the clan, Wallace accepted the invitation to the meeting but declined to join in the cleanup. He gave no explanation for his decision, instead promising Jim Maybin that he'd supply the posse with additional ammunition and firearms, if needed.

On the day of reckoning, like most townsfolk, Wallace Cole and his family attended Easter morning services at Mount Zion. Afterwards, his son, Caleb, explained that he was still feeling full from breakfast and wanted to meet up with some friends behind the church to play. Wallace went on to have lunch at the hotel, where Olivia discussed John West's beautiful sermon with Mrs. Rebecca Drake and her two daughters.

While they chatted, Wallace chewed his bites of glazed ham slowly, observing Fred Boss and Jess Cady behind the General Store. Men that Mr. Wallace knew personally, had even fished with, walked around the corner of the building and were immediately accosted at gunpoint. Wallace watched Jess Cady loop their wrists together and push them against the store's bricked wall. A third man, Wesley Xavier, demanded they remove their bullet-lined gun belts.

The cleanup posse had chosen this day to undertake their meticulous task, and all of a sudden Wallace Cole desperately wanted to be a part of it.

Wallace escorted his wife home after lunch. He demanded she stay put until he returned.

Olivia asked him where he was going with "that gun".

"To make things right," he said. "Nobody threatens me and mine."

By the time he made his way back to town, now very concerned about where his son and friends were playing, heavy layers of gun smoke hovered over the bodies of the accused riders. Too late to partake in the take-down, Wallace tied his horse at a post outside the hotel lobby and walked across the street.

Well, at least he could get a drink without Olivia verbally assaulting him about being a "common heathen" on the Lord's Day.

The vacant saloon felt welcoming, so he fixed himself a glass of Old Crow Whiskey and sat and stared at his reflection in the huge wall mirror. He'd aged in the last month since West and Kimbrell dropped by his home unannounced, threatened violence toward his family, and forcibly took his horses. New wrinkles had crept into his face and a sharper, meaner look had formed inside his once-soft brown eyes.

It wasn't the horses he'd been so concerned about. He could purchase more horses. But he could travel the lengths of the earth and never find another Olivia, or father a son as brave as Caleb Cole.

"That fool of a man," Wallace whispered to his glass. "I'll find him one day . . . send him dreckley to his grave."

Wallace set his drink down. Outside the opened window he heard a familiar voice: "Gimme three days folks! . . . Your financial woes will be no more . . . ."

He walked over to the window and saw John West standing large on a tree stump. West appeared nervous in the eyes of the crowd, promising folks bags of gold, untold wealth of unbelievable amounts, the frazzled desperation in his voice enough to lead them on and even make a person pity him.

That poor sinner needs help, Wallace thought.

Wallace aimed his Liege rifle out the window, took aim, and realized he needn't worry about the nightriders after all.

Boom!

The bullet broke through West's neck, propelling him off the stump.

The crowd backed away, horrified.

Wallace turned to the bar to finish his drink. Nearly empty, he grabbed the bottle and filled his glass.

He really did not want to be known as the man who killed John West. There always stood the chance that the cleanup crew might've missed a few riders during their sweep. If a loose cannon heard that Wallace Cole was the shooter, they'd surely track him down.

Wallace relaxed his shoulders and stood proud. Grinned.

The door opened slowly, and in walked Dan Dean.

Wallace raised his glass. "It's about time somebody killed that sack of pig shit, don'tcha think?" He filled another glass. "Have a drink, Mr. Dean. Far as I'm concerned, this is a celebration—not a funeral. Celebrate with me."

Dan smiled. "It'd be my pleasure, sir."

"Anyone else happened to see me?"

"Nobody, far as I could tell."

Wallace nodded. "That's good. I don't need any riders y'all missed in the roundup seeking me out . . . how about we keep this here between us for the time being?"

Dan walked over to the window and looked down at the mumbling, nervous crowd.

Blood spread out from under West's shoulders and head, carving curvy black streaks in red dirt. The bullet had torn open his throat and nearly taken his head off.

"Fine with me," Dan said. "I never liked the son of a bitch anyway."

*****

After most folks had left for home Caleb Cole stood at the forest's opening and confessed that he'd shot West's head clear off his body.

Wallace immediately emptied a burlap sack of feed on the back porch of the store.

John West's head lay face-up in pine needles.

"—but I didn't mean to, dad, he just scared me!" Caleb cried.

"Just nerves actin' up, son. You've done nothing wrong. He's long dead." Wallace grabbed the head by the temples and dropped it in the sack. He twisted the top half of the sack, sealing it tightly, swung the prize over his shoulder.

When he arrived home, Wallace set the stinking head on an anthill in his yard.

During several feedings days later, tireless worker ants freed the skull of skin, blood, tissue and muscle. Insects had even sapped sundried blood from bone, the head now ringed by fragile wisps of red hair rising and falling in the breeze.

Wallace Cole then perched his prized skull on a fencepost near a Hackberry tree in his back field. For several years that sun-bleached head smiled up at the sky, while the soul of its owner burned down below.

*****

That skull represents a constant reminder of the horrors the West Clan unleashed and how evil can be destroyed. No matter the obstacles I face, I strive each day to live life with a positive outlook . . . if nothing else but for the sake of my family's happiness and our survival. Not to mention my own sanity.

I spent my younger years getting an education, finally becoming a skilled carpenter—just like my dad, Wallace Cole.

I do not speak of the past to my wife and children. They're too fragile of heart. They just wouldn't understand.

Besides, there's no reason to dredge up those ghastly stories . . . .

About the Author:

John Ashley Blake was born and raised in the Great State of Louisiana and has been writing fiction for 28 years. He credits life in a small town for sparking his imagination to create entertaining stories on paper.

Mr. Blake is the author of the controversial thriller, *The Parent Killer*, his debut novel concerning child abuse and adult revenge. His second novel, *Dear Arial,* (a story about a psychopath searching for a so-called witch), was banned in several libraries upon publication in 2006 for its violent context, but has since been regarded as one of the most highly complex mysteries set in Louisiana. His third novel, *Dark Bayou,* explores the mystery of a treasure hunt for lost gold and—well, no sense in going into that story. You already know about the dark bayou, don't you?

He lives in Nashville, Tennessee, with an Alabama beauty.

If you have any questions or comments about *Nightriders*, please feel free to contact me. You may reach me at:

ablake277@hotmail.com

Copyright 2016 Ashley Blake
Jackknifed Publishing

ISBN 9781511590181

CPSIA information can be obtained
at www.ICGtesting.com
Printed in the USA
LVOW07s1810200317
527826LV00006B/1472/P

9 781511 590181